PRAISE FOR KHURRUM RAHMAN

'Told with striking panache. Announces the
arrival of a fine, fresh new thriller writer'
Daily Mail

'Combining humour and tragedy is one of the hardest
literary challenges, but Khurrum Rahman succeeds.'
TLS

'A brilliant thriller. You'd be mad not to buy this.'
Ben Aaronovitch

'A very funny but tense thriller... Think
Four Lions meets *Phone Shop*'
Red

'As much a coming-of-age story as a full-on action thriller,
East of Hounslow is thought-provoking and entirely gripping.'
Guardian

'Excellent book. Phenomenal writing.'
BA Paris

'Sweary, funny and, above all, an absolutely cracking
thriller that you'll tear through, this is the anti-
James Bond that the 21st century needs'
Emerald Street

D1245935

Born in Karachi, Pakistan in 1975 Khurrum Rahman moved to England when he was one. He is a West London boy and now lives in Berkshire with his wife and two sons.

Khurrum is currently working as a Senior IT Officer but his real love is writing. He has a screenplay which has been optioned by a Danish TV producer but is now concentrating on novels.

His first two books in the Jay Qasim series, *East of Hounslow* and *Homegrown Hero* have been shortlisted for the Theakstons Old Peculier Crime Novel and CWA John Creasey Debut Dagger.

RIDE OR DIE

Khurrum Rahman

ONE PLACE. MANY STORIES

HQ
An imprint of HarperCollins*Publishers* Ltd
1 London Bridge Street
London SE1 9GF

www.harpercollins.co.uk

HarperCollins*Publishers*
1st Floor, Watermarque Building, Ringsend Road,
Dublin 4, Ireland

This edition 2022

1
First published in Great Britain by
HQ, an imprint of HarperCollins*Publishers* Ltd 2020

ISBN: 978-0-00-838471-5

MIX
Paper from
responsible sources
FSC™ C007454

This book is produced from independently certified FSC™ paper
to ensure responsible forest management.

For more information visit: www.harpercollins.co.uk/green

This book is set in 9.5/15 pt. Meridien

Printed and bound in the UK using
100% renewable electricity at CPI Group (UK) Ltd

In memory of my beautiful Dad x

Prologue

In that very heartbeat, I knew what I had to do.

As I watched, his small hand emerged out of his pocket, a detonator gripped high above his head, high enough for me to see. In a hall full of guests, I alone was his audience and he had my attention. The serene smile on the face of the ten-year-old boy was one of no regret and no fear of death, only victory. There would be no second guessing, no degree of falling to my knees and begging to sacrifice my life for the lives of my family.

There was only one way it would go. This was my punishment.

His serene smile was the last thing I saw before a white light filled my eyes and an explosion filled my ears. He took his own life and snatched away everything that I had allowed myself to believe would forever be mine.

I held my family in my arms, tight to me, their faces and bodies burnt and broken and breathless. Through my tears and through my screams, I never once asked why.

I knew why.

The rage was the only emotion that I'd felt and I welcomed it back like an old friend.

I knew what I had to do, and I would allow the rage to dictate my actions.

PART 1

Fake News.
Definition: Bullshit information fed by bullshit media to
fit a bullshit narrative.

Chapter 1

Javid Qasim (Jay)

Flat on my backside, arms flopped to my side, laid out on a sun lounger with one of those big umbrella things above me, protecting me from the blazing sun, with nothing but another lazy day ahead of me. On the small plastic table next to me, a bottle of water sat upright on top of a book. Yeah, a book! Seemed like a good idea at the time. Seemed like a holiday thing to do, but really I could not be arsed. Give me some credit, though, I attempted it, ripped through a few chapters, but it just felt way too much like homework. Fuck, man, I barely did homework at school, I sure ain't doing homework on holiday! Next to the book was my phone, also taking a well-deserved rest, and some loose change that amounted to either a fortune or jack-shit. I don't know, I still hadn't sussed out the exchange rate.

I sighed the sigh of a man who had finally sat down. I accompanied it with a noisy stretch which turned into a big fat yawn. Good times, that may just get better from what I could see in front of me.

Through the tango tint of my replica designer shades I glanced across the pool and the brunette who was giving me the eyes yesterday was doing so again. I wasn't surprised, I'd hit the weights twice in the last couple of weeks, and possibly this attention was a result of that. I crossed my arms across my chest, hoping that the curve of a bicep might make an appearance. I lifted my shades onto my forehead, and gave her the elevator eyes. I decided against a wink, instead giving her the smallest of smiles, no teeth, not yet, just one side of my lips curling a touch. That's enough for today. I'd played this game before, with varying results. I'd keep it cool. With a flick of a finger I slid my shades down my forehead, but they fell too far down my nose and I had to quickly readjust. Great! She'd turned her attention elsewhere.

A member of staff approached. Unlike me he was showing teeth and smiling wildly. He towered over me, blocking my view. His too-tight shorts too close to my face, he handed me an already dripping lemonade ice-lolly that I'd forgotten I'd ordered, and didn't feel like anymore, and started jabbering on about some excursion or another, thrusting flyers in my face. I reached across to the table and picked up a couple of coins and held them up to my face, squinting, trying to figure out how little of a tip I could get away with. I handed him one Qatari Rial and took a flyer from him and waved him away with it as I considered jumping in the pool.

This had been my spot for the last two weeks, with another two weeks to come. And I didn't have the inconvenience of waking up at fuck-off-o'clock in the morning to come and plant my towel on the lounger, as is the international method of reservation. No, man, this was my mum's joint and she called the shots. It was actually the Marriott Hotel in Doha, Qatar, and Mum worked there on reception. She had a word with one of the lifeguards to keep the shaded lounger reserved for me during my stay, because she knew better than anybody how sensitive my skin was to the sun.

I had finally managed to get out to Qatar to visit Mum and Andrew, her now fiancé. His proposal was a long, convoluted story which I lost interest in pretty quickly when they told me, but there were dolphins, a hot air balloon and a lost shoe involved. He was alright, Andrew, made Mum smile and laugh. He made her happy. Even though they were settled in a Muslim country, nobody

6

questioned their so-called interfaith relationship. It would have been worse in Hounslow!

Yeah, man, life was good, you know. Well, it was good right then.

In a couple of weeks, I'd fly back home to an empty house and an empty life. I'd sit on my trusty armchair and face up to the fact that I was quickly running out of money, currently unemployed and had jack-shit to fill my days with. It crossed my mind that I should go crawling back to my old IT Helpdesk role at the London Borough of Hounslow. I mean, I never officially left. I just hadn't been in for the last eight months. I didn't even phone in my absence. I mean, what would I tell them? How would I explain the *death in the family*? That my old man was tracked down then shot down as part of a large-scale government operation that I was central to.

Can you imagine that conversation?

So instead I ignored the emails and phone calls from my team leader, then I ignored the emails, phone calls and letters from HR. I just couldn't be arsed to go back, figured that I had too much to sort out. Turns out I didn't have jack-shit to do. Abdul Bin Jabbar was dead and MI5 had no use for me. I should've been glad. It's what I wanted. What I thought I wanted.

My life came to a standstill and the world continued to spin without my interference.

It gave me time to reflect. Eight months of sitting in my armchair watching Piers, Lorraine and Holly and those crazy Loose Women, as I tried to work out what matters and what fucking doesn't. I was done with doing the right thing in the wrong way, and I was done thinking about those that didn't deserve my fucking attention. But, you know, sometimes your mind betrays you.

The fuck, man! *Stop with this self-pity bullshit.*

I had Christmas in the sun with Mum to look forward to. I realised that my nails were digging into my palms. I flexed my fingers and shook my head clear of that shit. Those demons could take a back fucking seat.

I lifted my head and peered over the rim of my shades across the pool to see if I could re-establish eye contact with my soon-to-be holiday romance. I watched her carefully, still perfectly poised, one leg stretched, the other bent at the knee looking like an Instagram post. She was no longer looking in my direction. She was chatting merrily away to a copper.

He had gallantly picked up her towel, which had dropped to the floor, and handed it to her. She smiled and flirted her way through a show of gratitude. I had been about to make my move on her, tomorrow or the day after. But I had no chance with him knocking about.

I laughed to myself in disbelief. If I'd had a pen and a pad, I'd have been taking notes.

I took him in. He wasn't in police uniform. In fact, he's wasn't wearing a stitch, apart from a pair of barely-there lime-green trunks that he'd probably borrowed from his ten-year-old nephew. He gave her a Sheriff's nod and sauntered away, her eyes tracking his movement as he rounded the pool and approached me with a perfect smile on his stupid face.

My best mate, and Hounslow's finest detective – his words, not mine – Idris Zaidi. I hadn't seen him in, I don't know, a couple of months? A few? A long time considering that we once lived in each other's pockets. Despite the fact that he'd got in the way of what could very well have been *The One*, Idris was just what I needed.

'They're letting anyone in here now, are they?' I beamed up at him. 'This is supposed to be a five-star joint.'

'They dropped a star as soon as you walked in,' Idris replied. 'You going to get up and greet me properly or do you want to do this horizontally? You know I'll do it!'

I laughed and straightened up, and we bumped fists before bumping bare chests. It was as awkward as it sounds.

'Mum?' I asked.

'Yeah,' he said, using a straight hand to shield the sun from his eyes. 'She called me, said you might need some company, so you know, thought I swing by.' He smiled and ruffled my hair. The girl from across the pool was laughing like a cheerleader as though the jock had just kicked sand in the nerd's face. I knocked his hand away.

'Swing by?' I said, fixing my hair with a flick of my hand. 'It's a six-and-a-half-hour flight.'

*

As sunny as my disposition allowed me to be, Mum had read me inside and out. She recognised that I was at war with myself. She'd made the right call to the right person. It was just what I needed. I'd never tell Idris this, but *he* was just what I needed.

In the evening Mum and Andrew joined us for a meal at one of the many bars at the Marriott. This one, can't remember the name, something corny, turned into a nightclub late on and I could already see it filling up with young hungry holiday-makers and well-dressed hookers looking to clean them out for a slice of dirty heaven.

'We should call it a night,' Mum said, joined at the hip to Andrew, opposite us in a booth.

Idris glanced at his watch. 'It's only just gone nine. Can I tempt you with a nightcap?'

Idris always did that, always spoke like that around certain company, a little hoity-toity for my liking. Who says *tempt you with a night cap*? Like he's just stepped out of a black-and-white flick.

'I wouldn't mind an early night, actually,' Andrew said, making eyes at Mum.

I wanted to believe that age was catching up with them, and that they were heading up to rest their old bones and not... you know. I made a face. Mum noticed, smiled beautifully at me, and they shuffled out of the booth. Idris stood up and gave Mum a cuddle, and shook hands heartily with Andrew, and told him what an *immense pleasure* it was to meet him. *Seriously Idris, keep that shit real, man!*

Mum beckoned me over to one side, away from Andrew and Idris, and softly asked me the same question that she had been asking for the last two weeks.

'Are you okay, Jay?'

It was a double-barrelled, fully loaded question. We both understood the meaning of it, but neither of us was willing to mention or even acknowledge the fact that my dad, her husband, was dead. We just had to read it in each other's eyes.

'Yeah,' I said. 'Are you?'

Mum smiled and replied. 'I am.'

I watched her watch me for a moment before landing one on my cheek and then rubbing off the lipstick with her thumb. She stepped away and linked arms with Andrew, then with a joint smile they walked out of the bar.

'Right.' Idris rubbed his hands together like he was trying to start a fire. 'Drinks?'

'Yeah, go on,' I said. I didn't have to tell him my order. He knew.

Idris went off and ordered the first round of alcoholic drinks of the night. It wasn't like we were hiding it from Mum, I think she knew, but I would never feel comfortable drinking around her. I did quit for a while, possibly due to the company I was keeping, but I was back on it. It helped, other times it hindered, but each time it numbed and clouded what I didn't want to see.

10

My stomach rumbled at the thought of drinking on empty. Once again, my choice of meal had been poor. I'd bent two knives trying to cut through the steak, so I gave up. The potatoes were too squishy, so I left those. The vegetables I didn't touch, because they were vegetables.

'Here,' Idris said, handing me my drink, a bag of crisps, and some sort of health bar. 'Figured you might be hungry,' he said, taking a seat opposite me.

'The hell is this?' I said, holding up the health bar, all raisins and berries.

'You don't want it?' he said. 'I'll have it.'

'No. I'll have it,' I said, taking a bite out of it. 'So, what's new?' I asked, through a mouthful.

'Honestly, I needed to get out of Hounslow. That place is starting to depress me.'

'Yeah, it's not what it used to be. Lost some of its charm.' I split open the bag of crisps longways and nodded at Idris to help himself. He shook his head. 'Gone are the days when you could sort out shit with a good scrap. Now it's all blades and shooters.'

'It's worse than that, Jay.'

'Drugs?' I nodded. Idris worked for the Met's Drugs Directorate; he was basically a Narc. It was a role that had taken its toll on him. 'Fucking junkies are taking over Hounslow.'

'Worse than that, Jay.' Idris took a sip and watched me over the rim. It was starting to become clear that he hadn't just flown over to work on his tan.

'What's happened, Idris?' I said, shifting my drink from one spot to another for no apparent reason.

'I've been meaning to chat to you, but I couldn't get hold of you at home. You could've mentioned that you were flying off on holiday.' Idris took his time clearing his throat. 'So when your

11

mum called, I thought, I'm due time off work, so why not. I'll fly over.'

Stalling…

'What's happened, Idris?' I asked, again.

He took a sip of his drink, and dropped his gaze. He wiped his mouth with the back of his hand and evenly and eventually, he asked, 'The name Imran Siddiqui mean anything to you?'

I sat back in my chair and measured the question. Yeah, that name meant something to me, but I wasn't quite sure what. Imran, or Imy as I knew him, used to knock about with this stoner, Shaz, and on occasion when I was juggling, they'd pick up off me at the back of the Homebase car park, Isleworth. Some shit-talk and that was it, everyone on their merry way. Once I quit dealing, I didn't see much of either of them.

Until one day Imy tried to fucking assassinate me.

From what little I found out, Imran Siddiqui was a sleeper agent for the terrorist cell, Ghurfat-al-Mudarris, and when said terrorist cell slapped a fatwa on my head, it was on him to carry it out. He couldn't go through with it, though. Living in London, in Hounslow, had softened him, I guess. The fuck do I know!? All I know is that I was looking down the barrel of a gun and then I wasn't.

'What about him?' I asked, drained all of a sudden. All that optimism dissipated out of me.

'Do you know him?' Idris said, one fucking word at a time, like I was a child.

'I've seen him around,' I shrugged. 'Way back when, when I was hustling, he used to pick up a little weed off me… You going to tell me what's on your mind, Idris?'

'You haven't seen him since?'

I wasn't about to give it up that easily.

'Yeah, knocking around town, probably. Fuck, man, what's with the questions?'

'He got married… Last week.'

I shrugged. 'Yeah?' The lights dimmed above me as the DJ took his place behind the booth, a ripple of excitement from the few early ravers. 'Good for him,' I said. 'What's that got to do with me?'

The DJ spun his first track, a Christmas classic remixed with a jaunty Euro-trash beat. Idris leaned in over the table so he could be heard over the music. I didn't know what he was going to say but I had a feeling I didn't want to hear it. I moved back even further in my seat and crossed my arms as I willed my knee to stop hammering under the table. He inclined with his head for me to join him at the middle of the table. I sighed, leaned in and met him there, our foreheads almost touching.

'Ten days ago, there was an attack at his wedding reception,' he said. 'A bomb went off,' he fucking said.

Chapter 2
Imran Siddiqui (Imy)

I used to have this itch. I'd scratch it and it would appear elsewhere. I'd scratch there. Then somewhere else. It would leave me with scrapes and grazes all over my head and body. At times I would break skin and bleed. It was a condition brought on by stress. Brought on by knowing with certainty that one day my past would catch up with me and destroy all those that I cared about.

I no longer have that itch. I no longer have that stress. My past caught up with me.

His name was Rafi Kabir, and at ten years old he was a child desperately trying to be a man. He reminded me of myself at that age, dripping in poison and ready to infect the whole world for a belief shared by millions but no longer by me. From the first time that I'd set eyes on him, I knew that he had the will to one day achieve what I never could.

I'd only spent a short time in his company, but Rafi often crossed my mind. The cocksure smile, the bravado, as though, at ten, he had it all worked out. Spitting out words with raw intention, the vicious promise to kill for his people, when at that age, his people should have been running around a playground, and not a battlefield.

But that's not how he was brought up. He was a product of his environment. His father, his brother and his mother, all had a part to play in polluting an innocent mind with sick thoughts.

I had walked away from him, desperately relieved that he would never cross my path again, and I would never again have to look at the hatred in his eyes.

Life has a way about it, though.

An uninvited guest at my wedding. Standing beside my son, Jack, my wife, Stephanie, and my Khala. Waiting, just waiting for the right moment for me to notice him, acknowledge him. With guests in my ear, hands out for me to shake, and pats on my back, I noticed him.

I noticed the detonator, too big in his small hands.

My eyes moved hungrily over my family, one last time. I was too far away to save them but close enough to see the smiles on their faces. They were the happiest I had ever seen.

It's how I would remember them.

*

My Khala was like a mother to me. I buried her the day after she'd been killed. As a Muslim, it had to be that way. Then I waited ten days locked away at home, lying on my side, staring through a small gap in the curtains as it shifted continuously from darkness to light to darkness. I ignored the knocks on the door, the phone calls and the well-wishers, and mourned them just as I had once mourned my parents. But I was older now, stronger, no longer a boy. And I had nothing or nobody left to lose.

On the tenth day, I put on the same black tie and suit and buried Stephanie, my wife only for a day, and Jack, my son. He would have turned six that day. We'd planned to celebrate on the beach in the Maldives, a joint celebration of our marriage, his birthday, and a future that I had been foolish to present to them. I had ripped the tickets into the smallest of shreds and then Sellotaped them back together and placed them in the inside pocket of my suit jacket.

15

I stood alone at the side of the graves, the rest of the mourners stood away on the other side. To them I was damaged, a disease, someone to steal glances at and blame. Stephanie's mother and father would have stood by my side, but they too had been murdered on our wedding day.

Somebody, I don't know who, had hired out an old tavern for the wake. And somebody, I don't know who, said a few words. The mourners, who had been guests at our wedding, sat and listened in grim silence, surrounded with cheap Christmas decorations, knowing how close they themselves had come to death. They drank, they ate, they whispered, they stared. I felt the blame directed at me and accepted every judgement. They walked away, leaving me on my own with ringing messages of consolation and promises of support. It meant nothing to me. They meant nothing to me. I'd never see them again.

Last to leave, I walked out of the tavern and into the early evening darkness that the winter brings. My Prius sat alone in the small car park, a thin layer of snow melting away as the weather changed to a cold rain.

I unlocked the car and lifted the boot. From under the spare tyre I picked up a roll of plastic food bags, a handful of elastic bands, and a Glock .40-calibre handgun and suppressor. I pushed the boot shut and sat in my car, placing the items on the driver's seat. I started the car and as I waited for it to warm up I felt a presence outside.

My hand reached across and instinctively I gripped the cold steel barrel of my gun and turned to look outside my window. A figure wrapped up in a black puffa and a woolly Raiders hat that I recognised, ambled slowly and uneasily towards me, each step more tentative than his last. I dropped the gun on the seat and placed my hands on my lap.

Shaz was the only other person left in this world that I cared

16

about. But the cards had been dealt and turned over and he had walked away from my life without a goodbye. Because of who I was. Because of what I had brought into his life.

We watched each other for a moment through the driver's side window, replaying the same events in our minds. I had once hurt him and I hadn't seen him since. I blinked away the memory and slid down the window.

'I'm… I'm so sorry.' He said the words I should have said to him a long time ago.

I took my eyes away from him and stared straight ahead at the Christmas lights running along the roof of the tavern.

'Steph… Jack… Khala… I don't know what to say… I'm sorry.'

I turned back to him. His teeth chattered and his body visibly shook from the cold or from facing me again. He looked at me for a response and I wanted to give him one. I wanted to get out of the car, put my arm around him and buy him a drink. I wanted to hear him regale me with the first world problems that always seemed to bother him. I wanted to hear his laughter. I wanted to hold him.

Instead, I nodded blankly.

'Anything I can do?' He shrugged softly.

I shook my head.

'I've moved away.' Shaz hesitated. I didn't blame him for not telling me where. I had once brought hell to his doorstep.

'It's okay,' I said.

Shaz looked embarrassed at what our friendship had become. He shifted his eyes away from mine and they landed on the passenger seat, on the roll of plastic food bags, the elastic bands, before resting on the handgun and suppressor. He blinked as though trying to find the common factor between the items. He couldn't. How could he?

I watched him jerk back, as though he had just been pulled back

17

from stepping onto a busy road. His eyes were wide, wild, worried, expressing what words could not.

'I have to go,' I said.

I slid the window up, my eyes not leaving his, and shifted the gear into D and drove away. In my rear-view mirror, past Jack's car seat, I watched Shaz get smaller and smaller until he disappeared out of my life.

Chapter 3
Jay

'Jay,' Idris called. 'Did you hear what I said?'

Imy got married? There was an attack? A bomb went off? Yeah, I fucking heard him.

Not able to bring words to my lips, I nodded and snatched my eyes away from his. Over Idris' shoulder, a gaggle of giggling girls moved onto the dance floor. A group of three lads followed, all tight jeans and tight T-shirts and perfect glow-in-the-dark teeth. They stood at a safe distance, eyes set on the girls as they coolly nodded their heads to the bass. In an effort to impress, one of them decided to break the monotony and bust a move. His body moved too fast to the music as he drew invisible shapes with his hands. *Too soon,* I thought, *bide your time, mate.*

'Aren't you going to say anything, Jay?'

'Is he dead?' I asked.

Idris shook his head. 'No… But there were fatalities.'

I nodded again, my eyes still over his shoulder. The over-enthusiastic dancer had peeled away from the group and shimmied closer to the girls. His friends watched and laughed on as though they were used to such an audacious move.

'Who?' I said.

'Imran lost his wife and son… He lost his Khala… He lost his mother- and father-in-law.' He held up an open hand. 'Five fatalities.

Six including the bomber. And a whole lot of guests were left with life-changing injuries.'

I nodded and kept nodding. The disco dancer had made himself a sixth toe, bang in the middle of the group of girls. He carried a huge smile, lighting up his face as the girls laughed and danced around him. I wondered what his biggest problem was. If he had any. I wondered if he would continue to live the rest of his life as free and happy as he was at that moment.

'How?' I said, not yet able to form any more than one-word responses.

Idris shook his head again, this time sadly, and took his time telling me. 'The bomber. His name was Rafi Kabir. He was ten fucking years old.'

I blinked and moved my eyes from the dance floor and they landed on the traffic light disco lights at the foot of the DJ booth. I watched them flash from red to blue to green. Red to blue to green. Red… Blue… Green. I focused on them until they were burning a hole in my eyes.

'Jay,' Idris said, putting a hand on my arm. I turned to him, the colours in my eyes moving with me. The bass thumping through my heart. 'You okay?' I nodded. He wrongly took it as a sign to continue. 'Rafi walked into Osterley Park Hotel with an explosives vest strapped to his chest under his sherwani. He detonated at the head table where they all sat.'

'But not Imy.'

'No.' Idris narrowed his eyes, picking up that I called him *Imy*, when I had told him I didn't know him all that well. 'Not Imran. He was at the other side of the hall, but he witnessed it.'

I let it sink in. I tried to visualise it. I couldn't. But I knew what it meant. Imy suffered a punishment worse than death.

'They only got married that morning. Less than a day they were husband and wife!'

'Yeah, alright, Idris.' I didn't need to know anymore. I stood up. 'I'm stepping out for a cigarette.'

I moved away from Idris with my name on his lips. I ignored him and walked through the half-empty dance floor in the straightest of lines, past the happy, and out of the bar into reception. The receptionist, a friend and colleague of my mum, said something to me, like a joke, something funny about my shirt, I can't be sure. I laughed politely without catching her eye and walked out to the pool.

I located my lounger and sat down heavily on it. The humidity, still strong at that time of the night, strangling me. I watched my cigarette shake in my hands all the way to my lips. I sparked up. The swimming pool was empty and blue and still and perfect. I wanted nothing more than to jump in. See how long I could hold my fucking breath for.

I took a long pull of my cigarette, not realising that I had smoked it down to the butt. The cherry was gently burning my finger tip. I let it burn.

Idris was walking towards me, drinks in hand, as if we could continue with this fucking evening. As if I would finally tell him what my life had become.

I wished I could.

He placed the drinks on the plastic table and pulled up a plastic chair and sat down beside me. I stubbed my cigarette out and slipped out another.

'Rafi Kabir was reported missing from his home in Blackburn by his parents eight months ago,' Idris continued, when all I wanted was for him to shut the fuck up. 'Did you not hear about it?'

I shook my head. A missing brown kid was never going to make any kind of waves in the news. The media is selective as fuck.

'The attack has made front-page news,' Idris said, as if crawling through my brain. 'The first few days, the country's media set up shop out on the Great West Road just outside Osterley Park Hotel. There were protesters from the left, from the fucking right. Gangs of Muslims from Luton turned up. Faces obscured with scarves. It kicked off, Jay! Fights and riots! The Four Pills pub and that Indian restaurant next to the hotel was smashed up and looted. Two stabbings and a fuckload of arrests.' Idris took a breath as I held mine. 'All because this kid decided to express his hatred in the most violent way possible, right in the middle of a wedding reception between a Muslim boy and a Christian girl.' Idris rinsed off his beer and wiped his mouth with the back of his hand. 'The press, as you can imagine, lapped it up.'

Yeah, I can imagine. The media. Instant fucking hard-on. Instant fucking narrative. *Bomb attack at Muslim/Christian wedding.* Reporting the level of racism, of hatred it would take for someone to react in that way. To destroy the coming together of two cultures after one had tried so hard to accept the other. I could picture the headlines, designed to prod and provoke, designed to escalate a war starting on social media before drawing blood onto the streets. It's bullshit, such *fucking bullshit*! Just another reason to avoid us, shun us, look at us and judge us. The press were not going to let go of this fucking bone. But once again they would be wrong. Because *I* know exactly why it happened.

It happened because of me.

Chapter 4

Imy

I pulled into our driveway. The front bumper of my Prius gently kissed the back bumper of Stephanie's Golf. The red and white Christmas lights draped across the houses either side of our bare home reflected and blinked lazily on the windscreen.

I didn't move for a moment, or a while. The soft, synthetic leather of my seat cradled me gently as the wind whipped and whistled around me and the rain beat down on my windscreen, making shapes in the darkness that resembled the holes in my heart. I could see her. In the driver's seat of her car, her blonde hair falling across her face, as she leaned across to pick up her work files before emerging out of the car, clumsily balancing the files and kicking the car door shut with the heel of her sneaker. She turned to me and smiled, transforming the storm into sunshine.

The wiper swooped over the windscreen and she disappeared.

I stepped out into the rain and rounded the car. I opened the passenger side door and picked up the Glock. I slipped it into the back of my trousers, letting the tail of my suit jacket conceal it. I slipped the plastic food bags and elastic bands into my inside pocket, along with the suppressor. As I walked past Stephanie's Golf I allowed my fingers to slide gently across the slick windows, leaving my mark.

I unlocked the front door and pushed it open with the palm of my hand. A dark empty hallway greeted me. Behind the darkness

I knew the coat stand was filled with jackets and hats and scarves and *them*. I knew Jack's handiwork was sprawled across the wall in red crayon as high as he could reach. I knew Stephanie's hairbrush sat on the shelf underneath a single Post-it note stuck to the hallway mirror serving as a school run reminder.

Book bag. Bottle of water. Lunch box.

It gripped me instantly. Paralysed me. My legs felt like the heaviest of weights and I was unable to cross the threshold. The wind howled in my ears, the voices and the laughter and the fucking hope that we once shared rushed at me like a physical force and dropped me where I stood onto my haunches. I reached out for support and my hand found the doorframe, my nails clawed into wood. I could feel a breath caught somewhere inside me, desperately trying to escape. I wrenched my tie away from my neck and ripped away the collar, the cold rain snaking its way down my back. I squeezed my eyes closed and pressed my teeth together. My jaw pulsed and my head pounded as their faces filled it. I screamed through gritted teeth, a guttural sound from deep within, willing me not to fall now, not to fail now.

In one quick motion I forced myself up to my feet and stepped inside the hallway and punched the lights on, slamming the door behind me into silence. Their faces disappeared and finally I released a breath.

I stood perfectly still in the hallway, the house now as still as me.

I had too much to do. Afterwards, the ghosts can take me.

For now, I had to focus. I slipped my phone out of my pocket and positioned it on the shelf. It would remain there and place me at home. I picked up my baseball cap and scarf from the coat stand, adjusting the cap low, finishing just below my eyebrows, and the scarf high, covering my mouth. With the cover of the darkness and storm, I didn't think that I could conclusively be picked up on CCTV.

I stared in the hallway mirror at what I had become, what I always was, and what I had tried so desperately to get away from. The black suit that I wore to bury Stephanie and Jack and Khala was drenched and clung to me. I wouldn't change. It felt fitting, somehow, for what lay ahead.

Chapter 5

Jay

Idris went to his hotel room and I went to mine. Thankfully he was seven floors below me. At that moment I needed that space between us. My room had been cleaned. Six pillows lined neatly against the head board, when all I needed was one. I threw the other five off the bed with unnecessary aggression, losing the complimentary chocolate in the process, and snatched the room service menu off the side table. I browsed through it intently, trying to prioritise my stomach over my heart and mind, which were ready to lead me astray.

Idris. Fucking Idris. I know in his own way he was looking out for me but all he was achieving was to bury me deeper into a hole that I was desperate to climb out of. The detective in him knew I was involved in *something*, and I could feel his concern, his disappointment that I couldn't share it with him. I wished I could. I wished I could share all of it with my best friend, but how could I put my shit on him? Instead my silence continued to drive a hole through our friendship.

Idris wasn't aware that I once had ties with MI5, but he was aware that I once had ties with a group of Muslims that had planned and failed to carry out a gun attack in the heart of London. Some of them were based in Hounslow. Fuck, man, one of them lived across the road from me, and I had considered him a friend. He died as result of his actions. If he hadn't, others would have. That should have been it, alarm bells should have been ringing, but no, instead, earlier this year, I grew close to a kid – much against Imy's advice – a kid who was touched by tragedy and decided to even it out by carrying out a fucking acid bomb attack against a right wing group. So, yeah, I get it! Idris was probably shattered from carrying the weight of *I told you so*s.

Given my track record it was only fair that Idris wanted to know whether or not I knew anything about the bombing, as if any shit that goes down in Hounslow has my name attached to it. If Idris had asked me, if he had brought those words and that question to his lips, I would have answered *Fuck no*. When the truth was entirely different.

Eight months ago, Imy walked into my home and pointed a gun between my eyes. I knew he was doing so against his will, and *he* knew that if he didn't pull the trigger then there would be consequences in the shape of his family.

And it came. The consequence, it fucking came.

This bomber, this *child*, exacted his plan to perfection, on what should have been the happiest day of Imy's life. Helpless, he watched his loved ones perish.

The one thing worse than death is watching the ones closest to you die.

The black and white of it. If Imy had killed me, his family would still be alive. But he just didn't have it in him to take a life.

I bet burying his wife and son changed that.

I had to get to him.

I made four phone calls. To reception, telling them that I would be checking out tomorrow. To Idris, telling him that I would be flying out tomorrow, and then cutting him off without explaining. Then a longer call to Mum with a bullshit excuse, telling her that I had to return home. And finally a call to room service, ordering myself a chicken burger, onion rings and a chocolate gateau.

I placed the receiver back in its cradle and eyed the minibar.

It wouldn't be the first time that I'd reached for a bottle to dim the madness.

Chapter 6

Imy

My Prius stayed at home. I couldn't risk the number plate being picked up by one of the many ANPR cameras. I needed a car that would be less likely for the police to notice, one they wouldn't expect me to be driving.

With a full moon for company I walked thirty minutes from our home in Osterley, to Kumar's Property Services in Hounslow West. I hadn't been back to work since, and I wasn't planning to, but I still had a key to the office.

I let myself in through the back door and blinked until my eyes adjusted to the dark. Each blink felt heavier than the last and I had to take a deep breath to push away the creeping exhaustion. I cut through the makeshift kitchen and stepped into the front office and stopped. To the left was my desk, as organised as I had left it. It sat opposite what had once been Shaz's desk. His inane observations and our laughter filled my head. I let it in. Let it add to the rage.

I keyed in the pin to the security box and picked out the keys to the company Ford Mondeo.

An hour later I joined the M40 and settled in for the four-hour journey to Blackburn. I let the radio run in the background, the incessant Christmas music reminding me of all that I would never have.

Rafi Kabir wasn't the only one to blame. If I'm honest, Rafi was the least to blame. The Kabirs, a seemingly normal, happy family, with good standing in the Muslim community, were in reality a channel for Ghurfat-al-Mudarris. Messages, weaponry and explosive materials would pass through many hands before arriving at 65 Parkland Avenue, Blackburn, straight into the hands of Saheed Kabir – father of Rafi and the head of the family. His responsibility was to secure the package in a safe place until it was picked up by a jihadi.

I was once that jihadi.

The Glock .40 handgun that sat beside me in the passenger seat had been provided to me by Saheed, with the intention of using it to carry out a fatwa that I think I always knew I wasn't capable of. I clearly remember the meeting. Kabir was a cheery man, full of life, content for the time being in his small role as he waited patiently for the day that his two sons, Asif and Rafi, would come of age and give themselves wholly to The Cause. He would happily and knowingly send his own blood, to shed blood. He didn't see it coming, though. He didn't see it coming that his youngest, the impatient Rafi, at ten years old, was ready.

He wouldn't see me coming.

I turned onto Parkland Avenue and drove at a crawl. The snow had settled heavier than in London. I parked the car in a tight spot outside number 34 and checked the time. It was near ten, still relatively early. The risk of being seen was high. I pulled the seat back and stretched out. Patience was key. I would wait until the early hours of the morning to give me cover.

I let the wipers sweep away the flakes of snow as I looked out onto the street. It was quiet, not a soul or a Christmas light in sight. This wasn't that kind of place. It was a thriving Muslim community, unashamedly proud at being segregated. I remembered from my last visit, each face was brown and every woman was covered top to tail in black with only her eyes visible. There were four halal butchers, located close together, and two masjids less than a hundred metres apart, with a third under construction. They were frowned upon in today's backwards Britain, but places like this do exist. I didn't have a problem with it. I know what it's like to find comfort with your own, whether that's family or whether that's someone who looks like you. It's only a problem when those values are forced upon you.

I remember clearly Rafi's elder brother, Asif, walking me up and down this street, proudly showing me the sights, revelling in the seclusion. He pointed out a newsagents, the only business on the street that was owned by a non-Muslim. I remember it being empty at the time, as a result of it being boycotted. Seeing it now, through my windscreen, it was boarded-up, out of business. Job done.

Across the road to my right, fifty metres or so in front of me, I could just make out the outline to the Kabirs' semi-detached home. I scanned for police presence, for the press that had set up camp outside the house after the attack. It had been widely reported by the media that Rafi was a cleanskin. He wasn't affiliated to any terrorist group or known in any capacity to MI5 or counter-terrorism. His family were looked at closely, but ultimately they also didn't appear on any watchlists. They hid their connections well. The press frenzy eventually fizzled out after Saheed Kabir had given his tearful doorstep interview to the world's media, about the tragic loss of his youngest son. His pain was genuine, even though his words weren't. His emotion blended easily with defiance as he stated that Rafi was innocent, and had been subjected to religious indoctrination from the day that he had gone missing to the day he took his own life. Not once mentioning that his *innocent* son had taken innocent lives. As for religious indoctrination, Rafi had been indoctrinated a long time before he went missing. By his father, his mother and his brother, who raised and nurtured him to exact madness against those who opposed their beliefs. The Kafir.

31

I couldn't wait any longer. The thought of Saheed's emotion in front of the cameras fuelled mine, and my body moved of its own accord. I don't remember stepping out of my car. I don't remember tucking the Glock into the waist of my trousers and slipping the suppressor in my inside pocket. All I know is that I was striding through the snow, the plastic food bags secured tightly over my shoes and hands with elastic bands.

The weather had picked up. The gentle fall of snow was now torrential rain, dropping from a black cloud that would forever follow me. I pulled my baseball cap low and my scarf high. It gave little protection against the strong wet wind, biting into me, trying to blow me back the way I came.

God's way.

But me and Him, we were no longer talking.

I lifted my eyes and through the storm I glanced at number 65 across the road. My eyes furtive and busy, taking in everything. Upstairs the bedrooms lights were on, shining a ray through the gap in the curtains. Downstairs, the living room light was off, but the glare of the television through the net curtains illuminated one figure.

I dropped my gaze and moved past the house. Further down, two houses next to each other had their lights switched off. Number 71 and number 73. Only a metal gate between the two houses separated them. I crossed the road and without breaking stride I rested one foot on the metal gate and scaled over. I hurried around to the rear of the house and into the back garden. The fences were head-height but the adrenaline made me feel light as I lifted myself over with ease. I ducked low under washing lines as I crossed from garden to garden to garden, until I was standing in the Kabirs' garden.

I craned my neck up. Upstairs the toilet light came on.

I pressed myself to the house and sidestepped to the back door.

I peered inside, through the frosted window. No movement, just the muted sound of the television. I removed the Glock from my waist and wrapped the tail of my scarf around the butt of the gun and then tapped it firmly against the window. The glass fell gently onto the kitchen mat on the other side. I put my hand through; the glass cutting into my forearm caused me no pain. My hand landed on the lock. I turned it and stepped inside their home as glass crunched under my shoes.

I looked around the kitchen as I attached the suppressor to the Glock. It was dark but I could make out a tower of mismatched Tupperware on the worktop. The neighbours. They would have rallied around at this *tragic* time and forced home-cooked meals into the hands of the Kabirs. I moved out of the kitchen and into the narrow hallway. Flashes of light and music from the television travelled from the living room. I stopped halfway into the hallway as an unwelcome memory hit me and I stood staring, just as I had eight months ago. Hung on the wall, the *Ayut-al-Kursi* in swirling Arabic written and engraved in wood. A prayer that once meant so much to me and was threatening to do so again. I squeezed my eyes shut and gripped my gun tightly and let them in again.

Smiling. Laughing. Living. Dying.

I exhaled hard and walked past the prayer without another look. With the Glock in my grip hanging low by my side, I stepped into the living room.

To my left the television was tuned into a music channel, heavy drum and bass accompanied by flashing lights. I turned to my right. Rafi's older brother, Asif, had already leaped up from his armchair and was hurtling towards me, the flashing from the television made his movements appear jerky. He cut the distance quickly. I blinked as a tight fist gripped around a remote control came towards me, connecting just above my eye, knocking my baseball cap off. I absorbed it. No pain. *No fucking pain!* The batteries dropped out of the remote and cracked loudly on the laminate floor. A second blow, same place, and I felt a trickle of blood above my eyebrow. I switched the Glock from my left to right hand and swiped across, blindly catching Asif flush on the jaw and dropping him. He looked up at me. Anger turned to recognition and then realisation.

'Imran?' he said, getting himself up on his knees. He spat out a bloody tooth. I lifted the Glock and pointed it to his chest. 'I couldn't have known… I didn't know Rafi was going to—'

I pulled the trigger and felt the bullet travelling through my heart and through my arm and popping quietly out of my hand and into his heart.

Asif dropped back, his head meeting the floor with his legs still tucked underneath his body. I breathed in three times through my nose and out of my mouth.

I would not let the guilt in. He had a hand in this.

I turned away and moved out of the living room. I passed framed family photos hung on the wall as I slowly climbed the stairs, the last of the family's memories. I stood on the landing, the Glock impatiently tapping against my leg. To the left, a light seeped underneath the bathroom door. To the right, a bedroom, door ajar. I pushed it open slowly. The room was lit dimly from a small football-shaped table lamp. Rafi's room.

By the side of the bed, Rafi's mother was standing on a prayer mat, hands clasped against her chest, her face a picture of peace. I watched her for a moment, just as I'd watched my Khala pray so many times. She moved her hands to her knees as she bent down towards Mecca, and then knelt in the *Sajdah* position, her forehead touching the floor as she recited *Subhana Rabbiyal A'laa*, three times.

The Glock twitched in my hand.

She sat up, back straight, such was the discipline, she kept her eyes fixed firmly on the prayer mat even though there was no doubt that she would have noticed in her peripheral vision a stranger in her home.

She turned her head slowly over her right shoulder to the angel who records good deeds and softy whispered, 'As-salamu-alaykum Rahmattulah.' She turned her head slowly over her left shoulder to the angel who records wrongful deeds and softly whispered, 'As-salamu-alaykum Rahmattulah.' It signalled the end of prayers.

She folded the prayer mat twice over and got to her feet. Turning her back to me, she placed the mat on the bookshelf, amongst Islamic literature mixed in with comics. She sat down on Rafi's bed, her hands clasped together on her lap, and for the first time lifted her eyes to me. She nodded.

The gun felt heavy as I lifted my arm and pointed it at her. I nodded back and shot her in the chest. She fell to her side, her head finding her son's pillow.

I would not let the guilt in. She had a hand in this.

I stepped out of the bedroom and waited on the landing for Saheed Kabir, faithful servant of Ghurfat-al-Mudarris. A man who helped fight a war that to many was justified. He was a small part of a huge movement, one that had become too powerful in the battle against the West, against the deaths of innocent Muslims across the world. He was a man who had educated his two sons with nothing but hatred towards the West and hatred towards the Kafir.

In the eyes of his ten-year-old son, I was that *Kafir*. I was that *Munafiq*. I was that *traitor*.

I heard the sound of the flush and then the sound of running water. I lifted the Glock and pointed it at the toilet door. The water stopped, the handle turned and the door opened.

Saheed met my gaze before his eyes moved towards the bedroom, then back on me. Filled with dread, his mouth moved, a silent question on his lips.

I answered it with a slow shake of my head.

Saheed fell heavily to his knees, a tear escaping from his eyes as his obese body shook and shuddered. 'Asif?' His voice barely above a whisper. 'My son?'

I shook my head again and his howl deafened me as tears flooded his eyes.

'My family,' he cried, at my feet. 'You took away my family.'

'You took away mine.'

I shot him twice in the chest.

I would not let the guilt in. Saheed Kabir had a hand in this.

Chapter 7

Sophia looked up at Easedale House, the tired-looking tower block standing tall but unremarkable amongst the surrounding identical tower blocks that filled the landscape within Brentford's Ivy Bridge Estate. Brentford had undergone – or was in the middle of – a regeneration project; Sophia wasn't sure which. It had been ongoing for years. Her crappy flat in her crappy tower block was a few minutes' walk away from the flats on the waterfront with price-tags she could never dream of affording. Nine figures had been spent on the regeneration, but not a drop on the Ivy Bridge Estate. Sophia despised having to walk past the smell of the rich, so close to her shit-hole flat.

Not even entertaining the idea of the piss-stinking lift, Sophia trudged up three floors. She walked past a whiny malnourished Alsatian tied to the railing on the first floor, and nodded curtly at a neighbour slumped on the landing of the second floor, who, judging by his eyes and blank stare, looked as if he'd fallen off whatever wagon he had been on. She entered the lobby of the third floor and let herself into her apartment. She closed the door behind her and double-locked it, aware that the cheap Homebase locks wouldn't withstand force. The door probably wouldn't even withstand somebody leaning against it.

As per routine, Sophia picked up the iron bar on the small hallway table and gripped it firmly in both hands as she walked from room to room, checking for chancers. She entered the bedroom last, dropped the bar on the side table and shrugged off her coat, letting it fall in a puddle at her feet. An ancient desktop PC sat on a desk in the corner of the room. Sophia lifted the monitor off the computer and placed it to the side. Her heart picked up as she clicked the two catches on the side of the PC and lifted the cover. Inside, sitting on the motherboard, right beside the hard drive, was a small stack of fifty pound notes, amounting to exactly ten thousand pounds. She sighed with relief, clicked the cover back in place and sat the monitor on top of the computer. And then, as she did every night after a shift, fell backwards with her arms out onto her unmade double bed, enjoying the thrill of her body bouncing gently before coming to rest. Strands of blonde hair fell across her face. She blew them away from her eyes and stared up at the damp patch on the ceiling, lit by the two working downlights. It was not a view she would get used to.

*

Sophia Hunt had arrived in London, aged 22, clutching hopefully onto her Performing Arts Diploma. She'd waited patiently for the opportunity – that one successful audition that would kick-start her career and give her the chance to live life on her own terms. Meanwhile, she worked hard as a cleaner. No, that's not right. She worked as a cleaner, but the effort was minimal, as were the wages and tips. Sophia's mother had been a cleaner. So had her grand-mother. Was it predetermined for Sophia to end up on her hands and knees, with a J-cloth and a backache, and to serve those who felt it was open season to grab, grope and fondle the fucking help?

Sophia's father had been a social worker, before he injured

himself, accidentally-on-purpose, and pissed off with his benefits. He wasn't big on sharing-is-caring. Sophia didn't blame him. At least he'd had some semblance of get-up-and-go when he'd got up and left.

Her mother, not able to afford childcare, dragged Sophia to her cleaning jobs, from the age of seven through to her teenage years. She couldn't bear to watch her mother crawl around grand homes with her bad back and her bad knees, making the place gleam whilst pocketing items that wouldn't be missed. It made Sophia sad. Sad to watch her mum. Sad that they were surrounded by money but didn't have any.

She died of a heart attack on the job, with an apron full of silverware. Sophia promised herself that she would not end up in the same position. But she was going up against life and patterns and a history of bloody cleaners in her family.

Sophia put in her all to achieve her Performing Arts Diploma, sacrificing sleep to study lines, skipping meals to stay skinny, taking extra classes to help improve her singing and dancing. But it had become quite evident, fairly soon after she'd arrived in London, that she was just one of a million starlets who shared that same hunger.

Working as an extra on TV wasn't as exciting as it had seemed. Hours of waiting around with all the other desperados, eating yesterday's sandwiches, until she was called to aimlessly sit in a coffee shop or a pub whilst the A-listers blocked her view of the camera. Regardless, she gave it everything, made each role her own. Once she had to push a pram across the road and she did it *method*. Making sure the road was clear as any mother would, looking left, looking right, and then left again, before tentatively crossing over, only for the director to shout, *'Cut! Just cross the bloody road!'*

Her diploma meant nothing, on top of which she couldn't remember where she'd put it, and these days all the networks could afford to make was reality TV. Brain-dead airheads with no qualifications or discernible talent, catering for the brain-dead viewer. Despite herself, Sophia adjusted, realising that it may be her only path to success, a platform from which she could showcase her talent to the world. She applied for the lot, and was turned down by the lot. Her only success, if you could call it that, came as she got through to the second round of *The X Factor* and the judges had to decide between her and some singing clown who couldn't hold a note for toffee. After some pretty dramatic deliberating, the judges chose the singing clown who sang sad songs with a frown.

Over the years, casual employment and the odd shoplifting spree helped her keep her head above water. She started to decline TV extra work, it was beneath her, and concentrated on promoting her talents on social media. Her presence was heavily felt on every platform by her twenty-three followers, who, if she was honest, were dirty old men, ogling her. She had lived in hope that a music producer or a film director would spot her undeniable talent, but all she'd received was creepy direct messages and dick pics.

And just as she was coming to another realisation – that the cleaning, the waitressing, the odd temping job, was no longer a stop gap, but just a stop – a man had entered her life and presented her with an opportunity.

*

It had been five days since Sophia had found the handset on her doorstep. She wasn't expecting it, and her first and second thoughts were that it had been wrongly delivered, and how much could she sell it for. She'd frowned when she noticed it was an old throwaway Nokia phone with physical push buttons, screen the size of a matchbox and no camera. It was worth next to nothing. She'd flipped it over and attached to the back of it was a small silver key and a white card. In neat handwriting the card read: *Call me*. With growing curiosity Sophia did just that.

A polite gentleman had answered. He told her his name was Samuel Carter. He sounded like a Samuel Carter, too, as though he had been brought up well, educated the expensive way, and never been referred to as Sam or Sammy. It was a particular quirk of Sophia's that whenever she met somebody new, or spoke to them on the phone, afterwards she would take her time deciding whether their name matched their face or voice. She had done this ever since she realised that her own name was so far from the mark. When you hear Sophia, you expect grace and glamour and a few quid in the bank. You don't expect a grubby apron and a damp ceiling and the high rise of Ivy Bridge Estate. And her surname: Hunt. Posh! As though she had come from old money, rather than a mob of cleaners and fraudsters.

Samuel had informed Sophia that he had located her online, sifting through her various profiles on social media. Samuel Carter wasn't in a position to help her further her non-existent career, but he was in the position to help her. Why he chose her, she didn't know or ask, but she was aware enough to realise that her online presence exuded a certain desperation and a willingness.

The job he had presented to her was easy, low-risk and with a pay-off to the tune of fifty thousand pounds. Ten that had already been delivered after their one and only conversation, left in a locker at Metro Bank – that's what the key attached to the phone was for. The money was there in a small bundle of fifty pound notes, which she had pocketed and transported safely back home and hidden amongst the guts of her computer. Samuel hadn't been in touch since.

Sophia reached across to her cabinet and from the drawer picked out the pay-as-you-go Nokia handset. She turned it on and waited a long minute for any alerts to come through. When that didn't transpire, panic didn't quite set in, but it was nearby. Had Samuel changed his mind?

Sophia shuffled up on the bed and rested her head back against the creaky headboard. She tried to relax, tried breathing techniques to force the panic from knocking on the door. If Samuel didn't get in touch, then what? Was it still on for tomorrow? Worst case, she still had ten thousand pounds. But ten wasn't exactly fifty. She'd already spent the fifty in her head. She was going to update her portfolio and replace cheaply taken selfies with professional shots. Then she'd hire a music studio and lay down the tracks that she'd been writing since she was thirteen and finally direct and star in her very own, high-production music video, possibly in Paris, possibly Rome, and share the hell out of it, until someone important sat up and took notice. Hadn't Justin Bieber got noticed online? She would stretch every penny of that fifty thousand pounds. She'd give it her best shot. Her last shot.

Sophia checked the phone signal, five solid bars stared proudly back at her. She checked the volume. She even called it using her own phone, and it rang loudly in her hand. Sophia considered her options. Samuel had treated her like an equal, she reasoned. It wasn't just a set of instructions, he had actually asked her for advice about the task ahead. Just like a partner. A business partner. She stared at his phone number. He hadn't said not to call, and surely one partner should be able to call the other.

Sophia pressed dial and butterflies the size of bats fluttered and danced away in the pit of her stomach. She cleared her throat several times as it rang once, twice, three times, before abruptly being cut off by a smarmy automated voice, telling her that Samuel Carter had found somebody better suited, or words to that effect.

'*Shit!*'

Sophia disconnected the call as the butterflies vacated, leaving her stomach feeling cold and empty. She stared at the phone until the screen dimmed.

'*Shit!*'

The small screen came to life and the unexpected ringing made her jump.

'*Oh, shit!*'

The butterflies were back with a vengeance, and they'd brought their butterfly friends with them. 'Hello,' she answered carefully.

'I apologise,' he said, and she thought she heard the slightest of accents, which hadn't been evident the last time they spoke. He lost it by clearing his throat. 'I had to find a quiet spot.'

'Oh, yeah, yep, yes. No problem. Not. A. Problem,' she replied, aiming for nonchalance but getting nowhere near it. She cleared her throat loudly and wondered how disgusting it would've sounded.

'You called, Sophia,' he said. 'I trust everything is okay?'

She loved how he said her name, like it was meant to be said. Samuel waited patiently and Sophia had to switch on and recall why she'd called. *Why had she called?*

'Are we definitely on for tomorrow? It's just I hadn't heard anything.'

'Yes, Sophia. We are planning to go ahead tomorrow, as discussed. But, as I said before, it's entirely your call. If you feel that you may encounter logistical issues, then, by all means, we can further discuss or… We can abort.'

She had never before, not once, been spoken to like that. He valued her opinion. He actually valued the value of her opinion. Sophia smiled as she wiggled her big toe through the hole in her tights. They were partners. *Partners in crime!* As for logistical issues,

43

all she had to do was leave the patio door unlocked, turn a blind eye, and then deal with the fallout with the police.

'I can't see there being any logistical issues,' Sophia replied. Check me out, talking logistics, she thought. 'I think we should proceed.'

'Excellent, Sophia,' Samuel said. 'It's been a delight dealing with you. Now, I'm sorry to say that this will be the last time that you and I shall be speaking.'

'Oh,' she said, her heart taking a sideways dive. She wasn't sure why.

'I'm afraid so. After this call, can you possibly delete this phone number and call register and dispose of the cell phone discreetly.'

'Yeah, sure. I'll dash it. Like, an outside bin? Or even in the river?' Sophia said, enjoying the drama of throwing away incriminating evidence in the river in the cold of the night, right under the noses of where the rich lived.

'Outside bin is fine. Just as long as the cell is cleared.'

'Okay,' she said, nodding thoughtfully to herself, as she recalled the *Jason Bourne* movie she'd seen the previous night. 'Should I take it apart piece by piece and put the battery in one bin, and the other bit in another bin, maybe on another street. And the sim card… I could destroy the sim card by frying it.'

Sophia thought she heard a sigh.

'It's fine to throw it away in one piece. It's unregistered.'

'If you're sure,' Sophia said, slightly cut. Maybe she was trying too hard. She should just say as little as possible, though that had never been her style. She had to think about number one. 'When do I get the rest of the money?' Sophia asked, carefully.

'A second key for a second locker will be posted to your address. The same as last time. The remainder of the fee will be there.'

Sophia had no reason to doubt Samuel Carter.

Chapter 8

Jay

The hotel room phone trilled in my ear. *Shut the fuck up!* I lifted the edges of the pillow tightly over my ears. The trill dimmed but just would not quit. Defeated, I reached out to it, blindly knocking a bottle of water off the side table as I located the phone.

'Good morning, Mr Qasim,' the smoothest of voices said. 'This is your eight-thirty wake-up call.'

'Yeah, I'm up, man. I'm up,' I slurred. My tongue felt as though it was wearing a fur coat and my breath bounced back at me off the phone. I turned my face away in disgust and noticed that the bottle of water that I had knocked over was actually a bottle of beer, steadily dripping onto the carpet. That damn minibar had broken my defences.

'Fuck's sake!' I groaned to myself as I straightened the bottle. That was going to cost me about seven quid in Qatari money!

'Excuse me?' the voice said, losing a little smoothness.

'No, not you… Thanks. Bye.'

I replaced the receiver and stared up at the ceiling, waiting for my vision to clear, trying to piece together my movements before sleep had eventually found me at… who knows when. The last time I had glanced at the clock, it was four something, closer to five.

The thought of meeting Imy had twisted me up inside, and I just wanted to forget about him, just for a minute. I think I had a moment of madness. Me. On my own. Wanting to let the fuck loose with total abandonment before I faced up to my responsibilities.

Not sure what happened after that.

I lifted my heavy head off the pillow and took in the state of the room as it sadly recounted the story of my night.

Yeah, it was coming back to me.

I remember wanting a drink but being too mentally drained to leave my bed. Rather than walk the three steps, I'd crawled to the foot of the bed and reached out to the minibar, which was just tantalisingly out of reach. I hung halfway off the bed, stretching, my shoulder screaming at me as I managed to pull open the door. The light illuminated my face and the miniature bottles neatly lined up greeted me like a surprise party. I started with a vodka.

I'd stayed at the foot of the bed, on my back, my head hanging off the edge as I watched the brilliant *Mean Girls* upside down, whilst knocking back drink after drink, unable to get Imy out of my head.

I'd pictured standing in front of him, meeting his eyes and letting him know, in no uncertain terms, that I recognised my part in his loss. I'd welcome whatever he threw at me. I'd fucking take it all.

Oh man, I got so wasted. Dotted around the bed were empty miniature bottles lying sadly on their sides, as though they'd been abused. I dropped my head back on the pillow, the pounding in my head taking the attention away from the ache in my stomach caused by all the food that I'd ordered from room service!

I knew that I should be getting up and packing, but I gave myself five more minutes just to get myself together. *It's always five more minutes* – How many times had Mum said that to me? Feeling sorry for myself, I turned on my side and curled up in a ball. Beside me was a chocolate gateau, some eaten, some spread across my pillow. I rubbed the side of my face. Some there, too.

I turned my back to it and flopped to the edge of the bed. I thought

46

about how much of a tip I should leave for housekeeping to clean my mess. Next to the bed was a bin, that I'd placed there in case I vomited. Next to that, a pool of vomit!

I groaned loudly and shot myself out of bed and went about carrying out a pre-emptive clean before housekeeping clocked on and, through Chinese whispers, Mum found out. I couldn't have that.

Satisfied, with the room looking semi-respectable, I spent record time brushing the crap out of my teeth and tongue whilst hopping around in the unpredictable shower. I had used the bath towel to soak up the vomit, so with an impossibly small hand towel wrapped around my waist I set about packing my holiday clothes before getting into my shitty-weather England clothes.

I had a flight to catch.

There was no way I was calling a bell-boy. I had already spent a small fortune on tips, so I belled Idris and asked him to help me with my luggage. He was at my door a few minutes later, looking annoyingly fresh and rested in his shorts and lairy Bermuda shirt. The total opposite of me.

'You sure you don't mind me staying on a few days?' he said, entering my room, sniffing and making a face. There was nothing I could do about the smell, but crack open a window. Idris took me in, jeans and Jordans where shorts and flip-flops should have been. A hoody on the bed to carry onto the plane, and my parka jacket in my hand luggage. Prepared for the wet, windy, vicious weather back home, back in Hounslow.

'Here, grab that,' I said, pushing my trolley his way.

'I still don't understand,' he said. 'Why'd you have to rush back?'

Why? A man's family had burnt and perished and I had a part to play. I had to find out how far a simple *sorry* would take me in easing the fucking guilt that I was drowning in.

'I just have to, that's all, Idris,' I said, knowing how unfair it was

47

to keep my closest friend in the dark. It wasn't the first time, and I'd started to realise, the way my life was turning out, that it wouldn't be the last, either.

'Obviously, this is about Imran Siddiqui,' he pressed, and I couldn't deny it but I could ignore it. I handed him my rucksack. 'Okay, fine! Be like that. Least tell me what bullshit you told your mum, just so we're on the same page.' Idris couldn't keep the frustration out of his voice, or maybe he didn't want to.

'Told her that...' I hesitated, knowing how it was going to sound.

'Go on. Told her what exactly?'

'Told her that I'd received an email inviting me for a job interview and that I really couldn't afford to miss the opportunity,' I said, looking suitably sheepish at the lame excuse.

'What job?' Idris asked.

'What's it matter what job?'

'Jay!'

'Project manager,' I mumbled.

'And she believed you?!' Idris scoffed, clearly not convinced that I could be a project manager.

'The fuck's not to believe?' I said, more than a little offended that he didn't think I could be a fucking project manager. I could *easily* be a project manager. Give me a project and I'll fucking manage it. Maybe it was the lack of sleep, or the hangover, or the prospect of flying back home and into fuck knows what, but Idris was getting on my last nerves. He always found a way – I know not on purpose – to make me feel a lot less important than him. As though being a Detective Inspector puts him on some elite level.

The fuck's he know!? I've done a shit load more than manage fucking projects. You ain't the only one making a difference. I did, too. A big fucking difference. Global. Fucking international! Not just plodding around after junkies in Hounslow.

I wanted to tell him just to shut him up.

'What is it?' Idris sensed. He edged closer, eyes on high alert.

It would have been for the wrong reason. Just so that I could prove to him that I was *somebody*, and I was worth *something*, and not just the fuck up he clearly thought I was. I shot him a look that said, *Sorry mate.*

'Alright.' He sighed, then like a friend he smiled. 'I'm coming to the airport with you.'

'Yeah,' I said, looking back at the room where I'd spent the last couple of weeks pretending all was okay. 'I thought you might be.'

*

The lift doors opened and I saw Mum before she saw me. She had taken position behind the reception desk and was dealing with a hotel guest. She'd already told me, on the phone the night before, that she wouldn't be able to accompany me to the airport as she couldn't get the time off at such short notice. It was better this way. I tend to get overly emotional at airports.

I moved myself in her eye line and gave her a small wave, she beamed when she saw me and I recognised the sadness behind it. She palmed off the guest to a colleague, picked up a large boxy paper bag and hurriedly walked around the reception desk. She placed the bag by her feet and threw her arms around me, one hand cupping the back of my head, the other hand lightly gripping my shirt.

I was going to miss Mum so fucking much, but I was determined not to show it. The last time we had said goodbye it was a cocktail of tears and snot and uncertainty. I couldn't show her that I was still that person. She had to know I'd be alright.

'It's cool, Mum,' I said, as she released me, my smile coming easily as she straightened my hair. 'I'll come visit soon.'

'Or I can come and see you in the New Year.'

And see the mess that my life has become.

'I'd rather come back to be honest, Mum. Keep the sun going for me.'

'Andrew is going to drive you to the airport, Jay. He's just bringing the car around.'

'He didn't have to do that,' I said. The last thing I needed was stilted conversation, but at least it would stop Idris from interrogating me further.

'If you need anything, *anything*, I'm here, Jay. I'll be here.'

I know what she meant. She would always be there just as my father wasn't.

'Oh, almost forgot.' Mum picked up the boxy bag and handed it to me. 'I popped into the mall this morning before my shift and got this for you.'

I snaked my hand into the bag and pulled out a smart, sandy coloured mac. I nodded dumbly at it.

'For your interview, Jay. You can't turn up in your parka.' Mum smiled and in that moment the hard fought determination not to cry threatened to crumble as my bullshit lie gained momentum. Not wanting Mum to see me break, I moved back into her, holding her tightly, releasing a deep breath over her shoulder, as Idris averted his gaze to the floor. I steeled myself and released her as she planted goodbye kisses all over my face. I took it all in, the smell, the touch, the comfort. A weird feeling swept over me – I couldn't shake it off – that a time was coming when I would desperately need to reach out and recall this moment.

Chapter 9

Imy

It wouldn't bring back my family, but pulling the trigger felt right. I didn't entertain the idea of disposing of the bodies. I left them where they fell and walked out of their home. The immense feeling of satisfaction was fleeting and I was overcome with an almighty tiredness as I struggled through the now torrential rain. Burying my wife and my son, followed by the long drive to Blackburn with nothing on my mind but avenging my family, had consumed me. I couldn't remember the last time I had eaten. Slept. The adrenaline that pushed me was gone, leaving me feeling more exhausted than I'd ever been.

The rain hindered my vision as I swayed and staggered and once stumbled to my knees as I tried to remember where I'd parked my car. I eventually found it after walking obliviously past it, before recalling that I had stolen Kumar's company Mondeo and not travelled in my own Prius. My mind and body, that had worked together perfectly to exact my revenge, had deserted me and the sharpness was replaced by a mist.

I turned up the heating the moment the car came to life, and held my hands close up to the vents, the seat beneath me shaking in rhythm to my body. I hunched over the steering wheel for support and gripped it tightly as I drove out of Parkland Avenue. With my phone at home and the absence of a satnav I drove aimlessly from one empty street to another until signs led me to the M6.

Thirty minutes on the motorway and I was startled back to alertness as headlights filled my car. I looked in the mirror, and saw a big BMW X5 with fluorescent markings. My heart thumped in my chest. They flashed again. What had I done to give myself away? I looked down and saw that the needle was hovering at forty-five mph, which on a motorway is almost as dangerous as speeding. I put my foot down, taking the car to sixty and beyond, hoping they wouldn't feel the urge to pull me over and ask me any questions or search my car.

The car slipped into the middle lane. Their eyes on me as they moved past. I noticed then that it was a Highways Officer – plastic police, not the real thing. Even so, I was shaking long after I lost sight of their tail-lights.

I released a sigh of relief which turned into a yawn. The heavy patter on my windshield was hypnotic, and yet again I found my eyelids starting to betray me. My body flagged and my shoulder moved towards something to lean against, causing the car to veer into the middle lane. The blare of an SUV shook me. I pulled back hard and the car swerved before settling back into its lane. As I straightened up in my seat I caught a glimpse of a young family, eyes wide and faces white with fright. I threw up a hand in apology.

There was no way I could complete the four-hour journey in that state. I had to take a risk before I became a risk to other drivers. I had to get off the motorway before somebody got hurt.

I managed to stay alert for the next five miles, and pulled into the first service station. I kept my cap low and my head down as I walked across the forecourt and followed the inviting light through the automatic doors. Despite it being the early hours of the morning, it was busy with families and groups of friends coming or going. Living a life that I would never have. I headed straight to the bathroom and splashed and scrubbed my face with cold water. I ran a wet hand through my hair, letting the water drip down my back.

Leaning against the sink I stared at myself in the mirror. The black suit I wore to bury my family. The same black suit I wore to kill another. I squeezed my eyes shut and questioned my actions. That of judge, jury and executioner.

I had no regrets.

Without making eye contact I purchased a black coffee, a chicken sandwich, and picked out the coldest bottle of water from the back of the cooler. I took a seat alone at a round table and tried not to focus on the two empty seats across from me. I removed the lid and emptied three sachets of white sugar, then took a sip of hot coffee followed by a bite from the sandwich, and then another before I'd swallowed the first. As I broke it down in my mouth I watched from under the peak of my cap. Two kids – brothers, judging by their features – were messing about at an internet kiosk under their parents' watchful gaze. Their eyes were darting between their children and me, as though they sensed a threat. As though they could sense that I had a gun tucked into the waist of my trousers.

I placed the cold bottle on the back of my neck and it sent an icy shiver down my spine as I glanced up at the security camera at the entrance. There were two more cameras on each side of the food court, plus the three that I noticed in the car park, that would have picked me up as I drove onto the forecourt. I had no choice. The state I had been in, I couldn't have stayed on the road.

Regardless of my carelessness, I would've been the obvious suspect. It was inevitable that the police would knock at my door. But I wouldn't be the only suspect. There had been numerous threats made to Saheed Kabir and his family. Vile threats, cowardly threats of death and rape and ruin from behind a keyboard by those looking to place the blame on them. It was a release of aggression, venting, trying to put the world to rights, but ultimately they were empty threats. Nobody was going to touch them. That right belonged to me.

The two brothers left their station at the internet kiosk and I watched them join their parents. They walked out of the food court, the father turning to look at me one last time. I held his gaze until he turned away, a protective arm around his wife.

I picked up my coffee and bottle of water and approached the internet kiosk. I slipped in two pound coins which allowed me thirty minutes of internet time and opened up a search engine. Sweat covered my back as I typed in his name. I hit enter.

The rage that had led me to kill Saheed Kabir and his family in cold blood was a different rage to how I felt about *him*.

He had social media accounts on Twitter, Facebook and Instagram but his activity was minimal. The only recent activity was two photos that he'd posted on Facebook. The location was tagged – Qatar.

The first photo was in a restaurant. Him and his mother in conversation, their hands meeting at the middle of the table, unaware at the time that their photo was being taken. She was looking at him like Khala had once looked at me. Like a mother looks at a child.

The second photo, he was in a swimming pool, his elbows resting on the edge next to a colourful drink with a small umbrella. He was smiling broadly behind orange-tint sunglasses. Like a man without a care in the world.

I looked at the date stamp – 3rd December. It was the date that I was married. The date where I'd lost everything.

Chapter 10

Sophia Hunt's alarm buzzed at 4.30 a.m., just as she was in the middle of a Beverly Hills shopping spree, a snobby shop assistant was questioning her means of payment, *a-la Pretty Woman*. But unlike Julia Roberts, she didn't have to rely on a smug-faced Richard Gere to come to her rescue. She hated that bit. Always had. It wasn't the fairy tale that she was looking for. This was different. A man and woman on equal footing, neither reliant on the other. A business deal, if a little crooked, but like her mum always used to say, usually as she slipped a trinket or two into her apron, *Robin Hood was a national treasure, if it's good enough for him…* It wasn't her best advice, but it wasn't her worst.

Sophia lifted the duvet and her feet left the warmth of her single bed and found the laminate floor, cold enough to send a walking-over-her-grave shiver through her bed socks. She snaked her hand under the duvet and located the fake Gucci cardigan that she had slept beside, so that it stayed warm. She shrugged it on and wrapped it tight around her as she took in the day in front of her.

There's crime and then there's *crime*, from petty to full-on evil, and all the degrees inbetween. A couple of nights ago, Sophia had popped into Londis. She paid for the tiger bread roll, but pocketed the cheese spread. Nobody got hurt. It was a victimless crime. But what she was planning to do, wasn't. But was it evil? Sophia didn't think so. If all went to plan – and how could it not? – then nobody would get hurt, and the *victim* would be compensated through insurance. Everyone's a winner. Okay, maybe not a winner, but, Sophia shrugged to herself, nobody loses.

Tonight, after her part was complete, she would have to face the police. She accepted that. It why Samuel Carter would be paying her so handsomely. The cops weren't a problem; her story would be straight. They'd believe her because, even though nobody recognised it, Sophia Hunt was a damn good actress and this would be her breakthrough role, one that changed everything.

Sophia picked up the pay-as-you-go handset from the cabinet and slid it into the side pocket of her cardigan. That was her only concern. That phone, those conversations, the secrets between her and Samuel Carter. It was the link that could see her swap her one-bed flat for a one-bed jail cell. Regardless of Samuel's somewhat casual attitude about the phone being unregistered, she would dispose of it as safely and securely as she deemed necessary.

Sophia got to her feet. The day had begun, and it was promising to be a long one. To help combat the cold, she pulled a pair of baggy jeans over her thin pyjamas and slipped on her navy blue coat, and matching bobble hat and gloves. At nearly five in the morning, armed with some burnt buttered toast, she walked ten minutes in the quiet and still darkness of the bitterly cold early morning, and made her way through Brentford Docks. Above her the rich slept soundly, the way only the rich can.

She arrived at the edge of the River Thames and leaned against the metal railing, her teeth chattering as the cold seeped from the slick, cold metal railing, through her gloves to her fingers. She faced the dirty grey, unimpressive river and shook her head as she wondered why people would pay hundreds of thousands for this crappy view? If she had that kind of money, would she? Absolutely, she decided.

Using her teeth, she pulled off her gloves and noticed her hands shaking. From the cold or from the nerves, she wasn't sure, but it reminded her of her dear old Nana's last years. She blew hot air onto her hands and rubbed them together hard and fast, before flexing her fingers and feeling the blood circulate. She removed the pay-as-you-go handset from her pocket and wedged a fingernail into the clip and released the battery. With a quick look over her shoulders, she lobbed the battery as high and far as she could, and lost sight of it before it had become part of the great river. She peeled out the sim card and lobbed the handset in another direction, again losing sight of it before it went under. *Would it go under, or would the waves carry it until it flows into the North Sea, on the way to France or Germany or even Norway?* Sophia impressed herself. Maybe some things had seeped in at school whilst she was scrawling her stage name – *Simply Sophia* – in pink and gold felt-tip all over her exercise book.

The last piece, the sim card, Sophia placed between her teeth and clenched down. She bent it back and forth until it weakened and snapped clean in half. Sophia placed both parts of the sim card on the palm of her hand and flicked one, and then the other, in two different directions, into the River Thames.

Chapter 11

Jay

I stepped off the aeroplane and cleared arrivals without any issues. More than could be said about the young Asian man that got hooked out of the queue and taken in for questioning, even though he was clearly Sikh judging by the turban wrapped neatly around his head. *Fuck, man,* how do these clueless fucks get these jobs, all they see is dark skin and a beard and it's hunting season. I could be wrong, he could have been pulled for a whole 'nother reason, but I don't think so. When the man appeared back, half an hour later, looking dishevelled and more than a little humiliated, I knew that he'd had his turban hand-checked and possibly removed. Do these clowns not realise how fucking offensive that is? It pissed me off, but was I surprised? Fuck no! If you're brown and travelling, you best have your affairs in order because fuck knows where you're going to end up. Airport security don't think twice, barely think once, they just react on some unfounded instinct. Happens all the time. But that doesn't mean we get used to that shit.

I could feel him, could feel the angst in his face. I watched him look around sheepishly to see if anybody noticed. *We all noticed, mate.* I caught his eye and nodded at him in solidarity He didn't return it and turned his back to me. Fair play.

I swear these things never used to bother me until that is, they did.

I picked up my luggage from the merry-go-round, and on a whim slipped on the mac that Mum had gifted me. I buttoned it up to the hilt and stepped out of the terminal. Even though I'd braced myself, the weather was a shock to the system. Only twenty-four hours ago, I was on my arse sizzling in the sun as I made eyes at my girl on the other side of the pool. And now this. Sideways fucked-up rain pelting me, and a strong wind not letting me spark up a much needed post-flight fag. I popped the collar shielding my face, and took the shuttle bus to the long stay car park. Just to elevate my bad mood I was charged for the full four weeks, even though I'd returned two weeks early. Bad mood didn't last long, though. Just for a minute everything was forgotten as, sitting there in Red Zone, Row 4, comfortably holding its own between a white Bentley and a silver Maserati, was my black BMW.

Restored to its full glory.

When Bin Jabbar had been killed, my Beemer had taken the full force of my anger. I'd taken a baseball bat and smashed the shit out of the one constant in my life. The regret was instant and overwhelming, and I didn't think twice about parting with the best part of five G to have it restored. That money was pretty much the last of the MI5 pay-off, and I was living off the kindness of strangers until somebody hooked me up with a job.

I placed the trolley and holdall in the boot, and then I did a couple of slow laps around my car, inspecting it for even the *slightest* sign of damage, a scratch, a nick, a fingerprint. I knelt down by each wheel and rubbed the built-up dirt away from the alloy with my sleeve. I nodded to myself, satisfied that my baby was as I'd left it. I pressed the button on the fob, and the interior lights lit up softly. I opened the door and sat behind the wheel, shutting the door gently on the world behind me.

And it just *felt* like home.

The car came to life on the button, as though it'd been waiting for my touch. Automatically it connected to my phone via Bluetooth. I opened up my playlist on Spotify and swiped my finger down, and watched all those killer tracks tumble down. I jabbed at one at random. 'Appetite for Destruction' – NWA.

Yeah, that sounds about right.

I wheeled my Beemer out of the car park and pointed it towards Hounslow.

First stop, find car wash. Second stop, find Imy.

*

I rolled my car into *American Jetshine* behind the Treaty Centre and requested the full complement. I walked out with my face in my phone and almost bumped into a car queuing to get into the car wash. I mouthed an apology as I checked out the car. Trust me, this car was built to be checked out. Latest model Mercedes AMG GT Coupe, dropped low on matt black 22s. The colour was a customised job, like a slimy green. The bodywork looked immaculate, and not at all like it needed a wash.

I couldn't make out the driver's face as the sun was bouncing off his windscreen, but I could feel his eyes on me. Typical cuts, I assumed. It's something you get used to living in Hounslow, a fuck-ing pastime, looking to make something out of nothing. He slid down his window and I moved away before he could start something. The last thing I needed was more friction.

As my Beemer was getting scrubbed behind the ears, I took a stroll through Hounslow High Street. It had been a long, stiff flight and I needed to stretch my legs and allow the cold air to slap me out of tiredness. I couldn't be a shattered mess when I faced Imy. I had to be on point.

60

I grabbed a takeaway cappuccino heavily sprinkled with chocolate for a boost, and strolled aimlessly, hoping for some of that Christmas magic to rub off on me. It didn't work, not like it used to.

It just doesn't feel like Christmas around Hounslow anymore, not like it does in neighbouring Kingston or Richmond or the like. I don't know what it is. Maybe the rise of the powerful pound shops, or the lack of a decent shopping centre. Sure, we have Treaty Centre, and it gets seasonally decked out, but it all seems a little half-arsed. It wasn't always like that. I remember Mum taking me to a giant Santa's grotto in the main lobby of the Treaty. She'd plonk me on the lap of a pretty decent Santa, surrounded by proper sized elves, year in, year out. It took until my early teens for me to clock that most of the kids queuing were younger than me. I didn't care. Christmas was everything. I'm not sure what changed, or when the mood shifted. Looking around now, it could be that there's just way too much culture and colour and other occasions that take precedence, and are celebrated with a little more gusto, to give too much of a crap about Christmas. Either way it was sad to see.

On a whim I nipped into Argos and picked out a six-foot plastic tree, and then hit the 99p store and left with a bag of decorations for under a fiver. I decided that I was going to make the most of Christmas, like it used to be. Like it should be. I refused to be on my lonesome like a sad Christmas commercial. I'd invite Idris over for some pre-Christmas-dinner drinks, and then I'd invite myself over to his place for his mum's halal chicken with all the trimmings, and watch whatever Harry Potter was showing on a satisfied stomach. I owed it to myself to end the year on a high, after the shit-circus of a year I'd had.

With two weeks to go before Santa was due to shoot down the chimney, I started to get that feeling, but I had to put it to one side. For now, I had more pressing issues to suss out.

I picked up my freshly cleaned motor, then steeled myself and headed towards Imy's place, a short drive down London Road. I only knew that Imy lived there because he and a stoner called Shaz used to session there, and I'd made the occasional visit to deliver some green. Seemed like a lifetime ago.

Across the road I could see workmen pulling temporary traffic lights from the bed of a truck, and I knew I was going to get stuck in traffic on the flipside. I pulled up on the opposite side of the road to The Chicken Spot. The strong smell wafting from there and through my open window made my stomach moan in anticipation, and I tried to recall the last meal I'd had. I'd never had the privilege to eat there before. According to the locals, the chicken was fried to crispy perfection, but I'd always been loyal to Aladdin's and their Inferno Burger. Either way, I wasn't there to eat.

Above the chicken shop was Imy's flat. The curtains were drawn. I watched intently for a moment, but couldn't make out anything other than that the curtains were drawn. I imagined Imy behind there somewhere, mourning. Or maybe he was past mourning and was intently plotting. Could be that plotting was his way of mourning. I could picture him sitting in an armchair staring at a wall covered with photos of all those who had wronged him, with maps and locations and bits of different coloured string connecting them. I wondered if I was on that wall. I wondered if he was waiting for me, watching me from a great height through the telescopic sight of a high-powered rifle.

I shuddered, killed the engine and stepped out of my car, not knowing what to expect. It could be anything from a slap in the face to *adios*, Jay. Whatever! I had to make my presence felt. I owed him that much. I looked both ways before jogging across the road and then slowing to a walk. I glanced inside The Chicken Spot and wasn't surprised to see customers queuing for a speciality heart-attack breakfast. I approached the door just to the side of it and pressed the buzzer. It sounded muted, like the batteries needed replacing, but probably Imy wasn't ready for household chores. I knocked on the door, respectfully at first, and then a little louder. I took a couple of steps back and looked up, shielding my eyes from the sun, which had made a surprise appearance considering the time of year. The curtains were still drawn. It got me thinking.

Imy had just got married. Would he have planned to live here with his wife and son, above a chicken shop? Doubt it. But in the absence of any other options this was as good a starting point as any.

I doubled back and stepped into The Chicken Spot, the smell of grease and onions and the hunk of doner meat smelt divine, and my stomach grumbled at me: *Fill me the fuck up!* I ignored it and leaned my arms on the counter.

'Mate,' I said to the guy with the greatest moustache in the world and a food-stained apron that I could easily have licked.

'Help you?' he said. Heavy accent, could have been from anywhere. I'm not hot on accents.

'Yeah,' I said, trying not to talk to his 'tache. 'Have you seen Imy? He lives upstairs.' I pointed up at the cracked, yellowing ceiling.

He took me in, paying special attention to my sandy mac, his eyebrows banging into each other in bemusement, maybe because I'd accidentally mistaken a chicken shop for the missing persons bureau. He leaned over the counter and his moustache was almost as close to my face as it was to his. 'You look like journalist,' he growled.

I gasped; I'd never felt so offended in my life.

I ventured out a smile. 'I'm a friend,' I said, playing fast and loose with the truth.

He snorted through his nose and something flew out. 'Where you from, boy?' he said from somewhere under his moustache.

'Here, Hounslow.'

63

'From newspaper!' he said, not letting it go. He picked up a meat cleaver in one hand and a blade sharpener in the other. 'I tell you what I say to all newspaper people. Get out of my restaurant!'

Restaurant! Probably best not to correct him. But I did need to convince him that I wasn't a journalist. I think it was my new sandy mac, it made me look exactly like a fucking hack. I assumed I was being judged by association. This shop had probably seen its fair share of reporters attempting to dig up dirt on Imy so they could write an inaccurate article.

'He's my friend, I just want to know where I can find him.'

He stared me down before turning his sizeable back on me and going about his business. I was losing him, and it made me do something I'm not proud of. Something which contradicted my friend status, and cemented that I actually was a fucking journalist.

I cleared my throat loudly. He turned back around to see near ten pounds, in coins, neatly stacked on the counter. I looked at the bribe and then at him. He looked at the bribe and then at me. His jaw tightened and his eyebrows collided. I swallowed and lowered my gaze, realising quickly what a shit idea it was. I had no choice but to abort mission and improvise.

'Can I have three pieces of chicken, fries, and a can of Coke, please?'

Chapter 12

Jay

I blasted the heat to max, dropped the gear and pulled away from The Chicken Spot towards London Road, only to drive into a standstill. Ahead of me were unnecessary road works galore. I was temporarily defeated by temporary traffic lights. I shifted the gear into neutral and checked my mirrors for the cops before firing up the web browser on my phone, hoping for some inspiration. I typed *Imran* in the search bar and Google ominously auto-filled *Siddiqui*. I ran my eyes down the first few hits.

Racially motivated bomb attack at wedding party.
Five dead. Many injured. Husband survives.
Ten-year-old Jihadi targets interfaith marriage.
Hostile reception for Prime Minister as she visits Osterley Park Hotel amidst protests.
Calls for tighter immigration laws.

Nah, I ain't reading any of that shit.

I shut down the browser and exhaled dramatically as traffic crawled slowly in front of me. It was killing me to be so stationary. Frustrated, I slipped the car into gear and pulled a daring U-turn and I was on my way. I glanced in the rear-view mirror, wishing away the suckers stuck in traffic, when I noticed a slimy green Merc pull the same manoeuvre.

There was no way that there were two of them in Hounslow. Not in that fucking colour. I'd seen that car twice in the space of a couple of hours.

Okay, so rationalise. It's not exactly unheard of to pull out of traffic and head in the opposite direction. The earlier appearance at the car wash was a little strange, though, considering the car already looked squeaky clean. But then again, if I was rolling around in a motor like that, I'd be getting it washed daily. I shrugged it off. I didn't have the time or the energy for paranoia. I put my foot down and put some distance between my Beemer and the Merc and took a turn and slipped down a quiet residential road.

Finding Imy was turning out to be a proper mission. There was one person who could help me in my search, but I really, *really* did not want to go there. The last thing I needed was for a next man to get involved, but with fuck all in the way of options, I had to consider it.

Using the dial on the centre console I scrolled through my phone book and stopped at S.

I caught myself smiling as his name appeared on the screen.

I wouldn't say we were friends; he was once my customer and I was once his dealer, that was the extent of our relationship. But I liked him, he was funny as fuck, mostly unintentional as he muddled through life like I once did. He and Imy were close, like only stoner-buddies can be. If anyone could point me in the right direction, it'd be Shaz.

My finger hovered over the screen. I swallowed the guilt at getting him involved and jabbed at his name. The phone rang through my car speakers, and eventually a small voice that I didn't recognise came through.

'Hello.'

I turned the volume up a touch. It didn't sound like Shaz at all.

His token greeting had always been a jovial 'What's cracking, Jay?' followed by an inexplicable laugh and a smoker's cough.

'Shaz?' I asked, unsure.

'Yeah. Alright, Jay?' he said through a sigh.

'It's been time, man.'

'It has. Look, I'm not looking to score at the moment.'

'That's cool,' I replied. 'I'm not looking to deal.' I laughed unnecessarily. He didn't, unnecessarily or otherwise. I cleared my throat. 'I wanted to chat to you about some next thing.'

I heard him sniff, as though he'd been crying or maybe he just had a seasonal cold.

'I haven't got long, Jay,' he said softly.

'What'd you mean?' I said carefully, wondering if he was ill, as I tried to recall the last time I'd checked my testicles.

'I've got a coach to catch in an hour.'

'Oh,' I said, relieved. 'I just need, like, five minutes, ten, tops.'

He didn't answer, and whatever he had said up to that point didn't seem like the Shaz that I knew. Considering the sensitivity of the situation, and the sensitivity coming off him in droves, I figured it would be better to meet him rather than chat about it over the phone. That way he wouldn't be able to cut me off.

'I can link you now, tell me where you are?' I said.

'Seriously, this is not a good time.'

'Please, Shaz. It's important,' I said, approaching the junction to the Great West Road, my hand hovering over the indicator, the direction dependent on his reply. It came in the form of a low moan. I was frustrating him, I know, but I couldn't let it go.

'Is this about Imy?' he asked, so fucking gently, that I had to think twice before answering.

'Yeah,' I said. 'It's about Imy.'

'Sorry, Jay,' Shaz said. 'I... I can't meet you.'

He disconnected the call.

Deflated, I slowed down, and without a destination I parked my car to the side. I let the engine idle as I slid down in my seat. I squeezed my eyes shut and pinched the bridge of my nose. The fuck was I thinking, calling Shaz? He'd probably been at Imy's wedding reception – scratch that, he was probably best man! He would have seen the tragic events of that night unfold in front of his very eyes. I should have let him be.

I exhaled deeply, trying to loosen a little of that frustration. I opened my eyes and in front of me that fucking slimy green Merc was creeping towards me. Any thoughts about coincidences curled up and died when it slowed down and stopped beside me.

His window slid smoothly down. He was a young Asian man, with a tight buzz cut and a small stud on the side of his nose. He was wearing a bright red tracksuit over his skinny frame, and he was watching me with an air of amusement on his face, as though Tom had finally caught up with Jerry. He twirled his finger, gesturing to me to drop my window.

I acknowledged him with a slight nod, and in no mood for bullshit, I said, 'I saw you at the car wash. What? You tailing me?'

'Nah, bro. Just trying to get your attention,' he said. 'You walked away just as I was about to say hello.'

'Do I know you from somewhere?'

'I think me and you should catch up,' he said, completely pissing over my question.

'Catch up?' I said, not a clue what he was chatting about.

He slipped his hand in the centre console and reached for something. My heart did a backflip. This is *exactly* how drive-by shootings happen. To my relief his hand emerged holding up a business card between two fingers. He passed it across through my window. I took it. It was a black and glossy, embossed gold trim bordering around an embossed gold phone number and nothing else. Not even a name.

'Call me,' he said.

I nodded and slipped away the card. 'I better go,' I said, making a show of putting my car in gear.

'Busy man, huh?'

'Just got a lot on, that's all.'

'Yeah,' he smiled. 'Just another day for Jay.'

Wait. *What?*

Before I could ask him how he knew my name, he'd roared away. My eyes flew to the rear-view mirror trying to pick out his number plate before he disappeared out of sight. The plates were private – OMA 22R – I repeated it out loud a few times before it escaped, and opened up the notes app and typed it in. It wasn't exemplary detective work, but at least I now knew his fucking name, too.

Omar.

The name didn't mean jack to me. He definitely wasn't someone I knew from dealing, that circle was small and I knew every one of my customers pretty well. I didn't recall him knocking about town either, flash little rich boy like that, I would have remembered. It's possible that we may have crossed paths at a house party or at a session, or his older brother was in my class at school and *why the fuck was I wasting so much time thinking about this shit*? I had more urgent matters to get my head around and getting hold of Imy should have been my only focus. And my only link to him had told me in no uncertain terms that he wouldn't help me.

*

Doing the right thing, I swear, is a bitch. Most of my life I've done the wrong thing and it's served me well. Responsibility is over-hyped. The last year or two, my attitude changed pretty quickly and pretty fucking dramatically, and doing the right thing has done nothing but cause hurt.

I dropped the indicator and turned right onto the Great West Road, when I should have turned left towards home. There was something I thought I needed to do but I wouldn't know for sure until I got there. If I couldn't face this, how the fuck could I ever look Imy in the eye?

Five long minutes later I wheeled my car into the grounds of Osterley Park Hotel.

Ground fucking zero.

The car park was empty and I parked in the first spot I saw. I exhaled loudly and stepped out. A toxic smell hit me like a force field and I found myself breathing through my mouth. The entrance to the hotel was at the far end, to get to it I had to walk past the hotel pub and the hotel Indian restaurant. Both haunts that I'd often kicked in, lifting my glass in one and stuffing my face in the other. Both now closed for business. I hoped the community spirit Hounslow is known for would soon see both of these businesses thriving again. Then again, people have long memories.

I gritted my teeth and moved quickly past, the presence of rioters, looters and protesters apparent as my feet crunched through a sea of discarded leaflets, patronising placards, broken glass bottles and improvised missiles. All that crap that comes when people lose their fucking minds.

There are six wide steps leading up to the entrance. I stood at the bottom, and despite wanting to puke out my heart, I lifted my eyes to Osterley Park Hotel.

The double doors leading into reception were hanging by a thread. Somebody had attempted to board it up, but somebody else had ripped it off again. The board lay by my feet, and scrawled over it in thick black marker was *Closed for Refurbishments*. It sounded a fuck of a lot more respectable than *Closed due to Terrorist Attack*. A few windows were smashed, and there were patches of a rough paint job, no doubt covering probably offensive or righteous graffiti. If I made the effort and looked closely enough, I could make out the message under the paint, but what the fuck for? To be honest the damage was minimal; it could be fixed. It was the screams that would be trapped inside forever.

I turned my back to the hotel and sat on the bottom step. I slipped out a cigarette, sparked it and pulled hard.

The fuck had my life become?

I'd lived my life in a lullaby, without a care in the world. Juggling a little weed to the bods in Hounslow and cruising through life in my shiny black Beemer, so blissfully ignorant. I never even used to watch the news or read the papers, and suddenly there I was, making the fucking news. I'd seen first-hand the destruction that most people only read, and cast their judgement about.

Fuck, man, this wasn't even the first bombsite that I'd had the misfortune to set eyes on. A hospital, located beside beautiful snow-topped limestone mountains in Afghanistan, was the first. It was built and funded by Ghurfat-al-Mudarris for the poor people of a poor village called Hisarak, and devastated by two US military drone strikes.

The result of a war – as was this, thousands of miles away in Hounslow.

The difference, and there was a fucking difference, was that the military action that destroyed the hospital was able to dodge the bad press. *Sorry about all the innocent lives but target has been met.* A round of applause and pats on the fucking back. Either way, the impact was felt, at the time and forever after. Points are scored as lives are lost. Shit escalates and then calms down for a beat, just before the next devastation. It's just where we are.

I sighed and it sent a shiver through me as I tried to figure out who was the egg in this fucked-up equation, and who was the chicken.

71

I took a last pull of my cigarette and added it to the littered ground, and looked out at the Great West Road. Cars were slowing down with purpose, necks craned, phones out, pointing, snap-snap-snapping away like it was a fucking tourist attraction, taking pictures that would burn through their phonebook, tagged with the same insincere message; *Look what I drove past today! It was harrowing.* Followed by a string of suitable sad-face emojis.

I threw a firm middle finger up at the rubberneckers. *Take a picture of that, you fuckers.*

Tyres crunched on glass. I turned to see a black cab pull into the grounds. The back door opened and a blue Adidas Gazelle hit the ground. A head popped out. His woolly Raiders hat was pulled down and it took me a moment to recognise him.

He recognised me, though. With his hand gripped to the car door, he remained rooted to the spot. I expected him to fall back in and leave. I looked away. The car door closed. I nodded knowingly to myself and sparked up another cigarette.

A moment later I felt Shaz stand beside me.

I looked up at him, trying to figure the right way to acknowledge him, but he was transfixed on the hotel. I let him be, didn't say a word. He'd had already made it clear that he didn't want to talk to me.

Shaz had changed. Obviously he'd changed! Shit like this chews you up, spits you out and then tramples on you. He looked like he'd put on weight and lost weight at the same time. I was used to seeing him carrying a quizzical look on his round face, as though he was trying to work something out, and then beam stupidly as if he had just worked it out. Now he just looked gaunt and sad. Yeah, Shaz looked sad.

'You alright, Jay?' he said, after a time.

I nodded. 'Yeah, you know.'

Shaz looked at the waiting cab before sitting down next to me on the bottom step.

'Yeah,' he said. 'I know.'

I pushed my cigarette deck towards him and he slipped one out. I sparked him up. He nodded his thanks and we smoked in silence for a bit as we both ran silent conversations in our head.

'I had to see for myself,' Shaz said.

'Me too,' I replied. 'I'm sorry. It must have been—'

'I didn't go.' Shaz cut me off. 'To the wedding, I didn't go... I went to the funeral.'

I could have addressed it, asked why he hadn't attended his best friend's wedding. I was curious enough, but it wasn't any of my business.

I changed the subject. 'Where you off to?' I said, nodding at the cab.

'Terminal 3. From there I'm catching a coach home.'

'You've moved. How comes?'

He replied with the smallest of shrugs. 'Just... I had to get away.'

I didn't push him, sensing that whatever Imy had gone through, Shaz, in his own way was going through, too. I didn't blame him for moving. He didn't ask for any of this shit. The person who he considered his closest friend had carried secrets that had devastated those around him. I know a little something about that. The secrets and the life I'd kept from Idris had strained our friendship, at times threatened to break it. I realised then that I couldn't allow what happened to Shaz and Imy to happen to me and Idris.

We sat in silence, looking across at the Great West Road through a cloud of cigarette smoke.

'I got to see him,' I said, before I could stop myself.

'What?' he said, his face scrunched up tight.

I didn't repeat it. He'd heard me. I waited for him to get his head

73

around it. He did so by bouncing to his feet. 'What is it?' he said, standing over me. 'You wanna pay your condolences? Fuck, Jay! Take my advice, stay as far as fuck away from him. He's... He's not right. He ain't thinking right!'

'I know he's not.'

'You don't know shit! And you don't know him!' His outburst had caused his Raiders hat to shift and I clocked the tail end of a deep scar. 'Fuck!' he hissed and pulled down his hat and stared at me in defiance, daring me to say something.

I didn't.

I watched a fat teardrop roll down his cheek followed by another. I stood up and clumsily rubbed his arm.

'Sorry.' Shaz apologised when he had no need to.

'Don't be.'

He swiped a hand over his face. 'It's bad,' he said. 'He's mixed up with some bad people. People that... Shit, Jay, it sounds so...' Shaz took a ragged breath and then he snorted out a laugh, and there was the tiniest glimpse of the Shaz I knew. 'These fucking guys!' He shook his head in disbelief.

'You and Imy, did you fall out?'

Shaz touched his two fists together. 'He was my boy, yeah. But he's got problems, he's got problems that I can't even begin to get my head around. I should have stepped up, but no. What do I do? I run. I up and move as far as fuck, don't even tell him. And now... This! *His family! Like that they've gone!* And here I go again, looking the other way, walking in the opposite *fucking* direction.'

Shaz closed his eyes tightly and bopped his head a few times as though he was struggling to find his go-to-tune and instead finding nails down a blackboard.

'He's got a shooter, Jay.'

Yeah, I knew he had a gun, I knew because he once threatened to put one between my eyes. I nodded my head without committing to anything. 'Tell me where I can find him.'

Shaz shook his head, and looked at the cabbie. I thought I'd lost him, but really I'd fucking broken him. He met my gaze, held it in his, and slowly he slipped off his beanie hat.

I stared when I wanted to close my eyes. I stared at the word *Kafir* carved into his forehead.

He placed the hat back on his head. 'You still wanna see him?'

Chapter 13

Imy

I returned Kumar's company Mondeo in the early hours of the morning and I was back home before the day had begun. I gave my phone a cursory glance. Numerous missed calls, texts and voicemails from well-wishers, same words, words of commiseration and finding strength. I deleted them all without regard as I climbed heavily up the stairs.

I stood outside Jack's room and looked in from a distance. His single bed still carried the small indentation of his small body. *Dear Zoo*, neatly sitting on the side table, by the lamp, never to be read again. A Buzz Lightyear poster peeling from the top corner, calling to be pressed back against the wall in line with the rest of his *Toy Story* posters. I still hadn't stepped into Jack's room since he was taken from me. And I wasn't ready yet. I closed the door.

I stripped off in the bathroom, peeling away my suit, which had stuck to me from the rain and the snow and the sweat. Placing the Glock on the edge of the sink I took a shower and scrubbed myself hard, cleansing the murder from me. I picked out an old grey tracksuit from the wash basket, put it on and headed downstairs to the kitchen. From the worktop I swiped a bottle of vodka by the throat and picked up a dirty glass tumbler from the sink.

I stepped into the living room and walked past the sofa that the three of us had spent so much time squeezed together on, and sat down heavily on the armchair that we hardly used. I poured myself the first shot of the day and waited for the police to knock on my door.

The Kabirs and I had one thing in common: we had paid dearly the consequences of siding with Ghurfat-al-Mudarris. For worshipping a man who I had never seen, yet I had betrayed. Abdul Bin Jabbar, known affectionately as Al-Mudarris by his thousands of followers, and known by the world's authorities as The Teacher. Such was his magnetism, he was able to make each one of his followers feel not like followers but like equals. Those who would lay down their lives for him, even though it would never have been asked of them. It was his teachings that had led me here, put me here. Given me everything and then ripped it away from me. All for a Cause that tried to change the world, but rocked mine.

I had once fantasised about meeting him, embracing him, but that fantasy had shifted. Now when I close my eyes I picture myself looking at him over the barrel of a gun. It would always remain a fantasy. A man who was worshipped by many, had many enemies. And he was killed before I could kill him.

I poured myself a second, heavier shot, and brought it to my lips. Over the rim of the glass, something caught my attention. I knocked the second shot back and wiped my mouth with the back of my hand as I watched his movement through the front window. If I applied even a fraction more pressure the glass would smash in my hands. The face that had fuelled my thoughts had dared to turn up outside my home. I breathed heavily and quickly through my nose as my heart slammed against my chest. I couldn't take my eyes off him, I couldn't blink. I watched him standing at the top of the drive, his mouth moving as though he was trying to convince himself that this was a good idea.

It wasn't.

I tracked him down the driveway as he moved past my Prius, past Stephanie's Golf, before losing sight of him as he approached the front door. I braced myself for the doorbell but instead the loud clang of the letterbox reverberated in my ears. I gritted my teeth and willed for him to leave and never think of making the same mistake again. Instead, he moved on from the letterbox and pressed the doorbell. Once, and then again: a short sharp burst and my heartbeat raced and my fingers gripped the arms of the armchair as he pressed it a third time. I pictured my Glock in the upstairs bathroom resting on the edge of the sink. It was just as well that it was out of reach.

Then a beat of silence. He'd left. I closed my eyes tightly before letting my eyelids relax as I concentrated on my breathing. I took a breath and another, as I tried to lose his face, stop it from playing on my mind. When I opened my eyes he had his nose pressed against the window.

Chapter 14

Jay

I walked across Imy's driveway and looked back at my Beemer, hoping that I would be getting back into it in one piece. I'd just had it washed, and my car had already seen too much of my blood shed. I walked past a Prius, which I knew belonged to Imy, and then past a Golf with a child's car seat in the back. That alone nearly made me spin on my Jordans and drive for the hills.

I took a breath and tried to clear the vision of when we'd last met. A gun planted between my eyes. Hands shaking, unable to pull the trigger. A decision that would irrevocably change his life.

I glanced through the bay window as I approached the front door, and wondered if his eyes were on me. I pushed the letterbox and it clanged loudly in my ears and I realised that I should have pressed the doorbell. So, I pressed the doorbell, too. I don't know why I did that.

I waited for the clanging and the ringing to die down before I jabbed at the bell short and sharp, but I wasn't sure if it had rung that time, so I pressed it again, just in case, and then jammed my hands in my pocket, so I wouldn't be tempted to do it again. He surely would have heard. I tried to work out his movements; the funeral had been the day before, I doubted that he'd be out. Chances were, Imy was curled up in bed, mourning his loss, with a pillow over his head, pissed off at the idiot insensitively jabbing at his doorbell like it's a musical instrument. But I was here now, and I had to see this through. I side-stepped off the porch and pressed my forehead against the bay window and peeked through the small holes of the nets into the living room. It took a second or two for my eyes to adjust.

On the other side of the window Imy was sitting in an armchair with a glass in his hand. He was looking right at me with dead eyes. I swallowed and pointed at the front door as though to gently guide him through the door-opening process. *Fuck, I was on form!* I watched him for a moment through the nets, as he tried his utmost to ignore my existence. I could have and should have come back another time, but would it have changed anything? I was never going to be welcome there. I side-stepped back onto the porch and got down on my knees and pushed open the letterbox and spoke through it.

'Imy,' was as good a start as any. 'It's me, Jay,' wasn't the best follow-up. 'Look, I... I... I wanted to chat to you... I heard... you know, I heard what happened... Can we talk... please?'

I let the flap drop and rested my forehead against the cold steel of the letterbox and sighed. He didn't want to see me and I couldn't blame him. I'd thought maybe the dark history that we shared would count for something, we'd both lost a big part of our lives to this. But I had to remind myself that my loss could not be in the same league as his. It was time to give the man some space. I pushed the letterbox and put my mouth to it.

'Listen, Imy. I'm gonna go. I'll try again later. Tomorrow maybe. Hopefully you'll—'

The door flung open and from my position on my knees I lifted my eyes up to him. He wrapped his fists around the collars of my mac, hoisted me to my feet and dragged me over the threshold. He kicked the door shut behind him and then spun me around in a waltz before pinning me to the wall with force.

He gritted his teeth in my face. No words, just a feral growl coming from somewhere deep inside him. I smelt booze on his breath as he shook me. I allowed my body to slacken and let him just fucking get on with it, which he did. He repeatedly bounced my head hard against the wall. I took it. I'd take it all. He dropped his hands and balled them into fists, his forehead scrunched tight over his face as he breathed heavily through his nose.

I did what I went there to do: I looked into his eyes and said, 'I'm sorry.'

His fist connected against my ribs, and again, two rapid jabs, painful as fuck. I slid slowly down the wall and crumpled to the floor. I lay on my side and held my stomach.

Imy leaned down, his breath in my ear, his tears on my face. 'You ever, *ever* come to my home again, I'll fucking kill you.' He left me there on the floor, and through heavy eyes I watched him walk away.

I should have, too.

Chapter 15
Imy

Jay was nothing to me but a reminder of a destination that I would never reach. I could not stand to look at his face. He had *his* eyes, *his* face, all I could see was his father in him. And I reacted. If I'd had a gun in my hand, I think I would have pulled the trigger without thought or hesitation.

I dropped down on my armchair and poured myself another shot. From the hallway I could hear Jay shuffling to his feet, muttering a swear word under his breath. I slumped back and took a sip of neat vodka. I placed the glass against my forehead to help cool a fast-approaching headache.

I know, I damn well know that Jay isn't responsible for my family's death, but if I'd never set eyes on him, they would be here and he wouldn't.

The front door opened. I squeezed my eyes shut and held my breath as I waited for the door to close behind him. And only when it had, did I exhale and feel my heartbeat slow. A moment later, when I opened my eyes, Jay was peering into the living room.

He pointed to his bright white hi-tops and said. 'Shoes off… or…?'

'What the hell is wrong with you?' I said, ready to dish out more punishment but not having the heart, will or energy to go through with it anymore.

'I'll just keep 'em on, if that's cool?' Jay tentatively stepped into the living room, holding his side from where I'd struck him. He stood around awkwardly for a moment as he regained his breath. His eyes wandered over to the coffee table, to the bottle of vodka and the tumbler and then back to me. 'In the kitchen?' he said.

I clenched my jaw as he disappeared, and I could hear him in the kitchen noisily going through the cabinets before popping his head around the doorframe.

'Can't find any. There's a couple of glasses in the sink, but they need washing.' He waited for me to reply, and when I stared back at him in open-mouthed disbelief, he said, 'It's cool. I'll wash them.' And with that he disappeared again. My fingernails dug into the arms of my chair, and my heartbeat started to race again, my head started to pound.

I heard the tap come on, then I heard him hiss, *Fuck! Hot!* He clattered around for a while, longer than he would need to wash one glass. I got to my feet and peered around the door and into the kitchen. Jay had taken his coat off and placed it on the worktop, and he was bent over the dishwasher stacking days-old dirty dishes.

I backed away as he closed the dishwasher door. A moment later he returned, a clean tumbler in his hand which he placed on the coffee table. I held his gaze. He tried to return it, but I could see the uncertainty in his eyes as he stood awkwardly in front of me.

'Do you mind?' Jay asked, nodding at the bottle. When I didn't answer, he poured himself a small shot and sat on the edge of the family sofa which I still hadn't sat on since.

He took a sip. It started small and then developed into a gulp, possibly for courage. He made a sickly face before wiping the back of his mouth with his hand. I reached for the neck of the bottle and Jay covered the top of his glass with the flat of his hand.

'Can't. Driving,' he said before realising that I was pouring one for myself. 'Oh, right, yeah, you go ahead.'

'What do you want?' I asked.

'Just…' He shrugged. 'Wanted to see you. See how you are.'

'Why?'

Jay took his time finding the right words and, unable to bring them to his lips, he said, 'You know why?'

My hand shook as I poured another for myself. 'You think that you owe me something. Is that it?'

'Yeah. Yeah, I do.'

'As if it all happened because of you?' I said. It sounded harsh, and maybe I wanted it to.

Jay's eyes wandered round our living room, stopping at the canvas of Jack dressed as a sheriff on a rocking horse. 'Is that how you feel?' he asked, carefully.

'Yes,' I said, 'it's how I feel.'

The words had left my mouth without regret and without meaning. I watched him, nodding his head in agreement, his eyes going back again to the canvas of Jack. He blinked away the tears.

My words were designed to cut him, and they did.

Chapter 16
Jay

Fuck, man! Tighten up. Don't cry now. If anybody should be crying, it should be Imy, not me. I didn't have the right. But, too late, the process had started, and I had to take a few undercover breaths to hold the tears from dropping down my face like a sap.

I turned away and quickly ran a hand over my eyes before he noticed. Not going to bullshit, his words hurt, but if that's how he felt, then that's how he fucking felt. I wasn't there to change his mind just so I could get a better night's sleep. Sleep and I didn't get along anyway, dotted with shit that I didn't want to see. What's one more thing to carry through the night?

I could feel him measuring me. He seemed pleased with the effect his words had on me. I think he was expecting me to up and leave. Well, fuck that. I wasn't done yet.

'I chatted to Shaz, earlier,' I said, measuring him right back.

He blinked at me with intent and challenged it with a 'So?'

'He's worried about you?'

'It's not his place anymore. And it's definitely not yours.'

Okay, still hostile. Understandable. But that was enough playing tag around the park. It was time to get to the point. 'He said that you've got a shooter.'

Imy shook his head slowly, incredulous, snorting through his nose as though I had no right to ask him. I opened my mouth to say more, but he got to his feet and grabbed me by the arm and lifted me out of my seat. 'It's time for you to leave.'

'What're you going to do with it?' I asked, and I noticed his face flinch. It set me on edge. 'What the fuck have you done, Imy?'

He dug his fingers into my arm and I just knew it was going to leave a bruise. I pulled away. He took a step into my face and it took a lot for me not to back away. I held my ground and locked into his eyes, they were red raw and his jaw was set tightly. I expected another beating. So fucking be it.

The doorbell saved me.

Imy kept his glare fixed on me as it rang impatiently a second time. He stomped out of the room and I heard the front door open. I inclined my head and assumed the eavesdrop position, but I couldn't quite figure out what was being said. It didn't sound like he knew them. I figured it was the time of the year when the God-squad did their rounds, and I expected the conversation to be short. A minute or so later, Imy walked back into the living room. He picked up his house keys from the coffee table and dug them in his tracksuit pocket.

'Let yourself out,' he muttered, without explanation. I opened my mouth to speak but he walked away before I could respond.

I rushed over to the bay window and stared out through the nets. He was walking across his drive flanked by a blandly dressed man and equally bland woman, towards a car parked across his drive.

I paid special attention to the motor; a Skoda Octavia, dark in colour and only two years old. It was clean and well kept. I couldn't see from my position but I'd bet my life that the dashboard was busy with communication instruments. No question, this was an unmarked cop car.

The man opened the rear door and Imy slipped into the back seat, and the door was slammed shut.

I did what I always did when I needed information: I placed a call to Idris. It did that weird international ring, reminding me that he was still in Qatar and not local. He wouldn't be happy with me for asking this of him, again.

'Jay-Jay,' he said, chirpily, obviously having the time of his life. 'Let me call you back, I'll Facetime you. You gotta check out this view.'

'No! Idris! *Fuck!*' I exclaimed as he cut me off. I watched the undercover cop car pull away and out of sight before my phone rang. I swiped to answer and Idris' big head popped up on my screen.

'Hang on,' he said, as he flipped the camera. Past his bare legs and hairy toes, I saw what he was seeing. White sand, the beautiful blue ocean and the sun out in force. 'Huh? Huh? Aaaah!' Imy cooed at the picture postcard!

'Idris,' I said over his appreciative murmuring, 'fuck's sake, turn the camera around. I have to chat to you.'

'I can't believe you walked away from all this,' he said, appearing again. 'What's up?' he looked past me and into Imy's living room. 'Where are you?'

'Will you shut up for a second and let me talk?' I said. 'I need your help.'

'Are you alright?' he said, some concern on his face, some urgency in his voice. 'I'm in Qatar, Jay. I can't get to you. What's happened?'

'No, I don't need you here. I need you to make a phone call.'

'Phone call? What d'you mean? To who?'

'Hounslow nick,' I said.

'Work! You want me to call work?! I'm in Qatar, Jay!'

'Yeah, I know, you don't think I can't fucking see that?'

Idris shook his head. 'I swear you take the piss. Are you going tell me what's going on?'

Shaz crossed my mind. The damage inflicted on him by the secrets Imy had kept from him.

'I can't,' I said. 'I'm sorry.'

Idris sighed in frustration, or disappointment, or both. He looked away and took in his surroundings. The sunny disposition long gone from his face, replaced by a wistful look as though things were soon about to come to an end.

'What do you want, Jay?' he said, ever the friend. A better friend than I was.

'Can you find out about...' I hesitated.

'About what?' he pushed.

'About Imy,' I said. 'Imran Siddiqui.'

'Oh, Jay! The hell is wrong with you?'

'He's been hauled in by a couple of yours and I need to know why.'

Imy glanced quickly at the top corner of his phone, checking the time, figuring out the time difference. I could tell he was curious.

'Bell me back when you hear something,' I said, disconnecting the call just as he made his disappointed face.

I pocketed my phone and looked around. It felt as though my presence there was invading precious memories. I had to get out of Imy's home, but the punch in the ribs that I'd taken was playing havoc on my bladder. I had to go before I went.

I climbed the stairs and stepped into the bathroom and took a really long, really guilty piss. I zipped up and washed my hands. But my eyes were fixed firmly on the edge of the sink.

From the little training that I'd once been given by MI5, and then the little training I'd once had at a Ghurfat-al-Mudarris training camp, I knew that balancing on the edge of the sink was an automatic Glock .40-calibre handgun.

I took two steps at a time down and jumped the last four, and left Imy's house in a fucking flash. I jumped in my car and even though I was in a rush to get home quickly I drove like I'd never driven before: considerately. I couldn't risk getting collared by the cops.

I pulled into my drive and opened the glove compartment and stared at the Glock that I'd taken from Imy's house. *What the fuck was I thinking?*

I took my eyes off it and looked up at my house. I hadn't been back since I'd stepped off the plane and I swear it was calling to me. It looked bare compared to my neighbour's sparkly number. First chance I got, I was going to drape a Christmas light or two around my yard and put up the plastic Christmas tree. Keep up with the Kumars and all that.

I reached for the Glock and shoved it down the back of my jeans.

I opened my front door and hauled my luggage in, trampling over the small mountain of mail in the process. I rushed straight up to my bedroom and my heart dropped. It took me a second to work out that I hadn't been burgled, and my bedroom was just in a fucking state. My heart dropped a second time when I patted my waist and couldn't feel the Glock. I fished it out from halfway down my jeans. *Calm, calm the fuck down*. Shaz, Imy, Idris were all jostling for space at the forefront of my mind. I took a deep breath, *one fucking thing at a time*. I dropped down and flattened myself to the bedroom floor and reached under my bed, pulling out my secret red Nike shoe box. I sat on my bed with the box on my lap and blew away the dust. I lifted the lid and inside was my old life.

My old drug dealing paraphernalia was all present and correct. The weed grinder that never quite worked. Two packets of king-size silver skins, perforated neatly for roaches. The zip-lock bags in various sizes that I'd bought to replace the cling film in an effort to polish up my image as a street dealer. A simple time.

I made some room and placed the Glock right at the bottom.

I think I knew why I'd nabbed the piece from Imy's house, but I wasn't sure if it was the right move. I hadn't thought that far ahead. All I knew was that I had confronted Imy about the gun, and a minute later he was being hauled away by the cops.

My train of thought – and this train only travelled for a few seconds before breaking down – was that if his place got raided on the back of some suspicion, and the cops located the gun, it could see him doing time for possession. I wasn't out to play Judge Rinder, but after what Imy had been through, I owed him *something*. The other reason I nabbed the Glock was that if I had it in my possession, then he was less likely to go on a killing spree. The only thing that was bothering me was, *what had he already done?*

And, *was it justified?*

When the time was right and when I'd figured out how, I had to get shot of the shooter.

I checked the time on my Batman clock. It was just approaching four, but that meant it was just *past* four and I needed to stick some fresh batteries up the Caped Crusader's backside. Idris would call me as soon as he found out why Imy had been taken in. Until then, I didn't think I had anything to do.

I thought I heard my armchair calling.

I made my way downstairs for a long-overdue reunion and noticed the scattered mail by the front door. I could have left it for later, but a small chore felt like a touch of normality. I bent down and picked up a stack of threatening bills and menacing bank statements. Amongst it all was a glossy black business card, the same one that had been handed to me earlier. I flipped it over. Scrawled on the back it read, *Bell me!*

I stood holding it. Through my living room door, I could see my armchair facing the television, so fucking inviting, and I wanted nothing more than to collapse on it. I could've. I should've. I'd done what I'd set out to do. I'd faced Imy. I could simply just stop.

But curiosity is a motherfucker.

Who the fuck was Omar and what the fuck did he want from me? I dialled his number.

It rang a few times, and when Omar answered, I realised that he knew a whole lot more about me than my name and address. The first thing he said made me want to turn back time.

'Well, well, well. If it isn't Jihadi Jay.'

Chapter 17

Imy

As soon as I'd opened my front door it was obvious from the way they were dressed and the dour look on their faces that they were plain clothes police. They flashed their warrant cards at me as confirmation.

DCI Humphrey assisted me into the back seat of an unmarked police car with a vice-like grip on my arm, as though he'd already decided that I was guilty. He shut the door hard behind me, just as I'd pulled my leg in, and threw me a look before settling into the driver's seat. I sat with my hands crossed at the wrists resting on my lap as if I was wearing invisible handcuffs.

DCI Taylor was younger, warmer. 'Truly, we're very sorry for your loss,' she'd said, twisting to face me from the front seat. Like the rest of the country she'd heard the news and I think the sentiment was genuine, but I couldn't be sure how she'd meant it. Judging by the colour that her cheeks had taken, she was possibly embarrassed that I was being hauled in so soon after my family had been killed.

DCI Humphrey didn't seem to agree with his colleague's sentiment. From my view in the back I could see from his hunched shoulders how tightly wound he was. He was much older and whiter than DCI Taylor. A well-worn look on his face that I read as a man set in his ways.

'When did you come to this country?' he asked me sharply, when

I think he wanted to ask, *Why did you come to my country?* Maybe it frustrated him that I'd taken up with a white girl and would've had a hand in raising her white son.

Or maybe he simply blamed me for the terrorist attack that I was a victim of.

I wasn't particularly surprised when they skipped the turning towards Hounslow Police Station and continued on the A4, eventually stopping at an industrial estate in Colnbrook.

I was led through the car park and into what looked like a low-level office block. Inside smelt of lemon disinfectant, and the only sound was the echo of our footsteps as we crossed the narrow corridor. They pushed open a door to a small square claustrophobic room with bare walls and a desk bare apart from a digital recording device.

They sat me at the desk, on the other side of it was an empty chair and I wondered who I'd be facing.

'Can I get you a cup of water?' DCI Taylor asked.

'He's fine!' DCI Humphrey was quick to reply on my behalf.

They both left the room leaving me to my thoughts. I could've simply got up and walked away. I hadn't been arrested and I knew my rights, but I was curious as to what they knew. The information that they would impart would only serve as knowledge. So I waited, sitting perfectly still.

It was almost two hours before the door opened.

DCI Taylor walked in first. She rounded the desk, and stood in the left corner, avoiding the one available chair. Her cheeks still coloured red and her eyes only met mine long enough for me to notice the uncertainty in them.

DCI Humphrey followed closely behind, and like DCI Taylor he didn't sit in the available chair either, instead he stood behind the desk in the right-hand corner of the room and communicated with me through a scowl.

I didn't turn to see the third person enter until she walked past me carrying a thin, A4 Manila envelope. She took the seat opposite me. Contrary to her colleague's, her face didn't show any obvious emotion.

DCI Taylor acknowledged her as 'Ma'am', whereas DCI Humphrey grunted his acknowledgement. She ignored them both and glanced at the recording device.

'Is that thing off?' She spoke over her shoulder.

'I think so,' DCI Taylor replied quickly.

'You think so?'

DCI Taylor hurried to the desk, her cheeks reddening further as she checked the recording device. 'It's not recording, Ma'am.'

The lady placed the envelope down flat on the table and covered it with her hands. She spent a moment looking at the cut above my eye caused by Asif Kabir striking me with the remote control.

'Imran Siddiqui,' she finally said. It wasn't a question, so I didn't answer. 'I am Chief Superintendent Penelope Wakefield.' She pushed a loose strand of hair behind her ear, a soft gesture at odds with her steely features, before slipping out four 6x4 photos. One by one she slid them across the table towards me. I held her gaze before I looked at each photo in turn.

Asif Kabir on his side on the living room carpet, his body contorted in a Z-shape.

Mrs Kabir in Rafi's bedroom, her head comfortably placed on the pillow, eyes closed peacefully and her mouth open as though a prayer were caught on her lips. A deep red hole where her heart once beat.

Saheed Kabir on the upstairs landing. On his knees, his legs trapped underneath him keeping his body up. One bullet wound in the chest. One in his forehead.

The fourth photo was of me. In a service station drinking coffee somewhere on the M40 between London and Blackburn.

I took my eyes off the photographs and gave Chief Superintendent Wakefield the same empty look that she was giving me. I held it for a moment before glancing over her shoulder. DCI Taylor simply blinked. My eyes moved across to DCI Humphrey, the outline of his jaw prominent and his fists tightly balled. I imagined his reaction if we had been the only two in the room. I pictured mine.

Chief Superintendent Wakefield picked up each photograph, collated them neatly and placed them back in the envelope. She had laid her cards on the table and as good as her hand was, this was a game that she could not win.

I'd once made a deal with the devil, and it was starting to show a return.

Wakefield turned her head slightly to her right shoulder towards DCI Taylor, a small gesture, an instruction.

'Imran Siddiqui,' DCI Taylor said in a small voice, 'thank you for assisting with—'

'*Ma'am,*' DCI Humphrey broke in with urgency. 'Do not do this!'

'DCI Taylor, please, continue,' Wakefield said, leaving no room for argument.

'Yes, Ma'am.' DCI Taylor nodded. 'Imran Siddiqui, thank you for assisting with our enquiries. You are free to leave.'

She held open the door. I stood up and walked out of the room without having said a word.

Chapter 18

Jay

I stopped at the traffic lights and clocked my mirrors for cops before checking my phone. Idris still hadn't left me a message. Despite his hesitation and frustration, I knew he'd make that call. He'd want to know why Imy was brought in, just so he could have further ammunition to further break my balls. He didn't know half the shit I'd landed in, let alone what I was walking into now. I wasn't quite sure myself.

I put my phone down and picked up the black business card sitting in my centre console. I had a good mind to rip it in two, one-eighty my car and head back in the opposite direction. The direction of my bed. I swear seeing my old Nike shoebox had set me off. The bare contents of my old life as a low-key street dealer, and now I had an automatic handgun in there. It had me scratching my head! Just how removed, *detached*, I had become, not only from my old life, but just fucking *life*.

I placed the business card back as the lights switched to green, and I made my way to the location Omar had messaged me – a coffee shop somewhere in upper-class South Kensington. It took me the best part of an hour and a half. An hour and a half of trying to figure out how Omar knew about my past.

The circle of people who had known that I'd once travelled and trained at a Ghurfat-al-Mudarris camp in North Pakistan was small.

It crossed my mind to call Teddy Lawrence, my old MI5 handler and regular piece of shit, but his number wasn't valid anymore – or more likely he'd blocked me after draining whatever he could out of me.

I wheeled my Beemer into an NCP car park and spotted Omar's slimy green Mercedes. There was a spot a couple of places along from it and I reversed in. I walked over to his car and glanced through the windscreen at the ticket. It was valid until midnight. It was approaching half five. *How long did he think we were meeting for?* I dropped a small fortune into the machine to see me through a few hours, not that I was intending to stay that long.

I slapped the ticket on my dash and walked out into the cold. I'd left my mac back at home as the weather had turned, and lifted the hood of my parka jacket over my head to protect me from the rain and the wind howling in my ears. With my phone directing me I walked five minutes to the location.

It was a double-fronted building, which didn't resemble any kind of coffee shop I'd ever been to. I stepped through the door and pulled my hood down. I was used to Costa and Starbucks, or the café behind Hounslow High Street that doubles up as a Vape bar. This was different. Above me there was a huge chandelier and circling it were smaller versions, but despite all that the lighting was moody, as though they were using those energy saving bulbs that never quite come alive. No obvious counter, no booths, just neatly clothed round tables and smartly dressed waiters serving smartly dressed clientele. On almost every table there was a three-tiered stand, holding picture-perfect cupcakes and some of the smallest sandwiches that I'd ever seen. Immediately I felt out of place, standing there in my dripping-wet parka and Air Jordans, wondering if I was violating some fancy-pants dress code. But I wasn't the only one.

In the far corner, sitting on his own at a round table fit for six, there he was, dressed as he had been earlier when we'd met, in a loud red tracksuit. He was watching me with amusement, clearly enjoying my discomfort. Maybe it's because he was the only other brown face in the room that I greeted him warmer than I wanted to, by throwing my hand in the air and waving at him. I walked past the mostly white, mostly middle-aged clientele. Well-to-do, in appearance anyway. They all took turns to discreetly check me out. I wouldn't have noticed if I wasn't doing the same to them.

I approached his table and I shrugged off my wet parka. I went to place it on the back of my chair, but some suit crept up on me and gently took it from me with a tight smile that said, *I'm watching you* before shuffling away with my jacket.

'Jihadi Jay!' Omar said, again.

'Maybe not call me that here?' I smiled nervously as I sat down opposite him.

'Never give up who you really are, regardless of your surroundings, Jay. You feel me?'

'Yeah,' I said, agreeing with the sentiment, but not quite in this case. 'I feel you.'

'Especially in a place like this. This is where you have to represent.' He made a show of looking around. His voice purposely raised just enough to be heard. 'Can you even begin to contemplate the arrogance of people that think there can only be one reality? One truth?'

It was a hell of an opening gambit and he knew it. He leaned back with a smirk on his face, twirling the nose stud in between his thumb and forefinger as I tried to figure out what the fuck he was chatting about. I felt every eye in the room on us. I glanced over my shoulder and nobody seemed to give a shit.

'So what's up?' I asked, because I really needed to know what the fuck was up.

'Busy as the Devil but doing the work of Angels,' he replied, smoothly.

It had only been a minute, but I swear he was starting to annoy me with his bullshit. If he wanted to play the Riddler, then, fuck it, I'd play the Caped Crusader!

'Alright, listen up.' I leaned in, appropriately aggressive, and pressed a finger into the table. 'You know my name, you know where I live. I reckon we should even the scores a bit.'

'My name is Omar.' I'd already sussed that from his private plates. I shrugged. He smiled. And then he dropped it. 'Bhukara. Omar Bhukara.'

The pieces fell heavily into place. I willed my face to express the right fucking expression, even though I almost shit out my heart. In that moment, that fucking second, I was back there again.

'Your father is a good man,' I lied. His father was a first-class evil fuck!

'Yeah,' Omar said. 'A great man!'

'He meant a lot to me,' I said. I was rusty and it sounded clumsy in my ears. It had been a while since MI5 had me in that position. But this was different, they hadn't put me there, I had gone seeking. It didn't matter; I was there and I had to switch on. Eyes and ears open. Taking in everything I could.

Omar leaned back and draped an arm around the back of the chair. I took my eyes off him and looked on the table between us. Two phones, a smartphone and a lesser phone, most likely a throwaway, sitting next to his Mercedes key fob. In front of him I eyed the tea pot and the crusts of a sandwich on a small plate. On a separate plate, the creamy remains of a cake. He'd been there a while and I wondered why.

'Last year my father was the happiest I'd ever seen him, leading up to the Boxing Day fuck-up! The way things turned out. It broke him.'

The Boxing Day fuck-up, as he so poetically put it, was a terrorist attack, young British Muslim men armed with sawn-off AK assault rifles and automatic handguns. They were let loose in the middle of the afternoon on one of the busiest days of the year on Oxford Street, London. Their target was to shoot and kill at will. Omar Bhukara's father, Adeel-Al-Bhukara had recruited them, educated them and made them think in the way that he wanted them to think. I was one of them.

'It broke us all,' I said. 'He wasn't to blame.'

'There's always somebody to blame.'

That, right there, was it. That was my cue: stand up, moonwalk out of the joint, go home and smoke a spliff. I'd only landed that morning and already I felt like I'd put in a shift in a job that didn't belong to me. But I couldn't walk away just yet.

I still hadn't worked out how much Omar knew, and I couldn't read if his screwed-up expression was directed at me. If word had hit him that I was on the opposite side of the table, in more ways than one, then this could be the last time that I'd enjoy high tea and cake. I nodded and then continued to nod as I looked over his shoulder, before casually scoping the room. There wasn't any threat, not that I could see.

'I wish things had turned out differently,' I said, softly, hoping he'd follow the lead and lower his fucking voice. 'Will you tell your father that I'm thinking about him?' That was nothing but the truth. I'd have to make room in my already busy mind for that terrorist fuck!

'You don't know?' Omar said.

'What? What don't I know?'

'Of course, how would you?' he said. 'My father is dead.'

Playing the part, I respectfully put my hand to my heart. 'I'm sorry. I… I didn't know.'

'Earlier this year. March. He was killed in Dubai.'

'I'm sorry, I didn't know,' I said, again, when I really wanted to ask, *how?* But I had a feeling the *how* would be revealed, and the *why* would follow.

'What're you drinking?' He switched, the smile back on his face. 'You seem like a frothy coffee type of guy. Am I right, Jay? Hmm? Am I?'

Without taking his eyes off me, Omar shot his hand up in the air and snapped his fingers. It got the attention of some of the patrons, and the waiter was at our table before Omar had put his arm down.

'I haven't decided yet.' I smiled at the waiter.

'It's alright, check out the menu. My man here will wait,' Omar said, looking up and down at the waiter. 'Won't you, Garcon!?'

'Very well, sir.' The waiter nodded.

I fumbled with the oversized menu and opened it. Considering the size of it there wasn't much of a choice. 'I'll just have whatever you're having,' I said, closing the menu.

'Alright, then,' he said to me, and to the waiter he said, 'Another pot of tea. Make sure it's brewed before it gets here. I don't want to sit around staring at it. And some more of those tuna sandwiches. Wash your hands first, though, I don't want you handling my food after you've handled haram. And get me another selection of cakes. Nothing with gelatine, because I'll know. You know I'll know!'

'As you please, sir,' the waiter said, and walked away.

'I love coming to places like this. Love how they look at me. You see, Jay, despite how I dress or the colour of my skin, money pisses over all prejudices. They have to treat me as though they would treat one of their own.'

'It's pretty exclusive for a coffee shop. Do you live around here?'

Omar shook his head. 'Did my growing up here, but I have a place in Copenhagen. I run my own PR company from there and my business takes me places, allows me to meet with some interesting people.'

'Is that why you're here? Business?'

'Amongst other things. I'm here to see you. I'm hoping you and I will do great things.'

The short hairs on my short-back-and-sides stood to attention. I placed a hand onto my lap and out of sight. I slipped my hand into my pocket and my fingers found my phone. Blindly, I used my thumb to quick-press twice on the home button, a shortcut to launch the camera function. The capture button was bottom middle, and to the left of it was the red record movie button. I pressed it whilst coughing to cover the beep. I wasn't trying to make a video of the inside of my pocket, but I hoped that it would pick up sound.

'PR has its benefits, you feel me?' Omar said, as I brought my hand back into view and placed it casually on the table. Every move I made now seemed to drip in suspicion. 'I scour the internet daily,' he continued. 'Social media sites, mainly. Looking for the king and queen of losers. The most desperate of desperados. Those willing to give their granny a black eye for a fiver.'

'For what, exactly?' I shrugged.

'Because,' he said, as the waiter parallel-parked a trolley by our table. 'They can be of use to me.'

He was about to reveal something, I could feel it. And I wasn't confident that his voice would carry to my phone buried in my pocket. I had to be sure that it was recorded. Omar watched the waiter clear the old crockery and place the new neatly on the table, no doubt looking for a reason to break his balls. I took the opportunity to slip out my phone from my pocket. Under the guise of casually checking for messages I glanced at my phone and *crap!* The clever manoeuvre in my pocket had led me to *like* an inspirational meme on Instagram. I raised my eyebrows and nodded to myself, as though I was reading an interesting text. Omar's eyes were still judging the waiter. I tapped quickly on the camera app and set the video recorder, the phone beeped softly to indicate that the recording had started. I coughed just in time to cover it, and placed the phone face down on the table. I think I did it cool, but I was sweating my balls off.

I picked up a small spoon and made appreciative sounds at the cake in front of me, as I cut smoothly through it with minimum crumble. I took a bite and it felt like a party on my tongue. The waiter walked away unscathed.

'So,' I said, getting him back on track. 'The king and queen of losers?'

'It's funny what lengths a downtrodden individual will go to, given a little respect and a cash incentive.'

I leaned in closer and in doing so I nudged my phone a touch closer to him with my elbow. 'I take it you found someone?'

'More than one. I've put together a small team. Two on the payroll, and one who is sympathetic to The Cause. You'll meet him.'

My mouth opened as my brain scrambled through a thousand questions. Omar had assumed that I would be part of this *operation*, as if Jihadi Jay was back in town.

One of his phones vibrated on the table and he picked up the lesser handset. 'Speak of the devil, and the devil shall call,' he said, talking shit again before answering. I poured us both some tea, positioning my body so that I could eavesdrop, but Omar dropped back in his chair and I could only hear one side of the conversation.

'Yes, Tommy. Hello… Are you in position…? Are you sure…? Clareville Road. Number 102…? Okay, alright, I'm just checking…! Of course she's going to let you in… Yeah, yeah, it's disabled… All good…? Drop me a text… I'm not far… We will be victorious, my Brother, Inshallah.'

Omar hung up and stared at the phone for a moment as though he was running through the conversation with whoever this Tommy character was. I wondered if he was one of those on the payroll, or the one who was *sympathetic to The Cause*. The use of *Inshallah* pointed to the latter.

'I'm afraid I'm going to have to call time.' Omar nodded over my shoulder, seconds later the waiter returned with my parka. I shrugged it on hesitantly with his help. I didn't want to leave, not yet. Omar hadn't given me much, but something was happening, and it was happening right fucking now. 'Keep your phone close,' he said.

'Huh?' I said, in a daze.

'If things go as planned, then believe me, bro, you are going to want to be a part of this.'

His words sent a cold shiver down my back and reality kicked the fuck in. I should've turned my back on the whole fucking thing and given whatever little I did know to someone more qualified for this shit.

Then again, who was more qualified for this shit than me?

I dug deep. I had to play the part and become *that* person again. I reached out and shook his hand warmly, and with my other hand on my heart, I said, 'It would be an honour to be a part of your Jihad.'

Chapter 19

How easy is it to get a gun in America? Tommy thought, as he sat invisible in the dark on the damp dank green. Walmart, or any other supermarket; apparently the checks weren't very rigorous and he could have walked out with a trolley chock-full of groceries and automatic weapons. The thing was, Tommy wasn't in America, he was in England, living in Southall, and regardless of what the news alluded to, it was near impossible to get hold of guns there. Unless, of course, he was running in those types of crowds which Tommy wasn't. Though he had found somebody who could place as many guns in his hands as he wanted. But it would come at a price.

Tommy repositioned himself into a cross-legged pose and snatched damp clumps of grass in each hand as he waited. From a distance he could just make out the metal railing that ran around the park. Beyond it, he could see the rear of the target house. He kept his eyes fixed to it. He could not get this wrong. Tommy really needed those guns.

His eyes flitted to his Casio calculator watch, which he'd stolen as a child, and pressed the well-thumbed button on the side which illuminated the small screen. It was time. This was the first step on the path that he had been searching for his whole life. It wasn't how he had envisaged making a difference, but sometimes you have to do something wrong to make something right.

Tommy stood up and wiped away damp grass from over his damp backside, as he stared into the darkness in front of him. He walked thirty steps, just as he had rehearsed twice already in the daylight, until he reached the black metal railing with the spear-top finishing. On the other side of the railing was a muddy path, running along one side of the park, popular with dog walkers and joggers. Tommy slipped out leather gloves from the side pockets of his black bomber jacket and pulled them on tightly. The railing was about chest height, so it didn't take much effort to heave himself up, place one leg on the flat between the spears, and lift himself over. He landed on his black boots and had to steady himself as he found his footing in the wet mud. In front of him was the back of a row of large, detached houses. The walls around the back gardens were low, with a break for a wooden gate, designed so that the home owners had a picturesque view of the park. Safety came in the form of Big Brother. Tommy could feel the numerous security cameras at the backs of the houses and hidden in trees, all pointing blankly at his face.

He crossed the muddy path, reached over the low gate and found the latch. He pushed open the door and stepped tentatively into the garden, expecting the motion sensors to flood him with bright light. That didn't happen. Somebody had done their job.

Tommy pressed the side button on his Casio. The timing was perfect. He looked across at the large patio door with the blacked-out glass, and could just make out his reflection. He crossed the garden path and walked towards it.

Chapter 20

Sophia's only cleaning job on Mondays was at 5.30 p.m. The majority of her jobs throughout the week were in the morning, but this particular homeowner liked to inspect her work when he returned home at seven. She didn't know the owner's name. In fact she hardly knew any of the names of the homeowners for whom she cleaned. They were just addresses to her. This one was 102 Clareville Road. It was the only house on her rota where she had to be vetted, her background thoroughly checked and asked to sign form after form, including a non-disclosure agreement.

Sophia had been cleaning this house two evenings a week for just over a year, and she hardly ever spoke to the homeowner. His phone was constantly attached to his ear, muttering his disdain through his red face at whatever was bothering him that day. He'd leave Sophia a tip on the worktop without so much as eye contact or words of gratitude.

The tips weren't great, and the tight shit never allowed her to put the heating on. It didn't disturb Sophia that he would soon be a target for a robbery. Maybe it disturbed her a *little*, like a pinch, but any doubt was quickly dissolved as she reasoned that his insurance would see him right. *It was a victimless crime.* Besides, wasn't it time that she had a break from the monotony of her crappy life?

Determined not to be late, especially today of all days, and not relying on the unreliable tube timings, Sophia left sixty minutes early for her sixty-minute journey.

On the tube she dipped marshmallows into her hot chocolate as she searched online for the cost of a professional photographer, and the cost of hiring a studio where she could lay down her tracks. She couldn't help but drift… *Simply Sophia* sprawled across an album cover, her sitting on the kerb of a busy road, looking moody as traffic passed her by. That's the image she would go with: moody, cute, sneakers, knee-length dress, leather jacket, a little like Lily Allen before she'd lost the plot.

With a jolt, popping a hole in her daydream and causing her to drip hot chocolate on her white uniform, she realised that when she's inevitably questioned by the police and they looked through her phone, they would surely notice from her search history that she was searching for a professional photographer and trips to Paris – as though she was expecting to come into a large sum of money.

Sophia cursed loudly under her breath and then apologised to the man next to her, who had been encroaching on her seat the whole journey. She shifted across closer to the window and his elbow slipped away from her arm. She gave him a look, indicating that he should get to terms with personal space, and shielded her phone away from him as she went about deleting the search history, knowing full well that it wouldn't make a difference. Someplace, somehow, everything is recorded. She put her phone away in her handbag before she could get herself into more trouble.

Sophia stepped off the tube at South Kensington. Not wanting to turn up half an hour early, she started to walk slowly, but it was so cold that she found herself pacing just to keep warm. She arrived twenty minutes before her shift. She'd never been early before – late plenty of times, but never early – and she wondered how suspicious that would look, especially as she'd always felt that the street was occupied by suspicious minds, cautious of anyone of a lesser standing.

Rather than hover outside in the dark, with twitching curtains around her, she decided to start her shift early. The house key was kept with the neighbour, and after every shift returned to the neighbour. Sophia knocked on the door.

'Good evening, Mrs Carson.' Sophia smiled brightly as Mrs Carson opened the door. She was wearing fluorescent lycra jogging bottoms.

'Sophie,' Mrs Carson said, frowning at her smart watch wrapped around her thin tanned wrist. 'You're early. I'm in the middle of warming down.'

'Sophia,' Sophia corrected for the hundredth time. 'I know. May I have the key please?'

'I was just warming down,' Mrs Carson reiterated, as if the whole world must stop so she could stretch out in front of her great big log fireplace, Sophia imagined, as her eyes fell onto the key *right there* on the mantel. 'You're going to have to wait, young lady,' Mrs Carson huffed. Sophia opened her mouth just as the door shut in her face. Not slammed, but loud enough to make a point.

God, Sophia thought, *how could I get in more trouble for being early than I do for being late?* She sighed, folded her arms tightly, and stamped on the welcome mat to stay warm, but the cold found a way through her cheap, knock-off coat.

At five-thirty exactly, Mrs Carson opened the door wearing a bath robe and a towel wrapped high on her head, looking flush from a hot shower. Sophia was frozen to the spot, colour drained from her face, her knees knocking and her teeth chattering.

'Next time plan your journey accordingly.' Mrs Carson handed the key over, and Sophia just knew that she was smirking under her snarl.

Sophia thanked her and walked away. Her hands shook as she inserted the key into the front door and let herself into the house.

Feeling rightly rebellious, she swiped the digital thermostat all the way up to thirty-two and slid down against the radiator in the large whitewashed hallway. As the heating kicked in and the shivering subsided, she leaned forward with her head in her hands. A bad feeling threatening to overwhelm her.

Nothing bad had really happened, not really. Yeah, those stupid searches on her phone, and that fat sweaty guy on the tube who had kept brushing his elbow against her like it was some sort of mating call. Then the little episode with Mrs Carson, leaving her freezing her backside off on the doorstep as she buggered off for a bubble bath. Nothing bad, just first world problems. But she couldn't seem to shake off that bad feeling.

With force, Sophia shook her head clear of it as her body warmed. She had a job to do. She removed her shoes and placed them on the door mat and padded through the hallway, the under-floor heating warming her nylon-clad feet as she stepped into the living room. There wasn't a Christmas decoration in sight. Not surprising, the homeowner seemed the type of person who despised festivities.

Like the hallway, like every other room in the house, the spacious living room was whitewashed and in stark contrast the furniture was black. Black sofa, black coffee table, black lamps, even the worktops and cabinets in the adjoining open-plan kitchen were black against white, giving the place a seventies monochrome effect. It wasn't in poor taste, but it wasn't to her taste either. It needed colour, it needed a woman's touch. Sophia snorted to herself. Even with the money coming her way, there was no way that she could afford a place like this, not even close enough for a deposit. It would be like a drop in the ocean. But it would be a start. It may be a cliché, but you really did need money to make money, and Sophia was going to make sure her unexpected windfall served its purpose.

At the back of the living room was a huge bi-fold, four-pane patio door, which led to the garden. Behind the garden was the park. In the park, Tommy was waiting.

Sophia walked across the living room, her body moving of its own accord as her mind tried to rein her in. She reached the patio. Her eyes fell to the key resting in the lock and her heart leaped. She averted her gaze and rested her forehead against the cold glass and looked out into the dark at the silhouette of a thick apple tree, its branches scratching softly against the thick glass. She stared at it as it stood perfectly at peace, never putting a foot wrong, literally. It reminded her of a children's fable that her parents never read to her. Not *Hansel and Gretel*, the other one, she couldn't remember which. The one with the poisonous apple. She could feel the tree looking down at her, in every sense of the word, taunting her, daring her to pick out the most delicious-looking apple and to hell with the consequences. Too late, she thought, she'd already taken a bite out of it and she was hungry for more. Without another thought, she snatched her eyes away from the tree and turned the key in the lock.

Job done. Her part anyway.

Sophia let out a long sigh, leaving a cloud on the glass, and watched it slowly disappear into nothing. She checked the time on her watch, and, not trusting the cheap time-piece, she turned to double-check on the huge black clock above the black mantelpiece on the white chimney breast. It was five-forty-five.

At six it would take place. By six-thirty it would be over.

All Sophia had to do was stay out of the way and get on with the cleaning. At seven, the owner would return home from work and deliver her a measly tip. He probably wouldn't notice anything amiss immediately. Sophia would return the spare key to Mrs Carson next door, and then head home where she would wait anxiously for it to kick off. The police would eventually knock on her door and question her about the break-in. She'd be ready. Her story would be straight.

The plan now out of her hands, and with nothing more she could do, Sophia wandered into the kitchen to get on with her chores. Out of her bag she took her own washing-up gloves – she hated the thought of using somebody else's. In the kitchen sink there was a cereal bowl, a plate and a jam-stained knife. She slipped on the washing-up gloves and rinsed the three items, and stacked them in the dishwasher, which wasn't near enough full to be switched on, but switch it on she did. She disinfected and wiped down the mostly clean black worktop, apart from where, if you looked carefully, there were small crumbs of toast. She ran a cloth over it and collected the crumbs in her hand and disposed of them in the kitchen sink and ran the water.

She checked the time on her watch, and then double-checked it again with the wall clock. It was five-fifty-five. Sophia risked a glance at the patio. She had been told that under no circumstances was she to make contact with Tommy. He would be in and out as planned.

Sophia willed her heart to quit beating so fast.

She glanced around the kitchen, it was gleaming without her having to do much. She could wipe the fridge door down, but she'd be doing it for the sake of doing it. Same with the fitted oven and hob. She could mop the floor tiles, but she'd just end up leaving water marks. It was better left alone. So, armed with her disinfectant spray and J-cloth, she moved into the living room, looking for something easy to clean. There was a film of dust on the Sky Box. She sprayed once and ran the cloth over it, and then looked around to see what else could do with a wipe. There was a faint coffee ring on the glass coffee table, and she knelt down beside it.

The patio door slid smoothly open and closed again, and she felt a presence behind her.

Sophia removed the high-end glossy magazines and broadsheet newspapers from the coffee table and placed them on the floor and sprayed the disinfectant twice on the glass, expecting to hear the man shuffle past her, out of the living room, into the hallway and up the stairs to the master bedroom, where, in the back of the fitted wardrobe, was a wall safe. Sophia had never seen it, but Samuel Carter had confirmed. How he knew wasn't her business.

Tommy was to empty the safe and then come back downstairs and simply leave with the contents of the safe, the same way that he had come in.

That was the plan. That's what was supposed to happen. Instead, she could feel a tickle at the back of her neck as she sensed him moving closer to her. Sophia braced herself as he sat himself down on the armchair by the coffee table that she was cleaning. Sophia didn't turn to look at him, but from the corner of her eye she could see black muddy boots planted firmly on the floor, legs spread in black jeans and two leather-gloved hands resting on his lap.

Samuel Carter had said it would take Tommy anywhere between ten and thirty minutes depending on the complexity of the lock on the safe. Sophia didn't know what the contents were, nor did she ask. These kind of operations and that kind of information, she surmised, was strictly on a need-to-know basis, but she imagined it was jewels, possibly cut diamonds in a maroon velvet pouch, or gold bullion, or even some highly confidential documents that would be worth a lot on the black market or the Dark Web. She had read something about the Dark Web recently. Either way, it was none of her business, she had carried out her part professionally. But this guy! What was he playing at? Sophia had to break protocol. Take control.

'Upstairs,' Sophia whispered, without looking at him. 'Master bedroom. At the back of the wardrobe.' Surely he'd been briefed! Sophia looked up at the wall clock, it had just gone six. 'You haven't got long,' she said, as she methodically ran the J-cloth in small circles over the disappearing coffee ring.

'It's okay,' Tommy said, calmly, as though everything was okay, when quite clearly it was pretty far from okay. He was on a clock, she knew that and he should, too! From whatever little she knew about Samuel Carter, it was clear that he wasn't the type to leave anything to chance. Everything had to run like clockwork. The hell was this guy thinking? Was she the only damn professional there?

'You haven't got much time,' Sophia said. 'He'll be back in an hour.'

'It's okay,' he said, again.

Slacker! His lax attitude could cost her. She was taking all the risks here. He would walk away, it was she that would have to face the police and provide a statement. Sophia had to put him in his place, pull rank; she was, after all, a partner.

Infuriated, or trying her best to act it, she threw down the J-cloth onto the coffee table with intent and shifted on her knees towards him.

'Go! Now!' Sophia snapped and then blinked slowly as she took him in.

Tommy was younger than she expected, and beautiful with it. Sandy brown hair flopped boyishly over his forehead. A smattering of light freckles around the bridge of his nose. His eyes were small and wide and caramel, protected by long curly lashes that had no place on a man. Sophia was immediately conscious that she was on her knees and that her uniform was stained slightly with hot chocolate, and that she was still wearing her bloody washing-up gloves whilst pointing the disinfectant spray at him. She tucked a loose hair behind her ear and her lips parted for an instruction that just wouldn't come.

Tommy seemed to blush, as though he wasn't used to such a reaction, and leaned towards her and she couldn't help but fall into his eyes. She wondered what their kids would look like.

He tentatively touched the side of her face, and with the other hand he placed the tip of a rather large knife under Sophia's chin.

Chapter 21

Jay

I started my car and cranked up the heating. As I waited for it to warm up I tried to get my head around what had just happened. It finally made sense how Omar knew me: his father was once like a father to me, but it didn't explain what the fuck he wanted from me.

Adeel-Al-Bhukara recruited me in the early part of last year, plucking me off the streets of Hounslow and plonking me down in a room full of wannabe jihadists. I was his favourite. I know that sounds wank, but it was true. Even though there were others in the group, stronger, more capable and fully committed to The Cause, Al-Bhukara always heaped praise on me, his arm around my shoulder a burden. I didn't understand it. I didn't know what he had seen in a small-time drug dealer. Until, that is, I found out that Al-Bhukara and my father had been close friends. Whilst my dad built Ghurfat-al-Mudarris, Al-Bhukara had been here in London keeping a watchful eye on me my whole life, and reporting it back to my dad until it was declared that I was fit for purpose.

Ultimately, it was my father who had engineered my recruitment and, ultimately, it was me who had engineered his downfall.

I located the video that I had made at the posh coffee joint. I turned up the volume and pressed play. The screen was black as the phone had been face down on the table throughout, and the

114

sound was a little muffled by the polite hubbub of customers. I wasn't hearing anything but noise. I hooked up my phone to the car system and changed the sound settings, dropping the bass and turning up the vocal, and replayed it.

Omar's voice filled my car.

I listened to it. Twice.

I tried to work out what could be used, but what exactly had he said that was of any use? Pretty close to jack-shit. He was Adeel-Al-Bhukara's son, so what? Didn't mean squat. What else? He was rude to waiters? Not quite terrorism. Then there was all this about creeping around the internet looking for someone to bend at his will for a few quid. What did that mean? I remember his old man used to chat in annoying riddles, too, jumping from one subject to another without fully committing to either.

Then there was that phone call to this Tommy character. Omar had called him his *associate*. What was Tommy doing for him, and what did he mean when he asked, *Are you in position?* Position for what?

I killed the video and ran it over in my head. There was nothing I could take to the police, and I no longer had the luxury of having MI5 on speed dial. Those leeches were keeping their distance.

Fuck, what was my move here?

I glanced at his parked green Mercedes, shining under the light, and I remembered that the parking ticket on his dashboard was valid until midnight. He was still around. Waiting. For something.

I replayed the video one more time and pushed the timeline forward to the phone conversation. Omar had mentioned an address.

Clareville Road. Number 102.

Chapter 22

'Just call Samuel Carter,' Sophia said, not for the first time. 'He'll clear it up. Me and him, we're partners!' It was starting to sound pathetic even to her.

Regardless of how things had turned out, were going to turn out, Sophia wasn't about to drop down on her hands and knees and beg for her life. It wasn't that it was beneath her, she just didn't think it would impress Tommy, and it may just irritate him into killing her earlier than planned.

Sophia had been on her knees opposite him for forty-five minutes. He hadn't said much, just made shy eyes at her and thrown in the occasional threat. She glanced at her cheap watch and double-checked it against the wall clock. It was approaching seven, just ten minutes before the homeowner was due to turn up. That had to be the plan all along. What else could Tommy possibly be waiting for? There never was a bloody safe. She'd been used, plain as day, and Sophia of all people should have known that life doesn't change that easily. Not for her. Never had.

She watched him carefully. He'd moved the knife away from her throat, but the threat remained. It was now resting on his knee as he caressed it with a gloved hand.

Sophia should have known as soon as she set eyes on him. God, she'd seen enough movies to know that once you see their face it

116

didn't matter how much you pleaded that you wouldn't say anything to anyone, they were going to kill you anyway.

'Why are you doing this to me?' Sophia asked, feeling sorry for herself.

'I'm not doing this to you,' Tommy replied. 'I'm doing it for a belief.'

'What belief? What's your belief have to do with me? I helped you. I can still help you.'

'Your part in this is over. But if you try to escape me, I'll find you. I'll find you and I'll have to kill you.' He said it with a sad smile, as though he was genuinely sorry at the idea of killing her.

'I won't try to escape you,' Sophia replied, her voice huskier than normal, her lips slightly parted. There was a naivety about him, a shyness. Sophia hoped that if she showed interest, his age and glaring inexperience with women could work in her favour. She didn't go as far as undoing her scrunchy and letting her hair tumble down, only because she hadn't washed it the night before and the scrunchy would get caught and she'd have to untangle it from her hair.

His phone vibrated noisily on the glass coffee table, he glanced at the text message and away from her. She could have used that moment to cause a distraction, throw something at him and then run out of the front door, screaming the quiet neighbourhood down. But the knife resting comfortably on his thigh was still pointing at her, and in the time it would take her to pick up the disinfectant spray, unlock the nozzle and squirt him in the eye with it, all he would have to do was lean forward and plunge the blade into her throat.

Tommy replied to the text message and his eyes were back on her.

'Was that Samuel?' Sophia asked. Tommy snorted and she felt stupid for asking. As if Samuel Carter would come to her rescue. She had to rely on herself. She had to be smarter than him, than both of them.

Sophia shifted on her knees and leaned in towards him. 'I meant what I said,' she said. 'I can help you... We can help each other.' Her hand crept onto his knee, inches away from the knife. He didn't flinch or tighten his grip on it. Sophia lifted her eyes to him, trying to make them as wide as possible. 'Take me with you,' she whispered, hoping he wasn't put off by the chocolate stain on her uniform.

'You're starting to become a nuisance.' Tommy lifted the knife to her face, the cold teeth resting on the side of her nose and the point an inch away from her right eye.

Sophia willed herself not to flinch, and to say something, anything, but only a soft breath escaped onto his hand, just as they both heard the faint rattle and motion of the garage door opening.

Tommy pulled the knife away but the respite was short-lived. He yanked Sophia by her ponytail and shot up to his feet, forcing Sophia up to hers. She held back a scream in exchange for the time that the distraction had bought her. He dragged her backwards behind him through the living area and into the open-plan kitchen, and headed towards the connecting door to the garage.

Sophia struggled to stay upright in his grip, her nylon-clad feet scrabbling to find purchase on the cold tiles. If she fell, he may not let her get up again. Tears stung her eyes. She gritted her teeth and blinked the tears away before they could obscure her vision, and searched frantically around the kitchen. Her eyes landed on the clean black granite worktop and then slid along to the knife block. Biting back the pain of having her hair wrenched out of her head, she reached out, her fingers brushing and then closing around a handle. The knife silently slid out of the block.

Sophia held it close to her leg.

Tommy stopped with his back tight against the wall beside the connecting garage door. Sophia was tight against him. She could feel his heart thumping in her back in rhythm with her own heartbeat.

The point of his knife rested against the side of her throat, hard enough to break skin. Sophia held her breath as she waited patiently to make her move. She mentally ran through her options.

The patio where she had let this hell in was closest to her; a direct run from the kitchen in a straight line, ten steps, a couple of seconds, she figured, and another two to slide the door open and then into the garden, out onto the beaten path and then run for her life. It was an option, but Sophia couldn't be sure if Tommy had locked the patio door after entering. She wouldn't have time to fumble with the lock with him on her tail. Those precious seconds could be the difference between her pathetic life and a violent death.

The other option was the front door. It was further away and not as direct. Sophia would have to negotiate her way around the three-seat leather Italian sofa and into the hallway and then out of the front door and onto the street. Again, not ideal, but the street would be more populated than the back of the house.

Sophia heard the chirp of the car alarm from the garage. The attacker tightened his grip around her. Sophia tightened her grip on her own knife. She evened her breathing the way she was taught in her Performing Arts course to combat nerves before a performance.

The adjoining door between the kitchen and the garage opened, shielding them.

The homeowner entered.

'Who the hell has had the heating on?' he puffed.

He turned to shut the door behind him and his eyes fell on Sophia, on the knife at her throat and on the stranger in his home.

'Do you know who I am?' he barked without fear.

'Shut up!' Tommy said.

'Do you know who I work for?' he shouted. 'I'll have your balls in a jar for this!'

'I said, shut the fuck up!' Tommy yelled back and moved the knife away from Sophia's neck and pointed it at the homeowner.

Now. It had to be now! Sophia brought the knife up and felt the sharp steel meet the flesh of Tommy's hand. He hissed, *'Bitch!'* under his breath and his grip slackened. Sophia bent at the knees and ducked out of his grip and ran out of the kitchen, determined, careful at each step not to slip on the floor. She ran through into the living room. She ignored the sounds of the scuffle behind her, she ignored the smack and the heavy thud and the homeowner's whimper.

Beyond the thumping of her heart, she could now hear the thumping of heavy boots getting louder, closer. She didn't have time to negotiate her way around the sofa so she placed one foot on the seat and leaped over the back, her heart in her mouth as she momentarily flew in the air before landing plum on her feet. She risked a look back. Tommy struggled with the same move, his boots too heavy, digging into the seat. Sophia slid around the door and into the hallway, past her shoes, past her coat, muttering to a God that she'd just that second started to believe in. Her shoulder landed painfully against the front door. She pulled down the handle and pulled open the door. The cold welcomed her as she ran as fast as she could onto the middle of the road.

To her left, headlights approached her at speed, flaunting the regulations of the quiet road. Sophia didn't want to be mown down after all her efforts. She waved both hands above her head as she ran full pelt towards the car. It skidded and screeched and finally stilled in front of her. She placed her hands on the warm bonnet, either side of the BMW badge, and locked eyes with the driver as she tried to catch a breath. The driver stuck his head out of the window and screamed at her to *'Get the fuck in!'*

Chapter 23

Jay

The woman pulled opened the passenger side door and scrambled in and slammed it shut behind her. I screamed at her to get down as I hunched low myself. My life was such that I expected my windscreen to explode in a hail of bullets.

I quickly carried out a hasty five-point-turn on the narrow road, my sensors doing most of the work, and shifted through the gears into second. My Beemer jerked and then flew away from whatever the fuck was behind us.

Her eyes were fixed on the wing mirror. 'See anything?' I asked, trying to keep the panic out of my voice, as I glanced through the rear-view mirror into the darkness, for a tail or the flash of a muzzle.

'I can't tell,' she said. 'I don't think so.'

'Okay, buckle up!' I said, as I tried to get my bearings, but I was pretty fucking far from Hounslow so I took the first right at speed, followed by a series of random turns until we eventually hit a more crowded street. We simultaneously expelled breath.

'Are you okay?' I finally got around to asking. 'Are you hurt?'

She ignored my questions and only opened her mouth to offend me. 'Does this thing go any faster?'

I ignored her right back as I hooked a left onto a road that I finally recognised. I looked out the driver's side window as I slipped past the coffee shop where I'd met Omar not an hour ago. The door opened and I couldn't miss him as his scrawny form stepped out dressed top to tail in his red tracksuit, with his phone clamped to his head, as he paced in the opposite direction. I shielded the side of my face with a hand, but he was too preoccupied finding out that his plan had gone a little sideways to notice the result of it sitting in my passenger seat.

At the first opportunity I hit the dual carriageway, and I was able to open up the valves, swerving and slipping easily past cars. Even with all the shit that was happening, a small part of me was hoping that she was impressed. I swear, a pretty face can do that. I put those thoughts quickly behind me and tried to take some control.

'Who's after you?'

She massaged her forehead and then ran her hand over her face. 'I don't know.'

I side-glanced at her and took her in; tied blonde hair, plain white uniform, and she smelt a little of disinfectant. That much told me she was a housekeeper. The lack of shoes told me she'd left pretty sharpish.

'I saw you run out that house. The hell happened back there?'

She shook her head in a trance. Playing for time, no doubt searching for a blag to entertain me with. I tapped my screen and brought up the telephone menu. 'I'm gonna call the cops!'

'No,' she said, and gently placed a hand on my arm before I could tap the last nine.

'Something went down,' I said. 'We *have* to call the cops!'

She pursed her lips tightly and I could hear her breathing through her small nose.

'From a phone box,' she said, quietly.

Obviously she wanted to make the call anonymously. Which suggested she was more than just the victim. She'd had a part to play in whatever went down, but she hadn't bargained that her part would lead to running for her life. Whatever had gone down, she sure as shit hadn't been expecting it.

'Cool,' I agreed. A phone box made sense. I didn't really want to be using my phone to call the cops. They traced that shit back to me and I'd get stuck in the mud trying to explain myself. I had to work out how this involved me, without the fuzz buzzing around me. I slipped off the dual carriageway and cruised slowly through Hammersmith High Street.

'There!' I pointed at a graffiti-decorated phone box and pulled up tight against it. 'I'll come with you.'

'I can do it myself,' she said stubbornly, stepping out of the car and into the phone box.

I watched her carefully through the passenger side window. She turned her back to me as she put the phone to her ear. I couldn't trust her to do the right thing.

'I *said* I can do it,' she hissed at me as I pulled open the door and stepped into the phone box with her, suddenly feeling overly conscious being in such close quarters with her.

I shrugged. 'Go on then.'

Her hands shook as she hit the first nine followed quickly by two more.

I placed my head next to hers so I could hear both sides. Only the phone receiver separating us.

'*What service do you require?*'

'Police,' she replied and then with a quick look at me, she added, 'Ambulance, too.'

'*What is the address please?*'

'102 Clareville Road. South Kensington.'

'*Thank you. Can you tell me exactly what happened?*'

'There was a break-in. The intruder had a knife. The home-owner... he... he was attacked.'

'Is he conscious?'

'I don't know.'

'Police and ambulance have been dispatched. Can I take your name?'

It didn't surprise me when at that point she disconnected the call. We stayed in the phone box for a moment in silence. She was looking at me as if daring me to ask the many questions that were running laps around my head. I let it slide. She'd been through it, and the police were on their way, so I gave her a small smile and nothing else. She didn't return it, instead she crossed her arms tightly around her body, her shoulders shivering. I looked down and noticed one shoeless foot was perched on the other and I wondered just how cold the concrete floor would be. I felt a little guilty wrapped up in my parka.

'Let's get in the car,' I said, when another part of me wanted to rub her arms and back for warmth. She looked out of the phone box as though considering other options, but something about her told me that this was a girl who never had options.

I opened the car door for her and watched her get in. I slipped my jacket off and handed it to her. 'Here,' I said, and she draped it up to her neck like a blanket.

I sat in the car. She ran a hand through her hair and in the process slipped off her purple scrunchy, then spent a moment untangling her hair before it fell gently over my jacket.

Yeah, she was definitely cute!

I cleared my throat. 'So... What now? Where can I take you? Where do you live?'

'I can't go home. Not tonight.'

I had a feeling that I knew the answer to my next question. 'Friends, family?' She shook her head gently. I nodded mine.

'Where do you live?' she asked.

It threw me enough to quickly answer, 'Hounslow.'

124

'Can I stay at yours for a bit?' she said, so softly that by the time her voice got to me I was already sweating bullets.

'My place?'

'Just for a few hours. I need to… work things out.'

'Uh, yeah, you know. That's cool, I guess.'

It was the first time that I saw her smile. It was only small but it was worth the wait.

'I don't know your name,' I said.

She leaned back against the headrest and closed her eyes.

'Sophia,' she said.

'I'm Javid,' I said, as my Beemer came to life. 'Call me Jay.'

Sophia opened her eyes and gave me another smile. 'Yeah,' she said, 'you look like a Jay.'

Chapter 24

Imy

The police had escorted me to the undisclosed location in Colnbrook but that's where their courtesy expired. I pulled up my hoody over my head as the rain picked up, and made my own way back.

Not ready to go home yet, I felt the need for noise, to drown out the noise in my head. I decided to cut through Hounslow High Street and let it all in; inhaling the smell and the constant stream of different tongues as strangers rushed and brushed past me looking for shelter from the rain. I allowed myself to escape for a moment, I allowed myself to be one of them. I didn't care that from across the pedestrianised road a man in a dark suit was walking in the same direction, keeping the same steady pace, his head hidden underneath a large black umbrella so he wouldn't be noticed by anyone but me.

I ignored him and stepped into a newsagents and bought a single bread bun. As I paid for it I glanced out of the shop window and watched him, his frustration apparent as he waited across the road.

I walked out of the newsagents and sat on an empty wet bench. My grey tracksuit darkened as the cold rain soaked through to my skin. Pigeons broke cover from shelter under the bench and approached me hopefully as I tore and sprinkled small pieces of the bread towards them.

I was in no hurry to see him and I wasn't in the mood for his bullshit. It turned out he wasn't in a patient mood. He wanted my attention now.

Beneath my hood his black leather brogues appeared in front of me. I kept my head down, the rapid patter of rain hitting and escaping like a waterfall from his umbrella. I continued to scatter crumbs around his feet as the pigeons surrounded him. He stamped his feet a few times and they dispersed in different directions before retreating to safety under the bench.

'You fool!' he said, sharply.

I looked up from his brogues, past his well-cut charcoal trousers and long black overcoat. His clothes were bone dry under his over-sized umbrella, and I met the eyes of the devil that I had sold my soul to. The hardness in his face shut down as I returned it with my own. He cleared his throat.

'We have to talk. My car is parked in that monstrosity over there. Top floor,' he said, inclining his head towards the Treaty Centre, and without another word Teddy Lawrence walked away knowing that I'd follow.

*

The first time I killed a man, it came easy. His name was Aba Abassi. He was known as Pathaan by those who loved him. I used to call him Pathaan.

From the age of ten to sixteen he was my mentor growing up in Gardez, a small working village located close to the Afghanistan/ Pakistan border. At times he was like an older brother. Other times he was like a father. He trained me in combat, educated me in the teachings of Al-Mudarris and sent me to England to strike fear amongst those who didn't believe as I once did.

It didn't work out that way. The ideologies slowly left me as I settled into the lifestyle that I had been brought up to despise. When the time arrived for me to make a choice, I didn't hesitate to pull the trigger and take him out.

I was looking at a long sentence for murder. Instead I'd escaped the clutches of one terrorist organisation and was now in the pocket of another: MI5, with Teddy Lawrence as my handler.

A few weeks before I was due to marry Stephanie, I was sent on my first mission. I had to tell her that a few friends had planned a stag-do to Berlin. Berlin was the only truth in the lie.

The Christmas Market at Alexanderplatz was a heavily populated event in the heart of the German capital, packed with vendors selling traditional Christmas crafts amongst fairground rides and beer stalls. The target was a small man called, but not named, Alfie. That's all I had, that and a few photos of him. His background was indeterminable from his appearance; pale like a white man, grey eyes like an Afghani, with thick, close-cut hair. He was responsible for selling bomb-making material on a mass scale to a Ghurfat-al-Mudarris splinter cell called al-Muhaymin.

In a crowded beer tent, I injected Alfie just below the ribs using a finger needle filled with cyanide. He flinched at the pinch and looked around amongst the crowd as I brushed past him. I walked out of the tent before screams for help reached me. The taxi driver, who had delivered the package containing the needle and photographs of the target, picked me up and dropped me back to my hotel. The next day I flew home and entertained Stephanie and Jack with stories and staged photographs of my stag.

Teddy Lawrence and MI5 ensured that they had full deniability of the operation. It was never officially authorised. Any victory would be quietly celebrated. Failure would've fallen solely at my feet.

That's what my life had become.

*

I didn't take my eyes off him as I approached his grey Volkswagen Passat on the top floor of the Treaty Centre car park. I opened the passenger side door and slid in, aware of Lawrence grimacing at my wet clothes against the leather seats.

'Seatbelt,' he said, turning the ignition.

We left the car park in silence and it stayed that way until Lawrence turned onto the Great West Road. If the silence was a tactic for me to speak first, then it wasn't working. I had nothing to say to him. He slowed down a touch as we approached Osterley Park Hotel. A cheap move, but not unexpected. I kept my eyes forward as I felt his gaze on me as we drifted past the hotel.

Lawrence turned off the Great West Road and pulled into Osterley Tesco's car park, finding a suitable parking spot at the very end away from prying eyes. He pulled in nose first and checked the rear-view and side mirrors. Leaving the engine running, he turned up the heat and pointed the vents towards me. A gesture that I wasn't buying.

'Imran,' he said after a long sigh, as though he'd realised that his rehearsed dressing down wasn't going to cut it. 'It was reckless.'

I said nothing.

'Do you have any clue what lengths I had to go through to protect you?'

He sounded selfless. I knew otherwise. There would be no gratitude forthcoming.

'What were you thinking? What did you hope to achieve, *Imran*?'

Frustration was creeping into his voice, and it pleased me. The cool calm demeanour that he wore for the world had never fooled me. Lawrence knew very well what I had hoped to achieve, and I couldn't care less if it wasn't sanctioned by the Secret Service.

'Saheed Kabir, you don't think that we knew about him?' he asked, speaking to the side of my head. 'Ghurfat-al-Mudarris is broken but that's not where this ends, Imran! We were getting close to al-Muhaymin. Their methods of operation have become volatile and unpredictable. Kabir was a member, a conduit for weapons finding their way onto our shores and into the hands of young British Muslims. He could have been imperative to us. You have to understand that, Imran. You can't dilute this with your personal feelings. You work for us!'

I turned to face him. He was sitting twisted on his side, leaning towards me, making himself bigger than his slight frame, spurred on by his credentials. I wanted to wrap the seat belt around his throat and bring him to the edge of death and show him how little his credentials meant to me.

He held my gaze for a moment before straightening up and placing his hands on the steering wheel, his Adam's apple bobbing as he swallowed. I turned away and through the windscreen I stared at the green bush that he had tucked us into. After a moment and a soft tone that wasn't natural to him, he asked, 'Is there anybody else left?'

I had killed Pathaan. The Kabirs had taken their punishment. Bin Jabbar's fate had been snatched out of my hands. *Is there anybody else left?* I blinked and Jay flashed before my eyes.

Lawrence's phone vibrated noisily on the centre console.

'Lay low, Imran. Get some rest,' Lawrence said, as he picked up his earpiece and clipped it on. 'When the time comes, I'll be in touch.' He gestured his head to the door. I stepped out of the car just as he greeted the caller. I shut the door behind me and lifted the hood over my head as I waited for the cloud above me to open up.

The reverse lights came on and Lawrence moved out recklessly. I took a step back, out of the way, and I saw his face screwed up and his mouth moving quickly as he shifted gears and sped out of Tesco's car park.

Whoever he was speaking to had delivered bad news.

Chapter 25

'*Fuck!*' Teddy Lawrence cried into the earpiece.

He wasn't the type to swear, too much armour in his vocabulary to resort to such language. The odd occasion he may throw around a '*damn*' or if the moment took him a '*Goddammit*', but all in context. Such as the situation that came to light earlier of Imran Siddiqui going on a '*goddamn killing spree*'.

Always looking at the bigger picture, Lawrence had to convince his seniors at Thames House to intervene in the arrest of Imran Siddiqui, and persuade the higher echelons of the police constabulary. Not an easy task. Chief Superintendent Penelope Wakefield of Hounslow Police Station would not take kindly to MI5 sticking their oar in.

Any other time, Lawrence would have thrown Siddiqui into the lion cage and watched him fight for his life. To be fair, it would have been a pretty even fight. But as it stood, Siddiqui was a key asset in the ongoing war against Ghurfat-al-Mudarris and its splinter cell, al-Muhaymin. Simply put, he was an asset that needed protecting by any means necessary. That, and that alone, was the bigger picture.

It took the might of Assistant Director of Counter Terrorism John Robinson and Major General Stewart Sinclair. They exchanged dialogue with the highly strung, highly frustrated Chief Superintendent. She dug in her heels, as expected, but two words, '*National Security*', uttered from the right mouth, had the power to open and slam shut doors.

Wakefield acquiesced, as expected. She wasn't pleased, of course, considering that she would have to exchange similar dialogue with the Lancashire constabulary who were investigating the Kabir murders in Blackburn. Whether that investigation quietly wound down over time, or whether they looked for some poor fool to pin it on, it wasn't Teddy Lawrence's problem anymore.

But this new revelation was. One fire out, another roared to life.

'*Fuck!*' Teddy cried again, slapping the steering wheel as he sped through Tesco's car park, his hand hovering over the horn, ready to blast away any trolley that dared cross him. He glanced in the rear-view mirror, a picture of Imran Siddiqui soaked in the downpour as Lawrence screeched out of the car park.

'Agent Lawrence,' the voice of Major General Sinclair boomed through his earpiece. 'Pull yourself together, man.'

'I apologise, Major,' Lawrence said, looking for and finding some composure. He took a long breath. 'What do we know?'

'An anonymous 999 call was placed from a phone box on the Hammersmith High Street at 19.21. The location of the incident given was 102 Clareville Road, South Kensington.'

'John Robinson's home.'

'The name associated with the address triggered the call to be intercepted by GCHQ and, rightly so, landed on our lap.'

'What did the caller say?'

'Not even close to enough. There was a break-in. The intruder had a knife. According to the caller, Robinson was attacked.'

Lawrence ran a hand through his overly-waxed hair. 'How bad is it?'

'We don't know.' The Major cleared his throat.

Lawrence filled in. 'He's been abducted?'

'It would appear so.'

'This is going to turn into a crap circus, Major. Front and centre of every goddamn newspaper. Speculation will shoot through the roof. Can we stop the story? Least delay it until we know. Is this a hostage situation? Have demands been made?'

'For now, we've put a cap on it. It won't be appearing anywhere. As soon as the call was intercepted we liaised with Kensington Police. There were no screaming sirens, no uniforms. Two of ours were quickly and quietly dispatched to the scene for recon. They let themselves in from the back. Blood splatter was found on the kitchen floor, but not enough to suggest anything worse than a bloody nose. For now, police are acting on advice only, and that circle is tight. God knows it could be leaked six ways from Sunday. But as far as the story is concerned, there is no damn story, nothing untoward happened tonight on Clareville Road.'

'Major, I think—'

'I haven't finished, Lawrence. I can see that this has come as a shock to you, especially after the day we've had with bloody Siddiqui, but I need you to pull your pants up and recollect yourself, because I want you taking the lead on this.'

'What do you need, Major?'

Lawrence heard the Major General sigh. It sounded tired, loaded, as though an old enemy that wouldn't lie had resurfaced.

'You have something, Major?'

'We do. I'm sending you CCTV images captured outside the phone box.'

'The caller?'

'Hold.'

Lawrence pulled over onto the hard shoulder of the M40 that he didn't remember getting on. In his ear Major Sinclair barked at somebody to send the images. Lawrence picked up his phone and waited for the message to arrive. It did by secure email. There were two files attached. Lawrence clicked on the first attachment and entered a unique pin to allow it to open. The picture wasn't of high quality but he could see a black car parked on a double yellow line outside of a phone box. Inside were two figures, Lawrence could make out the blonde hair of a female dressed in white. Standing close in front of her was the distorted figure of a man.

Lawrence quickly opened up the second attachment, the adrenaline rushing through him, and he entered the pin incorrectly twice. One more time and he could wave goodbye to that file. He took his time. The second attachment opened, a close-up of the two figures in the phone box, and it took Teddy Lawrence's breath away.

Chapter 26

Jay

I discreetly popped my head around Mum's bedroom door for a quick peek. I'd been doing it every thirty minutes on the nose between seven and midday. So what's that? Ten times. Each time Sophia hadn't moved from her position. Face up, head in the dip in between two pillows. Her blonde hair a mess around her and a pale ankle hanging out of the duvet.

I felt a little off with a stranger sleeping in Mum's bed. I should've slept here and she could have had my room. But Imy's handgun was still knocking about in a Nike shoebox under my bed, and fuck knows what direction this would take if she got her mitts on it.

A little after midday, I figured that I could be waiting around all day for her to wake up naturally, so a little intervention was required. I pumped up the volume on the television, but daytime TV is just too polite to do the job. I clanged around in the kitchen, opening and closing cupboards as I made myself a noisy cup of coffee. I hovered around outside Mum's bedroom, coughing and stepping purposely on a known creaky floorboard. Nothing worked, Sophia was dead to the world.

My next thought: what if she literally was dead to the world! I watched a bit on *This Morning* once about this lady who took a fall, her head meeting the edge of a kerb. Anyway, she got up, stuck a tissue to the cut on her head and soldiered on. That night she fell asleep and, well, that's it.

135

What if the same had happened to Sophia? Maybe there'd been a struggle and she'd been struck on the head, concussed, and her body had just now caught up, failing her. I didn't have time to Google *death from concussion* and it seemed unlikely, but in my experience unlikely was becoming the norm, and I couldn't have her dying on my watch. Especially not on Mum's bed.

I stepped off the noisy floorboard and pushed open the door harder than I expected to, and it collided loudly against the wall. She didn't stir. I crossed the bedroom and stood by the side of the bed and watched her. Her mouth was open slightly, but I couldn't hear her breathing. There were no two ways about it, I was going to have to risk a look at her chest and hope that there was some movement. I took a quick look but not enough to establish whether she was breathing. I leaned closer and took another look, longer, concentrating for any sign of movement, trying not to look at the red of her bra through the gap in her uniform. At that point my phone decided to ring loudly in my pocket. I slipped it out to disconnect it, but in my panic I swiped to answer. Idris' face popped on my screen just as Sophia's eyes flew open with my face in the vicinity of her chest.

I straightened up, not sure who to address first. I gave her a smile and she responded by lifting the duvet up to her neck and looking at me curiously. No, suspiciously! As though I was a dirty old man. I wasn't dirty or old, and I wanted to tell her that, but fucking Idris was in my face.

'Jay,' Idris's tinny voice said. I mouthed '*sorry*' to Sophia and backed away from the bed.

'Not now, Idris,' I said turning my back to her. 'I'll bell you back.'

Through squinted eyes, Idris asked, 'Who's that?'

I looked over my shoulder, Sophia had shuffled up against the headboard. I smiled stupidly at her and moved away so that she was out of the picture.

'You dirty dog!' Idris smiled and then broke into a laugh. 'Wait... Is that your *mum's* bedroom?'

'Idris. Can we do this later?'

'Yeah, okay, I can see you're busy. Bell me soon, I've got an update on... that thing you asked me about.'

'Yeah, cool,' I said. 'Later.'

'In your mum's bedroom.' Idris grinned. 'Seriously Jay, that's just weird.'

I cut him off and turned my attention to the stranger in my mother's bed. Her hair was tousled and sticking out at angles. I noticed that her nose was red and wondered if it was cold to the touch.

'I, um, that was... a mate.' I pointed at my phone. 'I don't know why he insists on video calling...' She didn't reply and the pressure was just too much and I blurted, 'I wasn't looking at your... you know.'

Sophia drew her hair back behind her ears like curtains, revealing her morning face, and what a morning face it was. I swallowed and continued to talk shit. 'I was just checking to see if you were breathing. I saw this bit on *This Morning*, I don't normally watch *This Morning*, but I couldn't find the remote, anyway, this woman had a head injury and...' She stopped me in my flow with a smile and I swear I forgot what I was chatting about.

*

I prepared a spot of convenience food for two as I waited for Sophia to come down. I listened carefully for her movements. The stubborn bolt of the bathroom door. The shower coughing before exploding to life. My armpits spiked as I silently prayed that there weren't any unwelcome visitors on my sponge. I flipped the fish fingers and waffles, and fired up the hob to get the baked beans going. I switched the kettle on, but, not sure if she was a tea or coffee girl, I decided to wait until I was informed. The shower stopped and I realised that I should have offered her a clean towel and maybe some of Mum's clothes. A moment later I heard the bolt slide across the bathroom door. I picked up a spoon off the worktop and checked my reflection in the back of it, as she padded down the stairs. I ran a hand through my hair and turned just in time to see her appear at the doorway. She was wearing my Batman onesie.

'Is this okay?' she said, pinching at it. 'I found it hung up behind the bathroom door. You don't mind, do you?'

'Yeah, no, yeah, it's cool,' I said, feeling my cheeks colouring. 'Cool, cool, cool, cool. I'm, uh, making some lunch. Take a pew.'

Pew! *Pew!* I don't say shit like pew. I take the piss out of people who say shit like pew. Sophia took a pew at the kitchen table and I turned away and took my time stirring the baked beans, as I made some award-winning small talk.

'Did you have a good shower? Sometimes the hot water can get too hot.'

Yeah, that's what I said.

'Fine,' she replied. 'I used your bath sponge, if that's okay?'

'Yep, that's fine.' I swallowed. I turned around to face her. She was leaning on the table with both hands cupped around my matching Batman mug, and I suddenly felt like I was seven years old again. 'I was just about to make you one, but wasn't sure if you wanted tea or coffee?'

'This is good,' Sophia said, taking a sip from my tea, which I thought was an intimate gesture, or possibly she just wasn't very particular.

I pulled up a chair and sat opposite her. I linked my fingers and then steepled them; it felt unnatural. I was acting weird and

I didn't know why. I couldn't disengage, not now, I had to own it, as though steepling was my thing. I took my time before speaking as she watched me with a measure of amusement over my mug.

'You feeling better?' I asked. 'You know… After last night?'

Sophia nodded gently at me, a smile playing in her eyes as she brought my tea to her lips. She had a way about her, I'll give you that. But fuck, I couldn't let a pretty face get me into trouble. I was quite capable of doing that shit all on my own. But *she* was in trouble, and just by her being under my roof, by association, so was I. Now I had to find out exactly what brand of trouble we were in.

'Wanna talk about it?' I prompted. 'We should.'

'Jay.' I loved the way she made the one syllable last, as though it felt as good on her tongue as it did to my ear. She placed the mug down and pushed it towards me. I peered in and it was still half full. I took a sip. There was something about sharing the tea and *I really need to snap the fuck out of this!* 'We've told the police. Let them deal with it. I really don't want to relive it.'

'Yeah, no, I know. Totally understand! But I can't have this coming back to me. *I* need to understand what happened last night. *I* need to know.'

In my thirst for information, to see how it all tied in with what Omar was jabbering on about, I had said too much, and I think Sophia had picked up on it. She narrowed her eyes to slits and wrinkled her nose and she looked like that cute witch from *Bewitched* that I used to watch with Mum.

I shrugged casually to throw her off the scent, and stood up. I opened the fridge door and looked inside for inspiration.

'What were you doing on that road last night, Jay?' she countered defensively.

'Nothing,' I said over my shoulder as I randomly picked up an apple that I'd bought with good intentions. 'I was on my way home.'

'Yeah?' she said, and I could tell that she wasn't buying it.

I shut the fridge door, and leaned back casually against the counter and crossed my legs at the ankles, and took a bite out of an apple for the first time in years.

'Look, Sophia, you're in my home. Don't you think I should be asking the questions?' It was a crap thing to say, but I had to flip the script before she started asking questions about what I was doing on that road in the first place. 'You called the cops anonymously. Why? They're going to want to chat to you. You were involved. And now I am, too.'

All of a sudden she looked smaller, a little vulnerable. It felt like the dynamic had shifted and I felt that if I continued to push, I'd lose her.

Sophia got up and approached the sink beside me. Her shoulders hunched forward and her head dipped as she turned on the tap and started to wash the mug.

'You don't have to do that,' I said, side-glancing at her as she placed the mug in the drying rack and started on my cereal bowl and spoon. 'Seriously, I can do that.' I palmed the tap shut. She stood motionless for a moment watching the tap drip before turning to me. The whites of her eyes cracked red as she turned to me. I straightened up from off the counter, which only made the distance between us tighter. 'I can help you,' I said. 'Trust me, I'm not as useless as I look.'

Sophia smiled, but it was small, and there was nothing behind it. She dropped her eyes and then dropped her head. There was a quietness for a moment, only the sound of her breath and the fast beat of my heart. She took a small tentative step towards me and rested the side of her head against my chest. The water from her hands seeped through the back of my T-shirt and onto my skin. I placed the apple on the counter and put my arms around her. I noticed over her shoulder that lunch was long past burnt as she spoke softly into my chest.

'He put a knife to my throat. He was going to kill me.'

140

Chapter 27

Tommy woke up on the sofa, in the living room, in a house that had once belonged to Omar's father. Despite having slept in his jacket and jeans and his socks, he was feeling the freeze. Omar had explained that the heating and electricity had been long turned off. The house was an empty shell of the home that it once was.

On the floor beside the sofa sat a tattered old brown leather holdall. One that Tommy found at home while rooting through his old man's wardrobe. It had been full of old photo albums, filled with memories that didn't mean a thing to him. He'd emptied it out and replaced the memories with tools. Tommy stretched the musty threadbare blanket tightly around his body and gently traced a line on the dry cracked leather straps, mentally picturing how he was going to use the tools.

He sat up straight when he heard the front door open, but kept the blanket wrapped around his shoulders. He blinked tightly to get the sleep out of his eyes as Omar appeared, looking well rested. He had spent the night at his own place. Tommy didn't know where that was, but he guessed the heating was in working order.

'Salaam, Brother,' Omar greeted him as he passed over a steaming hot drink in a polystyrene cup.

'Yeah, Salaam,' Tommy replied, the word still sounding unnatural to him. 'It's really, *really* cold in here.' His voice shivered in tune with his body as he wrapped both hands around the cup, despite the smell of coffee making him feel nauseous. The number of black coffees that he'd made daily for his half-cut old man had put him right off it.

'How's our guest?' Omar asked. Tommy could see the curl of a smile protruding from beneath the thick knit scarf. 'Comfy?'

'I've not heard a thing,' Tommy replied, eyes up at the ceiling. 'I was knocked out.'

'Alright.' Omar clapped his gloved hands twice. 'Drink up, and let's go say hello.'

Tommy followed Omar up the stairs, the tools in his leather holdall rattling in his hand. Omar was talking enthusiastically but Tommy was unable to make out his words, and didn't deem them important enough to ask. They stood on the landing, breathing plumes of warm vapour into the freezing air.

'Through there,' Omar marvelled, pointing at a closed door. 'That's where history was made.'

'Yeah. You said that last night.'

'Did I?'

Tommy was aware that Omar was itching to bring up his father's achievements again. How he had nurtured five young men in that very room, imparting great wisdom and turning them into brave Jihadis.

'Yeah. You did.' Tommy smiled, trying not to offend.

'Do you want to have a look inside?' Omar reached for the handle. 'For, uh, inspiration.'

'As you said, Brother.' Tommy still wasn't comfortable with that term. 'It's history. I'm looking to make my own history.'

'Yeah, of course.' Omar nodded, his face small as he dropped his hand away from the door handle. 'And I'm going to help you with that.' Omar's face lit up, the slight set aside. 'As agreed, I've reached out already. My contact has what you need. As soon as we're done here, you and I are going on a road trip to Coventry.'

Tommy had to trust him, and he did. It was clear that Omar wanted desperately to follow in his father's footsteps. Take on the role of the provider, to place tools in the hands of others and then stand back and watch the destruction from a safe distance.

'Let's get this over and done with,' Tommy said as they both lifted their eyes to the hatch door leading to the loft.

Omar stood on tiptoes and pulled the catch to flip down the hatch door. He slid the attached metal ladder down and moved to one side. Tommy climbed up through the hole and disappeared into the darkness.

'Bag.' Tommy's voice echoed.

Omar's slight frame struggled to lift the bag, let alone hoist it over his head, but motivation helped give him strength. A hand appeared out of the hatch and wrapped a fist around the handle. The bag disappeared into the darkness.

'The light switch is on your... Oh, you found it.'

Omar followed, and entered through the hatch. It was colder in the loft, much more so than the rest of the house. He tightened the scarf around his neck and stood beside Tommy, the holdall at their feet. They looked to the far end of the loft.

'Is he supposed to be that colour?' Omar asked, some concern etched on his face. 'Do you think he's alright?'

Tommy picked up his brown leather holdall, the contents clunked and clanged as he walked past the stuffed bin-liners and stacks of damp cardboard boxes filled with memories of Al-Bhukara family history. He stood in front of their prize.

Naked from the waist up, the hostage was secured to a wooden chair, his body a pale grey, flesh spilling over the thick rope that had been tied so tight that his shoulders had folded unnaturally inwards. His eyes were closed and his head dropped. His chin rested on his collar bone and his body shook from both the shock and the cold.

'Is he…?' Omar called. He hadn't moved from his spot and was rubbing his hands and stamping his feet for warmth.

'He's alive,' Tommy replied.

Omar walked across the loft and stood beside Tommy. 'Alright then,' he said. 'Wake him up.'

Tommy knelt down and unzipped the leather holdall, almost expecting to see old photo albums. He noisily scoured the contents, supplies that he had recently purchased from B&Q, and picked out a white paper suit. He slipped it over his clothes, zipped it up and lifted the paper hood. He rummaged further through the bag, and picked out a cordless hammer drill and attached a 25mm spade bit – a wide flat blade with a sharp point, primarily used to bore holes smoothly through wood. Tommy placed the sharp point on the thigh of the hostage and caressed the trigger. He looked up at Omar.

'Wait!' Omar turned his head away and grimaced. 'Do it!'

Tommy softly pressed the trigger of the hammer drill a quarter of an inch, just enough for the sharp point of the spade bit to rapidly rotate a couple of rounds. It ripped easily through the trouser leg and with the same ease pierced a red hole into soft flesh.

As though a string had been pulled on a toy doll, the hostage's eyes flew open. He cried. *'Do you know who I am? Do you know who the bloody hell I am?'*

Omar delivered his response, slowly relishing each word.

'As it happens, I do. John Robinson, Assistant Director of Counter Terrorism. Now, I'm going to ask you a question, and I hope you will give me the same courtesy of answering me.'

Robinson stared agog at the small red hole... in his thigh. He hissed through his teeth as the pain and the cold caught up. 'What do you want?' he asked, weakly.

'Where are you holding Abdul Bin Jabbar? The man known to the world as The Teacher?'

144

Chapter 28

Jay

No. Before you ask. We didn't sleep together. The fuck d'you think this is? I held Sophia for a bit, longer than I'd expected, but not as long as I wanted to. It was nice. Sophia was nice. But that's all it was. Didn't mean anything.

I'd come close a couple of times, but I'd never truly fallen in love. I liked the idea of it. I liked the feeling of my brain shooting in all directions as it formulated warm and fuzzy scenarios. A roaring fireplace, candles dotted on the windowsill, sinking into the sofa with limbs entwined watching Netflix on a full stomach after a take-away lamb madras. The images came quickly, then reality kicked in, and just as quickly they popped.

We'd moved into the living room. She made herself at home on my armchair. Both of us had lost our appetite for lunch, instead making do with a pack of Quavers and a Twix. I browsed the news channels and scoured online hoping for a mention of events from the night before. Absolutely nothing.

It's not like Sophia was imparting any further knowledge; she only fed me drops, when I needed chapter and verse.

'Did you get his name? The guy who…' I asked.

'I don't know his name,' Sophia replied quickly, avoiding my eyes, and hoovered down the back end of the crisp packet.

Of course she knew him, or at the very least knew something

145

about him. But to admit to that would be admitting that they were working together. 'What'd he look like?' I said, swallowing my frustration.

'He was young, good-looking.'

I shifted in my seat. 'How… How do you mean, good-looking?' I said, not coming across as jealous *at all*.

'Just…' She shrugged. 'He was attractive.'

'Look, I'm going to need more than *attractive* if I'm going to help you.'

'Light eyes, long lashes, maybe early twenties. Oh, and short red hair.'

'Ginger? He's a *ginger*?' I said, feeling a little better about myself.

Sophia nodded, followed by a sigh. 'I know you mean well, Jay, I just can't see how you can help me.'

'I have contacts,' I said, holding up my phone as if to prove my point.

She rolled her eyes at me. Even that was cute. But I couldn't just sit around sneaking glances at her as she went through her repertoire of expressions. I mean, *I could've*, but I had calls to make, people to see. Somehow I was part of this and I needed to know exactly what my part was.

The only thing was: could I trust her alone in my home? Probably not, if I'm honest, but I couldn't exactly take her with me. Not with this threat hanging over her. I did a quick mental run through of my house and tried to establish how much damage she could do. There was only that one thing.

I wiped the Twix crumbs from my mouth and shot to my feet, propelled into action.

She looked at me with a measured expression. 'What?'

'Back in a sec,' I said. Before she could respond I ran upstairs and into my bedroom. From under my bed, from my Nike shoebox, I retrieved the Glock. Not because I had any intentions of waving it around; I simply could not leave the piece at home with Sophia knocking about.

I shrugged on my parka and dropped the Glock in the bucket pocket and made my way back down. I stopped in my tracks halfway down the stairs.

Sophia was standing in the hallway, her back tight against the front door.

'Where are you going?' she asked, her eyes and voice both filled with apprehension.

'There's something I gotta do.'

She shook her head. 'You don't have to do anything.'

'I have to.' I walked down the last few steps and stood in front of her. 'Don't open the door to anyone and do not leave the house. I'll be back soon as.'

Sophia looked at me like she cared, or maybe that's just how I saw it. She stepped to one side and I opened the front door.

'Jay,' she said, as I moved past her. I turned back to look at her. She had her arms tightly wrapped around my Batman onesie and it almost broke my will. 'I don't want anyone else to get hurt because of me.'

It was the closest Sophia had come to an admission.

'Take my number.'

I read out my number and she put it in her phone and then she gave me a dropped call so I had her number. It felt weird, like the first step in a relationship, but this was nothing like giving out your number to a girl in a bar.

'Save it and check in on me later, if you want, you know, it's up to you.'

She smiled. 'I'll save it under J.'

*

I dialled Idris from my car. The international dial tone filled my car through my speakers.

'Yes, Jay.' Idris' voice came through, he sounded like he had his mouth full. 'The buffet in this place is killing me, I must have put on at least half a stone.' My heart bled; God forbid he might lose one of his abs from his precious six pack. 'So, what did I catch you doing earlier? In your mum's bedroom of all places. Jesus, Jay!'

We weren't video-calling, but nevertheless I could picture the stupid look on his face. 'You wanna tell me what you found out about Imy?'

'Not a thing, Jay.'

'What's that mean? They let him go?'

'No, Imran Siddiqui was never there. There's nothing on the system. He wasn't checked in.'

'I don't understand,' I said. 'Could they have taken him to another shop?'

'According to you he was picked up in Osterley—'

'What d'you mean according to me? He *was* picked up in Osterley! I didn't make this shit up.'

'Jay, you wanna calm down? I'm not saying you made it up. Look, if he was picked up in Osterley, nine times out of ten he's going to Hounslow nick. But if the crime is, let's just say *extreme*, then he'll get hauled down to Heathrow Police Station.'

'Extreme? *What?*' I waited for him to respond before answering myself. 'Extreme like terrorism-related? Are you saying they pulled Imy in on *terrorism* charges?'

'Fuck, why don't you say that word a few more times, just in case GCHQ missed it?'

'Is that what you think happened?'

'Nah, I don't actually. It wouldn't have gone down so… amicably.'

'Yeah,' I said, thinking back. The knock on the door. The exchange of words. Imy leaving them at the door to pick up his house keys and phone before voluntarily going with them. 'It was pretty fucking amicable.'

'If they had any inkling that he was up to… you know, they would have turned his house upside down.'

'So you don't think he's at Heathrow nick?'

'No.'

'And he definitely didn't get pulled into Hounslow?'

'No.'

I almost asked Idris for another favour. Another call. See what he could find out about what went down last night at Clareville Road. It was on my lips, but when he spoke next, I knew I couldn't ask him. Knew I couldn't keep taking the piss and not giving anything back.

'You gonna tell me what's going on, Jay?' he asked. It was token, his voice weary of asking me the same thing over, and me forever evading the question.

'Nothing, Idris,' I said, trying to inject a smile into my voice. 'Nothing to worry about.'

I ended up burning petrol as I took a tour of Hounslow trying to figure out my next move. I was expecting Omar to bell me at some point. What did he say? *If things go as planned, then believe me, bro, you are going to want to be a part of this.* The fuck's that supposed to mean?

I really hadn't taken to that riddle-talking motherfucker. His old man was a monster and it looked very much as though he wanted to do something to serve in his memory. I could easily tip him off to the cops, put him on their radar. Let them deal with him and whoever the fuck this Tommy character was. But could I trust the cops not to fuck this up?

How many times have we seen an attack take place by somebody who was known to the authorities, but they chose to sit on it?

As stressed as I was, my head was playing mind gymnastics, that feeling of doing something right, something important, creeping up and tickling the back of my neck, making my spider-sense tingle. It made me feel alive, it drove me, and no matter how easily I could have walked away from it all, I was involved because I wanted to be involved.

As I waited for Omar to bell me I thought I'd do a little homework, see what I could suss out. Knowledge is power, right, something like that? I filled up my Beemer, ready for a round trip to South Kensington.

*

In the daylight, Clareville Road was a pretty chilled-out street, well-kept homes belonging to those who liked to be well kept. There was nothing uniform about it, each house was detached and had its own character. It didn't seem like the kind of neighbourhood that had ever experienced violence, and as I slowly drove past number 102, at a glance, it still didn't seem like it.

Everything felt static, almost staged. As though the night before a woman hadn't run for her life from a knife-wielding attacker.

I wasn't quite sure what to expect; some police presence, door to door, asking questions. I guess there was a chance that the intruder had been jacked soon after we'd made our getaway, and the whole thing had come to a stop before it started. But, I don't know, that didn't fit either.

I dropped to the kerb about ten doors down from 102 and clocked the scene in my rear-view mirror. Between the house and my car, a man and woman walked towards each other, stopping by a post box. I watched them for a minute.

They were chatting and laughing as though they'd just bumped into each other after a dalliance at Uni some years back. Her hand playfully brushed his arm, as she ran the other through her hair. He shuffled confidently from one foot to the other as he went through his

150

repertoire of hilarious anecdotes with animated gestures. Not a hat, jacket or scarf in sight as though they were immune to the cold. They could have been neighbours who'd nipped out to post a letter and were just catching up, but my neighbours don't greet me like that!

I looked past them towards the house, and was dying to get out and have a nosey. I waited for the long-lost sweethearts to budge, but I knew they weren't going anywhere anytime soon.

Their actions seemed to loop, as if they had only rehearsed for a short period before stopping and repeating. Him hopping around from one foot to the other, holding court. Her hand on his arm and through her hair. The over-exaggerated laughter.

It could've been something, could've been nothing.

I removed the Glock from my pocket and placed it in the glove compartment, and stepped out of my car. I slammed the door deliberately hard, expecting them to flip their heads in my direction, but they were still wrapped up in each other.

I zipped up my parka and jammed my hands in the bucket pockets. I felt around and found a balled-up used tissue. I started to flatten it. It was time to put my theory to the test.

I walked casually towards the post box where they were standing. Even though I was in their peripheral vision they didn't even so much as glance towards me. About level with them I heard him say something like, '*And that's the last time I'll be using that plumber again,*' and she laughed with a flirty, '*Oh, stop it, Richard.*' I moved on past them, her continuous laughter still ringing in my ears. There's no fucking way his plumber joke could have been that funny. I made my move: *operation used tissue.* I had un-balled and flattened it as much as the room in my pocket would allow me to, and my hand emerged out of my pocket with it and I dropped it *accidentally* to the ground.

Now, check this out for tactical nuance: I could have dropped my keys but they would have hit the ground quicker; the flattened tissue would float slowly to the ground like a snotty parachute, and if my suspicions were correct, and they were watching me, their eyes would naturally be on the flight of the tissue gently floating to the ground and I'd have a small window to make my move.

I made my move.

In one swift motion, I spun and caught the tissue before it hit dirt. As anticipated, both their eyes were on it, and then wide on me. I busted them. They knew I'd busted them. And they knew that I knew that I'd busted them. Her fake laugh was suspended on her face, and he'd stopped hopping around as though somebody had shouted, 'Cut!'

They'd been watching me as soon my Beemer had made an appearance.

'Keep Britain Tidy!' I said, holding my used tissue up.

I turned my back to them and walked towards 102 Clareville Road, as I tried to piece together the significance of it.

Were they cops straight out of Undercover School? Were they watching me, or were they generally looking for any suspicious behaviour? Or, was I just being characteristically paranoid? My brain was still trying to digest it, but all of a sudden it seemed way too hot to be having a nosey around. If they were cops, they'd want to know what I was doing at that address, and I wasn't ready to spill just yet.

I moved casually past 102 without so much as a glance, as I tried to figure out an alternative destination that wouldn't put me on the radar. Before I knew it I was walking down the path of the neighbour's home.

I pressed the bell. It vibrated gently under my finger, and as I waited for an answer, I looked back at the couple. They had moved, like, ninety degrees, so that she had her back to me and he was in front of her, able to sneak a peek over her shoulder as they insisted on continuing their little charade.

I heard the chain rattle from the other side of the door. I hoped that a little charm would go a long way. The door opened. A woman, old, older than me anyway, dressed in a lot of Lycra, jogged on the spot like a cartoon about to take off. She eyed me with curiosity.

'Hi,' I smiled brightly, as though all her dreams had come true. 'How are you?'

She looked at her watch, a smart number, and she swiped the screen a few times. 'Yes?' was her curt greeting.

'My name is Jay.'

'Jay?' She said it with suspicion, as if I'd just made it up.

I cleared my throat. 'I was wondering if you could help me,' I said, as my brain tried to race ahead and figure out where I was going with this.

'You look lost,' she said, as though she knew that I didn't belong.

'No, not lost, Miss.'

'*Mrs* Carson,' she replied, and I think she instantly regretted giving her name away.

'Not at all, Mrs Carson, I'm looking for someone. She—' I started, but was rudely interrupted by my phone chiming from my pocket. I padded from pocket to pocket and blindly disconnected the call.

'She, whoever *she* is, is not here!' she snapped. 'Now, if you don't mind.' Her hand moved towards the door and I knew if I didn't improve my bullshit sharpish I'd be staring at a door number.

'She was working a shift yesterday evening. Next door,' I blurted and gestured with my head.

She narrowed her eyes. 'Sophie?'

'Sophia, yeah, that's her,' I said, and for no valid reason, added, 'She's my girlfriend.' I said it as part of the act, didn't mean anything by it, but weirdly butterflies fluttered through my stomach.

Mrs Carson took a moment to look me up and down, probably trying to picture us together, the coverage of the attack at Imy and

Stephanie's interfaith wedding reception probably still fresh on her mind. But, to her credit, and my shame, she said, 'Hope you're going to make an honest woman out of her?'

'Ha, yeah, no, it's still early days.' I swear those butterflies just would not quit! 'Thing is, Mrs Carson, Sophia was supposed to meet me last night. We had dinner planned at The Shard. It was my birthday, you see, but she didn't show. I tried belling, um... calling her, but her phone was switched off. I even went round to her flat. She wasn't there, either. So you know, I got worried that something happened to her. I tried knocking next door, but no one seems to be home. So... you know.' I shrugged softly at her.

'It's a bit of a stretch, isn't it, young man, to assume she's missing? Maybe she just forgot, she's not the most organised, let me tell you.'

'I know! Totally disorganised. That's exactly what I thought!' I said, starting to warm to the story. 'So I slept on it and tried to get in touch with her again this morning... It's just not like her. I knew that she had a shift here so...' I shrugged. 'I wondered if she turned up for it last night.'

She sighed, and then she followed it with a second, and then the lines in her forehead disappeared as her features softened. 'She did turn up for her shift. She picked up the house keys from me, she normally returns them after, but I guess she must have left in a hurry.'

I tuned out for a second as I pictured Sophia running for her life and scrambling into my car, into my home, into my Batman onesie and into my life.

'I gave her a hard time yesterday, I must admit,' Mrs Carson continued. 'She turned up early, was a little jittery by all accounts.'

'Did you see her leave last night?' I said, and carefully added, 'Or did you see anything out of the ordinary?'

Mrs Carson shook her head. 'No. Though I did hear some boy

154

racer screeching down the road. By the time I looked out of the window, he'd gone.'

'Right,' I said, sheepishly, and risked a glance at the couple at the post box. They were still in situ, freezing their bollocks off. Served them right for not wearing their jackets. 'But nothing happened after?'

'No.'

'Okay. I'll leave you to your run, Mrs Carson.'

'John is usually back home around seven, maybe he could shed some light?'

'John?'

'Yes, that's who that house belongs to. John Robinson.'

I didn't say much after that. Couldn't! I just plastered a smile on my face and nodded. I think I managed to mumble a few words of gratitude. I walked away down the path and I heard her call out, '*I hope you find her.*'

Hearing John Robinson's name simply dazzled me. But pieces were falling into place.

Omar had engineered, what? The kidnapping of a highly ranked MI5 officer? And Sophia had been paid off to give them access to his home and then turn a blind eye? That sound about right? And me, how did I fit into this bullshit? Okay, so it didn't all fit, but the pieces were staring me in the face.

I slipped past the couple still loitering by the post box, they were busting a gut trying to ignore me. I ghosted past them to my car. My phone connected via Bluetooth and I spotted the missed call. I recognised the number, it wasn't 666 but it wasn't far off.

I jabbed at the number and returned the call. He answered almost immediately.

'Ah, Jihadi Jay,' he bellowed, as though a man in control. 'We need to talk.'

Chapter 29

Jay

15 Jersey Way, Osterley. It's where it all started. This house. This fucking shithole of evil. I was one of many who had walked through the front door, up the narrow stairs, and into the unfurnished bedroom where I'd spent hours sitting on the hard floor alongside young and angry British Muslims with a seed planted in their heads for some fuck to water and flourish. We got close. Like brothers and sisters close. I understood why they felt they had no option but to lash out. I didn't agree, but I didn't know what the fucking answer was either. It took a giant leap of faith for them to trust me, and trust me they did. All the while I was giving them up one by one to MI5.

I pulled up my hood and knocked on the door, a silent unexpected prayer on my lips. It took all my will not to get back in my car and drive far, far away.

The door opened and Omar greeted me with a smile that told me things were going his way. He was wrapped up in scarf, gloves and coat buttoned to the top, with the collar popped. He stepped out.

'Let's go sit in your car. I've no heating in there!'

I didn't protest. I wasn't in any hurry to set foot in that place.

'Turn the engine on,' Omar said, through chattering teeth. I started my car and he turned the heat to max and pointed the vent in his direction. 'You got seat heaters in this thing?'

I pressed a button. 'Where's your ride?'

'Three roads down. I couldn't keep it here. You've seen my car, way too conspicuous!'

I could tell he was bursting to tell me, but I had a feeling he was going to milk this cow.

'Let me tell you about a man called Tommy,' he said.

I recognised the name from the phone call that he'd received when we'd first met. From what I could figure, he was the one who'd broken into Robinson's house and threatened to hurt Sophia.

I shrugged. 'That name supposed to mean something to me?'

'In due time, that name will mean something to everyone.'

'Why's that?' I asked, but in true Omar style, he switched the subject.

'Imagine growing up in a place where everyone is different to you. Their appearance, their language, their thinking.'

'You could be chatting about anyone of colour. We still talking about Tommy?'

'He grew up in Southall, right behind Central Masjid. The only white face in a sea of brown. His old man, the only reflection of him, was a weak man. Lost his job to a Brother, and then lost his wife to a Brother.' Omar smiled, revealing dazzling white teeth at odds with his stale coffee breath. I cracked the window open a touch. 'Abandoned by his mother, little Tommy, all eleven years of him, landed in the care of his useless bum of a father who spent the rest of his short life bathing in booze rather than taking care of business. You feel me?'

I nodded to indicate that I was feeling it, that I was feeling a little sorry for Tommy, but fuck, man, doesn't everyone have a story?

'So tell me, where do you think little Tommy found solace?' Omar asked.

'Within the community?' I replied, knowing it was more than that.

157

'Within the *Muslim* community, Jay!'

As if to serve as an exclamation mark, there was a sharp crack on the passenger side window. It made me jump as I looked past Omar to see a face staring in. I could see a smear mark on the glass, left behind from his knuckles.

'That him?' I asked.

Tommy met my eyes with intensity. I gave it back to him and then some. This was the ginger motherfucker that had threatened Sophia with a knife. I bit my tongue as Omar slid down the window.

'Get in the back, Bruv,' Omar said.

Tommy sat square behind us. I regarded him through the rearview mirror with no more than a nod as Sophia ran through my mind the way she'd run from him. I took his measure. He was nowhere near as good-looking as Sophia had made him out to be.

'This is Jay,' Omar said, proudly, arms out, expansive, as though he was introducing the Queen. Tommy leaned back in his seat and barely nodded, obviously not a fan of royalty. Omar squirmed in his seat; this wasn't the coming together that he had been hoping for.

Tommy dug into his pocket and pulled out a pack of twenty gold and I watched him slip one out and bring it to his lips. I'm a smoker, but seriously, not in my fucking *car*, and I wanted to impart that particular rule to him, but it already felt a little awkward between us, so instead, I said, 'You got a spare?'

'Running low, mate,' he said.

'No problem,' I nodded, even though I'd clocked the tops of plenty when he'd slipped one out for himself. Yeah, he really hadn't taken to me.

'We were just talking about you,' Omar said, a little put out by the frosty reception.

'How far did you get?' Tommy said.

'Just told him about your loser of a father.'

Oh, man, I couldn't believe he went there. Regardless of his father's shortcomings, you don't say shit like that about someone's old man. I watched Tommy through the rear-view mirror, expecting a reaction. He held the cigarette between two fingers in front of his mouth, as the smoke swirled and masked his face.

'Yeah?' he said, as the smoke cleared. His eyes were tight on me through my rear-view mirror. He tapped the cigarette, a beard of ash floated and dissolved onto my leather. I took my eyes off him before he killed me with the death stare.

'How'd you two meet?' I said.

'You know Central Masjid, Southall, right?'

'I know of it,' I said.

'Every day, just before *Zohar* prayers, a small crowd would gather outside the Mosque to listen to Ali Akbar.' Omar paused, expecting a response. Was I, *Jihadi Jay,* supposed to know this Ali Akbar guy? Should I have been on some sort of Jihadi WhatsApp group?

I dropped him a shrug. 'I've not heard of him.'

'He was an educator.'

I stopped myself from snorting through my nose. Educator! Hate preacher would be more accurate. The type who attach themselves like fucking cancer and spit hate in places of peace, and they do it with free speech as their protector.

'What about him?'

'The crowds would grow and circle around Ali Akbar's feet, but Tommy here kept his distance, as though he didn't belong, but he would hear everything. He listened to every truth, as Akbar spoke about every unjustified attack on Muslims around the world. He learnt how we developed our strength and resilience, that we weren't bound by uniform or the rules of war. How ordinary people performed extraordinary acts.'

I lifted my eyes and risked a look at Tommy through the rear-view

159

mirror. Thankfully his eyes were off me, but his face was set tight and his gaze was out of the window. I turned back to Omar, who in stark contrast had a face full of emotion, and was animated with it. He was in his fucking element.

'*We* showed them that what they have in weaponry and technology, we have twice that in heart. We *refused* to kneel down while they took us apart in our own homes. We retaliated in kind and devastated them. Berlin, Brussels, Paris. We fucking *devastated* them!'

From the backseat, Tommy said, 'London.'

'Yeah, Tommy!' Omar laughed cruelly. 'London, too. Especially London.'

We sat quietly for a minute with only the sound of my heaters on full. I stared out through the windscreen as the rain started to come down and hamper my view. I ignored Omar, who was glancing at me as if he wanted me to react, respond, fucking rejoice.

Omar – who else? – broke the silence. 'There's a war taking place right under our noses. We can't hide from it. Tommy here recognised that he had to pick a side.'

'I'm going back inside,' Tommy responded, and skulked out of the car, his presence replaced by the chill.

'Don't worry about him, he's just a little frustrated,' Omar said. 'The rain'll cool him down.'

I watched him through the watery film of my windscreen. Despite it pissing down he walked slowly and let himself into the house.

'Can you trust him?' I asked. If I could cast suspicion or mistrust on a next man then chances are I wouldn't be looked at with suspicion.

Omar considered my question for a moment. 'Who can you trust anymore, Jay? Everyone has an angle,' he said. 'As long as I can see the angle, that's good enough for me.'

'What angle?' I questioned, because once again I didn't know what the fuck he was chatting about.

'I wanted something from Tommy, and he delivered. He wants something from me, which I will deliver soon enough. Then we walk away in separate directions.'

'What's he want?'

Omar turned in his seat and with smiling eyes said, 'Guns, Jay! AK-47 assault rifle and a matching sidearm. Untouched, untraceable and enough ammunition to blast a hole in the history books.'

I fought to stay in his shadow, to stay perfectly still. I'd been here before, with his father. A road trip north.

Coventry.

'That's right!' Omar nodded and I realised that I'd uttered it out loud. 'My father told me how you accompanied him to Coventry to acquire weapons for the Oxford Street attack.'

I closed my eyes.

'Ten sawn-off AK-47s. Ten Glock 19s,' I said in a whisper. 'Yeah, I remember.'

When I opened my eyes he had his hand out, formed into a fist. I summoned up the energy to bump my fist with his and match the glint in his eye.

'What's Tommy got in mind?' I managed to ask. I had to know.

'I don't know, and I don't need to know. Too much knowledge can be dangerous, you feel me? I am merely a facilitator.'

'Alright, okay,' I said buying some time. I wasn't going to learn anything more about Tommy, but I needed to know more about the bigger picture. 'So you're the London connection for Ghurfat-al-Mudarris?'

'Shit, Jay, you really have been off the radar. Ghurfat-al-Mudarris has ceased operations. There's a new wave, which I'm part of. Have you not heard of Al-Muhaymin?'

'Al-Muhaymim,' I repeated slowly, committing it to memory.

'*Min*,' Omar corrected. 'Al-Muhay*min*. Definition: Bestower of

Faith. A splinter cell based on the teachings of Al-Mudarris, but the methodology is very different. Gone are those days of careful planning, years in the making. Al-Muhaymin attacks are at will.'

Omar was right. Things had changed. New York 9/11, London 7/7, articulated attacks, meticulous planning. Now there was an impatience, the surge of a new terrorist. Homemade bombs, acid attacks, using vehicles to mow down innocent bystanders, for fuck's sake. It was happening, and it was being carried out by those on both sides of the war.

'I visited Afghanistan earlier this year,' Omar continued. 'I met with some of the senior members of Al-Muhaymin. They kept me close, but they also kept me on the outside.' Omar turned and looked at his father's house. The way it loomed over us, I swear it had moved a few feet. 'It didn't matter that my father died for The Cause, they wouldn't reveal their secrets.'

'So you're not a part of Al-Muhaymin? You're just another sympathiser.'

'Maybe that was true, but not anymore.'

'What's changed,' I asked.

'I'll show you.'

Omar opened the car door and stepped out, the cold rushed in and rooted me to my seat. I looked past him, at the house of horror. Omar popped his head back through the open door.

'Come on, then. I have a gift for you.' He shut the car door behind him. I debated my next move for all of a second. I flipped open the glove compartment and wrapped my fingers around Imy's handgun.

Chapter 30

Major General Stewart Sinclair sat straight-backed at the head of the long table in Boardroom 3 of the SIS building. He sat alone. The rest of Thames House was abuzz with nervous energy. The breathtaking and calming view of the River Thames was unable to help him find the solace of the answers that he was searching for.

Sinclair was second to John Robinson in grade and nothing else. He was a military man who insisted on keeping his title. In 2016 he had been drafted by MI5 to help locate and capture The Teacher, the man they now knew as Abdul Bin Jabbar. It had been in this very room that Sinclair had insisted upon and initiated the move to enlist Javid Qasim.

Now, in the very same room, the Major was starting to doubt the decision of recruiting the son of the most wanted man in the world, and allowing him access to secrets vital to national security.

The door to Boardroom 3 opened without prior warning, and a head glanced inside as though it had popped itself around many doors before locating him.

'Ah, Lawrence,' Sinclair bellowed, the authoritative boom in his voice not diminished regardless of the developments concerning Qasim's involvement in Robinson's capture.

Teddy Lawrence glanced around the room, as if the conversations held in that room echoed back at him. 'Major, I've been looking everywhere for you,' he said, with only his head present in the office. 'We've established eyes on the location.'

Sinclair nodded, showing no sign of urgency, his head inclined towards the window, eyes on the grey river under the grey, overcast sky. Lawrence waited a beat for a response. He checked the time on his watch before shutting the door behind him, and took a seat adjacent to Sinclair.

'You don't seem yourself, my boy,' Sinclair said.

'It's been an incredible forty-eight hours. First the mess with Imran Siddiqui. And now this with Javid Qasim. So, yes, you could say I'm feeling a little—'

'Restless?'

Lawrence nodded. 'I should update you, Major. This morning we questioned a Ravinder Dhaliwal, a BT Openreach engineer. We made it abundantly clear that the odds were very much against him, and he didn't hold back. It would seem that he was contacted by one Samuel Carter to carry out private work for him. Highly illegal and highly lucrative, to the tune of ten thousand pounds, with ten more to follow on completion. Cash. An offer too good to resist for a family man with a gambling addiction. The job was to disable the fibre line from the exchange which sat at the end of the Clareville Road. Layman's terms, he disabled the broadband for the whole street, rendering the CCTV useless between sixteen hundred and eighteen hundred hours. The same window that John Robinson was taken.'

Sinclair shifted ever so slightly in his chair as rain started to spit at the window.

'We also contacted S&L domestic services, who provided us with the name of the young lady who was on duty at Robinson's home. Sophia Hunt. We still haven't located her yet. However, a search was carried out at her property and we seized ten thousand pounds hidden away neatly within her personal computer. Like Dhaliwal, Hunt is also in financial straits. We're not able to confirm until we have spoken to Hunt, but I'm certain that Samuel Carter is the benefactor.'

Lawrence had said much and wanted to add more, but Sinclair was staring into the distance and Lawrence wasn't sure if he was wasting his time and breath. So he waited, checking his watch again, and eventually Sinclair said, 'Qasim?'

'We have two two-man teams on surveillance at a location in Osterley, West London. And a helicopter circling two miles out. The house belongs to the late Adeel-Al-Bhukara who we know had ties to Ghurfat-al-Mudarris. We've been following Qasim ever since he left his home this morning. First he was sighted at Clareville Road, hovering around Robinson's house. And now we've followed him to the Osterley location.'

The rain picked up, silent in its attack through the thick glass. The River Thames looked angry and judgemental as the waves crashed against the Albert Embankment opposite. Lawrence itched to leave and be back in the Comms room, watching the developments unfold on screen, but he could feel Sinclair had something on his mind. Lawrence waited patiently, finding the will to not check his watch for a third time.

Then in a soft tone that Lawrence was not familiar with, Sinclair spoke.

'We've treated that boy badly.'

'Major?'

'Coercion, Lawrence. Lies! Repeatedly, for our own gain. We sent a young man, ill-prepared, halfway across the world into hostile territory in the full knowledge that what he would discover would have a psychological effect on him. A devastating effect! If that wasn't enough we dangled him like a carrot to an ass without any concern

165

for his welfare. And once we reached our goal, captured his father, we simply washed our hands of him. Now look! Look where he is now. Back at the house where we once sent him to be groomed.'

'With all due respect, Major. I don't think it's what it looks like.'

Sinclair thumped his fist on the table. The water in the glass jug in front of him rippled angrily, like the river outside. Sinclair turned his attention away from the window and met Lawrence's eyes.

'It looks like Qasim has finally decided which side of his toast he likes buttered, is what it bloody looks like. It looks like he's involved in the abduction of John Robinson! Possibly the murder! I would not be bloody surprised!'

'All due respect, Major. We shouldn't ever have used Qasim. Not like that anyway. But… bottom line, we reached our objective.'

'At what cost, son?' Sinclair said. 'The decision Robinson made behind his desk, the decision that I made in this very room, has had a very real and irrevocable effect in the real world! We have pushed and pushed that boy until his only choice was retaliation.'

'Retaliation? Is that what you think, Major?'

'You don't agree, Lawrence?'

'God knows Jay doesn't see the same picture as we do, but I just can't see him involved in the abduction. I can't.'

'But he is involved. You've seen the CCTV footage with Qasim and Sophia Hunt in the phone box. The same girl who we can place at the time and location of the abduction. How have we not found her yet?!'

'ANPR cameras picked up Jay's BMW on the M4, getting off at junction 3 towards Hounslow, after which he took back roads and kept under the radar of any CCTV.'

'Under the radar!' Sinclair snorted. 'That would be his past drug-dealing experience.'

'With all due res—'

'Stop saying that,' Sinclair snapped. 'Respect is implied. Speak freely.'

Lawrence placed his elbows on the table and leaned forward drumming his fingers gently. Sinclair allowed him the time to gather his thoughts.

'I just can't see it,' Lawrence said, evenly.

'Tell me, Lawrence, if not this, then what?'

'You're right. We have treated Jay badly, no question. And if we had to make the decision again… I think it would be the same. Time and again. Let me tell you how I see it, and bear in mind that Qasim and I have history, a semblance of a relationship, albeit not a great one. Despite how we've treated him, and despite his connection to Ghurfat-al-Mudarris, I believe Jay is on our side.'

167

Chapter 31

Jay

It chilled me. Made my heart dip way down into the pit of my stomach, and I knew it wasn't just the cold, it was this house. This hole of fucking evil.

'Upstairs,' Omar said as he climbed up the narrow staircase.

I placed a foot on the bottom step, gripped the banister and willed myself to follow him. Memories, so fucking unwanted, came rushing at me, the way my *Brothers* would skip up these very stairs twice a week in excitement and anticipation for sessions packaged as *Islamic Studies* with Adeel-Al-Bhukara holding court, spilling and spouting and indoctrinating impressionable young minds into believing they had no choice but to *stand*, to *fight* for a bullshit cause.

Here I was, back again, following Omar, the rotten apple who'd landed pretty fucking close to the tree. Each step I took was an effort, the stairs steep and neverending, the chintzy faded wallpaper closing in on me and making me gag. Halfway up and I wanted to drop to my knees and throw the fuck up. I managed to reach the top and tried to even my breathing, but I'd always been shit at that, so instead I just exhaled loudly, a cloud of warm air coming from my mouth. There was a pull-down metal ladder leading up to the loft. I held onto it, in case my legs gave way.

'Brings back some fond memories, huh?' Omar said.

I averted my eyes and they betrayed me by landing on the closed door which led to the unfurnished bedroom that I wished I'd never set foot in.

'It's where it all happened.' Omar smiled a sad little smile. I nodded and tried to mirror it. 'How many walked into that room determined? How many marched out of there like soldiers?'

I forced myself to meet his eyes.

'You, Jay, you were one of them. You were the most important.'

'That's not true,' I said, but the words barely left me.

'Do you want to…?' Omar gestured towards the room. 'Trip down memory lane?'

'No!' I said sharply, stupidly. 'Maybe later.'

'Right!' Omar clapped his hands loudly, breaking me out of my trance. He craned his skinny neck and looked up towards the open hatch. 'Hang back a minute, let me see if your gift is ready.' He climbed up the metal ladder and disappeared through the hatch.

I heard a hushed exchange, and realised that Tommy was already up there.

'I don't trust him,' I heard him say.

'Keep quiet. He's down there,' Omar said, in a whispered berating, his voice bouncing off the confines of the loft and making its way down through the hatch.

'Why'd you have to tell him all that shit about me?' Tommy hissed. 'You see how he was looking at me in the car.'

Fuck! He'd noticed. Obviously he'd noticed. I was so vexed at what he did to Sophia that my contempt must have been painted on my face.

'I need you to chill the fuck out. In fact, wait for me downstairs.'

'I'm staying put.'

'You had one job, which you have done and which you will be rewarded for. The rest of it is none of your damn business. Go wait for me downstairs.'

I took a step back as mud-encrusted black boots set foot on the ladder. Tommy climbed down and without acknowledging me he stomped his way downstairs.

Omar popped his head through the hatch. He rolled his eyes. 'Can't get the staff nowadays. Come up.'

I scaled the ladder and climbed inside. It was like ice up there, colder than the rest of the cold house, colder than I'd ever been. I zipped my parka jacket all the way up and lifted my hood tight over my head.

A dim light came from a bare bulb at the end of the loft, illuminating a figure. Through the tunnel vision of my hood I could make out the shape of an overweight man slumped on a chair. I'd never met him before, but I had no doubt that I was staring at John Robinson. I kept my emotions in check.

'My gift to you,' Omar said, gesturing like a magician. 'The Assistant Director of Counter Terrorism.'

I nodded my head within my hood, glad that he couldn't make out my reaction.

'We don't have much insulation up in here, it's the coldest part of the house,' Omar said, and I didn't have to look at him to know he was smiling. 'Let's go say hello.'

I took the smallest step, followed by another, and it felt like a journey. This was the man I held solely responsible for fucking up my life. For dangling me like a juicy fucking carrot to entice Bin Jabbar out of hiding, without regard for my safety. The same motherfucker who, despite what I had done for him, had always doubted where my loyalty lay.

I stood in front of him.

Robinson was tied topless to a chair, the rope eating easily into his flesh. His naked torso trembling from the cold. I looked down at the top of his slumped, balding head. The broken shell of a once

170

powerful man, who had made decisions from the safety and comfort of his desk, decisions that had seen innocent Muslims suffer. He was asleep or unconscious or near death, and I could hear a humming vibration through his closed mouth, an effort to stay warm. Blue veins mapped his body which had turned a patchy grey, and I counted seven holes drilled into his shoulders, arms and waist, encrusted in dried blood. I stopped counting and snatched my eyes away from his tortured, holey body and lowered my eyes to his wet-stained lap and the smell of stale piss hit me.

Sympathy did not come easy. My hands slipped into the bucket pockets of my jacket and my fingers brushed the grip of the Glock. Above me rain clattered onto the roof.

Omar took position behind Robinson and placed his hands on his shoulders. 'Honestly,' he said, 'it took longer than I expected. This fat fuck was a resilient one, let me tell you. But young Tommy had a bag full of toys that soon had him squealing and revealing.'

My brain was on the move and shooting, weighing up the one option I didn't want to reach for. Omar was grinning at me, Tommy was knocking about somewhere in the house and after seeing his handiwork on Robinson, I wasn't confident about facing him. I wrapped my fingers tightly around the Glock feeling the grip leaving an imprint on my palm.

'He told us everything, Jay!' Omar exclaimed. 'Everything.'

He was fucking swimming in anticipation. His face lit up, the words running from his lips as though he had dreamt endlessly about this moment.

'When my father told me who you were, Jay, I had to find you. I had to share this moment with you.'

I couldn't get a word out, a fucking question. The power of speech, of thought, sailed and I could do nothing but blink blankly at him.

'A message has reached Al-Muhaymin. Everything is in place. It's happening, Jay.'

I didn't want to know anymore. I didn't want to be there anymore. I had a Christmas tree at home waiting to be decorated. I had cigarettes waiting to be smoked. A bed to be slept in.

'We're going to set him free.'

My heart stopped. And then it started with a thump. Slamming against my ribcage. Threatening to rip a hole through my chest. I silently begged for him not to say it.

Please, not another fucking word.

But he did. He fucking said it.

'Abdullah Bin Jabbar, our great leader. He's alive, Jay... Your father is alive.'

PART 2

You're not supposed to be so blind with patriotism
that you can't face reality. Wrong is wrong, no
matter who does it or says it.

– Malcolm X

Chapter 32

Jay

Eight months ago, I reacted to Abdul Bin Jabbar's death in a way I didn't think I would. With emotion that I didn't think I could feel. I mean, who the fuck was he to me? He was my father in name and name alone. But some basic instinct within me took control and I let go of the fact that he had walked out of my life before I was born. I let go of the fucking fact that he was responsible for the loss of so many innocent lives. All I could see was that my dad had been taken away from me.

I remember knocking back shot after shot after fucking shot, slouched in my armchair, remote control in one hand flitting between every news channel, phone in my other hand furiously scrolling through Twitter. The demise of The Teacher was celebrated under the guise of journalism. On social media #VictoryfortheWest was going viral. One less monster in the world.

They ought to take a look a little fucking closer to home!

I felt anger, resentment, and really fucking drunk. I did not take it well. I needed answers.

Worse than worse for wear, and not knowing how I'd got there, I found myself standing outside the arched entrance of Thames House, MI5 headquarters. I beat down on their doors until my fists hurt. *'Let me in! I want some fucking answers!'* And those fuckers, those leeches that took and took and sucked the life out of me, were now ignoring me. With alcohol dictating my actions I demanded to speak to those who had made me. '*I wanna speak to Teddy Lawrence. I wanna speak with John fucking Robinson.*' When that had fallen on deaf ears, I screamed, '*I used to work here!*' I screamed, '*I risked my fucking life for you!*' I screamed until I was spluttering. I screamed until two security guards tried to grab me by the arms and I made myself into a little ball on the floor, like a toddler throwing a tantrum in the toys aisle in Asda. It wasn't my finest moment.

I was bundled into an SUV, blacked-out windows. The back of two heads in the front. Me at the rear, head in hand and a sore fucking throat. Somebody slapped a bottle of water in my hand which I sipped on greedily. An hour later, the car door opened and I stepped out.

Remembering my manners, I mumbled my thanks through the closed driver's side window and watched them pull away without a word.

I'd stepped into my house, knowing that was it. That was the extent of my mourning. I would not shed another fucking tear for him. He deserved it all. I spent the next eight months trying to forget him and piece my life back together.

But once again the world had lied to me. My father was alive.

*

'*Face him, Jay. Face the man responsible for your hurt.*'

Omar bunched whatever little hair Robinson had in his fist and wrenched his head up.

I felt light, as though my feet were hovering above the ground. I couldn't pick out a fucking thought. Each time I reached for one I was faced with just black. My brain wouldn't process, it simply just crashed and was replaced by a continuous loud ringing in my ears.

Robinson let out a low groan, his eyelids flickered before opening into slits, and through the slits he clocked me. 'Qasim,' he said, weakly. Then his eyes flew wide open in fury and his body thrashed from side to side, the legs on the chair rocking in rhythm.

'I knew it!' Robinson screamed into my face, his bloody spittle reaching impressive heights. *'Traitor!'*

Inhale.

Exhale. Exhale. Exhale. *Fucking exhale!*

The ringing in my ears stopped abruptly. My brain fired up and flipped to a new page that only I could write. My left hand emerged out of my bucket pocket with the Glock in my grip and I pointed it square in John fucking Robinson's fucking face.

He stopped thrashing. All his energy zapped out of him. He looked up at me, his teeth chattering noisily.

'Mashallah,' Omar bellowed from above him. 'My Brother came prepared.'

I smoothly flicked the safety off and retracted the slide, muscle memory from a time that would never leave me. I transferred the gun to my favoured right hand.

'Is it true?' a voice which didn't sound like mine asked.

Unable to hold my gaze, Robinson lowered his eyes, and then squeezed them shut. I pressed the barrel of the gun to his forehead. My finger resting firmly on the trigger.

'Look at me.'

His eyes opened wet. He looked at me. A measly *'please'* escaped from his lips.

'Answer me. Is it true?'

Robinson gently nodded his head and then let it drop to his chest.

Omar checked his watch. 'My work is done here, Brother. I have to leave for Coventry. Inshallah, our paths will cross again, but find

177

peace in knowing that your father will be liberated. A day is coming where you will once again stand by his side.'

'Shut up,' I muttered quietly to myself, practising the words, finding my voice as I desperately tried to compartmentalise all the shit that was tangled in my head.

'*Shut the fuck up!*' I screamed, swinging the gun away from Robinson and pointing it at Omar's face! I held it firm, I didn't allow my hand to shake.

His eyes stopped dancing and popped. His mouth made a small pout. His phone rang muted from his pocket.

'Is that your burner?' I asked.

'Jay.' He swallowed. 'Why're you pointing that thing at me?'

'Is that your fucking burner?'

He nodded, dazzled at the turn.

'Take it out of your pocket.'

Omar slipped it carefully out of his jacket and glanced at the screen.

'Tommy?' I asked.

Another nod.

'Answer it. Put it on speaker. Tell him all good.'

Omar shook his head in genuine disappointment as he accepted the call. He placed it on loud speaker. Tommy spoke first.

'We've got a problem!'

'Yeah,' Omar said, meeting my eyes. I took a step and moved the gun closer to his face. 'What's happened?'

'I've seen a black Q7 drive down the road, turn and then double back.'

Robinson lifted his head weakly and mumbled, 'It's over.' And then proceeded to burst into tears.

'Pack up.' Omar spoke into the phone, his eyes fixed on me. 'We have to go.'

He killed the call and placed the phone back in his pocket.

'I don't think I've ever been so disappointed in my whole life, Jay.'

'You'll get over it. Untie him.'

'Your father—'

'Say that word fucking word again!' I hissed, my finger tightening across the trigger. Any more pressure and I'd know what it felt like to kill a man. Omar knew better than to hold my gaze. His knees clicked as he crouched low and started to work on the rope tied around Robinson.

I relaxed my finger on the trigger and allowed myself to breathe a little, calm a little, get some time to myself and think a little. I had to hold on and stay focused. Help was close. There was no way I could do this on my own. The threat of the gun would only get me so far. I don't think I had it in me to pull the trigger, come what may.

'He needs to keep still,' Omar said, as Robinson's semi-naked body racked and shook with loud sobs. His relief was so fucking great that he was verging on hysteria. Loud, unnatural sounds were coming from him. I thought MI5 were supposed to be trained for this shit.

'Hold still,' I said. 'Take a breath and hold tight. Your boys are close.'

Robinson nodded and swallowed a whimper. With effort he looked up at me, his face a mixture of tears and snot and blood. Even though I was saving his sorry ass, I really couldn't stand to look at his face. I had a lot of questions and this motherfucker had a lot to answer for.

'Hurry up,' I hissed as Omar went to work untying him

Robinson's eyes widened and his mouth opened and just as my name escaped from his lips, I felt the most amazing pain in the back of my head. Stunned, I dropped heavily to one knee and with my head heavy as fuck, I turned over my shoulder to see Tommy towering over me, gripping a power drill by its nose. I spun on my

179

knee and swung the gun towards him, but the fucking power drill was again descending on me in a blur. It struck across my forehead and sent me sprawling onto my back. The gun slipped out of my hand and clattered to the ground.

I forced my eyes open and saw three Tommys pointing three guns at me. I blinked weakly and they merged into one.

'*Stupid!*' Omar screamed from somewhere, and then, helpfully, made his presence known by delivering a kick to my side. He bent down with his face over me like a pre-op surgeon inspecting a patient. He softly said, 'When did you turn, Jay?'

Turn, turn, when did I turn? I don't think I ever did. It's complicated. I didn't say any of that, I didn't even have the energy for a shrug and he definitely didn't have the time, what with MI5 prancing around outside. I watched him rise and stand next to his gun-toting-Muslim-convert-comrade.

Tommy tilted his head from behind the gun as if he wanted me to have a clear picture of his face before putting a hole through mine. He sneered, a barely controlled urge in his eyes as though he wanted to pull the trigger and just keep pulling.

'No.' Omar pulled rank. 'We have to get out of here, now!'

Disappointment painted Tommy's face. 'I'm holding onto the piece,' he said, tucking it into his jeans.

Their footsteps moved away and they dropped down the hatch, leaving me at Robinson's feet. He was looking down at me from what seemed like a great height. With glazed eyes and a glazed look on his face, he muttered weakly, 'I held on for as long as I could but...' He squeezed his eyes shut for a moment as though he was re-running the torture he had to endure in his head. 'They'll get to him before we will.'

I blinked at him twice in the hope that it communicated *fuck off* and took my eyes away and past him and followed the thick splintered wooden beams holding up the roof. On the other side, the rain had slowed. A gentle, steady, soothing patter, the way Mum used to pat me on my chest to sleep as a child. I closed my eyes knowing once I did they wouldn't open for a while. My final thought before sleep found me was, fuck Robinson, fuck MI5 and fuck you.

Nobody, and I swear *nobody*, is going to stop me from seeing my dad again.

Chapter 33

The Teacher

Eight months ago as Ghurfat-al-Mudarris crumbled, Abdul Bin Jabbar, very much a hunted man, found solace in a safe house close to the Afghanistan border. News had reached him that a fatwa had been placed on his son's head. Only Bin Jabbar had the power to lift it. To do so he had to come out of hiding and face his enemies.

Latif, his closest friend and confidant, had strongly advised him against it. The risk was too great. Capture was inevitable, but capture wasn't on his mind. Bin Jabbar would not succumb to the hands of the enemy. He would walk into certain death in the blink of an eye to save his son.

What Abdul Bin Jabbar didn't foresee was that his actions were to leave him hanging somewhere between Life and Death.

Despite reports of his assassination that had travelled across the airwaves around the world, and despite the news that was celebrated by the West, Bin Jabbar's followers did not dare stop, they did not dare rest. They would not dare believe the stories of his demise until they saw with their own eyes the dead body of their leader. It wouldn't be the first time that the world was fooled into believing that a revered Muslim leader had been killed. It was an unrelenting belief amongst his true followers that Al-Mudarris would stand once again and lead his people in the war against terror.

It wasn't what Bin Jabbar wanted anymore. But he knew that they would come for him.

*

Abdul Bin Jabbar watched the brass ceiling fan above his bed. He was hot, stiflingly so, but there was little chance of his captors turning the fan on. From his peripheral vision he could see, through the single-pane window, the white of the moon trying to get his attention. His dry mouth flopped open and a small breath managed to escape as his chest rose slowly and fell quickly. His pupils slowly glided to the far left. It took effort, and the strain made his eyes water, but Bin Jabbar had to know if the moon was full. He had to know if the stars filled the night sky.

It hadn't always been this way. At the beginning of his imprisonment, a man, stoic in expression, and a woman with a kind face, had watched him with care. To the world, the man was a farmer, and she a farmer's wife.

Each day, when the sun was at its strongest, the man would lift Bin Jabbar from his bed and bend and contort his body into a wooden chair placed in front of the window. With his bare feet pointed inwards and his limp arms resting on his thighs, Bin Jabbar would allow the sun to run over his burnt, seared body as he looked out of the small window and watched the baby lambs play on the green rolling hills just beyond the compound.

The woman had said her name was Fatima and he believed her. When the temperature dropped she would place a blanket around his shoulders; when it rose, she would turn on the fan to cool him. The man's name was Malik, and he would sometimes read aloud to Bin Jabbar, biographies mainly, other times sports headlines. But never current affairs.

Bin Jabbar had an affection for the couple. They didn't judge him, they were simply carrying out their duty. For a while, Malik and Fatima were the only two people in Bin Jabbar's life, aside from the neurologist who visited once weekly to examine him, to report no change, and then leave swiftly in his grocery truck.

Bin Jabbar counted the days and the nights through the window. After sixty days Fatima and Malik were transferred. A change of personnel. Two out, two in. One male, one female. A young Pakistani couple. Same as before, but not as human.

Communication was minimal and what there was, was aggressive. Bin Jabbar would be left in bed for days at a time without thought for meals or replacing the over-filled catheter. On occasion they would wake him in the early hours of the morning, a ghetto blaster held over him, an explosion of loud heavy metal music in his face. They'd lift his kurta and expose his stomach and point at the wounds caused by the bullets that had cut through him. They'd pose by him with wide, mocking smiles and take selfies. Keepsakes. To be shared with the small circle of those who knew that Abdul Bin Jabbar was still alive.

Alive.

The moon was full. The stars were indeed out. It was rare for the night to be so beautifully lit up. Bin Jabbar felt the strain in his eyes but he did not look away from the window. The pain was a welcome feeling when the rest of his broken body had long lost all sensation. Tightly, he blinked away the tears but they escaped in opposite directions and pooled by his ears.

Under the starry night, Bin Jabbar could see the clear outline of the rolling hills. They loomed larger, closer. A shadowy figure scurried down the hill towards the compound, followed by another. And another. The baby lambs had long scattered and were replaced by wolves.

The door to his room flung open and the light from the hall fell across his bed. Bin Jabbar kept his eyes on the window. The figures had disappeared out of sight. His pupils took the long journey to the far-right corner. He blinked slowly at the woman at his door. The light behind her cast her in silhouette as she stood with her arms stretched out above her head, her hands resting either side of the doorframe. She wore a T-shirt and nothing else.

'The world's most dangerous man,' she said, her skin brown, her accent middle England. She entered the room exaggerating her walk, her arms swinging playfully by her side, and walked past the foot of the bed and out of sight. Bin Jabbar's eyes took time to follow and catch up with her. She stood in front of the window, the glare of the moon seeping through the cotton of her T-shirt.

'Mmm, there's something about a full moon that makes me feel alive.' She smiled. 'Can't keep your eyes off me, can you?'

She took her time cutting the distance between them with one foot deliberately in front of the other. She leaned over him, the whites in her eyes veined red and her breath intoxicated.

'Darling,' she said, as she trailed a sharp fingernail slowly down the open collar of his kurta, 'you don't look very dangerous to me.'

'Zara,' a man's voice called, a voice that Bin Jabbar was familiar with even with the drunken slur. 'Didn't I leave you waiting in bed for me?'

Bin Jabbar was tired. Too tired to move his eyes across to the other side of the room, but he could sense the man enter his space. He walked around the bed and stood close behind Zara, a small towel around his waist.

'I got fed up waiting for you to shower, so I came hunting for a real man.'

'And, did you find one?'

She looked down at Bin Jabbar and gently rubbed a thumb along the trail where a tear ran from his eye to his ear. 'No,' she said.

Humiliation filled Bin Jabbar. Their laughter echoed long after they had left the room, only melting away into animalistic grunts and the rhythmic squeaking of their bed against the wall that separated their rooms.

Bin Jabbar's focus remained steadfast on the window. The face in the moon was smiling at him. It lent him strength. From the very far corner of his eye he felt as though he could see every thick blade of grass on the inviting hill. He could almost feel it to touch under his fingertips, almost feel it gently caress his neck as he lay under the stars. Bin Jabbar let the sensation embrace him as heavy boots against concrete steps rushed up the stairs.

The headboard that had been banging against his wall stopped. The grunting that had invaded his ears stopped. And for a glorious moment, silence filled the room.

And then started the desperate cries of begging.

Bin Jabbar kept his eyes at the window, for what he knew to be the last time. The moon looked smaller now, as though it was drifting away, until it was untouchable.

Abdul Bin Jabbar closed his eyes as two gunshots tore his captors apart.

The only thought that came into his head was seeing his son again.

Chapter 34

Imy

I'd had a drink. A few. Then I was sober. I searched through the kitchen cabinets, slamming the door shut harder each time as the bare shelves told me I'd had enough. I stretched my neck all the way back, wanting it to click and relieve the pressure on my shoulders, and stared at the kitchen ceiling. Beyond it was the bathroom and the bathroom cabinet. Within it the vials of tablets. I pictured taking one pill after another after another. The pressure in my shoulders gently eased, and the base of my neck released a series of small cracks as the doorbell rang.

I stretched my neck to the side, my ear brushing one shoulder and then the other. I checked the time on my watch as the bell rang a second time. I licked my lips and stretched my mouth as I walked to the front door and opened it without checking through the peep hole.

'Imran,' he said, and then hesitated, as if he hadn't worked out whatever needed working out.

'It's two in the morning, Lawrence. What do you want?'

'Are you going to invite me in or do you want to do this on the doorstep?'

'Do what, exactly?'

'I have work for you,' he said.

'I'm not interested.' I stood firm.

'I'm afraid that decision is out of your hands. Besides… I think you're going to want to hear this.'

Lawrence made himself small and squeezed past. I turned to face him in the hallway. Under the light, I noticed his suit was crumpled, and his navy tie was rolled into his jacket pocket.

'Shoes off,' I said, walking into the living room.

I sat down in my armchair. In front of me on the coffee table was an empty glass and an empty bottle of whisky. I couldn't care less how it looked. Lawrence stepped in, looking a little insecure with his socks on show. He eyed the sofa, *our sofa*, which I still couldn't bring myself to sit on. Though it frustrated me greatly, I'd allowed Jay to sit there earlier, but there was no way I was letting Lawrence.

'Over there,' I said, pointing out a dining chair.

Lawrence moved across the room and slipped out a chair and turned it to face me. He sat down and ran a hand tightly through his hair. I suspected it wasn't the first time that night. The wax used to style it had long disappeared with the day, leaving his hair greasy. He leaned forward on his elbows.

Though I had all the time in the world, I didn't have much time for him.

'I saw you earlier,' I said breaking the silence. 'What's changed?'

We'd never met at my home before. I recalled how the details were revealed to me for my first and only mission in Berlin. A meeting in a secure location. Names and photographs in a concealed envelope. A target. An assassination. Clean. Cold. It wasn't personal.

This felt personal.

This felt like something that Lawrence did not want to reveal to me but it was only me that it could be revealed to. I'd asked him what had changed.

'Everything,' Lawrence said. 'Everything has changed.'

188

Chapter 35

Jay

I woke up in a familiar setting, but I had never seen it from this position before. I was stretched out on the back seat of my Beemer. I lifted myself onto my elbows and peered through the window. I was still parked across the road from 15 Jersey Way, Osterley. The street was quiet, sleepy, no signs of blue and red lighting up the night sky, no signs of uniform. It was a carbon copy of my earlier visit to Clareville Road. A scene set as though nothing untoward had happened. *A conspiracy of silence.*

Even though it would have been nice to start from scratch, I wasn't fucking born yesterday. This was MI5. This was them tidying up. A concealed rescue mission without the heavy-handed interference from the police. They were looking after their own, which I wasn't.

I straightened up, my head heavy and dull, and let it drop back against the headrest. A man was sitting where I should have been.

'You better not have adjusted my seat!' I said it as if that was the biggest problem in my life right now. When he didn't answer, I asked, 'Who're you?'

He turned his head a quarter over his shoulder. 'How are you feeling?'

'Do you always answer a question with a question?' I said.

'Do you?' he replied. *Bastard had me.*

I caught a glimpse of myself in the rear-view mirror. A bandage had been tied tightly around my head. I reached for it. 'Don't do that,' he said. I moved my hand away and shrugged. He caught it in the rear-view mirror. 'You were in need of a little medical attention.'

'Yeah,' I said, recalling Tommy striking down on me with a fucking power drill. Twice. 'What time is it?'

'Two fifty-four a.m.'

Sophia decided to pop into my head. I checked my phone, missed calls galore from her number. God knows what thoughts were running through her mind.

'Do you think you can manage to drive?' the man asked.

'Tell me what happened,' I asked. 'Did you get—'

'Do you think you can manage to drive?' he repeated.

He wasn't going to tell me shit. Judging by his blank eyes, I didn't think he knew shit. I knew more. He was just some poor sap who'd been handed babysitting duties.

'Yeah,' I said, 'I'm alright to drive.' Then feeling a little more like myself I added, 'Get the fuck out my seat.'

He didn't react as though he'd been briefed about my gob. 'You are to go straight home,' he said. 'Somebody will be in touch tomorrow.'

'Yeah, well. I've got plans tomorrow,' I said. I had no plans. I just wanted to get in the last word.

Our doors opened in tandem and we both left seats that we shouldn't have been in. He held open the door for me and my manners betrayed me as I mumbled a thanks, and without another word, he walked away like a poorly paid extra from a bad movie.

I dropped myself into the driver's seat, adjusted it to my smaller frame, and started my car. I threw one last glance towards number 15 Jersey Way. It looked back at me like butter wouldn't melt. The lights were off and it looked like every other house on the street. But I fucking knew, I knew how many lies had been told and how many lives had been destroyed behind that door.

190

I swear if my numbers ever come up, the first thing I'm buying is that house. The second thing I'm buying is a fucking bulldozer.

*

I stepped through my front door late. Coming-back-from-a-nightclub late. *Simpler times.* Amongst all the crap clattering around my head I wondered if Sophia would still be there, if she had run.

I removed my Jordans without unlacing – that took twice as long – and I left them how they fell. I considered a smoke and a drink but I couldn't be arsed with the effort. Right now I needed my bed, to sleep and wish away the nightmares. Tomorrow, I'd deal with tomorrow.

I held onto the banister, placed my foot on the bottom step and readied myself for the climb. Through the open door of the living room I saw Sophia. She was curled up on my armchair, her eyes closed, her lips parted. Christmas lights reflected and blinked softly in her face.

She hadn't run.

I unpeeled my fingers off the banister and stood at the door, looking into my living room like an intruder. The Christmas tree that I bought from Argos a lifetime ago had been unboxed. It stood proudly in the corner of the room, red and white lights neatly wrapped around it. A silver star glittering on top.

I nodded to myself to stop myself from tearing up.

Sophia was still wearing my onesie, the sleeves stretched over her knuckles and gripped tightly into her fists. I liked noticing little things like that. I liked noticing little things like that about her. I stepped into the living room. The television was on low, set to The Comedy Channel. I wondered what her laugh sounded like. I picked up the remote and killed the TV. She stirred as did something inside me.

191

It tends to get a little chilly downstairs at night; I couldn't exactly leave her like that. A vision of Robinson freezing his fat ass off in the loft skipped through my head and I quickly swiped away that shitty thought before other shitty thoughts joined it. And I allowed myself, just for a minute, to let my mind drift away a little.

I imagined a present under the tree. Two presents. I imagined pulling Christmas crackers with Sophia and telling terrible jokes over a dried-out turkey. I imagined lifting her in my arms and carrying her upstairs and gently placing her on the bed, then I imagined the impracticality of it. I imagined introducing Sophia to Mum.

I was one step away from scrawling our names inside an exercise book and outlining it with little pink hearts. Fuck! I knew it could never be. Everything about that girl screamed trouble, and I had my own troubles to work through.

I fetched a blanket from the airing cupboard and placed it over her shoulders and lap. I considered moving a stray hair away from her face but decided that may be a line I didn't want to cross.

I left her breathing softly and walked away.

*

I couldn't sleep, obviously. I lay on my side counting sixty seconds in my head and trying to time the exact moment the numbers on my clock would tumble as I tried to both forget and recall the shit-show that had just taken place. *One Mississippi. Two Mississippi. Three Mississippi.*

After Tommy and Omar had left me bleeding and Robinson crying, I'd remained stock still and flat out on my back, staring up at his double chin as he rained tears over me. I think I must have popped in and out of consciousness because I could only remember snatches.

A glimpse of black, shiny and impractical shoes hurrying past me as if I was wearing Harry Potter's fucking invisibility cloak. Voices muffled because blood had gathered in my fucking ears. *'We've secured the hostage'* into their radio or up their sleeve or who the fuck knows. Grunts of exertion as they carried Robinson away. Black, shiny and impractical shoes along with Robinson's dirty bare feet going past me the other way. They lowered him down the hatch. It took them a while and a snooze before they came back for me. Their priorities apparent. I wasn't one of them.

What a shit fucking night.

Omar and Tommy would have been hauled down to separate locations with MI5 dogs let loose on them. Would they confess? I don't think it mattered. Omar had achieved what he'd set out to do. And I think... I think I was the only person in this world who could do something about it.

I reached for my phone and slipped out my bank card from my wallet and made a purchase to the tune of £470. I should have given it some consideration, thought it out a little, but I think the outcome would've been the same. Whether it was the right decision or not, well, I'd find out soon enough.

*

Fifty-seven Mississippi. Fifty-eight Mississippi. Fifty-nine Mississippi. Sixty-Mississippi. The digits on my clock tumbled to 4.28 a.m. Outside, dawn had broken. The sky was grey but birds still sang and still, sleep wouldn't come. But it felt like I was dreaming.

A dream where Sophia was standing at my bedroom door watching me. Her lips moving but my mind was too noisy to hear her.

I think she said my name.

I think she stepped into my room and knelt down on the floor by my bed and gently touched the bandage around my head. I think she asked me what happened.

I didn't know where to start. I didn't know where to finish.

I think I told her my dad was still alive.

She climbed into my bed and held me tightly, and she didn't let go.

I think I may have cried.

Chapter 36

Imy

After Teddy Lawrence had left I found sleep easily. A peaceful sleep. One that I didn't believe I would again find. I woke up fresh, invigorated, and the first thing I did was reach across for my phone with anticipation and checked for messages.

I dropped to the floor and pushed out thirty press-ups. It had been a while since I'd exerted myself and it took time for my body to adjust to form. I took shallow breaths before the next set and checked my phone again. The second set of thirty was quicker, lower, nose brushing the carpet, the adrenaline coursing through me doing most of the work. I gave myself a one-minute break, my eyes flitting towards my phone and away again, before I dropped into a final set. I purposely went slower, holding my position low, feeling the burn in my chest. I hit thirty and kept going, losing count along the way and only stopping once my arms and legs started to tremble.

I leaned against the side of the bed and took deep breaths. I hadn't trained to any level for a long time and though it was only press-ups it had exhausted me. I got to my feet and shook my arms and legs loose with one eye on the phone.

Still no word.

My body felt relaxed as I took a hot shower, my mind focused on nothing but the mission that Lawrence had put forward. It was one that, even if I had the choice, I could never have turned down. It would be my last. If MI5 had a problem with that, then they could come and say it to my face. I knew too much for them to be pulling my strings any longer. I had plans. Stephanie, Jack, my Khala, if there was a true heaven, a *jannat*, which I still believed in, then that's where my family would be. For me to join them, I would have to repent. To live my life clean. But first, I had to walk the sinful path in front of me.

I switched on the television in the bedroom and tuned in to Sky News and then flipped between CNN, Fox and BBC News. News that I was now aware of hadn't made it to the mainstream. If I carried out my task as I was expected to, it never would.

The news ran in the background as I browsed through my wardrobe. I'd always kept my clothes plain and simple, much to Stephanie's annoyance and Jack's amusement. The only items with a splash of colour or design, they'd bought for me, and I had worn for them. I left them behind as I packed a travel bag with light trousers and plain shirts. Clothes which I wouldn't be noticed in.

I knelt down, my legs felt heavy from the press-ups and it reminded me again how unfit family life had made me. At the bottom of the wardrobe was a small safe. I keyed in the pin number and pulled the door open. Three British passports sat neatly stacked on one side. I picked up the top one, flicked to the back and took my time taking in Stephanie's photo. Her hair was cut and curled at the bottom.

This passport has to last me ten years, I don't want to look like I've just woken up.

When you wake up is when you look best, Steph.

That's sweet, Imy, but I'm not buying it! I'm getting my hair done.

I picked up my passport, the photo portrayed a family man with hope in his eyes trying not to laugh as Jack did his level best to distract me outside the photo booth.

Remember, you're not allowed to smile, Dad. The airport police won't let you go on holiday if you're smiling.

I placed the passport on top of my clothes in my travel bag.

My fingers trembled as I picked up the third passport. I flicked to the back. His beautiful face, his beautiful blue eyes, his lips pursed, a picture of perfection in school uniform. A picture that had to be taken twelve times until it met guidelines. I clapped it shut before it made me weak.

Inside the safe there was an empty space reserved for my handgun, which I no longer had in my possession. I'd been reckless. After I was taken to the police station, Jay had taken it upon himself to go prying around my home. I know it was him who'd pocketed my Glock. *Why did he do that? What was his problem? What more did he want to take from me?* Qasim. Javid Qasim. *Jay*. I still could not believe he had the arrogance to brazenly walk into my home and back into my life with such an air of self-importance, as though his simple presence could ever be any comfort to me.

His name, his face would forever be intrinsically connected to everything that I had lost.

I closed the wardrobe doors and zipped up my travel bag and sat on the edge of the bed with nothing to do but wait. Jay had preoccupied my mind and I realised that I hadn't checked my phone for a while.

There were two messages. One an email. The other a text.

The email had arrived first, so I read it first. No subject, no message, only an attachment. An e-ticket under my name. PIA flight departing from Heathrow Airport tomorrow at 6.30 a.m. and landing at 2.10 p.m. local time at Islamabad International Airport.

The text was from a withheld number but I knew the sender was the same. The only information that was given was an address that I was painfully familiar with.

197

Chapter 37

Jay

I think it's pretty fucking fair to say that my relationship with my dad is pretty fucking complicated. For starters, there is no relationship but in name and blood. I've only ever met him once, and even then we didn't address what we were to each other. I hated him. But even in hate, there's passion. When I was told he had been killed, my reaction was immediate and angry and misdirected. It dissipated quickly as I convinced myself that I was mourning a monster.

Now fucking this. He's alive and it's fucking thrown me. Don't get it twisted, I know what he is and I know what he's done. *I fucking know!* To the world he's The Teacher. Al-fucking-Mudarris. The leader of a terrorist cell. In a world where you're either good or bad, he was the root of all evil. It's simply as black and white as that.

To me it's grey. To me, he's my dad, and all I want is to bring him back home and face justice the right way.

In bed next to me, Sophia stirred.

After I had told her that my dad was alive, we didn't address it. Maybe something in my voice told her that I didn't have it in me.

Sophia was nobody to me, but the fool in me felt as though she could be everything. We were simply two strangers who had been brought together by circumstance. There was a desperation about her that reflected my own. I naturally felt a pull towards her as though whatever crap life threw at us, somehow, we'd always find each other, understand each other.

But, as I said, that was the fool in me.

I slipped the dressing off from my head, and, careful not to disturb her arm draped over me, I shifted and twisted my body and faced her. It was a single bed, so her nose wasn't far from mine. I could see really small, really faint freckles on the bridge of her nose. I hadn't noticed it before, and now that I did, I wasn't likely to forget. Her eyes flickered. Said nose twitched. Her eyes moved behind her eyelids as though running the events of the night through her mind before having to face it. She blinked her eyes open.

'Morning,' I said, my voice morning hoarse. She moved the arm that had been over me and I felt its absence immediately.

'Sorry,' she said as though she'd crossed a line. I shrugged and smiled and wondered if it would ever be around me again. She tucked it out of sight and into the duvet. Things had changed, obviously, but not in the way they do after two strangers have to face each other in the morning after an awkward fumble. It felt softer somehow, like how I imagine a holiday romance to be; only without the exotic location, and the absence of any actual romance.

Though, I did rescue her. That was pretty fucking romantic!

'I've been thinking,' she said, glancing at the cut on my forehead.

'What've you been thinking?'

She smiled into my eyes and I drifted into hers. The moment didn't last long.

'I'm going to tell the police everything.'

I nodded gently. Sophia returned it with a shrug, a delicate movement of her shoulders under the duvet. She was part of a huge conspiracy to kidnapping and torturing a high-level MI5 officer. It wasn't something she could run from.

199

'I may have to go to jail.' She smiled as though she had said something altogether different.

'Maybe.' I smiled back at her.

'Probably share a cell with someone called Martha, or as she likes to be called, "The Duchess".'

'Maybe she'll smuggle in a mobile phone for you.'

'But at what cost, Jay? At what cost?'

I let out a small laugh. Her smile widened. It was nothing more than a moment. We both had a future ahead of us that we didn't anticipate and before shit got real, this... Well, this was nice.

'It's alright,' Sophia said, her smile smaller now. 'It's not like I've got anyone waiting for me.'

'I'll wait,' I said. 'When you come out, I'll be casually leaning against a convertible Cadillac. Elvis shades, toothpick in my mouth and a five o'clock shadow,' I said, trying to keep the moment going. But reality was looming over us. 'Seriously... I'll wait for you.'

I watched her take a breath, a soft sigh, and then her body shifted a touch closer to me. My eyes dropped to her lips which were slightly parted. I ain't a stranger to these signs. I played this game before with mixed results. I licked my lips, a subtle practised movement that if done correctly she wouldn't have noticed. I moved my face close, closer. And after calculating the trajectory of impact I angled my head off the pillow and closed my eyes. That's right, I was flying blind! But, man, I was rusty, and our noses bumped. After a quick recalculation I adjusted my head and our noses brushed gently before nestling side by side. And just before my lips could land on hers, an abrupt crack at my front door well and truly broke the moment.

The looming reality had finally kicked in, and was standing at my door wearing a crumpled suit.

*

I could have been spiteful. Unreasonable. Thrown a tantrum that a toddler would be proud of. Fuck, I wanted to. And maybe last night, I think I would have. But now, I felt calm, or as close to it as I could manage considering my old MI5 handler Teddy Lawrence was standing in my tight hallway.

At that time of the morning, I expected him to smell shampoo fresh, with every strand of hair clamped down perfectly in place. That was the smug, slick Teddy Lawrence that I was familiar with. But what was in front of me was a mess. I'd never seen him look so dishevelled. His hair – oh man, I wouldn't have been surprised if birds had set up a small village in it. And where the fuck was his tie? Yeah, his tailored suit probably cost more than my whole wardrobe combined, but it was creased. Fuck creased, it was crumpled, as though he'd slept and woken up in it. Though, judging by the passengers under his eyes, I don't think he'd yet been to bed.

'Sophia Hunt,' he said, without preamble. 'Where is she?'

I took my time before answering. 'She didn't know.'

'Didn't know *what*, exactly?' he said, frustrated.

'She didn't know what she was getting herself into.'

'I'm tired and I'm in no mood for games. Tell me where she is or I'll have this place taken apart looking for her.'

I challenged him with a stare. Lawrence knew me better, knew that his bullshit threat wasn't going to win me over. He shook his head. Wisely changed tack. 'We can help her,' he said.

'If she helps you, that is. Isn't that how it works?'

His eyes travelled past me and up the stairs. Sophia was standing on the top step. I watched her climb slowly down the stairs. She had her coat on over my onesie, and a pair of Mum's house slippers. She looked ready to accept her fate.

Sophia stood beside me and placed her hand in mine. She nodded gently at me and together we faced Lawrence.

'Sophia Hunt?' he said, smiling warmly but falling well short of the mark.

'What happens now?' I asked. Lawrence ignored me and continued to address Sophia.

'My name is Teddy Lawrence and—'

'He's MI5.' I jumped in and it cost me a glare from Lawrence.

'MI5,' Sophia mouthed to herself, and nodded as she took in that information. 'Why not the police?'

'For now, the police aren't involved, and if things go as I hope, they won't need to be.'

'So… I'm not being arrested?'

'No, we just want to ask you some questions.'

'Samuel Carter?' Sophia said.

'Samuel Carter is an alias. The man you spoke to is Omar Bhukara, responsible for taking hostage and torturing a high-ranking government officer. A conspiracy that you were part of.'

Despite everything Sophia let out a breezy laugh. 'Sounds a lot like I'm being arrested.'

Lawrence didn't reply. He'd said all he needed to. Sophia wasn't being arrested, not technically. She was being detained and questioned at a secure location without any counsel. That's what it amounted to. Her life had changed and I knew from experience that no matter how much she cooperated, she would forever be in their pocket.

Lawrence opened the front door. Sophia squeezed my hand. Together we looked outside. The wind had picked up. It had started to rain, again. Sophia pulled her sleeves over her hands.

'Do you want a hat?' I whispered. 'I've got a baseball cap upstairs. Or an umbrella? I've got one knocking about somewhere.'

'It's been nice, Jay,' she said. 'You're nice… maybe I'll see you again.'

I couldn't find the words quickly enough, and she was gone.

Lawrence led Sophia down my path and helped her into a waiting car. He tapped on the roof and the car was away. I watched her watch me from the back seat until she was out of sight.

I was going to miss her. *Fuck, man,* I was missing her already.

Despite the rain, Lawrence stood at the end of my path and took his time looking over his shoulders. He was waiting for somebody. He glanced at his watch before walking back down my path.

I closed the door behind him and he stood dripping in my hallway. 'We should talk,' he said.

'Tea? Coffee?' I asked, and then answered the question myself. 'Yeah, coffee, you look like you could do with one.'

He muttered his gratitude and made his way into the living room and I made my way into the kitchen. I almost turned back to ask him how he took his coffee, but fuck him, he'll take it as I make it. I knew why he was there, and it wasn't just about last night's events. It was about what I did after.

I balanced two over-filled mugs into the living room and placed them on the coffee table in front of him.

'How is he?' I asked, playing the game. 'How's Robinson?'

'Resting,' Lawrence replied.

I nodded as I decided if I should sit beside him on the sofa, or go solo on the armchair.

Lawrence picked up his coffee and took a sip, as if he was desperate for a caffeine hit. It was scalding hot and he rushed it back to the table. We both watched a wave of coffee spill down the side of his mug.

My eyes fell on the nest of tables. On top sat a tissue box and a stack of metallic coasters which I'd never before noticed. I plucked out a tissue and slipped out a couple of coasters. I lifted his mug, a stain was already forming into the wood. I ran a tissue across it before any long-term damage, and then slipped a coaster on the table and placed his mug on top. It felt like a fucking production, but I think there was a part of me that wanted to show him that I wasn't that same person. I had grown up.

'Looks like you could do with a little rest yourself,' I said, dropping on the armchair across from him.

'Who were they?' he asked. No beating, no bush. Worked for me, I was in no mood to dance. I'd tell him whatever I knew and then he could walk out the same fucking way he came in.

'Omar Bhukara,' I replied. 'His father was Adeel-Al-Bhukara.'

Lawrence nodded. 'I recognised the address.'

'A lot of young Muslims went in through those doors one way and came out another.'

'I know that, Jay,' he said sharply, as though I was wasting his precious time, and it pissed me off. It's always been the fucking case. No one cares how or why these Muslims turned, there's no preventive fucking measure in place, no education. All they give a fuck about is dealing with it, after. 'And the other?' he asked.

'Tommy. I didn't get a surname.'

'What do you know about him?'

'Lives local. Southall.'

'Convert?'

'I think so. I can't be sure?'

'There's doubt there,' Lawrence said, swooping a hand through his hair and making things worse. 'Why?'

'Something,' I said. 'I can't put my finger on it. Omar had said as much, but it didn't fit.'

'What didn't fit?'

I considered it for a second under Lawrence's watchful eye. 'Maybe it's lazy thinking on my part,' I said. 'Tommy didn't greet me with a *Salaam*, he wasn't throwing around *Inshallahs* or *Mashallahs*.'

'Nor do you, Jay.'

'I know, that's what I'm saying. Lazy thinking, tabloid thinking! Fuck, man, we come in all sizes and guises. It's just... A Muslim convert would, I don't know, try harder.'

I could see Lawrence trying to make sense of it, but I wasn't sure if there was any sense to be made. It was a feeling, is all. If the man says he's a Muslim, the fuck am I to argue? Lawrence wrapped a hand around the coffee mug and, being careful not to spill it again, brought it slowly to his lips.

'What I do know is that he's not part of Ghurfat-al-Mudarris. From what I understand his part in taking Robinson was just a transaction. It was Omar who wanted Robinson.'

'And what was Tommy's end in this transaction?'

'Guns. Omar was gonna supply him with a sawn-off AK-47 and a handgun, from a contact in Coventry that his old man used.'

'The same weapons that were used at the Boxing Day attack on Oxford Street?'

'And most likely the same contact. Wasim Qadir,' I said, from memory. Lawrence made a note on his phone.

'Did either Omar or Tommy mention a target?' he asked me carefully.

'No... Why are you asking me all this? I said, as the pieces fell heavily into place, in what was turning out to be the world's crappiest jigsaw. 'Lawrence... Tell me you've got them. Tell me they're sitting in a guarded locked room somewhere.'

He didn't tell me shit. I shot to my feet.

'You were watching the fucking place, you must have seen them walk out.'

'Sit down, Jay.'

'Fuck sitting down. What happened, Lawrence?'

'We had four agents in two cars on Jersey Way, and another in the house opposite with a camera on Al-Bhukara's place, feeding back to Comms. Taking into account the hostage we couldn't draw attention to the house, we had to be discreet. Two streets away we had Armed Response Units and SO15 waiting.'

'All that manpower and they still got away, that what you're telling me?'

'We didn't know what to expect, we even had a bomb disposal unit en-route. We were prepared for the worst. Yes, we saw Omar and Tommy leave the house, but you have to realise our *only* priority was the release or rescue of John Robinson. We made a calculated decision for two agents to tail them at a distance. They were followed to an underground car park in West Drayton. Our agents intercepted them as they tried to switch cars.' Lawrence took a moment to compose himself. Whatever he was about to say wasn't coming easy, and I wasn't going to make it any easier.

'And!?' I snapped and heard it echo in my head.

'One of them, and it's not clear which one, was armed.'

'Tommy.' I slumped back in my chair, leaned my head back. 'Tommy had the gun.'

'One of our agents is in a critical condition. The other died from multiple gunshot wounds.'

I closed my eyes tightly and Tommy's grinning face invaded my every thought. I was responsible for that gun. The same fucking gun I'd taken from Imy so that he wouldn't do anything stupid. I thought I was doing the right thing. And now, two agents had been shot, one killed, and I didn't think I knew what the right fucking thing was anymore.

I questioned all those past decisions that had led me there. I questioned the decision I'd made just a few hours ago. Was it the right one? It didn't matter. Nothing had changed.

'There's another matter that we need to discuss,' Lawrence said, trawling through my head.

'You know, don't you?' I said. 'Yeah, 'course you fucking know. Still keeping tabs on me like an obsessive ex.'

'Yes, we know. We know that in the early hours of the morning you booked a flight to Islamabad.'

'*So?*' One word. Two letters. Full of challenge and intent. My mind will not be changed.

'I'm not here to stop you, Jay. I want to help.'

I ignored him. I ignored him because my eyes were at my window, at the crappy Prius that had just pulled up across my drive.

No. There's no fucking way.

Chapter 38

Imy

I stood at the door struggling to keep my anger in check. I never thought I would be seeing him again, let alone this damn soon, and back in the house where my decision had cost me so dearly.

I couldn't bring myself to knock. I couldn't predict what my reaction would be upon seeing his face when he opened the door.

It turns out I didn't have to. Lawrence opened the door.

'Come in.' He was wearing the same clothes he'd had on when came to see me in the early hours. His state just as bad, worse.

'No,' I said, standing firm, as memories of what had taken place here flooded back. 'I don't want anything to do with him!'

'I *can* hear you, for fuck's sake!' Jay's voice came through from the living room.

I shrugged past Lawrence and stomped into the living room ready to give it to him. I stopped in my tracks. He was sitting in the same armchair where I'd once failed to kill him.

'I want my gun back,' I said.

He casually picked up a mug of whatever he was drinking and took a delicate sip without taking his eyes off me over the rim. I knew his play; I was on his territory now, and he was trying to dictate proceedings. I took a step forward and stood over him and leaned down into his face. 'Do you really want me to ask you again?'

'I haven't got it,' Jay said, without flinching.

'I know you took it. Do you think I'm stupid?'

'I don't know,' he said, 'do *you* think you're stupid?'

I straightened up, took my eyes off him and stared at Lawrence, who was standing at the door wearily watching us. 'Why am I here? I don't want anything to do with this… *child*!'

'If you can both allow me to explain,' Lawrence said, trying to keep the peace. He sat on the edge of the sofa. 'Imran, please, take a seat.'

'Make yourself at fucking home,' Jay said. 'Can I get you a drink? A sedative or something?'

Jay was circling, pushing the boundaries, there was desperation in his hostility. He wanted me to react, punish him, anything to alleviate the guilt he was carrying.

My head started to hurt. A pulsating pressure either side of my temple. I'd woken up that morning feeling strong, my mind focused on nothing but the task ahead. Being in that room, with Jay, it was starting to cloud my mind. It was starting to tire me.

I sat down on the armchair beside Jay.

'So when did you get in bed with MI5?' he asked, mocking. More than that, there was a sense of resentment.

'The Teacher,' Lawrence started, 'or Abdul Bin Jabbar as we now know, went into hiding December of 2017.'

'Can we skip the history lesson, for fuck's sake?' Jay spat.

'You need to hear the truth,' Lawrence said. 'Let me finish.'

'Your version of the truth,' Jay muttered. 'Go on, then. Let's hear it.'

'Despite numerous attempts we were unable to locate Bin Jabbar, until, that is, in early April 2018, he decided to come out of hiding of his own accord to lift a fatwa placed on your head.'

I glanced across at Jay and noticed his face colour slightly.

'The fatwa was placed by Sheikh Ali Ghulam who, in the absence of Bin Jabbar, had assumed control of operations for Ghurfat-al-Mudarris. We were able to track Bin Jabbar's movements as he crossed the Afghanistan/Pakistan border before sailing to Dubai. He was captured at the Sheikh's palatial residence where he murdered Ali Ghulam by way of strangulation. Bin Jabbar refused to give himself up, instead he opened fire. We had no choice but to return fire. He took shots to the heart and kidneys. Both lungs were punctured. His vital organs shut down. One bullet was lodged in his brain, another at the base of his spine. It's still in there now. How he didn't die, minds greater than most couldn't quite fathom. His nervous system collapsed. By all accounts, the man known to the world as The Teacher, is as good as dead.'

Jay stood up and slowly ambled out of the room as though we weren't there. This was probably the first time he'd got any answers about his father. I shook my head at Lawrence. Maybe the truth wasn't what was needed right now.

A few seconds after he'd walked out, Jay stormed back into the room, his eyes wide and on fire. 'But he ain't, is he? He ain't fucking dead and you spread that bullshit like it was fucking so.'

'If it was my decision, it wouldn't have played out that way. I think people should have been told the truth. The Prime Minister at the time was under intense scrutiny; this country was becoming a battle zone. Hundreds of Muslims, thousands across Europe, soldiers of Ghurfat-al-Mudarris held The Cause above human life. Innocent lives. In accordance with the teachings of your father.'

A part of me felt for a part of him. I had known Jay before all of this. He was nothing but a street urchin, happy to sell a little dope around town from his car and whittle his life away in blissful ignorance. He led a simple life that, if I'm honest, I'd envied. He didn't ask for any of this, it came asking for him. They, MI5, opened his eyes and kept them forced open. Used him, like they're using me, but what did they expect? For *us* to believe in what they believed in?

'You figured that if the world thought that The Teacher had died, the world would move on,' I said.

Lawrence shook his head up and down and side to side as though he was trying to dislodge an answer. 'Yes, actually. When Osama Bin Laden was killed, to an extent al-Qaeda died with him. Operations shifted from top down, the organisation was split and the attacks that continued were smaller scale, lone-wolf operators without facilitators and without funding. We're now seeing the exact same pattern emerge with Ghurfat-al-Mudarris. When it was announced that The Teacher had died, the cell split. Splinter groups were formed, *smaller* and to a degree manageable in regards to impact. Lone-wolf operators carrying out attacks all over Europe, but again, smaller, fewer deaths, less destruction. The attacks are no longer intelligent but crude in nature. The Foreign Secretary, along with the PM, made a decision – one that was heavily influenced by the Security Service and fully deniable.'

'Deniable?' I asked. 'To what extent?'

'We never said he was dead. We didn't say anything. The press, well… the press writes whatever it wants.'

Jay dropped down heavily in his chair, his mind processing it all.

'And you couldn't bring him back to England,' I said. Lawrence nodded. 'Too many eyes.' Another nod. He looked across at Jay.

'Your father was—'

'Don't call him that,' Jay said, softly.

'Bin Jabbar was transported to a safe house on the Afghan/Pakistani border. A functional farm for all intents and purposes, and was looked after by two of our own. A couple.'

'Is that it?' I said. 'You had the world's most wanted man and that was the extent of your security?'

'We had extensive CCTV, tripwires, sensors. The place was secured to the hilt. The couple were highly trained marines. We couldn't place any more manpower without the Pakistani Government asking questions, and risking a leak. We had a unit located thirty klicks south, four minutes' quick release by Apache attack choppers in the event the alarm was activated. But... It took us by surprise quite how speedily they were able to act upon the information they obtained. We couldn't get to Bin Jabbar in time.'

'How was this information obtained?' I asked.

Jay snorted through his nose. He ran an arm across it. 'John Robinson squealed like a stuck pig.'

Lawrence shifted uncomfortably in his seat. 'He was tortured. Either way, it's a rather unfortunate series of events. Events which we now need to control.'

'Yeah, you're good at that, controlling events, controlling people.' Jay said what was on my mind.

He gave me a look as if he'd forgotten I was there. He turned back to Lawrence.

'Bullshit to one side.' Jay jabbed a thumb over his shoulder at me. 'Tell me what the fuck he's doing here?'

Chapter 39

Jay

In less than twenty-four hours I'd be stepping on that plane. Teddy Lawrence couldn't stop me. For once MI5 didn't have jack to hold over me. Fuck, man, I'd just saved John Robinson's miserable life, they should have been lining up to spit-shine my Jordans!

'There's no way I can stop you from flying to Islamabad,' Lawrence said.

'Wait,' I heard Imy say. 'What did you say?'

'Trust me, Imy,' I said. 'This ain't none of your business and it definitely ain't none of their business. I can do whatever I like in my own time, and I can go wherever the fuck I want. And come tomorrow morning I'm stepping on that plane and there ain't a fucking thing MI5 can do to stop me.'

I said my piece as calm and as controlled and as black and white as I could, so they wouldn't be left with any doubt. I spent a second or two giving Lawrence a customary Hounslow stare before leaning back in my armchair. I waited for them to get the fuck up and get the fuck out of my house, but I think deep down I knew it wouldn't be that simple.

'I'd like to put forward a proposal to you, Jay,' Lawrence said, arms out, palms up, his butt balancing on the edge of his seat. 'I'd like Imran to accompany you to Islamabad.'

'You're out of your fucking head!' I exclaimed.

213

Imy did a little exclaiming himself. 'There's no way! I am not babysitting Jay.'

Babysitting. Did he just say babysitting? The fuck does he know? MI5 had me on missions whilst he was still earning a commission renting one-bed flats to families of four. Frankly, I was pretty fucking offended that Lawrence had approached Imy first, after everything I'd done for those leeches.

I bit back my natural reaction and coolly said, 'Do not underestimate me, Imy.'

Feeling pleased with my delivery I picked up my coffee and took a sip, but the metal coaster was stuck to the bottom of the mug and had come along for the journey, before slowly peeling itself off and clattering onto the coffee table.

'I think I estimate you just fine,' Imy said, winning the hand.

I turned my attention to Lawrence. 'Whatever hare-brained scheme you've got in mind, get this: I'm doing this alone.' I jabbed a thumb at Imy. 'I don't need *him* moping around, slowing me down.'

I stopped in my tracks as soon as the words escaped. It was insensitive considering that Imy was still in mourning. The guilt kicked in instantly. I turned to face him, a rushed apology ready to leave my mouth, but he had already bounced to his feet and was towering over me and effectively trapping me in my armchair. His face so close to mine that his scrunched features blurred in front of my eyes.

'I shouldn't have said that.'

'Alright! Okay!' Lawrence said from somewhere; I couldn't see as I was blocked by Imy's frame. 'Cut this out right now.'

Imy remained unmoved, baring his teeth at me like Cujo. 'Say that again,' he growled. 'I want you to say it again.'

I dropped my gaze and noticed his hands balled into tight fists. I readied myself for a much-deserved slap.

A voice that hadn't been in the room a minute ago said, 'What the fuck is going on?'

I inclined my head past Imy's frame, past Lawrence who was on his feet ready to pull Imy back from knocking my teeth out. There he was, at the tip of my living room, a travel holdall in one hand and a travel trolley in the other. Despite the wet weather, he was dressed in a half-sleeved white shirt to best show off his tan. I know Idris. I know how his mind works.

I slipped past Imy and with Lawrence's eyes on me, I stood by Idris.

'Alright,' I said to my friend.

'Yeah, Jay, I'm alright.' His eyes locked in mine. 'You?'

I looked back into the living room and tried to picture it through Idris' eyes. What would he make of it? A life that I had tried so desperately to hide from him stared back at us. My old MI5 handler and a man who once came to kill me. My two lives had finally collided like that middle bit of a Venn diagram.

'Yeah, you know.' I shrugged at Idris. 'All good.'

*

I left Imy and Lawrence in the living room. *'Back in a minute!'* I called out as I ushered Idris out of the room. We bombed it up the stairs and into my bedroom. The last thing I wanted was Idris to get involved with my crap, but at the same time, I was beyond relieved to see him.

Idris sat down on the plastic swivel chair by my computer desk. It wasn't the first time. He'd probably sat at my desk more than I had. Over the years in this room I'd taken the piss out his various hairstyles, and questionable facial hair choices, as we blagged our way through homework. Hours didn't feel like hours as we bit the bullshit about girls, friction at school, and family. Anything that was on our minds. Nothing was off limits. But nothing had been like this.

215

I shuffled nervously in front of him, burning a hole in the carpet.

'How'd you get in?' I asked, buying myself some time to figure what I should and shouldn't tell him.

'Still got your key, haven't I?' he said, flicking my key ring over his finger and then pocketing it. 'I did bell first but I guess you couldn't hear me over the raised voices.'

'Yeah,' I said. 'About that.'

Idris shook his head. 'Imran Siddiqui, in your living room. Feel free to correct me but didn't you say that you and him weren't that tight?' He said, taking little or no pleasure in it. 'Then again the way he was stood over you like he was going to rearrange your features, maybe you're not so tight.' Idris tapped away on his knee with his index finger as his mind tick-tocked away. 'And who's the other one, the stressed-out-looking fella. Didn't think you had any white friends, Jay.'

'I've got loads of white friends.'

'Yeah. Name one.'

'You, for starters,' I said.

'Who is he?' Idris was in no mood for a back and forth. I pursed my lips tight and blinked at him. 'Jay!'

'Fuck, Idris!' I said. 'His name's Teddy Lawrence and he ain't my friend.'

'I didn't think he was. So, twenty questions, or shall we save some time and you can tell me what you've got yourself involved in?'

I couldn't tell him.

My best friend, inseparable since the day we were born, at the same hospital, within minutes of each other. For so long we'd shared each other's secrets and so many times I wanted him to tell him this fucking secret and relieve some of that burden that was dropping me down to my fucking knees. Instead I had been spinning it, sprinkling seeds just enough to keep him at arm's length. I had

216

signed confidentiality agreements and non-disclosure documents, there was no way I could tell him even I wanted to.

But... There's a flip-side to that coin.

Idris. *Detective Inspector Idris Zaidi* had also signed similar agreements. Fuck, man, he had taken an oath and everything, but not once had he put that shit in front of me, in front of our friendship. I'd lost count of the number of times I'd asked him to use and abuse his position, and after some token huffing and puffing, he'd always, *always* come through for me.

'What you thinking, Jay?' Idris knocked me out of my thoughts. I took him in. My friend. Sitting there on the plastic swivel chair, as he'd done a thousand times, creaking as he swivelled a touch to the left, a touch to the right, in his stupid white shirt, showing off his stupid tan. I crossed the room and popped my head around the doorframe and glanced down the stairs. Lawrence and Imy were still in my living room, and I doubt they were making small talk. Judging by the silence, Lawrence was probably eavesdropping. I closed my bedroom door and sat on the corner edge of my single bed close to Idris and leaned forward towards him.

Idris stopped swivelling. The chair stopped creaking.

'You gotta keep this shit to yourself,' I started, and knew that I had to keep going.

Idris nodded quickly. 'Goes without saying.'

I cleared my throat and took in an almighty breath. 'For the last eighteen months... I've been working with MI5.'

The relief, I swear to God, was like nothing I'd ever experienced before. I'd finally been able to share with my best friend. Except my best friend was doubled up in the chair, holding his stomach as his shoulders danced and he laughed hysterically at my revelation.

'Fuck's sake, Idris. Shut the fuck up!' I said, but too late, the floodgates had opened, his dumb cackle had always been infectious

217

and I couldn't help but laugh along with him. He placed the back of his hand to his mouth to mute his laugh, but there was no stopping him. He gripped my shoulder and leaned against me for support, as if he was about to fall out of his chair. I watched his eyes starting to fill up and I couldn't remember the last time we had laughed like that.

I let it happen, didn't try to stop him or myself. I didn't care that Lawrence and Imy could hear us. I didn't know when I'd be laughing like that again.

It lasted a long minute until it died down. Idris rubbed the tears from his eyes as the last remnants of laughter died down with an almighty sigh. We sat in silence for a bit, both carrying dopey smiles on our faces as you do after a spell of hysterics, but I could see behind his eyes, the thought process putting it all together. My behaviour over the last couple of years, my actions that had put distance between us.

'Yeah,' Idris said, nodding slowly. 'I believe it.'

I told him the fucking lot, from spying on other Pakis to travelling to a training camp in North Pakistan. The gun attack on Oxford Street and my part in it. I told him how Imy had saved my life once, and spared my life another time at the expense of his family.

Idris listened carefully, only to interrupt me once when he muttered, *'Fuck, a fatwa!'* before getting off his chair and sitting beside me on the bed and placing an arm around my shoulder.

I told him about my dad, about who he was. His reaction was to take me into an embrace, and all I could think was, *why the fuck didn't I tell him all this before...*

We sat side by side on the edge of my bed in silence. I could see the goose bumps raised on his forearms, but couldn't tell if it was from what he'd just heard, or because he was dressed in a half-sleeved shirt in December. I slipped my phone out and it registered four missed calls from Lawrence and a text message. *Be down in a minute*, I replied back.

'You're definitely going to go?' Idris asked. 'Islamabad.'

I nodded. 'Ticket's booked. I fly out tomorrow morning.'

'How you going to find him?' he asked, hesitated, and then added, 'Your dad?'

I shrugged. 'I just will.'

'And then what's the plan?'

'He deserves it all,' I said. 'Everything that's coming to him. That man should suffer, but not like how *they* want. Not locked up in a fucking safe house in the middle of nowhere with the world thinking he's dead. He's not! Despite everything he's done they can't deny him his human rights. He needs to answer for his crimes, every single fucking one of them, but in a court of law... *Fuck*, what's that word?'

'Two words,' Idris said. 'Due process.'

'That's right. Due process,' I said, as my phone rang in my hands, I swiped it and answered. 'Alright, okay, I'm coming,' I said into it before disconnecting Lawrence. I got to my feet and stood in front of Idris. The echo of laughter a distant memory.

'What you going to do about Imran?'

I blew my cheeks out and followed it with a shrug.

'From what you've told me, he was once part of Ghurfat-al-Mudarris, he knows the terrain and he's trained in combat. I would feel a lot better if you went together.'

'I don't know,' I sighed. 'The man's just lost his family. He's half the man he used to be.'

Idris stood up in front of me and placed both hands on my shoulder.

'I know that, Jay,' Idris smiled. 'But he's still twice the man you are.'

*

A fist bump, a shoulder bump and a silent look passed between Idris and I, and then he was gone. I watched him jog down my path, into the rain, and step into an Uber. I closed the door behind him and then placed my head against it. I still wasn't sure what the right decision was. Nevertheless, a decision had been made.

'Jay.' I turned away from the door and Lawrence was standing in the hallway, a look on his face that screamed desperation. He needed me. Again, MI5 needed me.

I glanced over his shoulder into the living room. Imy was still in the armchair, cracking his knuckles one finger at a time, one hand and then the other. I could see arthritis in his future. It didn't look as though time had cooled his temper.

We remained in the hallway and keeping my voice low, I said, 'If I agree to this, what happens?'

'Full disclosure,' Lawrence said, with his palms up.

I snorted. 'I think you and I have pretty different definitions of full disclosure, but go on, I'm listening.'

'I want to make it clear from the off,' Lawrence started, all business now, 'we will provide you with the resources that you may require but we can offer you very little in regards to protection. The choice to travel to Islamabad is a choice that you have made. Our official position is to deny.'

I nodded in agreement and without argument. I'd been there before. This was the Secret Service keeping their hands clean, whilst somebody else did the dirty work. They would step in only when the target was met and then take all the plaudits. Fuck 'em, I wasn't doing this for plaudits.

Lawrence continued. 'You'll travel by road from Islamabad to the Ghurfat-al-Mudarris training camp in Khyber Pakhtunkhwa. We have intel that this site is now redundant, but the keeper still resides there. He will be your first point of contact.'

'Mustafa,' I said, pushing aside the harrowing memories.

'That's right. Mustafa Mirza, he trained you on your last visit. According to your debriefing notes, you still have a good relationship, a shared history. Use it. We need Mirza to talk.'

'And him,' I gestured vaguely in Imy's direction in the living room.

'Imran will use his contact to arrange transport from airport to camp. After that he will be relaying progress reports directly to me. Imran Siddiqui is still regarded as a member of Ghurfat-al-Mudarris so suspicion should not fall on him.'

I beckoned Lawrence closer to me, and dropped my already low tone to a whisper.

'What'd you mean still regarded as a member? He failed to carry out the fatwa on me. I'm pretty sure Ghurfat-al-Mudarris ain't that forgiving.'

'The fatwa was not common knowledge within the ranks. They kept that knowledge in very close quarters. Those in the know have been killed.'

I nodded. It kinda made sense. When Sheikh Ali Ghulam placed a hit on me, he kept that shit under wraps in fear of retaliation from Bin Jabbar and his band of loyal followers. So Imy's involvement wouldn't have been known.

'All right,' I said, summarising, 'Imy will arrange transport to the training camp in Khyber Pakhtunkhwa, where we'll meet up with Mustafa, and then. . . Then what?' I waited a couple of seconds, and then I waited a few seconds more. Lawrence pursed him lips. 'Are you telling me that's it? That's the plan!' I said, and I think I hammered a nerve.

'We can send out armed forces and turn the country upside down until Bin Jabbar falls out of whatever goddamn tree they've hidden him in, but we cannot risk the exposure. So, yes, Jay, that is actually it. It's you, and it's Imran! Now, am I wasting my time here or are you in?'

I let him sweat for a moment before I answered. 'Yeah, I'm in.'

'Good, that's good.' Lawrence nodded, trying his hardest not show his obvious relief, but the relief was incomplete. He walked back into the living room, I hung back and peered in through the door. Imy had stopped cracking his knuckles and was staring into the middle distance.

'Jay is on board,' Lawrence said. 'He'll be accompanying you to Islamabad.'

Imy got to his feet, he answered Lawrence as he glared at me.

'I don't need him. I'm doing this on my own.'

Chapter 40

Imy

I slammed the front door shut as I walked out of Jay's house, I slammed the car door behind me as I got into my Prius, and I slammed my head back against the headrest. I squeezed my eyes shut and breathed heavily through my nose as the rain beat against my windscreen.

When Jay had made the comment about me *'moping around'* I wanted to knock his head clean off his shoulders and crush his skull under my boot. He was sorry as soon as the words left his big mouth, but I wanted more. I wanted him to take it back, I wanted Jay to take it all back to how it used to be.

What the hell was Lawrence thinking putting me in the same room as him? How could he expect for us to work together after everything that had happened between us? I couldn't care less that he'd previously worked in some capacity with MI5; it was clear that he had been employed for who he was, rather than any discernible skill-set. The rain continued to snap relentlessly, threatening to break through my windscreen and drown my thoughts. I had to consider the angles and adapt. Tomorrow morning Jay would be travelling to Islamabad, regardless of my decision. His presence alone was going to throw everything into chaos. We'd be there at the same time, treading on the same ground, searching for the same man.

The only difference was that Jay had something that I couldn't offer.

He had something that neither MI5 nor any of the other authorities combined could offer.

He had his name.

That alone would give him an advantage. As soon as he set foot in Islamabad Airport, there was a strong chance his name would be flagged. Word would reach far and wide. It was an advantage that I didn't have, an advantage that could see Jay get to his father before I could.

I couldn't allow that.

The alternative, which I refused to consider, but which was now all I could think about: I travel with Jay. Work beside him. Guide and bend him to my advantage, in full knowledge that my absolute thirst for revenge would destroy him.

I started my car and shifted it into gear. I glanced in the rear-view mirror, the red glow of the brake light illuminated Jay. He tentatively walked towards the car. I gripped the steering wheel and took a breath, followed by another, deeper, as my eyes dully moved in rhythm with the wipers.

Jay knocked on the glass and from the corner of my eye I could see him half-crouched by the window. I turned to face him, his hair plastered over his forehead from the downpour. I watched him through the glass for a moment, his features distorted through the condensation, but I could see him, I could see his face. A constant reminder of what I'd once had, of what I'd lost.

He motioned for me to slide the window down.

I did.

For a moment he didn't say anything. Unsure, uncertain, his eyes everywhere but on me. He ran a hand through his hair, sweeping it back to something that resembled his hairstyle, just before the rain flattened it again.

'Will you come with me?' he said, his words barely reaching me as they dissipated into the rain. 'Will you help me find my dad?'

Chapter 41

The Ford Focus sat in near darkness in the disused aircraft hangar and in relative safety. Omar and Tommy had reached the meeting point in Coventry early, and without further incident. Omar's nerves had been shredded, his carefully orchestrated plan had almost come apart, but he was close now.

He twirled the nose stud in between his fingers as he waited patiently, casting glances at Tommy who was sleeping in the passenger seat. Omar wondered how, after everything, he could sleep so soundly. He would be glad to see the back of him, and the sooner the better. Tommy was starting to worry Omar.

How they had managed to make it there, Omar still couldn't get his head around. It had been going so well, too well. Robinson had sung like a bird and Omar had ensured that word quickly reached his Al-Muhaymin contact. The wheels were turning, spinning, and the rescue of Abdul Bin Jabbar from the hands of his captors was underway. Omar Bhukara had achieved what many thought was unachievable.

He closed his eyes and sighed, then shivered. It wasn't exactly the feeling of elation that he expected from his triumph. What he had learnt along the way disturbed him greatly.

His comrade, gently snoring next to him, was a fucking sociopath, and a liability. And Javid Qasim, the son of their great leader, was a traitor.

*

When Omar and Tommy had left the house in Osterley, Omar had expected them to be collared by dirty white hands. Instead they were able to walk freely to his Mercedes AMG, which was parked on a street parallel to Jersey Way. A second car, an unremarkable Ford Focus bought and paid for in hard cash, waited for them a short drive away in an underground car park in West Drayton to transport them to Coventry.

What Omar didn't anticipate was that they would be tailed to the underground car park. And what Omar didn't fucking anticipate was that there would be a shoot-out, or that he'd now be an accomplice to the cold-blooded murder of an MI5 agent. How could he have foreseen it? It was beyond anticipation.

Any other day, and from a safe distance, Omar would not have been more pleased at the news that the Kafirs had been on the receiving end of another lashing by a Brother. He would have rejoiced in it, taken to social media, under one of his many accounts, and waxed lyrical about it. Revelling in the hatred coming from those who felt the injustice, and the love from the like-minded.

Problem was, he wasn't at a safe distance. Omar had been right in the mix. Finding himself shrinking in his seat, his eyes locked on two MI5 agents carefully approaching his car. One white male. One Asian female. Dressed like civilians in dark jeans and black trainers, but holding official badges high in one hand, the other hand wrapped around the guns on their side holsters.

Omar had worked too hard and for too long, creating a role suited to his skill-set. His position was designed so he would never have to be in this position! He didn't want to die for The Cause, or be locked up for it either. He was too smart for that. But with the agents closing in on them, Omar had found himself lost in indecision. Next to him,

Tommy hadn't suffered from any such doubt. Without word and without hesitation, Tommy had stepped out of the Merc. Partially shielded behind the car door, he raised one hand in surrender with the other hand coming up behind holding the Glock that he'd taken from Jay.

A finger on the trigger, scratching an age-old itch.

Tommy put one in the shoulder of the white agent, and Omar watched him spin like a top before dropping. The other agent, in a series of small predictable actions, released her weapon from the holster, raised the gun and steadied her arm as she flicked the safety off.

In that time Tommy simply swung around a fraction, the Glock a natural extension of his arm, and unloaded into her chest with a little more intent, a little more menace, pulling the trigger until the gun clicked empty. She was dead before she fell.

Tommy ducked his head back in the car and calmly instructed Omar to '*Move!*' as he walked across the car park to the waiting Ford Focus. Omar stepped out of his Merc and tentatively walked around the squirming body of the white MI5 agent and the still body of the female agent with the brown skin.

They travelled the two-hour journey, covering 109 miles from West London to Coventry, with Tommy slouched in the passenger's seat like a man without a care. It had made Omar uncomfortable; the dynamic between them had altered.

But Omar was a man of his word. Tommy had carried out the job professionally. As agreed, and as deserved, Omar would pay him in the form of automatic weapons and ammunition, and the documentation for Tommy to start a new life under a new name. After which, Omar would shake Tommy's hand, wish him good luck in his Jihad and walk away, content, in the other direction.

Like his father before him, Omar was a facilitator, somebody who had the power and the contacts to put weapons of destruction into the hands of young Muslims, to carry out their God-given duty. But unlike his father, Omar did not have to impress upon them the importance of Jihad. Muslims were aware enough, angry enough, their people had *suffered* enough, to walk into war without guidance or recruitment.

From that suffering a new breed of Jihadi was emerging. One who had taken the teachings of Al-Mudarris and retaliated in kind. The Lone Jihadi was rising from cult to phenomenon. The longer that Omar had spent in his company, the more certain he was that Tommy was the very definition of a Lone Jihadi.

*

'Wake up,' Omar said, more confidently than he was feeling. But he had to exert some power. 'It's almost time.'

Tommy blinked open his eyes and checked his surroundings through the windscreen. It was hard to make anything out as they were in darkness. In the absence of vision, his ears tuned in to the rain hammering and rattling the arched metal roof of the old abandoned aircraft hangar.

'Sort yourself out. He'll be here soon.'

Tommy sat up in his seat. He leaned across to check the time on the dashboard and couldn't help but notice Omar flinch.

'What is it?' Tommy asked, knowing exactly what had Omar on edge.

'What is what?' Omar shrugged in his seat, trying not to show his discomfort.

'It had to be done.'

'I know,' Omar said, looking towards the large metal doors, waiting for them to slide open so he could make the deal and part company with Tommy.

228

Tommy turned in his seat to face Omar, waited until their eyes met. 'I did what I had to do. To survive. To keep my Jihad alive.'

Omar forced himself to hold Tommy's gaze. He took a moment before he replied. 'I know.' He snatched his eyes away, back to the metal gates.

'Don't get it the wrong way round, Omar,' Tommy said. 'I don't care that she was a woman and I don't care that she was brown. Like you and me, she chose a side.'

Omar nodded slowly, as the thoughts in his head organised themselves in justification. The Asian agent had pulled a gun on them. As Tommy had said, *she chose a side.*

The metal gate in front of them rattled before being pulled across. They both squinted their eyes as headlights lit up a single figure holding an umbrella over his head. Even from a distance it was clear from his form that it was Omar's contact.

'That him?' Tommy asked. Omar nodded. 'What'd you say his name was?'

Omar flashed his headlights once and the man turned away, collapsed his umbrella and got into the VW camper van.

'Wasim,' Omar replied. 'Come on.'

They stepped out of the car as the van pulled up beside them. Wasim switched the engine off but left the headlamps on. He stepped out of the van, tall and broad with fat that had once been muscle from his days as a promising Pakistani wrestler. Omar's father had told him many stories about Wasim. How his parents had sent him to England in the early seventies to study when his career was cut short by a knee injury. But studying had been duly avoided as he spent his early years warring against the growing presence of the National Front on the streets of Coventry and Nuneaton. It was these actions that had led him to cross paths with Adeel-Al-Bhukara.

His father had trusted him, and therefore so did Omar.

'Uncle Wasim, Aslamalykum.' Omar beamed, relief flooding him that he was no longer alone with Tommy.

Wasim wrapped his arms around Omar in a tight bear hug. He returned the greeting. 'Waalaikum-salam.' He pointed at Omar's nose stud and frowned. 'What is this? You look like a girl.'

'Yeah, it's nothing, Uncle.' Omar's cheeks flushed as he dismissed it with a wave of the hand, then felt as though he had to explain himself. 'Sometimes you have to look a certain way so the Kafirs' eyes aren't on you.' It sounded a lot better than, *I'm a huge Tupac Shakur fan.*

Wasim, satisfied with the explanation, nodded. 'Your father was like my older brother. I miss him, greatly. I'm happy that you have followed in his footsteps. It would have made him proud.'

Omar smiled away the compliment. Tommy, who was standing behind Omar's shoulder, took a step forward. 'Can we get a move on?' he said.

It sounded impatient and disrespectful, and Omar felt his cheeks redden. 'This is, uh, Tommy,' Omar said, by way of introduction.

Wasim took and shook his hand. 'Tommy?' Wasim said, tightening his grip. 'You see that open door?' Wasim gestured his head to the metal gate. 'Go close it, boy!'

Wasim released his hand. Tommy stood his ground for a moment, much to Wasim's amusement and Omar's horror, before crossing the hangar to slide the gates shut.

'You trust him?' Wasim asked as they watched Tommy.

'With the right tools in his hands, he is capable. He can do a lot of damage,' Omar replied, sidestepping the question.

'Yes. I know this. I heard what happened in London. I am surprised that you made it.'

'Allah's will, Uncle,' Omar said, as Tommy returned.

'As discussed, I have all the relevant documentation for you. Passports, drivers' licences and national insurance numbers.'

'And the oth'er thing?' Tommy asked.

'Yes, my impatient Brother,' Wasim said, meeting Tommy's eyes. 'I have the other thing.'

Wasim walked away to the back of the camper van. Tommy started to follow, but Omar reached for his arm. 'Have some fucking respect,' Omar hissed, but Tommy had already shrugged his arm away and joined Wasim at the back of the van. Omar gritted his teeth and followed.

Wasim pulled open the double doors of the camper van. An internal light lazily came on, illuminating a long black accessory bag, used to hold fishing equipment. The sound of Wasim slowly unzipping it echoed in the confines of the van. He pried open the bag, and stepped to one side.

Before Omar could inspect the contents, Tommy stepped forward. His hand snaked inside and emerged with a sawn-off AK-47 automatic rifle.

In all the time that Omar had known Tommy, it was at this moment that he first saw him smile.

Chapter 42

Jay

No turning back. No second thoughts. No fucking about. I'm doing this.

As I waited, I walked around the house, for the third time, making sure the windows were locked and the gas was turned off. All that grown-up shit. I even set a timer on the living room lamp to switch on/off throughout the day so it would bamboozle Hounslow's slow-witted burglars.

My travel trolley was waiting by the front door and I had wrapped a pink ribbon around it so I could easily recognise it when retrieving it from baggage reclaim. My passport was in the front pocket of my jeans, tucked in sideways so that the corner was constantly digging into my thigh so I'd know it was there.

I peeked through the net curtains of my bedroom window. Above, the sky was a weird purple; below, Imy was waiting in my drive, his luggage in the form of a sports holdall. *How has he managed to travel so light and how long had he been waiting there?* We'd agreed 4 a.m., which it was, but I expected a knock on the door, a phone call or the very least a text! Instead he just hovered outside my house as though I had nothing better to do but look out the window for him.

Fuck it, he wanted to be aloof, I could be aloof too. I'd fucking aloof the shit out of it. I walked downstairs slowly, took my time zipping up my parka and, not knowing when I would be coming back home, I looked around, saying a quiet goodbye to the place.

My eyes caught two mugs that I had placed on the kitchen counter beside a boiled kettle, thinking maybe Imy and I could have a cup of tea before heading to the airport. I felt stupid. That wasn't us. That wasn't our relationship.

I opened the door and casually flicked my head at him as a greeting. He nodded back at me with the same enthusiasm. I watched him watch me as I pulled my pink-ribboned trolley behind me, with my rucksack against my back. With the press of a button my Beemer tweeted; another press of a button and the boot flipped opened. I placed my trolley inside and gestured to see if he wanted to put his *one piece* in with mine. He shook his head. I closed the boot as he let himself into my car.

I exhaled and joined him.

Imy placed his bag by his feet and pulled the seatbelt across. 'From here onwards,' he said, 'you watch your step and you *watch* your mouth around me.'

I opened said mouth but he shut me down with a look that I didn't want to fuck with at that time of the morning.

My engine roared to life and I flicked on the window heaters, but before it could kick in, Imy had leaned forward and used the sleeve of his jacket to haphazardly wipe my windscreen, leaving smear marks all over it. It took a lot for me to bite my tongue.

I dropped my car in the long-term car park and we sat next to each other on the shuttle bus. I kept my headphones on and watched him in the window reflection, hoping that the tinny sounds escaping from my cans would annoy him. He sat with his hands on his lap, perfectly still, which for some reason annoyed me. As soon as the shuttle bus pulled up outside Heathrow Airport, Departures, he was up, bag in hand and stepping off the bus as though we weren't travelling together.

I stood at his shoulder at the PIA check-in desk, as he showed his passport and exchanged his e-ticket for a boarding pass.

'What seat did you get?' I asked. As he passed me by, he mumbled something that sounded a lot like he'd been upgraded to first class! Best Jordan forward, I approached the desk, smiled charmingly at the lady, and spoke in my best voice. She eyed me with suspicion, as though posh wasn't my default voice, checked in my luggage and slapped an economy boarding pass in my hand.

I turned away with the smallest of thanks and searched for Imy, knowing full well that he'd already sauntered off to airside. Fuck, man, I understood that this was far from a lads' holiday, but at the very least he could show some civility.

I crossed through security with the usual checks, and an additional body check thrown in for good measure, eventually finding Imy sitting at a table for two at Huxley's Restaurant & Bar, a hot drink in front of him. Just the one. I sighed. Seriously, I was getting tired of him already. I placed my rucksack on the chair opposite.

'I'm gonna go get myself a cappuccino. Want anything?'

'You can't leave your bag unattended at an airport,' was his reply.

A vision popped into my head. Outside my house, kneeling down by Imy's car as the rain pelted off my head. *Help me find my dad.*

I didn't know what lay ahead for me when I landed in Islamabad, but it was becoming increasingly evident that Imy was not going to make it easy for me. There would be no relationship, nor camaraderie or any of that shit. He did not like me, and though my vanity took a hit, really, I couldn't give a shit. I'd made the effort, I'd apologised and taken whatever he threw at me. If he still wanted to carry that around, then he could be my fucking guest.

234

Chapter 43

Imy

I couldn't help myself. Those small actions weren't designed to slight Jay, I just could not allow myself to have any relationship with him. Not with what was on my mind.

I studied him, in the queue, his head bopping slightly along to his headphones. His movement felt out of rhythm, as though he was trying too hard to aim for nonchalance. He had his rucksack attached to his back, both straps, making him look like a kid on a school trip.

Jay returned to the table, coffee in hand, the bump in his walk a little forced. He shrugged his rucksack off and sat down opposite me, keeping his headphones on and reading my mood correctly. I saw him jab the volume repeatedly until the tinny obnoxious hip-hop racket escaped. If he was trying to annoy me, and I think he was, then it was working.

Jay's eyes fell on the throwaway mobile phone laid out in front of me on the table. He slipped his headphones off.

'That a burner?' He picked up the handset and examined it. 'Teddy give this to you?'

I nodded. 'It's got two numbers in the call register. Yours. And Lawrence's. When we've completed our mission—'

'Mission!' Jay snorted through his nose.

'Once it's done, I'll call it in.'

'Then what?'

'Whichever military unit is closest to our location will take over and detain Bin Jabbar.'

'Yeah, is that how it's going to play out?' Jay leaned back in his chair and drummed his fingers on the table. We both had a very different vision of how it was going to *play out*. 'How comes I didn't get a burner?' Jay asked.

'I'm the primary point of contact.'

'That why you'll be sitting in first class and I'll be stuck in coach? Quite tight with MI5, are we?' I didn't entertain that with a response. 'It's a shit phone, anyway,' Jay said, and handed the burner back to me. It buzzed in my hand.

'Lawrence?' Jay said, leaning over, trying to get a glimpse of the screen. I angled it away from him. "Course it's Lawrence,' Jay muttered. 'Who else is it gonna be?' He jabbed at his own phone. 'Why didn't I get a text? Why's he just texting you? Shouldn't we have, like, a WhatsApp group?'

I took a breath. His mouth just did not quit. He reminded me of how Jack could easily fill silence. But Jack had been five. Jay was a grown man. As I read the message from Lawrence, I realised it would be the last time I would make that comparison:

Do not get close to him.

There was no danger of that happening. I pocketed the phone as an announcement called for first-class passengers to board.

'Get some rest on the plane.' I stood up. 'I'll see you when we get there.'

Jay crossed his arms and shrugged at me in a *maybe you will, maybe you won't* manner. It was becoming increasingly clear to me that despite my age and experience, he wasn't there to follow. Jay would do whatever he felt was right and I had no doubt it was going to land him in trouble.

I made my way onto the plane. The next time I would see Jay would be in Islamabad.

Chapter 44

Jay

'I wasn't expecting to see you so soon,' Imy said, looking up at me from the luxury of his first-class cabin. 'What do you want?'

It was a valid question. As soon as the plane had taken off, adrenaline had rushed through me as though a spirit had taken over my body. My eyes fixed on the seat belt sign, waiting for it to dim. As soon as it did, I unbuckled and shot to my feet without a destination in mind. I was buzzing as I walked the aisle one way and then back the other, seeing the same air stewardess twice, compelling her to ask, 'Are you okay?'

I told her, 'I'm just stretching my legs.' Her expression said, *we've only been in the air for fifteen minutes!* I was a bag of nerves, a bundle of fucking energy, and I couldn't just sit in such a tight space for the next seven hours and forty minutes. I brushed past the stewardess and hustled my way to the toilet, and not for toilet reasons either. I needed to be alone for a minute, needed to calm the fuck down before the passengers noticed my behaviour and started to get para.

I closed the toilet door behind me. *It's happening! Fuck! It's happening!*

I placed my hands on the tiny sink, willing myself to be still. I looked at my reflection in the mirror, looking at myself through my dad's eyes. *What would he see? What would he say?* He'd be angry. Angry that I'd fucked his shit up. Thrown a whole fucking toolbox

237

in the works. Well, fuck that, and fuck him. I was a lot angrier that he couldn't be bothered to be a father.

I took a deep breath and followed it with a series of smaller ones, before splashing my face with cold water. I stepped out of the toilet. To the left and down the aisle was my crappy seat, and to the right was the little curtain that separated the riff-raff from the first class. It was drawn tightly. An impenetrable iron wall.

I went back to my seat.

My flying companion looked at me curiously, as though seeing me for the first time, and shifted to make room. I squeezed past him one way and rustled through my rucksack, picking out my shareable pack of M&Ms, and then squeezed past him the other way just as he had got comfortable. It cost me an eye roll.

Sorry, mate, I've got an iron wall to penetrate.

I popped my head around the curtain and peered in. It was glorious. I inhaled the smell of privilege and stepped through, letting the curtain fall behind me. I spotted the back of Imy's head and made my way through, walking like I belonged, past the passengers all stretched out and stress-free, giving it large with tall champagne flutes in hand. But this was Pakistani International Airways, and I knew these suckers were sipping on nothing stronger than apple juice.

'You shouldn't be here.'

'Yeah, no, I know.' I shoved the pack of M&Ms in front of his face. 'Want some?'

I knew he wouldn't be able to resist. He snaked his hand into the shareable packet and pulled out two green and one yellow. I glanced over my shoulder and clocked a stewardess taking my number. I smiled sunnily at her.

It felt weird standing over Imy, so I got down on my haunches and rested my arm against his arm rest. That felt weird too; I was too low and in danger of being hit by an oncoming food trolley.

'I was thinking, we haven't really chatted properly. I assumed we'd be sitting together so we could discuss, uh, strategy, but you're up here in first and I'm back in the nosebleeds.'

Imy squeezed his eyes shut, as if that would make me go away. I was aware that I was frustrating him, but, fuck, there had to be some sort of plan and structure. If he was thinking of bullshitting his way through, then what was the point of him being there? I could do that by myself.

Imy got to his feet and gestured for me to do the same. He stepped into the aisle and walked with me hot on his tail. He slipped through the curtain and held it for me to follow. We stood by the pressurised aircraft door. The temptation to pull down the handle was almost too much.

The same stewardess who'd had words with me earlier, eyed us from behind her food trolley. Two Pakis talking in hushed whispers on an aeroplane. I smiled at her. It wasn't as sunny as the last time, it was tighter, more of a *shame on you, I know what you're thinking, lady.*

'You have to calm down,' Imy said, but I could sense he wanted to say something altogether different.

'I'm calm,' I said, 'but—'

'But what, Jay!?' Imy spat, actually spat, spittle coming at me in numbers but falling short somewhere between us. 'There's nothing to discuss. When we land you follow my lead. Is that clear?'

Yeah, it's clear, it's fucking crystal! Imy was going to use me as he saw fit and as soon as he reached his target he'd probably discard me. Typical fucking MI5 move, and he was up their backside further than I'd realised. I should have taken my chances and done it solo; now I had MI5 casting a shadow over my every move.

Imy locked his stare on me, but fuck him if he thought I was going to back down. I held his gaze right back. I saw in his eyes the loss. I saw that he was still searching for someone to blame. And I was the closest he could find.

Chapter 45

Jay

The passengers stood up in unison and filled the aisles. I stayed seated, the long flight had zapped the adrenaline out of me. I looked out of the window. I was in no hurry to face whatever the fuck was waiting for me. I switched on my phone. Imy had texted me cold instructions, telling me to meet him at the pick-up point outside of the terminal. Would it hurt him to use a fucking emoji?

I kept my head down and made my way to border control, and handed my passport over to the officer in a bright white shirt and the most convincing comb-over I'd ever seen. He took his time, flitting between my passport photo and my face a few times. Fair enough, that picture had been taken at a bad time in my life, when the barbers that I usually went to in Hounslow West was unexpectedly closed, so I had to hit the Treaty Centre and pay more for a lesser cut. They'd butchered it! On top of which, I'd been going through a Tony Stark phase and as a result I was rocking the world's worst box beard. Fuck it. You live and learn.

'*Javid. Qasim.*' Comb-Over repeated my name slowly back at me.

'Yup,' I said, adding, 'That's me,' for good measure.

He ran a hand through his thinning hair as though he had a full head of it, before handing back my passport and sending me on my way with a crooked smile.

My Jordans squeaked on the large marble tiles as I crossed the lobby, following signs to baggage reclaim. I could already see the pink ribbon around my luggage moving proudly down the belt. I reached for it and before I knew it another pair of hands were on it, brown, weathered, and lifting it effortlessly off the belt.

'No, no, no,' I said to the porter, knowing that I had no money to tip him as I'd forgotten to exchange pounds into rupees, and there was no way I was dropping a fiver for something I could do myself. 'It's okay. It has wheels. I can take.' But he had already placed my trolley on his baggage cart and moved away at speed. I caught up with him, as he incorrectly picked up on my accent.

'American?' he said. 'Donald Trump?'

'No,' I replied. 'English.'

'English!' He grinned. 'Brexit?'

'Yeah,' I sighed. 'Brexit.'

He laughed to himself. 'Big problems, huh? Big problems for you?'

I didn't like that, his mocking laugh, as though some sort of imaginary *I told you so* for living in a country that wasn't mine. In England, if somebody badmouths Pakistan, I get pretty pissed, but now, the other way around, I found myself feeling equally offended. Pakistan was the motherland, but England was home.

I ignored him the rest of the way, feeling pretty justified after all that I wasn't going to tip him. I stepped out, my parka draped over my arm, not knowing what kind of temperature December would bring. I shrugged it on as soon as I stepped outside; it was colder and darker than I'd expected.

'What time is it?' I tapped at my wrist where a watch would be, and then immediately felt ignorant about the gesture.

'Eleven thirty in the night,' the porter replied in broken English that was a far sight better than my broken Urdu. He lifted my trolley off his cart and wheeled it towards me before hovering around for a tip. Despite my intentions, I dug deep and pulled out a scrunched-up fiver. I flattened it and handed it to him and he was away before I could thank him. I adjusted the time on my phone and scanned the area for Imy.

He was in the middle of an embrace with his contact. It looked genuine and warm and I couldn't help but wonder as to the extent of their relationship. I approached them just as they separated, and instantly I recognised him.

He hadn't changed one bit, he even wore the same fake, misspelt *adihash* T-shirt, and just like our previous meeting, the smell of skunk came off him in waves, making me long for a joint. I ran through a list of names in my head before landing on – 'Aslam!'

I wasn't expecting an embrace, but at the very least a handshake or some recognition. I put my hand out, Aslam reached past and took my trolley and rucksack, leaving me hanging. I styled it out and patted him on the back as he roughly threw my luggage into the back of his rusty-ass, open-top jeep.

'I know him,' I whispered to Imy. 'From when I was here last.'

I expected a reaction. Did it change anything? Probably not, but still, give me a fucking reaction.

'We've a long journey ahead of us,' Imy muttered, before turning away and planting himself in the front seat without calling shotgun.

I climbed into the back as Aslam secured the luggage. 'You and Aslam seem close.' When he didn't fill in the obvious blanks, I pressed, 'How'd you know each other?'

'We grew up together,' Imy said, quietly. I had to lean forward and pop my head between the front seats so I could hear him better. 'He was my neighbour. We were in the same class together.' I glanced at Aslam; he looked like he had ten years on Imy and a hundred years on me. 'Life's been tougher on him,' Imy said, hopping onto my thought train.

Aslam got into the driver's seat. He nodded and smiled fondly at Imy. Imy returned the gesture. Aslam started the car and set off with a jerk.

'So… What happened?' I prompted, before Imy shut down again.

'We were just kids when our village burnt down. Ghurfat-al-Mudarris took us in, provided us with shelter and food, and quickly put us to task. Those who were weak, those who mourned for their parents, were given menial duties.'

I sneaked another glance at Aslam. I wondered, if he'd understood English, would he have been offended? He just stared forward, on autopilot, his eyes red from whatever he'd smoked earlier. He slapped himself hard on his cheek as though a fly had landed on it.

'He's been a driver ever since he could reach the pedals. These roads are all he knows.'

'Did you not…' I stopped midsentence, knowing that my line of questioning could potentially see me on the back end of Imy's wrath. But he was on it. He turned his head slightly over his shoulder so he was meeting my eyes. I had the urge to lean back and away from him.

'Did I not mourn for my parents?'

'I didn't mean to… Forget I asked,' I said, backtracking. Some things were none of my business.

'I mourned for them every second of every day,' Imy answered, 'but it didn't break me.'

'It must have been hard,' I said. It was all I had, and it sounded as lame in the open as it had in my head. 'But, I guess, it made you hard,' I recovered.

For a moment he watched me, like a hawk watches a worm, or whatever a hawk fucking watches. He took a breath in through his nose and let it out again, before finally speaking.

'It made me determined.'

Chapter 46

At Benazir Bhutto Airport, Comb-Over checked the time on his watch on repeat. He desperately needed his mobile phone but it wasn't permitted on duty and was stored in his locker. His other option was to tell one of his colleagues about it – he wasn't the only one on their payroll – and they could easily pass on the message. But he needed it more, he needed the light to shine on him. He needed the money that would befall him as a reward. Five children, and a wife who refused to earn a living, wouldn't feed themselves.

He checked his watch again and then compared it to the time on the clock on his computer. It was five to midnight. Five more minutes before he finished his shift, and almost twenty-five minutes since he'd learnt of the news.

There was a queue forming in front of him. He went through the motions, giving passports a cursory check before letting them into the country. At two minutes to midnight, he rushed on his uniform blazer over the stripes of his uniform white shirt and slipped the locker key into his hand. He held onto it tightly, the teeth of the key biting into his palm, and counted down the last sixty seconds in his head, and then half-leaped out of his booth.

His head down, he paced across the terminal, into the staff room, ignoring the small talk coming his way from his colleagues. He jammed the key into his locker and removed his phone, switching it on immediately as he headed for the toilets. He checked underneath every stall as his phone picked up a signal, and then he located the number which he never believed he would have to dial. As it connected, Comb-Over ran through how he would spend his new-found fortune. A new Kawasaki bike seemed more appealing than replacing a weather-worn roof.

The 'Salaam, Brother' caught him off guard.

Comb-Over looked in the mirror above the sink and grinned victoriously to himself.

'He's here,' he said. 'Javid Qasim has just arrived in Islamabad.'

Chapter 47

Jay

It was half-five in the morning when we arrived at the training camp. I slipped both arms through the straps of my rucksack and picked up my trolley from the back seat before Aslam could get his heavy hands on it. Imy stood by my side. He cracked his neck by dipping his head from one shoulder to the other as together we took in the camp.

It seemed different, somehow. Smaller. The trees at the foot of the mountains that acted as a barrier around the camp were thinner, skeletal, almost hunched, as though standing sentry had finally tired them. The ground itself, once red earth, was dark, dank, covered in patches with sodden leaves. To my right was the entrance to where I had once stayed, a cavernous opening with a wooden rifle rack bolted into the rock. The rack was empty, and I suspected it had been for some time. This place that had broken so many souls now suffered the same fate.

I scanned the camp, looking for the man who was as big and as invincible as this camp had once been. An ex-American soldier who had broken ranks and switched sides to fight for his own people, rather than against them. His name was Mustafa Mirza.

Aslam placed a hand on the horn to signal our arrival. It was loud and offensive and because I was still standing so close to the jeep, it was right in my ear. I turned to Aslam; he grinned at me before running his tongue along the length of a rolling paper. *Yeah, you go get high, mate.*

A hammer of a hand clapped me on my shoulder. Any harder and, I swear, I would've dropped. My shoulder vibrated. I turned and came face to face with a green army T-shirt, tight against a ridiculous chest. I craned my neck up a degree and then a few degrees more, and smiled at Mustafa.

'You,' he said, his American twang apparent in that one word. And then again, '*You?*'

'Yep,' I said. 'Me.'

For the next ten seconds I was on a fairground ride. Squeezed tightly in his arms, being lifted off my feet and twirled around getting a blurred 360 of the camp, not quite knowing if this treatment was of friend or foe. He put me down gently.

Friend.

I found my feet and my head slowly stopped spinning. I could see Imy looking at me curiously. 'Me and him go way back,' I said, punching Mustafa gently on the arm, then worrying slightly about the retaliation.

He introduced himself to Imy with a handshake. 'My name is Mustafa Mirza,' he said, before turning to Aslam who had his bare feet up on of the steering wheel, a tight joint behind his ear, smiling like he was winning.

'Aslam,' Mustafa boomed. 'A breakfast of eggs fit for kings.'

Aslam stumbled away to prepare us breakfast. Mustafa turned back to me, placed his meaty hands back on my shoulders. He shook his head in near disbelief.

'Javid Qasim, as I live and breathe. The great pretender,' he smiled. 'Or the heir to the throne?'

Chapter 48

Imy

Aslam prepared breakfast. With Mustafa's blessing, Jay showed me around the site. It was clear that there was a closeness between him and the camp. A place where he had formed and broken friendships, a place where he had grown.

Jay was in control there. That was fine. As soon as I sensed him losing a grip on it, I'd take over.

He led me towards a deep-set opening within a rock formation. Outside of it sat an empty rifle rack. I sensed that with the current state of Ghurfat-al-Mudarris – defunct, both operationally and functionally – it would remain empty. This camp would no longer see the lethal successes it once had. There would be no more training of zealous young Muslims. Not without a leader.

In contrast to the strong sun, inside of the cave felt cold, and to the touch it was. An array of threadbare rugs overlapped each other on the floor. There were two openings, one to the left and one to the right.

Jay pointed to the left: 'That way is a tunnel, about thirty metres. Leads straight into Mustafa's cabin. You saw that, right?'

I had seen it. A decent-sized, well-constructed wooden cabin, that sat adjoined to the foot of the mountain. There was a huge clock attached externally, central to the structure above the front door, with five moveable markings to indicate prayer times. The next one would be *Zohar* prayers at 1 p.m. I'd make sure I wasn't around for it. There was nothing I had left to say to Allah.

'And to the right is our quarters.' Jay shrugged. 'You know, if we're staying. Are we staying?'

'Let's see.'

Jay spun right and I followed him into the room. A small generator was buzzing in the corner with a thick white cable trailing along the skirting and finishing between two sleeping bags where there was a single power point.

'Only the one point.' Jay wagged a finger at it. 'Best we charge our phones while we can.' He sat low on the sleeping bag and took out his charging cable from his rucksack. He slipped out his phone and connected it. He stayed sitting on the sleeping bag, for once at a loss for words – either that or he was lining up what was going to come through his mouth next. He pulled his knees in towards himself and rested his arms on them.

'Did you hear what Mustafa said?'

'I did.'

'*Heir to the throne!*' Jay whispered loudly at me. 'He knows that I'm *his* son. The fuck's he know that?'

I placed my bag down and sat on the sleeping bag opposite him. 'I don't know.'

'So, how do we play this?'

'Breakfast first. Eat whatever is put in front of you, we don't know when our next meal is coming.'

'I mean how we going to bring it up, you know, about Bin Jabbar?'

'Mustafa is sure to bring it up again. Any member of Ghurfat-al-Mudarris is incapable of going five minutes without bringing up their precious leader.' I instantly regretted saying it. I'd been so busy trying to rein in Jay and his mouth that I hadn't paid attention to what came out of mine. Despite Jay's intentions, it was clear to see that there was still a relationship between father and son, regardless of how dysfunctional that was. I had to tread more carefully. 'Let's freshen up. Once we're out there, follow my lead.'

Jay exhaled loudly, and followed it with a shrug. It was the closest he'd get to acquiescing.

There was no sense in instructing him any further; he didn't seem to have a character that took well to instructions. I stood up and removed my shirt and jeans.

Jay made a face and gestured with his head. 'There's a stall down there. If you wanna get changed.'

I unzipped my bag and took out a fresh shirt, half-sleeved, and cotton trousers, both off-white. I slipped them on as Jay took his eyes off me and busied himself. He reached for his trolley and opened it up. I caught a glimpse of its contents, unnecessary and unsuitable to say the least. I removed my shoes and socks and took out footwear chosen to suit the terrain.

'Crocs?!' Jay exclaimed, and for some reason laughed behind his fist. 'Oh, man.'

'They're more suited than those.' I nodded to his high tops.

'Sorry, I wasn't laughing at that. A friend of mine swears by them. Lives in them!' His smile was smaller now. '*Lived*.' He corrected himself before hissing to himself. 'Fucking past tense.'

'He's dead?'

'His name was Parvez. And, yeah, he's dead.'

I nodded. It was nothing that I didn't already know. Parvez had been another victim who was killed fighting for Ghurfat-al-Mudarris.

Jay got to his feet and met my eyes and for the first time I saw fire in them.

'No two ways about it, we have to find Bin Jabbar,' he said. 'That man has blood on his hands, and I'm going to make sure he fucking pays for it.'

Chapter 49

Jay

I wasn't about to strip and get changed in front of Imy like he'd just done. No thanks. I didn't want him casting judgement on my body, especially as my gym sessions over the last few months hadn't yet kicked in. Though, from the quick glimpse I clocked of his torso, I was surprised to see more than a little squish there. Didn't exactly inspire me with confidence. Thought he was supposed to be a badass! I expected muscle, a six-pack, at the very least a flat stomach, not a Dad-bod.

I got changed in the bathroom. Not a bathroom like you and I are accustomed to, let me tell you. It was a stall. Barely there swing-doors and a rubber pipe attached to a tap, used to wash, shower and clean your backside with. Don't even get me started on the hole-in-the-floor squat-toilet that was currently housing a couple of loved-up cockroaches. I slipped out of my clothes into something more suitable for the climate, balled up my England clothes, and got the fuck out of there as quick as I could.

Even from deep inside the mouth of the cave I could hear voices. They were muted, but I was still able to discern the boom in Mustafa's tone and the short measured responses from Imy. I checked that my phone was charged, and unplugged it before walking out. The heat embraced me like a second skin. Even in Pakistan, December shouldn't have been that warm, especially in the North amongst the rocks. I swear, if it ain't people killing each other, fucking nature is.

251

Mustafa and Imy had taken places on the floor and sat themselves cross-legged around a straw dastarkhwan mat. Aslam hovered around setting down plates filled with a form of egg that I didn't recognise. Armed with my bottle of Tabasco that I'd had the good foresight to pack, I walked towards them, clearing my throat loudly for no particular reason.

Imy's eyes travelled up, down, up and away again, and I knew immediately that he was judging the sailboats on my sky-blue Hawaiian shirt. *Oh, I'm sorry, I haven't got any dull clothes for the occasion.* I sat down opposite him, decked out in his stupid safari outfit, with Mustafa at the end in his usual green military T-shirt and combat pants. It looked like we'd all misjudged the theme on the party invite.

I saw Mustafa's arm swinging towards me, and tensed just in time to absorb the heavy clap on my back. He beamed at me. 'We were just talking about you?'

'Yeah,' I said, searching the mat, knowing full well that Aslam still hadn't been cutlery shopping since my last visit. I placed the Tabasco next to the bowl of bread and signalled a *help yourself* gesture.

'I was just telling Imran about your antics last year.'

'Weren't exactly antics though, were they?' I said.

Mustafa turned his attention to Imy. 'From the moment I laid eyes on young Qasim here, I must be honest, I had doubts.'

'Shouldn't judge,' I muttered, picking up a strand of egg and holding it up for close inspection. Just past it I could see Imy staring at me: *eat your food.* I split open a bread roll and carefully picked out any bits of egg that looked some way cooked, and laid them out into a sandwich, before dousing the crap out of it with Tabasco.

'He didn't share the same enthusiasm as his fellow comrades,' Mustafa continued. 'Switched off, I think is the best way to describe him.'

'In the zone is another way to describe it,' I said, mouth full; it wasn't all that bad.

'We have a training course eight kilometres that way.' Mustafa pointed into the distance. 'We would jog in the hottest part of the day, assault rifles strapped to our backs, with just enough water to teach them a thing or two about rationing. Javid here,' he laughed, 'drank half and emptied the other half over his head before we had reached the two K mark, and then he suffered the rest of the way, stopping and starting, moaning and groaning, slowing everyone down.'

Yeah. It's true. It happened. Fucking inhumane is what it was. I noticed Imy, with the smallest of smiles. He was enjoying this! I poured some grey water from the jug into my barely standing crumpled plastic cup. Then thought, I'd better do the same for the others.

'After the first few days,' Mustafa continued, 'it wasn't just me that had doubts. I could sense fear in the others. We were days away from unleashing hell in the heart of London. Plans had been cemented, weapons had been placed in hands. But... Questions were asked. Could Javid Qasim walk into a war shoulder to shoulder with his brothers? Could he be trusted?'

I'd just about had enough. I was ready to get to my feet and skulk away but it was exactly that attitude that these stories were made from. I kept my head down and stayed put, waiting for the next batch of tales, of which there were many. Instead, Imy spoke.

'That's not the Jay that I know.'

My head popped and my ears tuned in.

'Looking at him, I'd have to agree,' Imy said, looking at me. 'But past the mouth, the attitude and the inability to follow a simple instruction...'

Fuck, man, get to the good stuff.

'There's a directness to him, a determination. A drive which you'd be forgiven for missing when you first experience him.'

Experience him. Not sure what Imy meant by that, but I took it as a compliment.

Mustafa considered it with a creaky nod. He smiled and squeezed my shoulder as gently as he could. 'Who knew that this troublesome young man would turn out stronger than most? Braver! To this day it shames me that I had judged the boy who would one day lead us all. For through him runs the blood of Al-Mudarris.'

At a loss for words, and probably better that way, I turned to Imy. 'This,' Imy said, 'is common knowledge?'

'Go back twelve months, and things were very different,' Mustafa said. 'Ghurfat-al-Mudarris was known to the world by name and name alone. Our enemies, the authorities across the West, despite their so-called intelligence, their resources, and the obscene amount of money that they steal for a war of their own making, they were drowning in desperation. For many years our beloved Teacher was allowed to roam freely amongst his people, knowing never a word would escape their lips. Our training facilities and camps on both sides of the border remained hidden from Kafir eyes.'

Mustafa stopped. Took a breath. I opened my mouth but Imy shot me a look. Mustafa wasn't done.

'We had it all,' he continued. 'Prominent figures around the world. Imams, scholars, politicians in a position to cast influence on the young minds who had seen their *Deen* blackened, those who'd lost loved ones as the Kafir tore through their homes. They were shown that they had a God-given right to reply.'

A heavy silence followed.

Mustafa's eyes wandered past us and pensively around the camp that once was. I had no doubt that what was running through his mind wasn't far from what was running through mine.

254

The excitement, the anticipation, the laughter of those *young minds* who had once lit up this camp would never return. The rifle rack would remain empty. The assault course that had broken many, before building them back up, would no longer feel the stain of blood and sweat. Young angry Muslims would never again stand side by side five times a day and pray to Allah for strength to make their presence felt. Not here.

'So,' Imy asked. 'What happened?'

Me. I happened.

Chapter 50

Imy

It was a loaded question and I searched Mustafa for a reaction. I knew the truth. It was a buried truth and I needed to know if it was pushing up against the surface. Mustafa quietly considered the question.

'Secrets were revealed,' Mustafa replied, his soft voice at odds with his appearance. 'In an instant everything was over.'

'Somebody spoke?' I said, holding Mustafa's gaze, but I could see Jay shoot to his feet, before trying to disguise it by stretching noisily.

'I might get some shut-eye,' Jay said through a fake yawn.

'You can rest later,' I said, and with the slightest gesture of my head told him to sit back down. He held his position just enough to prove a point and then resumed his place.

Mustafa didn't seem to have noticed Jay's dramatics, or possibly he was used to them.

'Trust,' he said. 'The foundations of Ghurfat-al-Mudarris were built on trust. Its success. And its failure. Yes, somebody spoke.'

'Who?' I asked.

Jay fixed me with a glare, and I could almost hear the long list of profanities running through his head.

'It's known,' Mustafa replied. 'Just not to me.'

I nodded. Jay nodded. I could see the relief set in his face.

'However,' Mustafa continued. 'There were rumours. Many, many rumours. Young Qasim's name was mentioned.' Jay spluttered into his cup, coughed, water spilled down his chin. Mustafa gently rubbed his back. 'Easy there, Javid. Easy.' Jay wiped his face with the back of his arm. 'Your father, before he was forced into hiding. He called me.'

Jay swallowed.

Mustafa nodded. 'I remember it word for word. The man who I'd worshipped but never before met, the man who I would lay down my life for. Now all is lost, his voice, his words still carry me through. He… he thanked me for my work, my loyalty. I'll never forget it.' Mustafa jabbed at a tear from the corner of his eye. 'And then,' he said, 'he asked about you.'

'What did he want to know?' Jay asked, softly.

'Everything…'

Jay dropped his eyes, his finger tracing circles in the dirt.

'I told him about your progress, but he wanted more; how you interacted with others, if you ate properly, if you'd been comfortable in your quarters. No matter how much I gave him, he hungered for more.' Mustafa shook his head. 'Even before he told me, I knew then that this was not a leader asking after one of his own men. This was a father asking about his son.'

The conflict in Jay's face was clear to see, the blood of a man that he despised running through his veins and colouring his cheeks. He didn't have it in him to say another word.

'Did he say anything else?' I asked.

'He told me that there was a small faction waiting for him to go under. Men who he trusted, men who had lost faith in his ability to lead. Men who would try to divide Ghurfat-al-Mudarris and turn his followers against him with lies. I told him, I believe only in him.'

I tried to understand what had been said.

Bin Jabbar had played his final hand.

Mustafa gripped the back of Jay's neck and worked his fingers,

257

massaging him. Over Jay's shoulder Aslam appeared in the distance. I squinted as the bright sun around him gave him a filmic appearance. He moved in long strides, cutting the distance quickly. I smiled at my old friend; he returned it with a look of nothing in his eyes.

Aslam stepped onto the mat as though he hadn't seen it. His foot got caught on the bread bowl but that didn't slow him down. I uncrossed my legs from underneath me as he continued to trample over the mat, knocking over the flimsy plastic cups and spilling water until he was standing above Mustafa.

I was now on my haunches, I caught Jay's eyes and hoped he could read what were in mine. He understood enough and got to his feet and backed away just as Aslam pushed a knife into the side of Mustafa's throat.

'Go!' I screamed.

Jay took another step back, but no more. His eyes were transfixed on the knife embedded in the side of Mustafa's thick neck, as he scrabbled aimlessly, finding and popping the buttons off Aslam's shirt.

Aslam gripped the knife but struggled to remove it from Mustafa's throat. He used his spare hand to push Mustafa's head for leverage and, with force, pulled the bloody knife out. Mustafa's body fell forward heavily onto the mat.

Aslam turned to me and blinked; any recognition of the boy he'd grown up with was lost. He moved the knife from one hand to the other.

Jay sprang into action. Brave but clumsy. Running, picking up speed, head down and blind, he made contact with Aslam's lower back and wrapped his arms around his waist. It only served to push Aslam and the blade closer to me. I shifted to the right and swung, my fist aiming to meet his jaw but glancing off his chin. It was enough to stun him into a stumble. Jay was still grasping onto him. I didn't need his version of help. I needed him away.

'Let go of him!'

Jay released him and scrambled away. Aslam wildly lashed out with the knife at me. I let it come, let it whip close to my torso; it threw his balance. I sidestepped and swung again, this time connecting and cracking his jaw.

Chapter 51

Jay

'Move!'

Fuck, he didn't have to ask me a second time. I got to my feet and ran into the open space towards the eye of the sun and away from the hell of camp. I risked a look over my shoulder to my right. Imy had peeled off in another fucking direction! He was shouting something to me but my fucking heart was in my fucking ears. I figured it out when I saw Aslam's jeep in his path.

I stopped at a skid, and shifted direction, my Jordans better suited to a basketball court than the gravelly earth. Imy was in the driver's seat as I caught up with him. I thought about asking him to shift so I could drive. The man drives a Prius! Last thing we needed was considerate driving, but we didn't have the time to switch. I jumped in the passenger seat.

'Go!' I said, looking back at where we'd just run from. Mustafa was still dead! Aslam had regained consciousness and reminded himself that he was on a killing spree. He got to his feet and faced us. The sun reflecting off the knife in his hand. He started walking towards us before breaking into a sprint.

Imy had taken the ignition apart and was fucking about with the wiring.

'Quick, he's coming fast.'

Something sparked and the car exploded to life. 'Seatbelt,' Imy said, as he clicked his into place.

'Seriously?! Just fucking go!'

Imy clicked it into gear and put his foot down, the wheels screeched and spun on the uneven ground, before launching. On second thoughts, I pulled the seatbelt over me and took another glance behind. The wheel-spin had kicked up dust and I couldn't see shit but a dirty brownish swirl. I watched it carefully as it dissipated, and Aslam flew through the cloud, a mask of sheer determination on his face as his legs pounded and his arms pumped, gripping the knife like Usain Bolt gripped the baton in the last leg of the relay.

'He's on us, Imy!' I cried.

'It's okay. He can't catch us on foot,' Imy said, just as a shiny sharp object flew into the open-top jeep, clattering onto the dash in front of me and dropping into the footwell.

'Fuck!' I reached down by my feet, grabbed at the blood-stained, jagged-edged knife and threw it out as though it had a mind of its own.

'You should have held on to it,' Imy said.

'I know! I wasn't thinking.' I glanced in the wing mirror. Aslam appeared very small and appeared to have stopped. I imagined him shrugging to himself, before turning away and walking calmly back to the camp to roll himself another joint.

'Our luggage,' I said.

'Do you have your passport with you?'

I patted the hundreds of pockets of my combat shorts until I felt it. 'Yeah. You?'

Imy nodded. 'It's all we need.'

We drove aimlessly and in silence for around twenty minutes. Everything looked the same, just mountains and vast space every-where. Eventually we saw signs leading us to a main road towards the nearest town.

'Do you wanna have a go at explaining what the fuck just happened?'

After a beat, Imy replied. 'It's not Aslam's fault.'

'Think a jury of his peers would feel a little different, don't you?!'

'Best guess,' Imy said, 'is that between picking us up from the airport and attacking Mustafa, Aslam received a phone call. Simple instructions were delivered.'

'So, what, he's a mercenary now?'

'He's a cook. A cleaner. A driver. He's anything you ask of him. No questions asked. This was not personal. He doesn't do it for money. He does it for those who he's indebted to. Believe me, it's not his fault.'

'Yeah, you said.'

Did I buy it? I think I did. You play the cards you're dealt in life, and old Aslam had walked into a casino with plastic ducks and one shoe. I waited for Imy to fill me in. I felt that he'd caught up quicker than me.

'Your father—'

'Let's just stick with names, shall we?' I jumped in.

'After Bin Jabbar was captured, or presumed dead, whichever way you look at it, he was no longer in a position to lead. That position was handed to Sheikh Ali Ghulam—'

'The fuck who put a fatwa on me!' I put my hands up in apology and pursed my lips and gestured at him to carry on.

'Sheikh Ali Ghulam was the natural successor but his reign didn't last. There was an absence, a vacant position. The world's eyes were on Ghurfat-al-Mudarris, on their network. By any and every means the organisation became dysfunctional. It literally ceased to function. History has shown us, from the IRA to Al-Qaeda, when organisations of such magnitude cease to operate, splinter cells are formed. Objectives shift, as do the method of operations.'

'You're talking about Al-Muhaymin?'

Bestower of Faith – I recalled Omar banging on about them. It was only a matter of time before they made their presence known.

'Right.' Imy side-eyed me, a little surprised that I was up on my terrorist trivia.

'So you're saying Aslam took an order from Al-Muhaymin?'

'It's possible,' Imy said, stopping just short of confirming it.

I stopped myself from asking *why* and let it sink in as we saw our first sign of life.

Cars, locals, shops. A small but bustling working town. Imy followed signs to a car park and pulled up at the flimsy red and white plastic barrier. A short squat guard appeared at the jeep with a respectful, 'Salaam Saab.' Imy greeted him with a nod, and showed his two fingers to indicate the time we'd be staying before handing him a fistful of rupees. The guard lifted the barrier and went back to his newspaper. We wheeled into the quiet car park, passing spaces until we were near the back. Imy reversed into a spot where he had a view of the grounds and anyone approaching. He killed the engine.

I chewed the inside of my mouth, a worrying theory forming in my head. I looked across at Imy, wondering if I should share it, hoping, *really fucking hoping*, that if I voiced it Imy would pierce a thousand holes through it.

'Imy,' I said. He kept his eyes front and centre but grunted that he was listening. 'The order Aslam received from Al-Muhaymin. It wasn't to kill Mustafa, or you. You just happened to be in the way.'

Imy took his sweet time turning his head over his shoulder and face me. I knew then, but if I'm honest I think I always knew.

'The order was to kill me.'

*

263

After what had happened back at the camp, it was a risk to be seen in public, but our rumbling stomachs made the decision for us. We hadn't eaten since the flight, and breakfast had been rudely interrupted by a killing spree. Imy reasoned that we were far enough away from the camp, and in relative safety, but we still walked out of the car park not knowing what or who to expect.

The street was narrow and the traffic tight. A barrage of car horns and dated Bollywood music spilled out of a small radio hastily wired up to a large speaker from a stall selling bootleg CDs and DVDs. We walked silently past shop to shop and I could feel every eye on us. It didn't matter that our skin was on the same colour palette as everyone else's, locals could establish just from a glance that we were pretty far from home.

If you thought about it, I mean, really took the time to dwell on it, it could drive you nuts. At home, back in so-called *multicultural* London, we were looked at as if we didn't belong. Jump on a plane and visit your Motherland, and we were still looked at as if we didn't belong! That shit is pretty fucked-up: having no sense of belonging or proper identity or acceptance. Never really able to embrace home in places which *are* home. Maybe you get me, maybe you don't. Maybe now wasn't the time to think about it.

'What's wrong?' Imy asked. He was a perceptive one, I'll give him that.

'Nothing,' I said. 'Just, you know.'

'Yes, I know. Just keep your eyes to yourself and walk in a straight line until we find somewhere to eat,' Imy said.

'Everyone's looking at us,' I muttered.

'Your shirt,' Imy said. 'Couldn't you have worn something a little less conspicuous?'

'Says the man dressed like Safari Edition GI Joe. Couldn't you have worn something a little less bland?'

264

'I don't want to be noticed.'

'Well, you are. You look like you're on an expedition.'

He smiled, it graduated with honours into a small laugh through his nose. It was the first time I'd seen him express anything other than sadness, anger, or just plain annoyance. It was nice. It suited him. I still didn't trust him.

A couple of kids, about seven or eleven years old, I couldn't tell, decked out in traditional shalwar and kameez get-up, standing on opposite pavements with the road separating them. They were playing catch, looping a tennis ball back and forth over barely moving traffic. The boy on our side of the pavement clocked us and grinned, before shouting across the road to his friend in slang Urdu that I just about understood.

'Did you hear what that little shit just said?'

Imy shook his head. 'It's not my language.'

I translated. 'We're going to be walking back the way we came. Naked.'

'Ignore it,' Imy advised, and I was tempted to accidentally nudge him onto the road, if it hadn't been for the man watching us. He was leaning against a black and gold auto-rickshaw, a cigarette hanging from his lips, a phone to his ear.

'Four o clock,' I mumbled behind my hand.

'Put your hand down, Jay,' Imy hissed at me.

'By the rickshaw. Think he's watching us.'

'Along with everyone else. Don't make eye contact, just keep moving.'

We moved past a fabric shop, where a woman emerged victoriously. A defeated, bag-laden man, who could only have been her husband, tagged behind her. The same the world over. No threat detected. We passed a well-used outdoor Aga, where a heavy-set man punched his podgy fists into dough that smelt so fresh that

I could have consumed it in that form. '*Taza naan, Saab. Doh rupee.*' He called out to us and pointed to two rickety chairs either side of a rickety table.

I looked up at Imy in the hope that we could park here for a bit and enjoy fresh naan bread, heavy on butter, heavy on garlic.

'Too open,' he said, and stomped right past it.

'I didn't get a chance to change pounds into rupees,' I said, looking around for a bureau de change.

'You're not going to find anything here.'

'I'm gonna need some walking around money.'

'It's fine. I have enough money for the time being.'

'Can you drop me, like, twenty quid's worth, and I'll sort you out as soon as I hit a money exchange place?' I asked as I glanced back over my shoulder, and I swear it was like everyone – the two kids playing catch, the roti maker, the smoking rickshaw guy, the woman and her weary husband, *everyone* – had slowed down almost to a stop and were gawping at us.

I flinched as a motorbike ripped close past me. Imy grabbed my arm and pulled me closer to him. 'You're veering towards the road!'

'Sorry,' I apologised. 'How about here?' I pointed at what looked like a place that may sell a cuppa and a little something to eat. I walked through the open entrance, not giving Imy a chance to protest. I was too hungry, too thirsty, too fucking tired. I needed a time-out. I stood just inside the restaurant. It was spacious and clean and smelt like I wanted it to smell.

To the left was an elderly man. He sat alone, bare feet up on a chair, reading a book through a magnifying glass.

A curvy woman who – judging by her tight pink duppata-less kurta – seemed proud of her curves, smiled a welcome at us. She approached us from around the counter and swayed her hand over a table as if to say, *best table in the house.*

Imy slipped past me and took a seat and I sat opposite. A jug was placed on the table, filled with surprisingly clear water.

'*Shukria*,' I said, and she grinned at my effort to speak my own tongue, making me feel a little self-conscious. 'Can I get a… Amritsari paneer bhurji,' I said, looking up at the boarded menu. 'Doh parantha, and, uh, masala chai. Cheers.'

She turned to Imy. 'Same.' He grunted.

The old man with the magnifying glass watched her sway away through the magnifying glass, before winking at me through the magnifying glass! I turned away quickly and noticed Imy had placed a stack of rupees on the table.

'Walking around money,' he said.

'Thanks, I'll sort you out first chance I get,' I said, and just for a split-second, I pictured him as a friend and not an MI5 asset out to use me for their gains. That reassurance lasted as long as the blink of an eyelid, because I knew the man sitting in front of me was keeping secrets.

Chapter 52

Imy

I'd taken a seat across from Jay which faced the entrance, but the glass front to the restaurant had left us vulnerable. It wasn't the location I would have chosen.

Our host had disappeared through beaded strings and into the kitchen to prepare our meal. The old man on the opposite side got bored of us quickly and went back to his paperback. I could feel Jay watching me intently, and I could tell that he was looking to get into it.

'You knew all along?' he started, as soon as he caught my eye.

'Keep your voice down,' I hissed at him.

'Even before we set foot in Pakistan, you knew that my life was in danger.'

'No, I didn't know. Not for certain,' I replied and waited for the onslaught.

'Don't play me for a fool. You knew! And Teddy Lawrence knew! It wouldn't be the first time MI5 used me as worm.'

'Will you listen to yourself?' I said, trying to keep my voice neutral in an effort to pacify him. 'Nobody sent you here, Jay. You alone made the decision to come searching for your father.'

'His name! Use his name. *Bin Jabbar, Al-Mudarris, The Teacher,* whatever! Fuck, man, how many times do I have to tell you?'

There was no pacifying him. He was in full-on-Jay mode now.

I glanced at the old man, we again had his attention. I threw him a look and he dropped his head quickly. 'My point is,' I remained calm in the face of frustration, 'nobody forced you to be here.'

'It would have been a little fucking polite if somebody had given me a heads-up!'

'Would it have changed anything?' I asked.

Jay buttoned up. It wasn't a question to which an answer was deemed necessary. The desperation to see his father again was painfully obvious, matching only my desperation to find him. I looked through the beads leading to the kitchen in the hope that our waitress would emerge with our meal.

Jay leaned back in his chair, a touch calmer, and I had to make sure he damn well remained that way, but I could see behind his eyes a busy mind.

'Al-Muhaymin,' he said. 'They're out to get me. What d'you know about them?'

I hesitated, tried to think it through. How much did he need to know? If I divulged, what impact would it have in what we were trying to achieve? What *I* was trying to achieve?

'I know as much as you do,' I said, calmly.

A small smile played on his face and he nodded softly to himself as his eyes moved around the restaurant. I could read the signs. Jay was building himself up towards something, like a small ticking time bomb.

He pushed his seat back dramatically, the legs screeching against the lino. He shot to his feet and jabbed a straight finger close to my face. 'I promise you, I will walk out of this joint and do this shit on my own if you don't start talking.'

'Sit down, you're causing a scene,' I said, wanting to snap the finger pointed at me.

I didn't have to tell him a damn thing. I waited for him to sit the hell back down with his tail between his legs. With the attack on his life still fresh on his mind, Jay knew he wouldn't last a second without me.

He needed me.

'You think I'm playing?' he said, unrelenting, a foolish determination plastered across his face. 'You really wanna test me?'

I took a breath, and another, taking my time to read him. There was an unpredictability in him. Would he rather walk away, out of sheer stubbornness, than be kept in the dark? I couldn't take the risk.

I needed him, too.

'You've made your point,' I nodded. 'Sit down, I'll tell you what I know.'

'Yeah, do that!' he snapped, before taking his seat. 'Start with Al-Muhaymin.'

'They're small but quickly growing in numbers,' I started, keeping my voice low in the hope that he'd follow. 'But unlike their predecessors, they're reckless. Ghurfat-al-Mudarris went decades with little indication of their presence.'

'Reckless how?' Jay asked. To my relief he'd dropped his tone.

'GCHQ picked up communication, slow at first, trickling into a PR firm based in Copenhagen. Over the last few days there was a flurry of chatter to a pay-as-you-go phone in London. It all stopped the moment Bin Jabbar was located and rescued.'

'I know that,' Jay said. 'Al-Muhaymin are responsible for releasing him. Omar told me as much.'

'Right. Omar Bhukara. He's the one that initially made contact with you?'

'Yeah, he's the one who pulled me back into this fucking mess. What else you got?'

'You know as much as I do,' I said, which was near enough to the truth, or as close to it as I could give him.

270

'Alright, put that shit to one side for a minute. Tell me this.' Jay pressed a finger onto the table, his voice a rising whisper. 'Bin Jabbar told Mustafa who I am? Who else knows I'm the son of that son of a bitch?!'

'I think Bin Jabbar made sure that his people were aware,' I said. 'And I think you know why.'

Jay sat back in his chair, his shoulders slumping as realisation dawned on him. He stared at the empty space on the table between us and he quietly said, 'He's trying to protect me.'

It signalled a stillness in him.

Abdul bin Jabbar had handed his people the ultimate test.

I know what it's like to be a follower, the fierce loyalty, the unbridled passion, the belief that whatever Bin Jabbar feels, no question, you feel it too. It's by that token that Bin Jabbar had revealed that Javid Qasim was his son. It had bought him a degree of protection.

However, Al-Muhaymin were a different beast altogether. Though their love for Bin Jabbar was as passionate, they wouldn't be as forgiving. There was an anger, a hatred; they wanted to place the blame and they knew who to place it on. Jay had betrayed his Brothers to MI5, and brought about the end of Ghurfat-al-Mudarris.

'You didn't sleep on the plane, did you?' I asked.

Jay fixed me with a glare.

The waitress emerged through the beads, balancing two thaals filled with much-needed goodness. She rounded the counter, her eyes on Jay and Jay only. She placed the thaals on the table. I nodded my gratitude and Jay muttered his. The waitress nodded and smiled before walking across the floor to the frail old man.

'*Ooht*!' she snapped, asking him to get up. He took his time placing a bookmark into his paperback. The waitress impatiently snatched it off him and hoisted him up by the arm and marched him to the door. I don't think Jay noticed anything but the food in front of him.

I noticed, though. I noticed the way the waitress ushered the old man out in a hurry, the way she stood at the entrance and looked out onto the street over her shoulders before rushing back in our direction.

'Jay!' I whispered.

'What?'

'I think we should go.'

Before he could respond the waitress was bearing down on us, smiling sweetly at Jay. He returned the smile. It encouraged her to pull up a plastic chair and sit between us. She twisted so her back was to me, and she faced Jay.

'My English,' she said, holding up her thumb and forefinger into a pinch. 'Little bit.'

'My Urdu,' Jay said, holding up his thumb and forefinger into a pinch. 'Little bit, too.'

They grinned at each other at the breakthrough, while every instinct told me that we had to move now! I took out my burner phone from my pocket and under the table I composed a message sharing my location.

Chapter 53
Jay

'My name,' the waitress pointed to herself, 'Jameelah.' She looked over her shoulder at Imy, who couldn't have made it more obvious that he was *secretly* texting under the table. She turned back to me and carefully, *very* carefully said, 'Your name Javid... Qasim?'

Without thought and without paying attention to Imy's stare, I gave her a small nod. A tear ran smoothly down her face and her smile was that of someone who would never see me come to harm. 'Mashallah,' she said, as she measured her next words. 'You talk very loud.'

I couldn't help but laugh. She joined in. Imy decided to remain stony-faced.

'Your father...' she said, and the laughter came to an abrupt stop. 'A great man.'

I had one question, and it was the natural one, and I said it quickly before Imy tried to intervene. 'Do you know where he is?'

Jameelah searched her limited vocabulary. 'On TV... They say he died.' She shook her head like she meant it. 'But we don't believe.'

'No, not dead. Alive,' I said. 'He escaped,' I said, making cartoon running action with my fingers. 'I'm trying to find him.'

Jameelah placed a hand on top of mine. 'Some say Ghurfat-al-Mudarris finish,' she said, 'because you.'

Imy had put his phone away, and I could feel his leg hammering under the table. '*Jay!*'

I ignored him, and gave Jameelah some space. Despite what she'd said, my hand in hers didn't feel trapped. With her other hand she tore a piece of parantha from off my plate, expertly scooped up some paneer, and brought it up to my mouth.

Imy glanced at my plate before fixing me a look and a small shake of the head, as though the Amritsari paneer bhurji had suddenly grown horns. Jameelah smiled sweetly, her hand still hovering in front of my face. I thought of the last time Mum had fed me like that.

I opened my mouth.

She placed a perfect-sized bite, with the perfect parantha to paneer ratio, into my mouth.

'I… don't believe. People… here… don't believe.' Jameelah placed a finger under her eye. 'But dangerous for you, beta.'

'Someone is watching me?'

'Yes. Watching,' she said. 'Angry with you. Open!'

I opened my mouth and she fed me another bite.

Imy was on his feet, he walked to the entrance and had a good old nosey outside, before rushing back to the table. 'We have to move.' He took out more rupees than necessary and slapped them on the table.

'What is it?' I said, through a mouthful, another bite already lined up.

'People are gathering.'

I looked towards the entrance, and yeah, people were gathering, all wide-eyed and broad smiles, hands and faces pressed against the glass. But they didn't try to enter the restaurant. I felt their hesitance as much as their curiosity.

'You are safe here, Javid. They not hurt you. They are… looking only.'

The crowd was growing, the two kids who we had passed, tiptoed, craning their necks, trying to get a peek in. Traffic had come to

274

a standstill, people stopping, getting out of their cars and climbing on the roofs.

Word had ripped through this town.

These people knew who I was, and who I was meant something to them.

'Thank you, Jameelah,' Imy said, looking anything but grateful. He gripped my arm and helped me to my feet. 'Is there a back way out of here?'

'They not hurt you, Javid,' Jameelah repeated.

I caught myself considering it: *How it would feel to walk out and into their arms*. They didn't see my dad as a monster. He had once made them feel safe, when the rest of the world meant them harm. He gave them hope. And now that he was gone, did I? *Did I give them hope?*

I moved towards them.

And, I swear, it felt as though they all took a step back as though it was too much for them.

Imy was on me again, pulling me back, his hand vice-tight on my arm. I turned to him and I read in his face what he wanted to say.

Don't be stupid, Jay.

I wrenched my arm away and rubbed it. I got it! My actions, playing spy, bringing down Ghurfat-al-Mudarris, there was a big fat fucking 'kick me' sign on my back. Yeah, I got it! But my dad, fucking monster that he was, played his hand, his last move, one that was designed to test the *love*, the *trust*, of those who worshipped him.

He had revealed that *I* was his son.

And despite everything that came before, despite all that I had done, it all came down to one thing.

To hurt me was to hurt him.

Chapter 54

Imy

As soon as Jay set foot into this country, I had no doubt that it would not go unnoticed, but this, I wasn't expecting. I could feel the sheer energy, the powerful pull, and Jay, dumbfounded, wanted to be amongst it, to feel the overwhelming love that these strangers felt for him. It was clear what Bin Jabbar meant to these people. A man who had sacrificed his own family, his own life to devote himself to his people. To ensure that they were able to stand on their own two feet and fight back. He showed them glimpses of victory when defeat was, and still remained, inevitable. I know this. I was taught this.

But *history* has taught us, repeatedly, no one man can receive absolute adulation. There is, without fail, somebody ready to go against you.

I had to get Jay away from there, from them.

'Jameelah,' I said, 'is there a back way out?'

'Through kitchen,' she said, hurriedly packing the food away in a tinfoil container.

'Come on, Jay, we have to move,' I said, with one eye on the entrance. A man was slowly but surely shouldering his way through the mass of bodies.

Jameelah handed Jay the container, and gently cupped his face. 'Eat!' she said. 'Be strong.'

Jay nodded, his Adam's apple bobbed. I could feel him getting emotional, and I knew if I pushed him, he would dig his heels. I placed a hand gently on his shoulder and guided him away from Jameelah as the crowd watched our every move.

We rounded the counter and slipped through the string beads into the small kitchen. There was a splintered wooden door at the end. I took a breath, not knowing what was on the other side. 'Wait here,' I said, pushing open the door and stepping carefully out.

It was an alley about a metre and a half wide, but it felt tighter, with bin bags buzzing with flies lined up against the backs of the shops. Running parallel was a six-foot grey brick wall. I stood on my toes and looked over. Beyond was a vast crop field. We could scale the wall with ease and we'd have plenty of room to manoeuvre, but we'd be an easy target.

I checked the burner. Live location was still active; I watched the red dot move slowly towards the blue dot that represented us.

'What you waiting for?' I heard Jay over my shoulder. 'Which way?'

'West,' I said, stepping out.

'Which way's that?'

'Left. You go first, I'm behind you. Walk. Calmly. Do not run.'

We moved in single file. His mouth was going but I couldn't hear him, but from snatches of what he was saying, it didn't seem like anything of note. I looked back over my shoulder. A man had appeared at the far end of the alley behind us. He stood stationary, watching as he smoked a cigarette.

'A little faster,' I said.

The man finished his smoke and threw it down onto the ground and stamped his sandal on it before walking away out of sight. I faced forward, forty, forty-five metres to go. Another glance at my phone, the red dot was getting closer.

Jay shook his head. 'Did *not* see that coming? Those people…
They knew who I am. Unbelievable! One of them must know where
Bin Jabbar is being kept? We should have asked? I think we should
go back and ask?'

I heard the splutter of a motor behind me, the push and pull of
a throttle.

'No. Keep moving.'

'I think it's the wrong move,' Jay said. 'Like Jameelah was saying,
we're not in any danger. Not here. They could help us… What's
that noise?'

I glanced back over my shoulder as the growl of an engine grew
louder, a small front wheel turned slowly into the mouth of the alley,
followed by a rusty black and gold body. The man behind the handlebars
lit up a fresh cigarette and took a deep pull and let out a cloud of smoke.
And through that smoke the auto-rickshaw came hurtling towards us.

'Go!' I pushed Jay. The tinfoil container slipped out of his hand,
and he instinctively stopped to pick it up. His eyes were wide as he
noticed the rickshaw moving towards us. 'Run!'

The alleyway was tight, and the sides of the rickshaw scraped
against the walls slowing it down a little, but not much. My eyes
moved for a weapon, a stick, a rock, anything, but everything was
flashing by me at speed. I reached an arm out and dropped anything
that wasn't clamped down, mainly bin bags, a stack of dirty pots and
pans and a jahroo brush hanging off a hook. I risked another glance
back. The rickshaw had adjusted to the narrow path, it was dead
straight now and picking up speed as it blew away the obstacles I'd
placed in its path.

Jay wasn't moving quick enough, his ridiculous heavy footwear
slowing him down. I pulled up a little so that my feet wouldn't hit
the backs of his ankles. Over his head, I could see the end of the alley,
no more than twenty metres away, and then an opening to the left.

278

A red Honda hatchback reversed into the alley, effectively cutting off our path.

Jay skidded to a halt. 'Fuck!' he screamed. 'We're boxed in.'

I screamed back at him, *'Keep going!'* I brushed past him, bunching his shirt in my fist and dragging him behind me.

In front of us a tall man calmly stepped out of the car. He shielded his face by looking over his right shoulder, and walked away out of sight, leaving the car door open and the engine running.

Chapter 55

Jay

Man, I never thought I'd be so happy to see a Honda!

It took me a second or two to work out that whilst I was tending to my hungry stomach, Imy had been tending to business. As Jameelah hand-fed me parantha and Amritsari paneer bhurji, Imy had sorted us out a getaway. We were metres from escaping from the auto-rickshaw-assassin.

Imy had moved past me. He was quick, quicker than me. My Jordans were weighing me the fuck down; maybe there's something to be said about Crocs after all. The gap between us grew bigger and it crossed my mind: *Once Imy reached the idling Honda, would he wait for me or leave me behind?* He'd already made it clear I was the weakest link, maybe he'd sussed he'd be better off without me. Fuck, this wasn't the time to be having doubts. I pumped my arms harder, closing the gap a little, the chainsaw growl of the rickshaw felt like it was down my fucking throat.

Imy slowed down a touch and slipped through the open car door and into the driver's seat. The way the hatchback was parked, there wasn't physically any room for me to go around. So, without breaking stride, I lived out a childhood fantasy by sliding across the warm bonnet and landing flush on the other side. *Fucking rush!* Imy had already reached across and opened my door, and I felt stupid for having thought that he might abandon me. I leaped in head-first.

Imy glanced over his shoulder; I glanced over his shoulder. The fucking kamikaze rickshaw was showing no signs of slowing down. 'Go!' I screamed.

Imy dropped the car into gear, but the rickshaw was on us. We had barely moved when we felt the impact, the rickshaw smashing into the side of the car. Our little hatchback rocked and wavered and stalled. Imy turned the key, and despite appearances the Honda roared back to life before shooting forward.

Imy ripped a right, expecting to floor it and leave the town behind us, instead he was forced to slam his foot heavily on the brakes.

'Shit!'

I'd never before heard Imy swear; it sounded strange coming from his mouth, but something stranger was happening outside my window.

The crowd had gathered directly in front of us, and they moved in a pack towards us, around us, until they swallowed the car whole.

With the press of a button, Imy central-locked the car. He searched the rear-view mirror for the auto-rickshaw driver, but there was no way he was going to catch sight of him through the sheer mass of bodies.

The car started to rock, gently. Hands pressed against the glass, faces peering in. I moved from face to face to face to face. Nervous smiles and looks of bewilderment and disbelief stared back at me, as though committing me to memory. I acknowledged them with a small smile and watched their smiles grow. It was all too fucking much. My hand reached for the window control.

'Don't do it, Jay,' Imy warned.

I pressed the button.

'*Jay!*'

Too late. The window was sliding down; the noise entered the car like a fucking force field, drowning out Imy's protests.

I took a breath and reached out. My hand was touched, held, squeezed and kissed. It was a love that I'd never before experienced and it led me to desperately cry out, *'My father? Do you know where he is? Anyone? Bin Jabbar! Al-Mudarris! Do you know where I can find him? I have to find my father. Can you help me find him?'*

What came back to me was a growing chorus of *'Al-Mudarris Zindabad! Al-Mudarris Zindabad!'* – translation along the lines of, *long live Al-Mudarris, long live the revolution.* They chanted it over and over again, increasing in volume, turning my stomach inside fucking out as they chanted my father's name.

Imy slid my window back up, the glass edge knocking my arm and forcing me to pull my hand back in. He slipped the car into first gear and kept his hand on the horn as he edged slowly forward. The crowd started to part leaving us a long stretch of road in front of us.

I turned in my seat, and looked through the back window. They held their arms aloft, pumping their fists, their chants still reaching and ringing in my head. I kept watching and watching until I couldn't see them anymore, couldn't hear them anymore.

*

I felt warm, as though a giant blanket had been wrapped tightly around me. Imy hadn't spoken in a while. I hadn't. I don't know what was going through his mind and, honestly, I didn't care.

It was after maybe thirty minutes or so of hitting the road at speed, that he finally broke his silence.

'We have to be more careful,' he said, evenly and eventually.

All that time stewing and that's the best he could come up with.

'I know,' I replied, just as unimpressively.

'There's a lot of love for you here, because…' He cleared his throat. 'Because of who you are. But you have to understand, it's blind love.'

'That supposed to mean?' I said, with a little unintended bite. I didn't like where this conversation was headed, but I knew it was one we had to have.

'They want to believe in you,' Imy continued. 'They need to believe in you. Here you're not Jay, here you're Javid Qasim, the son of the man they worship. They cannot see past that.'

'But not everyone feels that way.' I stated the obvious and what was obviously on his mind. 'That's what you're saying, yeah, Imy? You don't think I fucking know this, you don't think I've noticed that the last two times I've sat down to eat, someone has tried to fucking kill me?'

'We have to be careful,' Imy said, again.

Ahead a motorbike cruised at a steady speed towards us. The rider wasn't wearing a helmet, but he was wearing a leather jacket and reflective shades. His swept-back, thick black hair didn't budge in the wind. A woman sat pillion and held him tightly, her fingers spread over his chest, her head resting on his broad shoulders. Normally, I'd think: *good on you, mate, you go be a fucking freshy hero*, and not give it another thought. But normal hadn't been in my life for a long fucking time.

I tensed; I could feel Imy next to me tense.

The bike growled past us without as much as a glance. I checked the side mirror, Imy eyed the rear. Both expecting something but getting nothing. They disappeared into the distance and it was becoming increasingly obvious that every minute of our stay here would be dripping in paranoia.

'Are you hungry?' Imy asked.

'Nah,' I said, 'kinda lost my appetite.'

'Maybe some sleep then?'

'Yeah,' I nodded. 'I wouldn't mind some shut-eye.'

'Sleep. We're not stopping for a while.'

'Destination?'

'Far from here.'

I kicked off my Jordans, pulled the seat right the way back and reclined. 'We'll swap shifts,' I yawned. 'Wake me up in about thirty and then you can get some sleep and I'll drive.'

'That won't be necessary,' Imy said.

'Nah, half-hour, it's all I need. I'll set a mental alarm.'

Imy nodded. 'Okay. You sleep now.'

And I did. It came easy. The gentle glide of the Honda spiralling down a windy sloped road, wrapped around a cold grey mountain, easing me into a comfortable slumber. One without dreams. One without nightmares. Just black! My mind as tired as my body, too tired to form any pictures.

Chapter 56
Imy

The Honda hatchback was as much as I had expected. Sturdy enough, reliable enough, and a tank full of gas. It had always been in our vicinity, never more than five kilometres away, and always at my disposal. The driver was the MI5 asset who had taxied me on my mission in Berlin, and provided me with the cyanide to assassinate the high value target of Al-Muhaymin. I hadn't yet checked what package was provided to me this time; my immediate objective was to put some miles between us and those who wished Jay harm.

My long-term objective was to put Jay right in the middle of it.

I looked across at him, curled up in a ball, his back to me and his faced pressed up again the inside of the car door. So much for his thirty-minute mental alarm. I had been behind the wheel for two hours, and with the destination that I had in mind, there were at least another four to drive.

Jay showed no signs of waking up, his back rising and falling gently, and I knew that it would take intervention for him to wake. I let him be. For now. Part of me was glad that I didn't have to put up with any more inane chatter, whilst another part wanted to nudge him awake and let him fill the air, as that very same nonsense chatter would help pass the time.

A destination fixed in my mind, I headed east, cutting through the outskirts from town to town until the population and the roads became light. Each car, each face, posed a potential threat, and I kept moving until I found somewhere relatively safe to stop for a break.

I was curious as to what package had been left for me.

I saw faded street signs for Jinnah Medical College, a place that, if you looked very carefully, was mentioned in the news about two years ago. I turned into the grounds. As expected, the car park was empty. As expected, the wide six-storey structure was abandoned. Another victim of war in a place where the next generation were trying to make the world a better place.

I parked facing the building and let the car idle for a moment and stared at the college. The lower storey was perfectly intact and still standing proud despite the collapsed upper left wing. The casualty count was just a number.

Beyond the structure were overgrown, unkempt green fields which once boasted sports facilities including a hockey pitch and a running track. Over the other side of the field was a road crossing which led to a bus station. Behind the bus station was a small operational Ghurfat-al-Mudarris compound.

That had been the target. The target had been met.

The bus station, the medical college, the innocent lives, were all chalked up as collateral damage.

I turned off the ignition and stepped out of the car, glass and debris crunching under my shoes. I took a breath and stretched. Bending forward and touching my toes, feeling my spine stretch, then crack. I straightened and twisted my torso from side to side, counting a full minute in my head before walking around to the rear of the car and flipping open the trunk.

The interior light lazily came on. Neatly to one side there was a mid-size plastic Tupperware container. I pried open the lid. It was filled with mixed nuts and dried fruit. I took a handful before placing the container on the roof of the car. From the trunk I unzipped a red and black square cooler bag. Inside were six 500ml chilled bottles of water. I took one out and took a long overdue sip. I took another bottle for Jay and placed both on the roof beside the nuts. In the side compartment there was a first aid kit, a torch and a digital compass.

I lifted the inlay. There was no spare tyre, in its place was a large Go-Bag, camouflaged in the universal army pattern. Two flat zipped pouches at the front and two at the rear. I pulled the long zip in the main compartment. Secured neatly inside was a high-powered semi-automatic Browning handgun. Taking up the main was a tactical mat, a bean bag, a brown camouflage rifle cover, and a pair of radio receivers, all neatly piled on top of a Remington MSR sniper rifle.

I browsed through the front pouches. Matches, a tourniquet, lighter fuel, supplies that may be of use.

I pulled the zip across the Go-Bag and let the inlay drop over it. I closed the door of the trunk carefully, so as not to wake up Jay, and made an overdue phone call.

It was answered quickly.

'Jinnah Medical College.' As expected, Teddy Lawrence was tracking our movement. 'Any significance?'

'Apart from the two military drones that destroyed the school?' I said. 'No. No significance. It's just somewhere quiet to stop.'

'The school wasn't the bloody target and it wasn't us. It was the Americans,' Lawrence mumbled. 'Do you really want to get into this now, Imran?'

I looked across at the devastated structure and tried to picture how it once stood. 'No,' I said.

'Progress?'

'Twice there's been an attempt on Jay's life. Twice, we've managed to escape. Just.'

'Christ, you've been there for just over twenty-four hours!'

'His presence has been noticed. But it's... strange.'

'What? What's strange, Imran?' Lawrence prompted impatiently, and I wasn't sure exactly how to explain.

'The reaction,' I said. 'The people here, the majority, they have an affection for him. Actually… it's more than that: they have faith. They look upon him as though he's the second coming.'

'Two attempts on his life tells me something altogether different, Imran.'

'They were isolated incidents. As soon as Jay set foot in this country, word reached far and wide. Orders were rushed, the attempts on his life were reckless. Characteristic in the way Al-Muhaymin operate. But if we are careful, here in the North, he is relatively safe.'

I didn't go further. I had planted the seed. The instruction had to come from Lawrence.

'You're going to have to cross the border,' Lawrence said. 'You have to be in the place where people don't feel that way.'

It's what I expected. I had second-guessed him to the point where I was already en-route to the Angoor-Ada border. Once that line was crossed there would be no turning back. We would be deep in Ghurfat-al-Mudarris territory, where the splinter cell Al-Muhaymin had taken control. If they were able to place eyes at Islamabad Airport to flag the arrival of Javid Qasim, then, no question, they would have eyes at the border. Al-Muhaymin would not be as appeasing as the people of North Pakistan.

'And Imran,' Lawrence said, 'the world believes Bin Jabbar is dead. I'd like to keep it that way.'

*

Three vehicles bristled in front of us. Our small hatchback was noticeable, crammed tightly between freight trucks and lorries. We had no right or business to be there, and none of the required documentation. Not for the first time, I scoped the surroundings. Two men, dark, hot and agitated, stood patrol under the blue banner that read, *Goodbye Pakistan. Have a safe journey.*

The open-bed truck in front, carrying fresh fish in netted crates, moved. I slipped the car into gear and moved one step closer.

To the right, set back, six armed US troops stood evenly spaced out by the barbed fencing. A provision to aid against the possible spill of terrorism from the uprising Al-Muhaymin. The angry blare of a horn from behind indicated that the truck in front of me had moved again. It caught the attention of the armed troops. Attention that I didn't need.

I moved forward.

The truck in front reached the checkpoint, documents and passports switched hands followed by a search of the bed of the truck. My mind wandered to the contents of our car.

The truck moved past the blue banner and crossed the border.

I loosened my grip on the steering wheel and moved to the checkpoint and slid down the window.

'Passport!' A pin-thin man wearing aviators barked at me. I handed it to him and he took a moment to consider the UK passport. He flicked to the back and compared face to photo before handing it back to me. He looked past me, at Jay, who was still curled up with his back to me. 'Passport!' he barked again, and I knew if he wanted to he could back it up with a bite. I handed him Jay's passport. 'Face!'

I nodded and pulled Jay by his shoulder flopping him across onto his back so his face was in view. He stirred, squirmed and let out a frustrated *mmm* sound, but he didn't wake. If the guard requested papers detailing our business, then we were stuck there. If the guard decided to inspect the trunk, then we were stuck there.

The car was in gear and alive, my foot on the brake. I could wait for a decision but if it was the wrong one then we'd remain on the wrong side of the border. That wasn't an option. All I had to do was lift my foot off the brake and place it hard on the accelerator and cross without consent and to hell with the consequences. I looked past the guard's shoulder, at the US troops, and quickly realised that the consequences would catch up with me all too easily.

The guard flicked to the back of Jay's passport and spent longer scrutinising it than he had mine, his eyebrows knotted and deep lines appearing in his forehead.

I willed myself to breathe calmly through my nose as I focused on my distorted reflection in his aviators. His eyes flitted from Jay to passport and then back to Jay. A drop of sweat rolled down his forehead and disappeared under his sunglasses.

Jay sprung back onto his side, facing away from us again.

The guard nodded to himself and handed back the passport.

Decision made. He tapped the roof of the car.

I lifted my foot off the brake and crossed over the Angoor-Ada border and into Afghanistan.

Chapter 57

Jay

I opened my eyes and blinked several times until the blurred vision came into focus. I was in beige hell. I stayed put for a minute, as the rest of my body caught up with me being awake. From the back of my throat I made loud inappropriate waking-up noises, as I stretched an arm above my head and peeled my forehead away from the cheap beige plastic door interior.

I lifted my head just enough to peer through the window and squinted as daylight hit me. All I could see were browns and greens and greys. The cluster of tall mountains in Khyber Pakhtunkhwa had been replaced by a cluster of untended pine trees standing on unkempt overgrowth.

'Where are we?' I said, through a yawn which bounced back off the glass and attacked me.

Imy said nothing.

'Imy?' I unfolded my legs, my feet finding the floor. I shifted in my seat to face him. Again, Imy said nothing because Imy wasn't fucking there!

'Shit!' I shot up in my seat, fully awake and alert. I patted the pockets of my shorts and pulled out my phone. I checked the phone signal: no bars presented themselves. '*Shit! Shit! Shit!*' Something, not very nice, entered the pit of my stomach and lifted the hairs on the back of my neck. *The fuck has he gone? The fuck has he left me in the middle of nowhere?* I had to stay put, no way was I wandering through the forest. There could be grizzly bears or killer snakes out there. I hit the central locking button and the locks hammered down, sending an echo through the car.

In the centre console there was a box full of nuts. I made a face, but desperate times, desperate measures. I had to keep my energy up. I placed the box on my lap, and with eyes furtive, I rifled through the nuts, chucking a bunch in my mouth, noticing, too late, that there was dried fruit in there, too.

Fucking insult to injury!

Wanting to get rid of the taste, I reached for the bottle of water sitting in the cup holder, checked the seal was intact before breaking it open and downing it. There were still bits of nuts and fruit in my mouth, a mixture of soft and hard, all floating about in a gulp of water. I swallowed. Something had to stick, and it did. Halfway down my throat. I started to choke.

I dug my fingernails into the dashboard and forced myself to cough, to puke, but it wouldn't come, just a dirty dry heave. I dropped my head down in between my knees, maybe gravity would sort me out. I could see my Jordans parked neatly in the footwell. I couldn't die, not like this, not like a fucking eejit, on some nut and dried fucking fruit choking accident, not in my socks.

The locks flew open with a jolt scaring the shit out of me. The door flung open and the smell of nature and shit entered the car making me gag further. A hand gripped my shoulder.

I turned my head to see Imy on his haunches looking at me, nowhere near as concerned as he should have been. 'Breathe,' he said, rubbing my back. 'In through your nose, slowly, and out through your mouth, slowly.' I did. In through my nose and out through my mouth. 'Some water,' he said, calmly. 'Small sips.' I did. Small sips. I swallowed, cleanly. 'Okay?' he asked.

I nodded fast, and kept taking breaths until I could speak.

'I choked on the nuts. There was dried fruit in there. Think it caught me by surprise.'

Imy nodded. 'Looks like you were having a panic attack.'

'Where were you? I woke up and you...' I didn't finish the sentence as I was in danger of sounding like a sap. I noticed carrier bags by his feet. 'Did you... did you go shopping?'

'I went to get supplies. I left you a note.'

My eyes searched the interior in an effort to prove him wrong. 'Where?' I spotted a white corner of paper wedged between the driver's seat and the centre console. 'You couldn't find a better place to put it?'

'I left it on the dash,' Imy replied. 'You must have knocked it.'

'I think I would've noticed,' I countered with conviction, knowing that I probably did knock it during my episode. 'I can't believe you left me by myself and went shopping,' I said, not yet ready to let it go. 'What if somebody came for me? What then?' I waved the note at him. 'Am I supposed to origami some sort of weapon out of this?'

'I couldn't risk taking you with me, not after last time. You're well hidden here.'

'How far are the shops?' I asked.

'About seven kilometres.'

'*English*, Imy?'

'About five miles.'

I unfolded the note and read it out loud to myself.

'*Gone to get supplies at 2.30 p.m. Will return by 3.30 p.m.*'

Imy glanced at his watch. I glanced at his watch. 3.20 p.m. He raised his eyebrows at me as though I should be fucking impressed with his timekeeping. When I didn't acknowledge it he only went and took a dig at my timekeeping.

'What happened to your thirty-minute mental alarm?' He smiled. 'You've been asleep for almost six hours.'

'Oh, I'm sorry, two attempts on my life tired me out a little. Is that… Is that alright with you?'

Imy considered that for a moment, then said, 'You should have slept on the plane.'

'Don't. Seriously.'

He turned away and rooted through the carrier bags. I slipped on and laced my Jordans and stepped out onto uneven ground. Imy had placed two foil containers on the hood of the car. I walked over to inspect them and immediately the rich masala aroma attacked my senses and made my mouth water. I swallowed in anticipation and licked my lips.

'I played it safe,' Imy said. 'One is chicken, the other, lamb. Do you have a preference?'

'I'll get on better with lamb. Unless…'

'That's fine.' He handed me a plastic fork. 'I'm good with chicken.'

Imy pried off the cardboard lids to reveal yellow rice topped with a thick sauce and a generous helping of meat.

'Oh, man. Lamb Biryani,' I said, as I bent over the makeshift table, elbows planted on the bonnet and went to town on it. I didn't say a word. Imy didn't. We just munched hard with a soundtrack of birds rustling through the trees and appreciative murmurs, mainly from me, until every grain of rice had been consumed. I even went one step further and scooped up any remnants of masala with my finger. 'That hit the spot!' I said in my review, before knocking back the bottle of water. 'Did you get more water?' I asked, as an afterthought.

'We have plenty.'

I leaned back against the car and looked at the dense forest in front of me and asked a long overdue question. 'So where we at?'

'The nearest town is Sharana.'

'Never heard of it,' I burped.

Imy hesitated for a moment, before saying. 'Come with me. I'll show you something.'

'Nah,' I said, holding my stomach. 'Can't move. I'm seriously full up.'

'It's not far,' Imy said. 'The walk will help you digest the food.'

Imy led as we walked through trees that all looked pretty much the same to me, but he seemed to know his way around those parts. I kept my eyes frosty for any signs of wildlife and made sure I stayed no more than an arm's length behind Imy in case I had to use him as a shield.

'Any bears around these parts?' I asked.

'Yes. Lots.'

'Fuck, Imy, this ain't the best time for you to develop a sense of humour.'

'No. No bears,' he said, reverting back to form.

Something had happened whilst I was asleep. Imy was in a better mood, more open. Was he warming to me? I mean, I wouldn't have been surprised. Whatever it was, I didn't want to address it in case it spiralled him back to a non-communicative state.

We continued to crunch on whatever was beneath our feet: twigs, branches, stingy nettles, crap like that biting at my bare ankles. In the far distance a road came into view. Imy stopped and crouched down by a tree. 'Get down.'

My knees clicked as I got down on my haunches with a view over his shoulder. Imy dipped into his pocket and pulled out a... I don't know, it was too small to be a telescope. He put it to his eye. 'What's that?' I asked.

'Spotting scope,' he replied, gently adjusting the dial around it.

I nodded, knowingly. 'Sik! Where'd you get it?'

'From the trunk of the car. It's an attachment.'

'Yeah? What's it supposed to attach to?'

'A sniper rifle.'

'We got a sniper rifle in the back of that crappy Honda?' I whispered loudly in his ear.

He moved his head away. 'Yes, amongst other supplies.'

Imy handed me the… Shit, I'd already forgotten what it was called. I put it to my eye. It felt proper cool. 'What am I looking at?' I said, as a banged-up, seemingly abandoned car with a dirty mattress strapped to the roof came into view.

'We are currently on the outskirts of Sharana,' Imy said. 'You see that old car?'

'Yeah, Toyota. I see it.'

'Okay, if you follow the dirt track to the east, it meets the main road.'

East? *Never Eat Shredded Wheat.* I moved my head to the right.

'At the end of the main road,' Imy continued, 'there's a junction about a mile down.'

'Yeah, I can see. That's a mile down? Man, this thing is powerful!'

'If you take a left, a few miles down is a market.'

'That's where you've just come from. And to the right?' I was so in awe of how powerful this thing was, and trying to figure out if I could somehow swipe it and take it home with me, that it took me a moment to realise that Imy hadn't answered.

I removed the piece from my eye and asked the back of his head, 'Imy, what's to the right?'

Softly he replied, 'Home.'

Ah, shit. No wonder he'd loosened up. We were close to where he grew up. I couldn't imagine what was going through his mind. Bittersweet, I guess. A place which once held happy memories, before those memories were burnt down to the ground. I wanted to put my hand on his shoulder, or rub small circles into his back. The situation called for a sympathetic move, but I couldn't do it because a fucking realisation was slapping me across the face.

I bounced up from off my haunches. 'Are we in fucking *Afghanistan*?'

He wrenched me back down by my arm. 'Get down,' he hissed. 'And keep your voice down.'

'You crossed the border. You didn't think about running it past me? The fuck, Imy, you can't treat me like a fucking passenger.'

'You were asleep.'

'Yeah, asleep. I wasn't in a fucking coma!'

Imy stood up. 'Back to the car. We'll talk there!'

'No, I want to talk now!' I said, not giving it up that easily, but he was on the move, stomping away quickly. I followed close behind in fear of getting lost in the fucking woods. My mouth going off without permission from my brain. 'I still had business in Pakistan. I know people there. You can't just fucking drag me on a trip down memory lane on a whim.'

My foot bumped into his heel. I looked up to see that Imy had stopped. That he'd turned around. I instinctively took a step back and he took one forward, I could see clearly the outline of his jaw. His face snarling in mine.

I should've been sensitive to the situation, considering what this place meant to him, but fuck, my point was valid. Crossing the border without my consent and without discussing it with me was a first-class dick move. Maybe he was pissed off. Well, I was, too.

I stopped cowering, straightened up and stood my fucking ground.

He spent a moment destroying me with his gaze. I waited for a verbal, physical or emotional attack. It didn't come. Behind his anger he knew I was bang to rights.

I kept my mouth firmly shut on the way back to the car and I kept my distance.

*

The Honda sat in the same place where we had left it. I leaned against the door. Imy slowly circled the car.

'What're you doing?' I said, but I didn't think he was in any mood to chat to me just yet. I watched him carefully, his eyes focused on the ground. I think he was looking to see if any of the growth had been trodden on whilst we had stepped away. I would never have thought of that. He went one step further by getting down on his hands and knees and looking under the car, for a tracker, I assume, or explosives.

Once again I silently questioned my motive for being there, and once again I justified them.

Imy opened the driver's side door and sat inside and stared longingly out of the windscreen. I jumped in next to him. 'So what now?'

'We wait until the cover of night before we move,' he said, all mysteriously.

'Where exactly?' I asked, leaving no room for him to spring any more surprises.

'There are five Ghurfat-al-Mudarris safe houses all located close to the border. One of the safe houses is located close to a weapons storage facility. If Bin Jabbar is being protected by Al-Muhaymin, then he's being kept in one of those. If I had to take a guess—'

'It would be the one near the weapons facility,' I filled in. 'So they're armed in case someone comes knocking.'

Imy nodded. 'That's right.'

I nodded right along. I knew there was more to it, but I didn't want to voice it just yet.

I checked the time on my phone. I figured we had an hour or so to kill before darkness, and I knew exactly how to kill it.

From the thigh pocket of my cargo shorts I pulled out a pouch of rolling tobacco. I lifted the flap and tucked inside the opening was a Bic lighter, rolling paper and a small bag of weed.

He gave me a curious look, before sussing it out.

'Aslam,' he said.

'I had a nosey around his glove compartment,' I said. 'Found his stash. Thought I'd pocket it. Serves him right for trying to kill me!' I shrugged and held up the small bag of skunk. 'What you saying? Wanna blaze?'

Chapter 58

Imy

I think it was being so close to home. I felt the temptation to just dwell in my surroundings and reach out to those sweet memories before it was all taken away in the blink of a child's eye.

Jay toffee twisted the top of the joint and handed it to me. 'Normally, it's wrapper's privilege to spark up,' he said, 'but, on this occasion, this being your home town and all, I'ma let you go ahead.'

It came from guilt, I know, but it needn't have. Being so close to home, I had overreacted, expected Jay to understand. Why? Who was he to me, to my past?

I took the joint and nodded my appreciation at the tight wrap before biting off the end and spitting it out of the window. I placed it between my lips and Jay flicked the lighter and sparked it.

'Good?' he asked, as I held it deep in my lungs.

'Yes,' I coughed out a broken cloud. 'Good. Strong.'

Jay switched the car stereo on and fiddled around with the functions. 'Bluetooth!' He shook his head in disbelief. 'This car is constantly surprising me.'

I took another pull, the effects instant as I slouched down a little in my seat. Jay was busy connecting his phone to the car stereo. 'Some music?'

I nodded. The joint switched hands. Someone rapping softly about needing love filled the car.

'LL Cool J,' Jay said.

'I don't know who or what that is?'

'It's a tune, is what it is.' Jay turned up the volume, slid down in his seat and drowned in the music.

I let him get on with it as I tried to compartmentalise why I was there and what the place meant to me. I was home. Or as close to home as I thought I could manage. Those secluded woods remained acutely familiar to me. A place where my friends and I, at the age of eight and nine, would steal our fathers' tobacco and rolling leaves and escape into these very woods until we were sick from chewing sweet paan. We'd return home red-tongued and guilty, expecting punishment in the form of the back end of a slipper. It never happened. Our parents knew what we were getting up to, and with the increasing fear of Taliban presence in our small village, they were happy to turn a blind eye to us escaping to the relative safety of the forest. What our parents didn't fathom was that it would be Ghurfat-al-Mudarris, and not the Taliban, that would turn their children into orphans.

'Give me that joint.'

Jay handed it over. I took a long drag and held it in until my lungs felt like they were going to burst. I let it out in a neat plume through my nose. Aslam's gear kicked in quicker than anything I'd smoked in Hounslow, the flow was smoother and the high was intense, adding to the already surreal situation – and if it wasn't surreal enough, I was sharing a joint with someone who I'd once tried to assassinate.

I glanced across at him, his eyes still closed, his head moving gently through a heavy cloud of smoke as he mouthed the lyrics. I noticed the phone display in his hand, the song was called 'I Need Love' and the playlist was titled *Sophia's Mix Tape*. The song faded out and another song, along the same lines of young love, started.

301

'All I Need' by somebody called Method Man. A small smile played on his face.

'You've got someone?'

Jay turned to me. The high had hit, judging by the red in the whites of his eyes. 'Nah,' he said, but his smile said otherwise. 'Not really.'

'What's her name?'

'Sophia,' Jay replied, unable to stop his smile from blooming.

It made me sad for him. Sad that the path he was set on could only lead to loss. I couldn't tell him that, though. If somebody had told me, when I'd first met Stephanie, there's no way I would have listened to reason. You live in hope, no matter how little.

I didn't say anything more, wishing that I hadn't brought it up. Jay still carried a lazy smile on his face, and I knew that wouldn't be the end of it. He sat up in his seat and turned to face me.

'We ain't, like, *together* together! But... I think there's something there. *Something!* I can feel it. The way she looks at me, *trust me*, I've clocked it and she knows I've clocked it. My Jay-dar is *on* and *popping*, you know what I'm saying?'

I knew that Jay was peaking when he winked at me before jabbering on.

'Let me tell you, she is trouble, I swear, proper trouble. Capital T! Actually, no, the whole word in caps lock! Like large flashing font lit up Vegas-style! I don't mind, though. Like for like, yeah?' Jay's smile froze and then quickly disappeared, replaced by mild panic. 'Oh, shit, oh fuck, oh man! I'm sorry.'

'Don't be.' I didn't have to ask. I knew exactly what he was sorry for.

'*So fucking insensitive!*' he mumbled. 'Why didn't you just tell me to shut the fuck up?'

'It's fine.'

Too late, the guilt had kicked in and the high carried it on a wave. He fiddled with his phone and quickly put an end to the song, concluding wrongly that listening to a bullshit love song would be too painful for me. I opened my mouth to tell him otherwise, but he was clumsily jabbing at his phone, exiting out of *Sophia's Mix Tape* playlist, and searching frantically for something more suitable to fill the silence that now sat awkwardly between us.

'There!' he said, as he put on something harder, full of profanities and violence. 'That's better.'

I handed him back the joint. 'Finish it.' He took it off me and spent the next few minutes smoking it silently down to the butt. He flicked it out of the window and turned to me with red eyes and his mouth open. I was already dreading what he was going to say next.

With tumbling words he said, 'For what it's worth, and I know it's not worth shit, *I know that, I do*, but, honestly, truly, I'm *so* sorry about...' Jay squeezed his eyes shut.

'Stephanie.'

'Yes! Stephanie.' Jay's face reddened. 'And, uh...'

'Jack.'

'Jack, yeah, I know, Stephanie and Jack.'

I turned away from him and through the windscreen I focused hard on a spot, trying so hard to control my emotions, but it was difficult as Jay was tapping me repeatedly on my shoulder.

'Imy?' *Tap, tap, tap.* 'Imy?'

'What is it?'

'You do believe me, yeah?'

'Believe what?'

'That I'm... I'm really sorry, about... '

'You're not very good at this, are you?'

Jay slumped down in his seat and out of frustration whacked his knuckle on the plastic dash. Contrary to how I was feeling – possibly it was a combination of the high and Jay's clumsy attempt at con-dolences – but out of nowhere, trapped somewhere deep inside me, escaped a laugh.

'The fuck, man?' Jay shook his head. 'What's so funny?'

'I think the two of you would have got on.'

'Me and Stephanie?' He beamed at me. 'You think so?'

I suppressed a smile.

'Oh, you mean me and Jack?'

I burst out laughing again. Hard, harder, harder than I had done in a very long time, and over the barrelling sound I could hear Jay joining in, filling the small confines of the car and escaping through the windows and echoing amongst the trees, just as it had once done many years ago.

Afterwards, we both sat quietly for a moment or so, carrying the afterglow on our faces. It was the first time that I'd thought about Stephanie and Jack and been grateful for what I'd had, rather than raging at what I'd lost.

'We cool?' Jay asked.

'I want you to know something, Jay.'

'Yeah. What?'

'If I'd stopped and thought about the consequences of sparing you,' I said, 'no question, I would have killed you in a heartbeat. I want you to remember that.'

Chapter 59

Jay

Fuck! Talk about ruining the moment. That bombshell sobered me up and put me in my place all at once. Before I could respond, Imy stepped out and disappeared amongst the trees, leaving me alone, his words still ringing in my head.

It wasn't exactly a bombshell, though, was it? In hindsight, of course he would have put a bullet through me. I mean, obviously I wouldn't have been pleased about it, but, honestly, I think I would have taken it.

Family first.

It meant something to him and it fucking meant something to me.

I'd been pretty pissed that Imy had dragged me across the border into Afghanistan, but I was starting to understand the reason. It was apparent that Bin Jabbar's many loyal followers in the North of Pakistan would open their arms and their homes and lay down their lives for him. But they were just that, they were his followers. They weren't his men. There's a difference, I think. His followers hang on his every word as though the man was a prophet, and if Bin Jabbar says *'that kid is my blood'* then I was starting to believe that apart from the odd crackpot, I would've stayed pretty safe in North Pakistan.

Afghanistan, though, that's a whole different ballgame. The men are more than followers, they believe wholly in a cause, one that I royally put a hole in. Regardless of who I was, or my relationship with their leader, they would be a lot less forgiving. By the same token, if anyone was protecting Bin Jabbar, it'd be his men and not his followers. So yeah, right now Afghanistan seemed like the place to be. But it wasn't going to play out like Imy had planned.

I stepped out of the Honda, stretching and yawning, ridding myself of the last of the haze. The lamb curry that I'd devoured was making itself known in all sorts of forms. I rubbed my stomach and thought about dropping one in the woods. I even went as far as to establish a bunch of soft green leaves I could use for the clean-up process, before checking myself. *There's no way I'm doing that.* I wondered if that's what Imy was up to, and made a mental note not to shake his hand or offer up a high five any time soon, not that Imy was the high five type.

It was good to see him laugh, though, open up a little. I'm pretty sure there was no one left in his life that he could talk to. If he wanted to, I would step into that role. It was the least, the very fucking minimum I could do.

I waited for Imy to return, and with next to nothing to do I aimlessly walked around the little hatchback Honda, checking out its little biscuit wheels and rust on the rear arch. I tried not to turn my nose up at it, after all it had saved my life, but seriously, MI5 really scraped the bottom of the barrel for this little number.

I approached the rear and located the latch for the boot and flipped it open. Inside there was a red cooler bag, which, upon closer inspection, stored chilled bottles of water. Beside the cooler bag, in the side compartment, was a torch. I switched it on. It worked. I switched it off. I picked up a compass and watched the hand fly around until it landed on South. Not sure what that told me, so I put it back. And finally, there was a first aid kit containing first aid shit.

Bored already, I sighed and looked over the roof of the car, hoping Imy had finished contemplating his life. I thought about calling out to him, but decided to give him a little break from me. I slipped out my phone, hoping for a signal, but fuck all presented itself back at me. I placed my phone on the roof of the car and continued to look around the largely empty boot space.

There was a small handle to lift the inlay. I pulled it up carefully to reveal a pretty serious looking holdall decked out in army colours. I remembered what Imy had said about the eye scope thing, that it was an attachment to a sniper rifle. This I had to check out. With both hands I lifted the heavy bag out of the boot and placed it on the ground. Kneeling down next to it my hand reached for the zip, just as my phone decided to come to life in the form of a series of short beeps.

As is the way of the world, I abandoned whatever I was doing to check my phone. Three bars had appeared, and I had three missed Facetime calls from Idris, and three text messages.

Two of the text messages were from Sophia. The other number I didn't recognise.

I read Sophia's message first with a feeling in my chest that could only be described as fuzzy.

Sophia
FYI, I told Lawrence everything I know. Truth and nothing but the truth your honour. Hoping no jail but am under protection until all gets sorted out. S x

It was good news at a time where I could've done with some good news. As feisty as Sophia made out to be, I didn't think she would fare well in jail. It wasn't all good news though: *until it all gets sorted* meant that MI5, or whoever the fuck was tasked with the job of bringing Omar and Tommy in, were still chasing their tails. It was a concern for Sophia and, bigger picture, it was a concern for everyone else.

I read and reread the message, trying to suss out the meaning of the *x* at the end of the message. Back when I was dealing, I had a customer that would end his messages with an *x*, and I was pretty sure he didn't have feelings for me. It's just a way people sign off these days. I'm sure that was the case here; it was probably just how she signed off all her messages. I was ready to brush off any significance of the *x*, and then I read the second message from Sophia.

Sophia
Another FYI, I'm thinking about you. S x

It's like she knew that the *x* in the original message would perplex me, and felt the need to clarify matters. That fuzzy feeling that was hovering around my heart was now climbing up my back and working its way up my neck. I flexed my fingers and thrashed out a reply. It sounded crap. I deleted it and composed another. Again, crap. Delete. I did this a few times before deciding to keep it real.

Jay
Xx

It felt good. I felt good. I had something to look forward to. Something away from this hell. She'd be trouble, no question, but I could handle trouble. Trouble was fast becoming a companion.

I wondered if she'd spend Christmas Day with me.

When all was said and done, maybe I'd pop into duty free and buy her a Christmas present, maybe a bottle of perfume. Ah, man, *perfume*, that's so lame. Maybe a cheesy Christmas jumper. She'd like that. I could picture her wearing it. Though wasn't that the kind of thing you got after you'd been with someone for some time? I'd figure it out. I read her text again and smiled to myself.

Yeah, I'd figure it out.

In the meantime there was still a message from an unknown number that sat unread. I tapped it open and read it once and then read it again, really fucking slowly.

+93 070 234 7855
You are in grave danger. Return home immediately. A friend.

I heard the rustle of leaves and then the crack of twigs, and Imy was at my shoulder. His eyes on the message. Without a second thought, or even a first, I jabbed at the number and slapped the phone against my ear. Before the line could connect, Imy snatched the phone away from me.

'Give my phone back,' I said with my hand out.

'Can we talk about this for a minute?' Imy said.

'Like we chatted about crossing the border? Give my fucking phone back!' I reached for my phone and like a dick he lifted it out of my reach.

'Calm down, Jay. Talk to me.'

Calm had left the building and Outrage had rocked up in its place. I pushed him, the heels of my hands slamming against his chest. He didn't so much as budge, so I dug my back foot into the ground for leverage and pushed him harder. He stumbled a step back and before I could revel in the smallest of satisfactions, that cold look in his eyes had returned.

Imy pushed back.

It knocked the wind out of me and dropped me to my backside. He stood over me and I steeled myself for a kick in the ribs, instead he lobbed my phone towards me and I flinched as it landed by my head.

Typical Imy, non-fucking-descript, the drop of emotion that he'd displayed earlier in the car had disappeared, as if he'd rebooted himself. He shook his head. 'It's not the right move,' he said.

'You don't know that. Let's call back and at least find out who it is. That's all I'm saying.'

'We stick to the plan.'

'You mean to travel down to the safe house guarded by Al-Muhaymin, that fucking plan? You think we're going to spot Bin Jabbar out front watering the fucking plants? No, I tell you what's going to happen: you're gonna dangle me like a carrot in the middle of Al-Muhaymin territory.'

'That's not true,' Imy said, and I couldn't determine if he was telling me the truth because of his lack of fucking emotion. I wasn't taking the risk.

'I'm tired of being a fucking carrot!'

I unlocked my phone with intent, expecting him to intervene again. When he didn't, the stubbornness left me and uncertainty filled me. I read the message, again.

+93 070 234 7855

You are in grave danger. Return home immediately. A friend.

'You think it's a setup, like, reverse psychology?' I said, feeling a lot less confident.

'I think, on this side of the border, you have no friends. It could possibly be a trap.'

I turned the phone over in my hand, my mind ticking over as I chewed the insides of my mouth. Imy and Lawrence had a plan from the off, and to some extent it was working. My name was flagged, first at Islamabad Airport, and then at the border. The only hiccup in their plan was that the rumour of my involvement in taking down Ghurfat-al-Mudarris seemed to be widespread. It was more than a hiccup, it was a full-blown vomit. Knowing Lawrence, and knowing how his devious mind worked, he was going to use it to his advantage.

I wasn't having that. I wasn't playing their fucking game. I made the call.

The phone connected and I put it on speaker. A man answered.

'Javid.'

I licked my lips. 'Who is this?'

'Go home. Please do not call this number again.'

I sensed that a disconnect was on the cards. I spoke quickly, unable to hide the anguish in my voice. 'I... I need your help. I have to find my father.'

There was a moment of stretched silence, followed by a sigh. He wanted to say more, I know he did! Imy leaned in closer, our heads almost touching, our eyes meeting.

'Goodbye, Javid,' the man said, leaving me with dead air.

Imy and I separated. He said something disparaging like '*I told you so*', or some shit, but I'd tuned him out. Because the man's voice, it had thrown me.

I was expecting a regional accent, but what came through in those few words was unmistakably middle class British. Clipped and educated the expensive way; somebody who had chosen to use that education to further a cause.

'I know him,' I mumbled quietly to myself, before letting it out. 'I know him!'

'What?' Imy replied frostily.

'I think his name is Latif.'

'You think?'

'It's definitely Latif. I met him last year, here, in Afghanistan. I travelled with him and my dad.'

'He's Ghurfat-al-Mudarris?'

'Fully pledged, paid-up member. Logistics, I think. He dealt with the finer detail of the operation. Always carried an iPad with him.' It was coming back to me quickly, years of smoking weed not having any lasting effect on my memory. 'But he's more than that. They're close, Latif and my dad, like brothers, he's his...' I clicked my fingers as I searched for the word. 'Confidant! His fucking confidant. He knows things that no one else knows... Maybe I *do* have a friend here.'

Imy leaned back against the car and looked up at the sky. I followed his gaze, the sun had done a runner, and it felt cold and grey and depressing. I looked across at Imy in the hope that I could convince him to consider our options, given this new information. I think he sensed it and walked away in that brusque manner of his before I could speak.

He rounded the car and noticed the army bag that I'd taken out of the boot and placed on the ground. 'You don't go anywhere near this bag!' he chided, before mumbling to himself.

I ignored him. I could no longer allow him to dictate to me.

I let myself back in the car.

Imy busied himself packing the bag of supplies back into the boot, and slamming it shut to prove a point. He joined me a moment later, no doubt ready to give me the high and mighty. He looked across at me, and then at the phone in my hand.

I smiled at him. It was sheepish at best.

'Jay?' Imy said. 'What have you done?'

'I've sent Latif our location,' I said, without hesitation.

'You fool!' he said tiredly and without bite. I think he knew I wasn't going to let this go.

I shrugged. 'It's done now.'

'Latif made his position clear. He doesn't want to speak with you, let alone see you. What makes you think he'll turn up?'

'Because,' I said, 'I'm the son of Abdul Bin Jabbar.'

Chapter 60

Imy

I could feel the realisation within him. The change. I noticed the way he started referring to Bin Jabbar as his father, and himself as his son. It meant something. It meant his emotions were hitting the surface. I didn't need him emotional, I needed a clear head.

He should never have texted Latif our location.

That was the one place that we should have kept to ourselves, somewhere secluded to retreat to. It would have been safer to drive to the nearest village in Sharana and arrange to meet Latif there, somewhere less exposed with fewer points of entry.

I left Jay in the car, with the car keys and the task to charge both our phones. I gave him a radio receiver and a crash course on how to use it. I made my way to wait for Latif a couple of hundred yards from the dirt road, where I had the height advantage.

Partially covered by a tree I watched the road through the spotting scope. I'd left the sniper rifle secured in the car. If Latif was indeed a friend, as his communications suggested, there would be no need for it. But I wouldn't know that until I'd met him and taken measure. If it turned out that Latif anticipated this, and we were walking into a trap, then I had with me the Browning.

I checked on Jay every thirty minutes.

'All good?'

'Yeah, all good.' His voice, surrounded by static, came back through the two-way. 'The phones are fully charged. Anything from your end? Over!' Jay insisted on playing at soldiers. I didn't indulge.

'Nothing as yet.'

'It's so dark,' Jay said. 'Can't see shit outside the window, or in the car. It's pitch fucking black! There could be a family of four sitting in the back seat and I wouldn't know. Over!'

'Do not turn on the interior light. Or use your phone. Any light will attract attention.'

'Like I don't know that! How about you, can you make anything out in this light? Over!'

I could. The spotting scope was equipped with night vision and thermal imaging and at that moment I was watching a dark saloon moving shakily along the uneven dirt track. It was the first car I had seen in the two hours that I'd been there. Despite the narrow track, the car moved at speed, bumping and veering and I couldn't get a clear view of the driver. However, the thermal imaging helped me identify that there was only the driver present.

'Yo, Imy, you still there? Over.'

'I see a car. Wait.'

'Shit! Is it Latif? Over!'

'I don't know. Stand by.'

'Stand by for what? Over!'

I turned the volume down on the two-way as I continued to track the saloon. I expected it to slow down and park at the foot of the forest, but it continued along, its acceleration constant as the dirt track met the main road. It then slowed smoothly and stopped at the junction. I focused in on the driver.

I turned the volume back up on the two-way. 'What does Latif look like?'

'A few years older than me. Short, slim, think he wears round glasses. Looks like a librarian.'

Without indicating, the car turned left but didn't continue in that direction, instead it looped around until it was facing back the way it came. This time it moved slowly and the driver was bending his neck towards the forest. The car stopped directly below me. The driver turned off the headlights.

'Is it Latif?' Jay asked. 'Over.'

The interior light came on as the car door opened. The man stepped out and stretched his neck as he looked up towards the forest. Long frizzy hair escaped from underneath a brown Pashtun hat and framed his hard face. Around his mouth was a neatly trimmed goatee beard. Jay had said Latif was short; this man wasn't tall, but tall enough not to be labelled short. He wore traditional shalwar kameez and draped over his shoulder was a gun strap. This wasn't Latif. Whoever it was removed the gun from the strap and held it low by his leg and started to climb the hill leading to the forest.

'It's not him,' I said. 'But I think he's sent somebody.' A barrage of foul language came through the two-way radio. I tried not to allow the tension in Jay's voice to feed mine. 'Listen to me very carefully. To get to you, he has to get past me, and I've got him in my sights. But I want you get yourself in the driver's seat, start the car and keep it running. I'm shutting down communication now. There's no need for panic. I'll be there soon.'

Chapter 61
Jay

Jesus fucking Christ! I jabbed at the central locking button on the dash, the thud of the locks echoing down as I scrambled over to the driver's seat, my knee knocking painfully into the handbrake in the process. *Motherfuck!* I landed awkwardly on the driver's seat with my butt to the steering wheel. I manoeuvred around and dropped my legs into the footwell and my feet came reassuringly into contact with the pedals.

I stared at the Honda logo on the steering wheel. I swear it was mocking me. I jammed a hand into the side pocket of my shorts searching for the car fob. My hand came back empty. *Okay, breathe! Stay the fuck calm!* I checked the other side pocket, same result. *Not now, please!* I still had two pockets at the back and two thigh pockets to check. *Damn combat shorts with your multiple pockets.* My hand snaked in and out of each pocket, visions of Imy being overpowered running through my head. I couldn't remember which pocket I had checked so I started to pat and slap my shorts. *Shit, breathe, just breathe, just breathe.* I looked out of the windscreen and saw nothing but a wall of black. Fuck breathing, I had to find that fob key.

I couldn't believe how wrong I'd been. Latif had set me the fuck up! Why did Imy let me make decisions? The hell was he thinking? Whoever Latif had sent could be on his way right now, he could be standing beside the car pointing a gun at me, right fucking now!

I resisted the urge to switch on the interior light, and ran my hand over the passenger seat in case the fob had slipped out. If I didn't find it, I was going to have to knuckle up and fight, and fuck knows what he was armed with. Imy had taken the handgun and I had nothing in the car but a box of nuts and dried fruit.

The sniper rifle in the boot.

I paused and thought it through.

I'd have to leave the relative safety of the car and go into the darkness, and if I did manage to get to the boot without getting felt up by a bear, then what? The fuck do I know about a sniper rifle? I barely know how to use a handgun. I could just point it menacingly at him. But he'd know, wouldn't he, just by the way I was holding it, and chances were he'd snatch it off me and proceed to beat me to death with it.

Yeah, I had to find the fob.

I dropped my hand in the small gap in between the driver's and passenger seat, something sharp scratching at my hand as I delved tighter and deeper. The tip of my fingers just about managing to touch the floor. I felt around, felt something, felt something small and plastic, just like a car fob! Relief was short-lived as I heard rustling from outside.

I remained stock still, only my ears standing to attention. I tried to rationalise it, after all I was in a forest and a little rustling was to be expected. I could feel the fob with the tip of my fingers, it had landed flat, 'course it fucking landed flat, and my hand didn't have room to manoeuvre.

I gritted my teeth and, using my index and middle fingers, managed to flip the fob onto its side. The rustling remained around me, and I was unaware of which direction it was coming from, just that it was getting clearer and closer. I gripped the fob precariously in my fingers and carefully extracted my hand painfully from in between the seats. My hand emerged scratched to shit but victorious.

I wasn't like those chumps in horror movies whose hands tremble so much that they can't start the car – fuck that! My survival instincts were switched on. I pressed a small silver button on the fob and the key popped out. I inserted it smoothly into the ignition and flicked it clockwise. The little Honda growled like a lion cub and the automatic headlamps came on illuminating the scene in front of me just as a body slammed heavily against the hood of the car.

My heart beat out of my chest as I pushed myself back into my seat trying to gain distance between me and the man laid out on the bonnet. He was wearing a Pashtun hat, the kind that makes you crave a cheese and onion pie, and wore a cream cotton kameez top. I could just about make out his face even though it was squashed against the hood and he had a gun pressed against the side of his head.

I opened the door. Imy screamed, '*Back in the car!*' just as my foot found the floor.

'It's cool,' I said, stepping out. I inclined my head, giving myself a better look at the man.

'Get him up,' I said.

Imy pulled the man up by the scruff of his neck so that he was facing me. His pie hat fell to the ground, and his hair fell over his face, concealing his features.

He drew his hair open like curtains and through it he said, 'Javid Qasim, Mashallah.'

'Haqani!' I said. 'You nearly gave me a heart attack. The fuck you doing?'

'I here to talk with you,' Haqani said.

Imy moved the gun so that it was tickling the back of his neck. Not quite reading the severity of the situation, Haqani smiled at me. He'd lost a front tooth since we'd met a year ago. Haqani was Ghurfat-al-Mudarris through and through; he and Latif were ever-present by my dad's side. Where Latif was the confidant, Haqani was the muscle and occasional chauffeur.

'I not here to hurt you.'

Imy reached around and pulled out a piece from his waist and handed it to me. 'Your *friend* had that on him,' Imy said.

'He ain't my friend,' I replied, and the expression on the big bad terrorist's face changed. He dropped the smile, his eyes widened and his mouth opened up in a little pout. I'd offended him! I took my eyes off him and checked out the gun that Imy had handed me. It was less gun, more revolver, well worn, faded black. With a little pressure I thumbed the revolving chamber, which popped out, six bullets dropping to the floor. 'You won't be needing those,' I said, styling it out, as though emptying the gun was my intention.

'You are like my brother, Javid,' Haqani said. 'I would never hurt you.'

'The last time we met, you knocked me out with the butt of your rifle.' I touched the back of my head. 'You remember that?'

Again, misreading the scenario, Haqani laughed out loud, his head tilted back, the sound travelling through the forest. 'Be quiet!' Imy dug the gun into his neck.

'Yes. I remember,' Haqani said. 'Your father very angry with me.'

'What're you doing here? Is Latif in the car?'

'He came alone,' Imy said.

'Latif no come. Too dangerous.'

'That why're you packing?' I asked.

'Packing?' He frowned.

'Gun! Why have you brought a gun with you?'

'Not for you. I soldier. Soldier always carry pistol. I also have hunting knife.'

Fuck's sake!

'Pat him down,' Imy said.

319

'Didn't you do that already?' I said, not really wanting to put my hands on him.

'Pat him down, Jay.'

I tentatively patted his shoulders and down his arms; they weren't huge, but they were taut and springy, as if he could reach out and break my neck quicker than Imy could pull the trigger.

'Check his waist,' Imy said.

I patted his waist half-heartedly, and immediately I felt something. To get to it, I would have to lift the front of his kurta. This was way too personal for my liking, but Imy was staring at me to get a move on. I lifted his kurta, catching a glimpse of his hairy but flat stomach. Clipped to the top of Haqani's shalwar was a black leather sheath. I gripped the handle and slowly removed the knife, it kept coming and coming, until all twelve jagged inches were out.

'Fuck, Haqani! I'm having a little trouble believing you here.'

'Why, Javid?' he said, genuinely confused. 'Why I want to hurt you? I have no reason.'

'Then what? Why are you here? Why isn't Latif here?'

Haqani didn't answer straight away and Imy was clearly getting frustrated. He dug his gun harder into the back of his neck, and leaned into his ear and hissed, 'Answer him!'

'Tell your friend to be calm, Javid. I not happy.'

I saw that. He wasn't happy at all. It was the first time I'd seen anger flash across Haqani's face. 'Easy, yeah, Imy.'

Imy held my stare but didn't relent. I couldn't understand why he had to stand so close to him, why the gun had to be pressed up against Haqani. Never understood why people do that, all it takes is a slick Steven Seagal move and that gun can be easily disarmed. Why not just go and stand over *there* and point it at him? It's a fucking gun, it'll do the same job from a couple of feet away. I didn't say

320

any of that to Imy though, he looked like he was in the zone. But it made me tense. These two were not going to get on.

'Latif send me,' Haqani said. 'I came to give you message. You must go home.'

'Yeah I know that! I got the message!'

Haqani shook his head sadly. Even though he was wedged in between Imy and the front bumper of the car, with a gun on him, he calmly took a step back, forcing Imy to do the same. He then walked towards me and took me tightly in his arms. I accepted the embrace, but couldn't bring myself to return it, my arms hanging limply by my side, the knife that I had liberated from him gripped in my hand.

'Young Brother, you should not be here,' Haqani whispered in my ear.

'Please,' I said. 'I have to see Latif. He knows. He must know. I'm not going anywhere until I find my dad.'

I could feel his breath as he sighed wearily and whispered in my ear.

'*Inshallah.*'

Chapter 62

Imy

I didn't trust Haqani, but Jay seemed to, or at least he was coming round to the idea. If Latif was playing a hand, he was playing a good one. He and Haqani had given us every chance to walk away. Giving the impression that they cared for Jay's wellbeing. It's possible that I was being distrustful, but it wasn't without reason.

From experience I knew that psychological warfare was an important part of Al-Mudarris' teachings. It'd been hammered into me; the emotional state, the disguise that I once portrayed when I was sent to England at the age of sixteen as a sleeper agent who never quite woke up.

It could be that I was over-thinking it. It's only natural that Latif would want to protect the son of the man that he worshipped. The fact that Jay had a hand in bringing down Ghurfat-al-Mudarris seemed less of a problem than I'd anticipated. According to Mustafa, they were rumours and nothing more, but two attempts on Jay's life told me that somebody believed it. Somebody was giving these orders.

I was behind the wheel. Jay was in the passenger seat giving a running commentary. Haqani in the Mercedes in front leading us. He drove recklessly. When we first set off, it seemed as if he was trying to lose us, but Jay explained that Haqani simply liked to put his foot down and that I should *'Fucking keep up.'*

He kept to back roads where the terrain was rough and unoccupied, but that wasn't always possible. At one point we drove an hour along a main road through the Terwa District towards Gardez. Haqani adjusted, kept his speed in check, aware that close behind him was a wanted man.

Jay stayed slouched in his seat, a state of disquiet paranoia, his eyes furtive, moving from mirror to mirror, his paranoia hitting heights when we approached dense traffic due to road works – I felt him physically tense.

I pulled up behind Haqani. His eyes meeting mine through the rear-view mirror. He lifted a calming hand. I slipped the car into neutral.

In Jay's footwell was the revolver and hunting knife that we had taken from Haqani. The Browning handgun was wedged under my thigh for easy access. In the trunk was the sniper rifle.

We waited in silence.

'Check out the guy with the lollipop board.' Jay leaned forward and pointed at a man in an orange hi-viz jacket, who every couple of minutes flipped the board from red to green. 'Why's he looking at us like that?'

I lowered Jay's arm. 'He's not looking at us, just towards us. He's directing traffic flow.'

'I don't know. He's had that lollipop on red for well over two minutes. I timed it!' Jay held up his phone, the stopwatch showed that it was approaching the two-and-half-minute mark. 'He should've flipped it by now. I think he's buying time, trying to keep us stationary.'

I nodded, casually, trying not feed his paranoia, but I was starting to learn not to underestimate Jay. I glanced in the rear-view mirror. Behind us there was a grey van, tight against our bumper. Due to the height of the van and its proximity to us, I was unable to see the occupants. In front, our Honda was tight to Haqani's Mercedes. In effect we were boxed in.

I wrapped my fingers around the grip of the Browning. My thumb finding and resting on the safety.

'It's moving.' Jay leaned back in his chair and exhaled. The board had flipped to green and the two cars in front of Haqani moved forward, as did he. I moved my hand away from the gun and flexed my fingers. I put the car into gear and followed Haqani with one eye on the man directing traffic. He didn't so much as glance at us.

'Man, the paranoia is killing me,' Jay said, as the road opened up and we started to move freely.

'It's good to be observant. It'll serve you.'

'Speaking of which, I think I know where we're going. I've been here before, on these roads, in that car.' Jay nodded his head at the Mercedes. 'Haqani was behind the wheel, driving all mental, Latif was in the passenger seat, his head buried in an iPad, reading aloud the itinerary. And I... I was in the back with my dad.' Jay cleared his throat. 'So, yeah, it all feels pretty familiar.'

I didn't feel the need to say anything; realisation was dawning on him. The conflicted feelings he had for his father, clearly eating away at him.

'The moment we set eyes on him,' Jay started, his tone harder now, desperate to make a point. 'You make that call to Lawrence. Get the military or whoever the fuck to take him away. Throw away the fucking key!'

'We're not there yet, Jay,' I said. 'We don't know what Latif will tell us.'

'We're close,' Jay said. 'I can feel it.'

I should have shut down the conversation there. But I was curious to know the extent of his feelings for his father. I needed to know how much damage I was going to inflict on him.

324

'What does he mean to you?'

Jay shot his head around. 'The fuck, man, what kind of question is that? He don't mean shit to me!'

I didn't push him because I knew he wasn't finished.

'This *bullshit* MI5 cover, convincing the world that he's dead. He ain't. He ain't fucking dead. And believe me, I'm going to make sure the whole fucking world knows that he's alive, that the whole fucking world sees him pay for every one of his crimes. That man deserves to spend every second behind bars getting his head kicked in for the rest of his pathetic days. I don't care. I really don't fucking care!'

'You don't care?'

'Didn't I just say that?'

'So why you? Why are you here?'

Jay clenched his jaw, his knee jackhammering, eyes ablaze and fixed on the road ahead. His lips pursed tight.

'Well?'

'Because he's *my* fucking dad!'

*

We didn't speak for a while. Jay busied himself connecting his phone to the stereo and choosing music to suit his mood. Harsh, angry lyrics spilled out of the tinny car speakers. He slouched in his seat and nodded his head in and out of the rhythm. It was clear the thoughts in his head were drowning out the music.

Haqani slowed a touch and without indicating took a turn off the road. I followed at a distance as we entered a built-up residential area.

The Mercedes pulled up at tall metal gates where a smartly uniformed night-watchman stood guard. He nodded at Haqani and pushed opened the gates. Before driving through, Haqani motioned him over, and pointed back at us. The night-watchman considered us, nodded and smiled gratefully as Haqani placed money in his hands. The night-watchman happily waved us through.

The gates clanged closed behind us. Jay straightened up in his seat and whistled appreciatively at the gated community. The houses were high and wide, and well maintained. The parked cars were expensive and recent, a combination of high-spec saloons and high-powered SUVs, mostly all German. Despite the evening, a small team of uniformed gardeners gently watered the manicured front lawns. The grass greener, the strands thicker than I'd ever seen. There were no lampposts, but on either side of the road, palm trees were lined up, with lights fixed at the foot of each tree, giving the street a warm, dreamlike glow. It felt like a small piece of utopia in a country which had suffered much dystopia.

I turned the volume low. 'Have you been here before?'

Jay shook his head. 'We still in Gardez?'

'On the outskirts.'

The brake lights came on. Haqani stuck an arm out of the window and gestured with his hand for us to park the car roadside. He pulled away and turned into an opening, automatic sensor lights illuminated the drive as he pulled up next to a gleaming white Audi Q7.

I pulled up slightly before the house so that I had a view, and parked tight against the kerb underneath a palm tree. The small Honda hatchback looked out of place. I switched off the headlamps but left the car running.

Chapter 63

Jay

My old man had money, I knew that. For years he had sent Mum monthly cheques to the tune of three G in the name of maintenance. That was his idea of playing the good dad, the caring fucking husband. From what I'd learnt about him, he didn't lavish money on himself, lived in pretty much near poverty up a mountain or in a straw hut or whatever. Truly a man of the fucking people! But since his so-called timely demise, it would seem as though Latif had taken a slice of that sweet terrorist funding and set himself up nicely. I figured that, in a roundabout kind of way, the big white double-fronted motherfucker of a house, the gardener, the private security and the killer motor all belonged me. In my head it made sense, and, probably, a half-decent lawyer would agree. But in my heart I knew I could never accept gains that were built on the foundations of bricks, mortar and the blood of innocent lives.

Haqani stepped out of the Merc, a lot dirtier than when it had started its journey. He gestured to the gardener who abandoned watering the neat rectangle of front lawn and changed the setting of the hose from lazy spray to a faster number, and went to work on the Merc. Haqani jogged over and approached my window. I slid it down and he knelt down and folded his arms on the window frame.

'What's up, Haqani?'

'What's up, Jay?' Haqani imitated me with a smile.

'This it?' I asked. 'We here?'

'Yes. You wait here. I come back.'

'Wait? Wait for what?'

'I go speak with Brother Latif.'

'He knows we're here, right?'

'He not,' Haqani replied.

'Seriously?' I said, frustration creeping up on me. 'You didn't tell him?'

'If I called Brother Latif and he say no, then we have big problem, yes? You here now, he must say yes. Yes?'

'Yeah, I guess.' I shrugged at his logic, but I was feeling uncomfortable at just showing up at Latif's doorstep without a heads-up.

Haqani looked down in the footwell. Beside my Jordans were his pistol and blade. 'You leave in car. No weapons in Brother Latif house.' I nodded, and Haqani patted me softly on the arm and bounced to his feet before scurrying towards the house. I noticed he hadn't addressed Imy once, not even glanced in his direction.

'Listen, Imy,' I said, clearing my throat. 'Was thinking...'

'What were you thinking?' Imy said, as he pulled out the gun from under his thigh. I didn't even know it'd been there.

'For starters you can't take that in with you! You heard what Haqani said.'

'It's coming with me.' Imy leaned forward and tucked the piece into his waistband. 'What were you going to say to me?'

'I was going to say maybe you should wait in the car. I mean, Haqani clearly doesn't like you, you're just going to make everyone edgy.'

'No. I'm coming.'

'I could call your phone and you can listen in, first sign of trouble and you come abseiling down the roof and somersaulting through a fucking window, guns blazing, for all I care! But for now, for right now, I think that you should sit tight for a bit.'

Imy didn't reply. It didn't matter. I'd been harsh how I'd said it, as though I'd used him to get me there and now that I was done with Imran Siddiqui Protective Services, I could simply cast him away. But it was the right decision. Since Imy had met Haqani, I could see that he was looking for it, an excuse to start something. Last thing I needed was for Imy to be there with a shooter tucked into his pants, making everyone nervous.

Haqani appeared at the lip of the drive, he threw a hand up and waved me over. I checked my appearance in the sun visor mirror and patted and matted my hair in place, before stepping out of the car. I walked towards Haqani, wondering how Latif would greet me. Behind me I heard a car door close, and before I knew it, Imy fell into step with me.

'The fuck, man!' I hissed at him. 'I asked you to stay in the car.'

'And I told you I'm coming,' Imy replied.

I couldn't make a scene a few yards outside of Latif's yard, so I let it slide, but I gave him a sideways glance sharp enough to cut. But with his eyes fixed on Haqani, I don't think he noticed.

'This way,' Haqani guided us. I took a heavy breath in through my nose as I slipped in between the Audi Q7 and the Merc and stood outside heavy black double doors with gold accessories.

Haqani pushed the door open. In the large hallway stood a little girl and a little boy, toddlers possibly, definitely not babies or grown-ups. They were decked out in matching his-and-hers dungarees. I stepped into the hallway and flashed them a smile and the little girl replied in perfect English, 'I like your shirt. It has sailing boats on it.'

'Nice one,' I smiled.

'What's your name?' the boy asked.

'Jay,' I said.

The boy incredulously replied, '*J?* That's not a *name*. That's a *letter*.' The girl covered her mouth with her hands and they giggled in unison.

'Ha. Yeah, I guess it is. How about you? What are your names?'

'I'm Cookie Monster,' the boy replied. 'And this is Dora. She's an explorer.'

'Is that right?' I laughed, just as Latif appeared in the hallway.

He was just how I'd remembered him: small, round Lennon glasses sitting on a small nose, and a shiny bald spot. He stood behind the boy and girl and put his arms protectively around their shoulders. Stood together, it was clear that they were his children and all of a sudden this seemed like the worst idea. It didn't matter that he was a terrorist, it didn't matter that he may be the only lead to my dad, all that mattered was I was bringing fuck-knows-what into his home. He acknowledged me with a nod. I returned it with a small smile.

Latif tapped Dora the Explorer on the shoulder. 'This is Malaila.' He tapped Cookie Monster on the shoulder. 'And this is Misbah.'

I could feel Imy behind me, could hear his shallow breathing, knowing he had a gun concealed made me want to spin on my heels and walk away. I didn't want any more fucking consequences from my actions.

'I can come back… If this a bad time.'

It sounded as stupid in my head as it did coming out of my mouth.

Latif took his eyes off me and tapped his kids on the shoulder. 'Get ready for bed. I'll join you soon.'

'Yes, Papa,' they choroused. 'Goodbye, Uncle Jay.' They smiled sweetly at me, before nudging each other mischievously as they raced up the stairs.

'There's no way those kids are getting ready for bed,' I said through a nervous laugh. I looked back at Imy. He wasn't laughing. I looked across at Haqani. He wasn't either.

I looked at Latif.

He seemed at a loss without his children by his side. I watched him for a reaction, a handshake, something that would tell me where I stood with him, but he remained still and without expression. It felt like we'd been facing off in the hallway for ages before he finally said, 'Come into my study.'

I flashed Imy a reassuring smile and gestured for him to follow me. The study was a moody number, dark wooden flooring and wood panelling on the wall giving it a cabin feel, which felt out of place to the rest of the airy house. The only light came from a floor lamp which stood beside a wall map of the Afghanistan/Pakistan border. My eyes flicked to it in the hope that Latif had helpfully stuck a pin in the exact location where my dad was being kept.

There were only two chairs in the room. Leather, high-backed and pretty grand, as though they were designed to admire and not park on. Latif took a seat and motioned for me to do the same. I did. As suspected, the chairs were as uncomfortable as fuck. I resisted the urge to fidget.

Haqani stood behind Latif. I looked over my shoulder, and Imy was stationed behind me. They could make eyes at each other for all I cared. I wanted to say my piece, hear his, and then walk away leaving him to put his kids to bed.

Latif looked as uncomfortable as I was, but more from nerves than anything else. He sat right at the edge of the chair, his small hands wringing in his lap.

'Haqani,' Latif said, without looking at him. 'Will you arrange refreshments for our...' he searched for the right words, before landing on, 'guests?'

'No, that's fine. We're fine,' I said, even though refreshments were exactly what I needed.

Latif nodded, and we both waited for the other to speak and then started to speak at the same time.

'Please,' I said. 'You go first.'

'Very well,' he said. 'News reached me about the terrible business in Khyber Pakhtunkhwa Camp. Very distressing indeed.' Latif placed a hand to his heart. 'Mustafa was a loyal servant; his loss will be greatly felt. However, Javid, you must understand, I am no longer involved.'

Not very nice to start with a lie.

This seemed very much like a *with all due respect* moment.

'With all due respect, Latif, you know about Mustafa, and according to your message, you know that I'm in danger, so, please, don't tell me you're not involved.'

I tried to say it passively, and Latif didn't seem to take offence. But over his shoulder Haqani looked at me as if to say, *careful*.

'Remnants, Javid. That's all. Information passes through me and largely it goes without my attention. On this, however, I had to intervene, out of courtesy for who you are, for what Bin Jabbar meant to me. When news came to me that you were in the country I had to look my son and daughter in the eyes and determine how my intervention would affect them. Do you understand, Javid?' Latif's voice rose a touch. Behind him, Haqani poured a glass of water from a tall bottle and handed it to him. Latif took a small sip and placed the glass on the table between us. 'I beg you, Javid, do not let this courtesy become a burden.'

'I just want to know where he is,' I said, softly.

Latif removed his glasses and ran a hand over his face, stopping only to massage his forehead with his eyes squeezed shut. I understood I had him in a corner, his loyalty to my dad split with protecting his children.

'I have something for you,' Latif said, sidestepping my question. He signalled for Haqani to leave the room. We sat in silence, with my question still floating in the air. Haqani returned carrying Imy's travel holdall in one hand and pulling my trolley with the pink ribbon intact in the other.

Latif cleaned and slipped on his glasses. 'I had your luggage transported across the border.'

My heart dropped a couple of notches. 'I wasn't expecting to see our bags again.'

'It was reckless for you to leave them behind,' Latif added.

'To be fair,' I smiled, 'we *were* running for our lives.'

'And again at the market,' Latif said, trying to hammer home the point. 'It seems that you caused quite the commotion.' He leaned back in his big fuck-off chair and crossed his spindly legs. A little more assured now. 'You really ought to be more careful.'

It's the way he said it. It seemed like something had changed.

Haqani retook his position behind Latif. His face a little harder than his default hardness, and I wondered if when he'd popped out to get our luggage, he'd come back armed. I ran my eyes over him but couldn't tell from all the loose material of his kurta. My brain ticked quickly and I struggled to catch up. The change in Latif's tone, less conversational, more cautionary. Haqani stared at me without expression, his fingers loose and relaxed by his side. The luggage, our only belongings, were here. With us. All in one place.

Did Latif know, despite his protests, that we would track him down? Did that mean what I thought it meant? Because it was starting to look like Latif wanted to make us disappear along with our belongings.

As if we were never there.

Chapter 64

Imy

Jay twisted in his chair, turning his back on Latif and Haqani and looking over his shoulder at me. 'We've got our luggage back. Pretty cool, huh?' he said, casually, but at the same time he threw me a look that expressed what I was thinking.

I know, Jay. Just turn back around and be calm.

I watched Haqani for the smallest of movements. He mirrored my look, his eyes trailed down my arm which was slowly moving behind me, ready to lift the tail of my shirt and release the gun from my waistband. From the corner of my eye I noticed Jay slouch down slightly in his chair. Latif's mouth opened and closed as his gaze moved from me to Jay and then back to me.

No secrets. No turning back. Everyone present had the measure of the room. The only sounds were the muted laughter and high-pitched voices of Latif's children from above us.

Haqani moved first and he was quick.

My fingers brushed the handle of the gun before they wrapped around it. I released it smoothly from my waist and my arm tracked Haqani.

He took two steps forward, his leg knocking onto the small table and sending the glass of water smashing onto the hardwood floor. The sound reverberated around the room. I flicked the safety and pointed the gun square at Haqani's chest.

'Drop it,' I said, as he held a small pencil knife under Jay's chin.

'You drop,' Haqani said.

'Haqani!' Latif snapped.

Haqani moved the knife away immediately. He backtracked and returned sentry behind Latif. I wasn't going to relinquish my position as easily.

Latif puffed his cheeks out. 'What is the meaning of this?'

'You knew we would come to you,' I said.

'You think I want you here?' Latif replied, his voice pained. 'Here! Near my children! You think I want this?'

'You have our bags. You damn well knew we would find you.'

'The bags?' Latif pushed his glasses back up his nose and took a moment to consider it. 'Is that what this is about? You think we were going to… Eliminate you? And remove any trace of you? This! This is your line of thinking? Please put down the gun and let me explain.'

I shook my head. 'Explain first.'

'After I learnt news of Mustafa's death, the very first thing I did was to remove any sign that either of you were there. If your belongings were found at the scene, believe me, my hot-headed young Brother, the police would be looking to pin the murder on your head. I had the bags transported here as a matter of urgency. I didn't believe for a second that you would find me and turn my world upside down.' Latif turned his head a quarter-turn towards Haqani. 'You should never have brought them to my door.'

Jay finally lifted his head above the parapet and straightened up in his seat. He got up and stood by me. 'It's cool,' he said gently. 'It makes sense.' He placed his hand on my arm, and I lowered the gun. Jay breathed a sigh of relief before turning to face Latif and Haqani. 'Talk about misreading the situation!' He laughed nervously. 'It's all good. We all good, right?'

335

'Under no circumstance will I allow a gun in my home.'

Jay nodded his head enthusiastically. 'Of course, Latif, your home, your rules, and can I say, it's a great rule!' Jay made a show of putting his hand out towards me. I stood my ground. 'Come on, Imy. There's kids here. Let's lose the gun, shall we?'

'It stays with me.'

'So be it.' Latif got to his feet. 'Please leave my home and my family in peace.'

I wanted to grab Jay by the scruff of the neck and march him the hell out of there.

'No, no, no.' Jay plastered a desperate smile on his face. 'Nothing has happened, nobody got hurt. It's just a misunderstanding, yeah. Seriously, can we all just calm down?' He turned back to me, a tight smile to pacify, but I could see his frustration hitting boiling point. 'Imy, give me the gun!'

'No. We're going,' I said. 'I don't trust them.'

'You wanna go, then fucking go!' he hissed. 'This has nothing to do with you.'

His breaths came heavy, as heavy as the words that sat between us. He puffed his chest and bore his eyes into me, standing by his every word. He had come this far and he knew he could find his father without me.

But I could never find Bin Jabbar without him.

I gave up my gun.

Jay would soon know that, despite his words, this had *everything* to do with me.

*

Haqani led us through a large modern kitchen, rounding the ivory marble island to a door on the far side. He pushed it open and stood to one side. I peered in, I could sense Jay doing the same over my shoulder. The room was similar in size and shape to a second lounge, and it was in the latter process of being converted. Two La-Z-Boy armchairs, still sealed within protective plastic speckled in paint, pointed towards a large flat screen. Beside the TV was a still-boxed PlayStation console. The walls had been primed, and there were small brush strokes of bright colours – pink, blue and yellow – as if a colour scheme had yet to be determined. It looked very much as though this room was on its way to becoming a spot for his children.

'Go, go,' Haqani gestured. 'Room no bite.'

My eyes dropped instinctively to the key in the lock on the outside. I stepped into the room. Jay followed pulling his trolley behind him.

'Still work to be done, but you be relaxed here, yes?' Haqani said. 'Latif bhai make telephone calls to help you. You rest, sleep.' He pointed at a small basin in the corner of the room. 'You can wash there for prayers.'

That wasn't going to be happening.

'Nice one,' Jay said.

'I leave you now.' Haqani turned away and before shutting the door he said in all seriousness, 'Leave plastic on chair, okay?'

Jay wheeled his trolley and parked it beside a La-Z-Boy. He sat heavily down and adjusted himself noisily on the plastic covering before pulling the lever so the footrest shot up. He kicked off his shoes and let them drop as he murmured sounds of appreciation. I sat down on the armchair next to him, slipped off my Crocs and placed them neatly by my chair. I pulled the lever and stretched out.

I stared at the television. It wrongly reflected two normal guys casually sitting on La-Z-Boys in front of the TV. We sat in silence for a moment, the earlier incident no doubt running through Jay's head, as it was mine.

Latif had forgiven us a little too easily for my liking. He'd told us that once he'd put his children asleep, he'd make some calls, but couldn't promise anything. It was exactly what Jay wanted, *needed*, to hear – the nerves and excitement coming from him were tangible. I could sense it, but I was seeing things very differently.

I'd given up my gun and we were in a room with one lockable door.

I got to my feet.

'Where you going?' Jay asked.

I ignored him and padded my way to the window. I tried to push it open. It was locked. I ignored Jay's stare and moved across to the door. I put my ear against it before turning the door knob.

I pulled it open just enough for light to seep through. I shut the door.

Jay twisted in his seat. 'You thought they'd locked us in?' He shook his head. 'You got to stop being so paranoid. We both do.'

I sat back down. 'I've been thinking,' I said. I didn't have to look at Jay to know that his sigh was accompanied by an eye-roll.

'Of course you have,' he said.

'Do you remember how Mustafa greeted you at the camp? The waitress, too?'

'Jameelah,' Jay said. 'Yeah, what about it?'

'And all those people in the village, the love and affection they held for you because of who you are, because of what Bin Jabbar meant to them.'

'Do you wanna just get to the point?'

'Latif was Bin Jabbar's confidant, like brothers, that's what you told me. You don't think it's strange that Latif didn't show you the same affection as everyone else?'

'That it? That's what's on your mind?' Jay shrugged. 'I wasn't exactly expecting Latif to embrace me.'

'You must have expected something. Some emotion, a little

respect, even. Instead, Latif kept his distance. He didn't even shake your hand. You don't think that's a little off.'

Jay twisted in his seat and glanced at the closed door, before leaning in closer. He kept his tone to a whisper. 'It's like this. When I was here last year, I was the centre of Bin Jabbar's world. And he, *Latif*, did not like it. Trust me, it was written on his face. Yeah, I did say that they were like brothers, but, honestly, Latif looked up to my father as though he was *his* father. He was under the impression that he would be the natural successor.' Jay cleared his throat. 'Until Bin Jabbar made it clear that role would one day belong to me. So yeah, there's some resentment there.'

I nodded. Did it fit? I wasn't sure. But it did explain the animosity.

'You're looking for something that's not there,' Jay said, settling back into his chair. 'If anyone can find Bin Jabbar, it's Latif.'

'Let's say that he does manage to give us Bin Jabbar's location,' I said. 'How do you think it's going to play out?'

Jay shifted in his chair. I wasn't the only one keeping secrets.

'Jay.'

'*What?*' The frustration in his voice was barely restrained. He tried to even it out. 'What is it?'

'Have you thought this through?'

'The fuck, Imy! 'Course I've thought it through. I've thought of nothing else.'

'So you think the authorities are going to bring him back to England? That the world is going to find out he's alive? That he'll get his day in court?! Come on! You must know that they're going to lock him up in an unknown location again, and no matter what fuss you kick up, people will believe what they are told.'

Jay laughed, but it didn't come easy. 'You think I'm naïve.'

I hesitated. 'No, I don't.'

'It wasn't a question. You think I'm naïve.' He shook his head, as though he was tired of having to prove himself. 'You think I don't know how Lawrence and fucking Robinson and all those pieces of shit at MI5 operate? Check this, Imy: they used me once, trust me, I won't let them use me again.'

'And how will you do that? We're leading them straight to him. You're being used as we speak.'

'They've underestimated me,' Jay said. 'And so have you.'

Chapter 65

Jay

'Can you see the TV remote anywhere?' I said.

It was an odd thing to say considering all the shit he was throwing at me, but I just needed a fucking break from Imy, some distraction. I was getting beyond frustrated with him casting doubts on me.

'No,' Imy replied through an almighty yawn. He squeezed his eyes shut and then forced them wide open in an attempt to stay awake. The last time he'd slept would have been on the plane.

'Get some shut-eye,' I said.

'I'm fine,' he said, looking anything but. 'Do not let me sleep. You see me close my eyes, you wake me. Is that understood?'

I nodded. Everything he said felt like an order, as though he didn't trust me to be alone. Rather than reply and escalate it, I let it slide. If he did go to sleep, I'd be tempted to slap him awake.

I spotted the edge of the remote control hidden behind the legs of the TV. I reached for it without having to get out of my seat and switched the TV on. I flipped through the channels and nothing but snow came back at me. Not even Freeview. I muttered my disdain under my breath and eyed the PlayStation still sealed in its box. I was tempted to hook it up, but I couldn't bring myself to take away the pleasure of unpacking it from the kids. I pictured Latif and his children setting it up. That new smell. All that polystyrene.

Malaila and Misbah sitting on the La-Z-Boy, their feet barely reaching the footrest, game controller in hand. Latif proudly watching on.

Fuck, man! I hated that this fucking monster was a good dad. What's worse, now I knew where Latif lived, I had no choice but to pass on that information to MI5, and then I'd have to live with the fact that I was responsible for leaving his children without their old man. They'd have to go through the same shit that I did when they found out that their father was a terrorist.

The fuck is it with dads?

It got me thinking. What kind of father would I be to Jay Jnr and Jaya? What kind of mum would Sophia be? I shook my head clear of that straight away. I hadn't even asked her out, and already I was picturing her as mother to my children!

I laughed quietly to myself, and then feeling self-conscious I looked across at Imy, who was purring gently through his nose. Sleep had finally defeated him.

Despite what he said I wasn't going to wake him.

I killed the TV. The plastic cover on the armchair rustled loudly as I lifted myself off the chair. With little to do but wait, I twisted at the waist a few times to loosen up. I thought about dropping down and knocking out twenty push-ups, but, honestly, it was never going to get past the thought process. I glanced around the room for something to keep me occupied. My eyes landed on my trolley.

I knelt down beside it and untied the pink ribbon and laid it down on its side. I unzipped it. It didn't look as though Latif or Haqani had interfered with it. The contents were exactly how I'd left them. My black leather toiletries bag wedged between shirts and shorts and a spare pair of Jordans. I removed the toiletries bag and moved to the newly installed basin in the far corner of the room, hoping that the plumbing had been put in place.

I flipped the tap and to my relief water ran. I looked up above the

342

basin where a mirror should have been and wondered what I looked like. Only my shadow stared back at me. Even that looked like shit, my hair sticking out at odd angles. From my toiletries bag I took out my toothbrush, toothpaste and some moisturiser; the weather and the environment had not been kind to my skin.

I splashed cold water on my face and over my hair. Brown dirt pooled in the basin before disappearing down the drain. I scrubbed my face hard over and over until the water ran clear. The same effort with my whites: I squeezed out a double decker of Colgate onto the toothbrush and went to town, paying attention to my gums and tongue until my mouth fizzed.

I knew what I was doing, if Latif managed to come through for me. I didn't want to admit it to myself, maybe it was a subconscious thing, but I wanted to look my best for when I saw my dad.

There was no towel, but I had one packed in my trolley. I dried my face and finally applied moisturiser. My forehead and nose – the T-zone – required the most care. I picked out a clean pair of boxers, a half-sleeved shirt, light blue with a repeat shark print, and cream combat shorts.

With no privacy to get changed, I stood behind Imy's armchair and got dressed. I realised half-way through that if Imy woke up right now, he'd see me in the reflection of the TV screen, hopping on one foot trying to get my boxers on. My shirt was the last to go on and as I buttoned up I took a moment to consider, *how much chest is too much chest?*

I checked myself out in the TV screen and tried to picture myself through my dad's eyes. A light caught on the screen and I spun around to see the door open. Haqani filled the doorway.

'Javid,' Haqani whispered loudly.

I moved across the room towards him, but stopped a distance from where he was standing. Haqani noticed and I felt stupid for doing so. If Latif wanted me dead, I'd be pretty much dead by now. I moved closer until I was standing in front of him.

'No sleepy?' he whispered.

'No, no sleepy,' I whispered back.

'You want pillow? Blanket? I can get.'

'Nah, it's all good... Any news?'

'Latif make many calls. No luck. He trying very hard for you, Javid.'

'Oh, okay,' I said, keeping my disappointment in check.

'You hungry? Come with me to kitchen. I make you best sandwich.'

I turned towards Imy. I had a sudden urge to wake him up before quickly realising I had no reason to. He'd only want to tag along and bring his paranoia with him. I really didn't need another incident, not whilst Latif was actively trying to find news on my dad.

'Yeah,' I shrugged. 'I could eat.'

Chapter 66

Jay

I left Imy counting Zs and stepped out of the room and into the adjoining kitchen. Haqani shut the door behind him gently and pointed me to a high stool at the island. He buried his head in the fridge and took out ingredients at will and got busy fixing us both a chicken sandwich. Thick white bread, heavy on mayo, light on salad, and heavy-handed with the hot sauce. Just how I like it.

I watched him carefully, making sure he used the same ingredients for himself. He placed two identical plates on the island for me to pick. I noticed a wry smile on his face as if he had read my mind. I pulled forward a plate without deliberation and took a bite.

'Hmm,' I nodded my appreciation. It was a damn fine sandwich.

'Hmm,' he nodded back, appreciating his own work. After a minute of munching he said, 'You are... how you say... crazy, no?' He chuckled to himself. 'Too much problem for you here.'

'Yeah,' I said, wiping my mouth. 'I know.'

'But I...' he started, then shook his head. '*We*... never forget who you are. What you did for us. We very proud, yes?'

I nodded. I wasn't sure what I'd done for him to feel such pride but it hurt me a little that he did. He was just one of many that saw me as somebody that I wasn't.

'Look,' Haqani exclaimed, his eyes as big as his smile. He gestured at the sandwiches. 'I not believe I make food for the son of

345

Al-Mudarris. You tell him, yes? When you see him you tell him I feed you with my own hands.'

'I'll tell him.'

He took another bite, and I did too. He kept his eyes on me, his features soft, that same look of adoration that I was getting used to.

I understood that, here, I was not Jay. I was Javid Qasim.

'You want we eat sandwich and watch movie?' Haqani suggested. 'Latif have big TV.'

I approved in the form of a shrug and he led me out of the kitchen. We stepped into the hallway by the wide staircase that the twins had disappeared up. Haqani stepped into the living room, and, opposite me, across the hallway was Latif's study. The door was half open. I couldn't help myself. I glanced in.

Latif had his back to me and was standing facing the large map that I'd clocked earlier. His white shirt was half tucked out, half tucked in. One hand was massaging his lower back. He sounded proper stressed as he spoke on the phone.

'Every safe house. Yes! Every single one! Three in Gardez... Yes, yes, including the godown. Wake up Ahmed, send him to the bungalow in Jalalabad... I don't care what time it is! And, find somebody to go to the house in Kandahar. Is this understood...? Good. Now repeat it back to me.'

I stood watching until Haqani reappeared in the hallway. He reached past me and gently shut the door to Latif's office. 'It's okay. Latif trying to help. Come.'

Haqani asked me to select a DVD of my choosing as he mumbled something and disappeared again. The selection was vast and I picked out *Fast & Furious 8* when really I wanted to watch *A Few Good Men*, but thought that Haqani may not be able to keep up with a court-room drama, and may prefer to watch cars racing fast and furiously.

Haqani returned and placed a bowl of crisps and a mug of hot

346

chocolate on the coffee table. 'Will help you sleep,' he said, like the caring terrorist that he was, and sat down on the armchair adjacent to me, leaving me to stretch out on the three-seater.

The hot chocolate with the pink marshmallow floating on top looked inviting, so I took a sip of that first. So good! The milk was thicker and creamier than I'd ever had. I took another, bigger sip. The hunger hit me suddenly and I went to town on the remainder of the sandwich, taking bites too big for my mouth. I took another sip to help wash it down. My body relaxing to the extent that I felt as though I was at one with the sofa.

It felt nice. Dreamy. I sunk deeper and deeper into the seat, aware that I had a milky moustache, but not finding the energy to run an arm over it.

The sandwich in my hand started to feel heavy as though I was holding up an anchor. The harder I tried to bring it to my mouth, the further away it went. Unable to carry the weight of it any longer, I let go of it and watched it come apart on my lap. I opened my mouth to apologise but the words wouldn't come. I let my arm flop down by my side and my head felt as though it was spinning clockwise and then anticlockwise and I didn't know how that was possible.

Fuck's sake! They had me.

My mind dimmed, like a low battery, only able to execute the most basic of functions. I took a breath. On screen Vin Diesel and The Rock were facing off, and I wondered if it was true what was said about them in the tabloids. *Did they really hate each other?* If so, this fight had an extra edge. I tuned in. Focused. Ready for these two screen giants to kick the shit out of each other.

From the corner of my eye I could just about make out that Haqani had been replaced by Latif. I turned to him and slurred, 'You drugged me, you fuck!'

347

I think he nodded and I think he was wearing different clothes, as though he was heading out.

I glared at him, but honestly I had no idea what expression my face was making. Everything was so fucking numb, as though all my features had melted away. For all I knew I could have been dribbling over myself and smiling stupidly at him. I couldn't straighten my mind. That shit had made me so fucking lethargic that I wanted nothing more than to just stop and watch TV.

I focused back on the film. I wasn't pleased that I'd missed the dust-up between The Rock and Vin Diesel. I had the sudden urge to know the outcome. I tried to reach for the remote control so I could rewind the scene, but my arms didn't want to know. I tilted my body forward hoping my arms would follow, but gravity kicked in and I took a slow motion dive off the sofa and landed face-first on the really comfortable fucking rug.

Haqani was right, the hot chocolate did help me sleep.

Chapter 67

Imy

A dull thud, and my eyes opened. I wanted nothing more than to close them again. I blinked away the sleep from my eyes and checked the time on my phone. The brightness of the screen stung my eyes. I'd been asleep for forty minutes and my body craved so much more. I slipped my phone away and I could see from the dark reflection of the TV that Jay was no longer in the room.

He wasn't one to follow instructions, particularly from me. It was understandable. I'd been cold and distant, refusing to form a relationship, knowing what I knew, knowing what hell I was about to unleash on him.

I stayed rooted to my seat, unwilling to hold back the unease that was creeping up my back. My eyes moved around the room. There didn't seem any signs of a struggle. Jay's trolley was lying open on its side and the clothes that he had been wearing were discarded beside it. On the other side of the room his toiletries were sitting on the basin edge, beside a toothbrush and toothpaste.

He was anticipating seeing his father and he wanted to be at his best.

But he was gone.

It didn't mean anything, but at the same time it could have meant everything. His curious and foolish nature were troubling. I forced myself not to give in to the paranoia and decided, against my better nature, to trust Jay. I dropped my head back against the headrest and decided to wait a moment. But after sixty seconds I heard the front door close.

I eased myself out of the armchair and slipped on my shoes. I crossed the room to the window. It overlooked a well-kept side lawn and not much else. But I was close enough to hear a car start, a diesel engine growl, and the wheels spin with urgency.

I rushed to the door and put my ear to it, only the muffled sound of the television came back at me. I reached for the knob. If the door opened, I'd put it down to an overreaction and when Jay did return, believe me, he was going to feel the force of my anger. If the door was locked, I'd know that Jay would never be returning.

I held my breath as my fingers wrapped around the door knob. I twisted it one way. And then the other. Immediately fear set in.

I spun around scanning the room for something to strike down and break the lock. Something that would double as a weapon. I pictured the contents of my holdall, quickly dismissing everything as useless. My eyes landed on the small basin in the corner of the room. It was far from ideal.

I swiped away Jay's toiletries, and kicked the pedestal holding up the basin dead centre. The contact was loud and I knew my action would not have gone unnoticed. The pedestal tilted at an angle, leaving a gap underneath the basin. A leak squirted at me as I squeezed my hand through the gap and disconnected the pipes, whilst glancing over my shoulder at the door.

The basin was free from the pipes, only hanging on by the sealant. I gripped it with both hands and ripped it away from the wall as water rushed up the tail piece and hit my face.

I moved to the door and lifted the basin to chest height ready to strike down on the door handle and snap the lock, praying that

I wasn't too late and cursing myself for closing my eyes and leaving Jay to his own devices.

Keys jangled on the other side of the door. I sidestepped, my back against the wall. I balanced the small basin in one hand and with the other I reached over my shoulder and clicked the light switch off.

The lock retracting echoed through me. I held my breath and held the basin tightly at chest height.

Haqani was no fool. He waited.

'Imran…' His voice came clearly through the door. I didn't reply so as not to risk giving away my position. 'Javid is on his way to die. You want to join him?'

A burst of fire erupted and reverberated loudly in the darkness. I slid down against the wall and made myself small, lifting the basin above my head as bullets ripped through the door.

The shooting stopped as quickly as it had started. Rays of light beamed through the bullet holes in the door. From the gunfire I recognised that Haqani was in possession of my Browning handgun. Before I had handed it over, I'd inserted a full clip. Fifteen rounds plus one in the chamber. Seven had been spent. Haqani had more than enough remaining.

The echo of the gunshots stopped ringing in my ear and was replaced by piercing screams. 'Look what you have done.' Haqani's voice came through. 'The children are awake.'

I got to my feet and pushed back against the wall. The door handle turned and the door slowly opened. The light from the kitchen illuminating the room. Haqani led with the arm and I recognised my gun in his hand. I brought down the basin with force, and it met his wrist with a sickening crunch. Haqani screamed through gritted teeth as the gun fell from his grip and dropped softly onto the carpeted floor. I had to move fast before his arm retreated and locked me back in. I let the basin slip from my grip and grabbed at his broken wrist, dragging him sprawling inside.

Haqani landed on his stomach. The gun closer to his reach than it was mine. I moved for it but his fingers were already looping around the trigger guard. He inched it towards him until it was in his grip, his body already twisting around to face me, his holding arm coming quickly around.

I kicked the door shut, plunging the room back into darkness. He pulled off a round but I was already moving. My foot knocked against the discarded basin. I bent low and reclaimed my makeshift weapon just as another shot rang out, whistling close. The round shattered through the basin and shards of porcelain rained upon me.

I struck down blindly with whatever was left of the basin and, unmistakeably, I felt it make contact with his face.

*

Two faces, wide and teary-eyed, appeared at the top of the stairs, watching a stranger holding a gun to their Uncle Haqani.

'It's okay,' I said. 'Go back to your room and call the police.' They scuttled away and I heard a door shut and lock. I moved Haqani into the living room. An action film that I'd never seen before was playing out on the television. I sat Haqani down on the armchair, the gun trained on his face with one hand and with the other I reached for the remote control and muted the sound. The ingredients from a half-eaten sandwich lay scattered on the sofa next to him. On the coffee table was a bowl of crisps and an empty mug with brown residue. I picked it up and brought it to my nose.

'Where is he?' I asked.

Haqani smiled through his bloody broken nose, as he examined his limp broken wrist. I launched the mug over his shoulder and it smashed against the wall. He didn't so much as blink, but it wiped the smile off his face.

He glanced casually at his watch. 'If he's not dead, he will be soon.'

I released the clip from the Browning and checked the rounds. Seven of the fifteen remained. I slid the clip back in, retracted the slide, thumbed the safety off and held the gun in his face.

Haqani tilted his head past it, brimming confidence with the knowledge that I didn't have.

'You are not our problem, Imran. You walk, no problem, I can drive you to airport or I can call you taxi,' Haqani said. I dug the gun into his left thigh and pulled the trigger. His scream was muted as he gripped my shirt. I shrugged him away.

'Take me to him.'

*

Haqani divulged the information and it wasn't out of fear. He believed that whatever I was walking into would be more of a problem for me than for them.

The Honda was parked in the same place. Haqani hobbled with his arm around me as I helped him to the car. I unlocked the car door and helped him into the driver's seat. I walked around to the trunk and looked over the roof. The gardeners were trying their best to avoid what clearly wasn't their business. I whistled to get their attention. A boy in service uniform, who couldn't be more than sixteen, looked up. I gestured him over.

'What's your name?'

'Tashfeen.'

'Okay, Tashfeen, I want you to listen to me very carefully.' I pointed to the Latif's house. 'Two children are alone in there.'

'Miss Malaila and Master Misbah.'

'Right. The front door is open, I want you to go inside and wait in the living room. The police have been called and should be arriving soon. Do you understand?'

He stared at me blankly. I took out a thousand Afghan Afghani which amounted to ten pounds and placed it in his hands.

'Yes, *malik*.' He nodded his head vigorously. I watched him all the way until he disappeared inside. Latif's children were about to lose everything, just like I had once.

I rounded the car and lifted the trunk, relieved to see that the Go-Bag was still in place. I sifted through it, ensuring that the sniper rifle and ammunition was present, before taking out some much needed supplies. If this was going to work I needed Haqani not to bleed out in the five-hour journey ahead of us. I wrapped the tourniquet tightly around his left leg and gave him a handful of painkillers and a bottle of water. I slid into the back seat directly behind him and placed a length of rope next to me.

'Better?' I asked. Haqani removed his Pashtun hat, his forehead was slick with sweat. He ran an arm over his face and nodded. 'Okay,' I said, as I held the gun through the gap in between the headrest and the seat so he could feel the cold barrel on the back of his neck. 'Now drive.'

Chapter 68
Jay

One of the chair legs was shorter than its counterparts, which in itself was annoying enough without the rest of it. My arms were pulled so tight behind me it felt as though my shoulders were about to pop, and the rope around my wrists was secure enough to break skin. Some boy scout had done a fucking number with the knot. I couldn't move.

My head was covered with a hessian hood. I knew this to be the case because it wasn't the first time that my head had been covered with a fucking hessian hood. The cloth was coarse and it scratched against my skin like little ants that needed their toenails clipping were marching along my face. My breathing was somewhat limited, so I kept it in check by taking shallow breaths when all I wanted to do was scream away the suffocation.

I tried to tune in to my surroundings, my eyes and ears straining within the confines. If I squinted and didn't fidget, I could *just* about see through the smallest of gaps in the woven fabric, a row of green hills in the distance.

Intuitively I knew it was the only thing of beauty around me.

A figure stepped in front of me and whatever little I could see was replaced with black. I flinched. The chair tilted to its right and I expected it to topple over. It corrected itself and a rough hand roughly ripped away my hood, almost pulling out a clump of my hair in the process.

355

The sun hit the side of my face. I blinked several times before squinting at the man in front of me. I couldn't see past him as he was pretty much standing over me, so I started with him. He was decked out in a black boiler suit zipped up to his throat and tucked into heavy boots. Somewhere in the middle he held a shiny sharp machete and his grey eyes peered at me from underneath a balaclava.

'Alright,' I said. He didn't reply in kind, so I decided to establish how much trouble I was in. 'The balaclava? Is that to intimidate me? Because I gotta tell you, the machete is intimidating enough.'

I gritted my teeth and braced myself. The handle of the machete came crashing into the side of my head, catching and splitting my eyebrow. This time the chair did topple and fall onto its side. I landed heavily on my shoulder, my head bouncing off the ground, twice. I tried to blink away the white sparkly stars in my eyes just as a heavy boot ground my face into the dirt.

'Get him up,' an annoyed voice said.

The boot obediently left my face. My head rushed as the chair was lifted back into place. I could feel the moist earth stuck to the side of my face and a little had entered my mouth. I noisily spat out the dirt and used my shoulder to brush the crap off my face.

I looked at Latif. He looked tiny standing next to the giant who'd knocked me down.

'I don't know why he's being so sensitive,' I said. 'I was only giving him some fashion advice.'

'You must learn, Javid, when to keep your mouth shut.'

'I'll work on it,' I said, as I finally had the opportunity to take in the scene, and just as I suspected, it was fucking terrifying.

Five metres or so in front of me there was a tripod with a mounted video camera pointing at me. I know what that fucking meant! A home movie starring me soon to burn through the internet as a moral fable. I snatched my eyes away and looked past the camera.

To my right, was a set of green corrugated iron huts. Beside it was parked Latif's Q7, where I had spent hours curled up in the fucking boot!

Set back to my left, six men stood stock still, a few feet apart. Black boots, black boiler suit, black Ghutrah scarves bound tightly around faces. I wondered if they all went shopping together; stopping to eat, bitching about their Jihadi brides and you know, just making a day of it.

I tried to balance out the pros and cons of my impending death; would I prefer a clean swoop of the machete or would I prefer to be riddled with bullets by the firing squad? Or was there a plan C that I wasn't seeing?

I exhaled loudly, the beginnings of a migraine stirring; it was the last thing I fucking needed. Past the six men and into the distance there was the row of beautiful green rolling hills that I had seen earlier through my hood. I imagined cute little lambs scattered across the hills, eagerly ready to congregate when the show started.

I stretched my neck back, and stared at the tall tree directly above me. Past its thick branches I searched the heavens, hoping to spot a Chinook ready to swoop down to the rescue, but the bright blue skies were clear. Only the sun smiling down on me, even if nobody else was.

My fingers moved quickly as I fiddled with the restraints around my wrists. When Balaclava had knocked me to the ground, the knot had seemed less tight. Not much, but something to work with. If I could manage to get my hands free, then all I had to worry about was getting past the seven bloodthirsty men armed with rifles and knives.

'Do you know who we are?' Latif asked, knocking me out of my delusion of grandeur.

'Shot in the dark? I'd say you were Al-Muhaymin.'

He nodded softly, his face colouring, as though a hint of embarrassment. 'It wasn't how it should have been. But it's how it is.'

I couldn't have cared less about anything he had to say, but I needed to buy a little time. Delaying the inevitable was all I had.

'What's that supposed to mean?' I asked.

'Ghurfat-al-Mudarris has always been misunderstood. At times it's misunderstood by its own people. There's a belief, an incorrect one. The Cause was never been about hardline Wahabbism or spreading Sharia Law. It wasn't about being a pure Muslim or even fighting a religious war. In its barest form, it was about protecting our own. An eye for an eye.'

'For an eye, for an eye, for an eye,' I said. 'Yeah, I know that.'

'We were in the midst of a storm and our leader was a hunted man. In accordance with the teachings of Bin Jabbar, we expected to retaliate, to lash out like a cornered tiger.' Latif shook his head sadly. 'But no... It's not what happened. Our esteemed leader, he had a weakness.'

I looked at him blankly. Latif didn't go so far as say it was *me* that was the so-called weakness, but it was clear that the name Qasim did not hold any gold here.

'Men,' he continued, 'good men who laid down their lives for The Cause quickly became disillusioned... They came to me... They begged at my feet. I had no choice but to give the people what they wanted.'

'You've finally got yourself your very own terrorist cell. Congratulations! How's that working out for you?'

Latif didn't reply with words, his eyes firing at me as his calm demeanour took a hit. I'd pissed him off, which should have told me to stop, but seriously, how much more trouble could I get in?

'Let me tell you how I think it's working out for you,' I continued, getting a grasp on it. 'As soon as I set foot in Islamabad, I'm guessing

358

your eyes must have just lit up. You made some phone calls, sent some emails, passed a note to a man on a donkey, something like that? Either way, you put the word out, far and fucking wide, but you quickly learnt that apart from a couple of losers, no one gave a shit, no one dared to go against Bin Jabbar.' I ventured a smile. 'Gutted!'

Balaclava took a heavy step towards me. At the very least I was expecting a slap. Latif put a small hand across his barrel chest and stopped him in his tracks. If he'd allowed Balaclava to strike me, it was as good as admitting that I had got to him. Latif was too clever for that.

'I underestimated his followers,' Latif said quietly to himself, the calm, calculated demeanour returned to his face. 'But I didn't underestimate you, Javid. You came crawling to me in desperation. You trusted me.' A smile appeared on his face just as it was wiped off mine. 'How did that work out for *you*?'

Bastard stole my line!

'Javid,' Latif said, with something close to glee in his voice.

'*What?*' I spat with the practised attitude I'd picked up thousands of miles away in Hounslow, when really I just wanted to cry and beg for my life.

'I'm afraid, this… All this,' he gestured expansively with his hands, 'it's your own doing.'

'I'm pretty fucking sure it's not,' I said, my hands working double-time behind my back, knowing that my time was coming to an end.

'When will you learn that every action has a reaction?'

'Yeah, and what action is that?' I said, just as my thumb had squeezed its way into the restraint. I stretched it as far back as I could until the tight rope opened into a small loop.

'Your treachery!' Latif replied.

I peered past him, past the camera, at the men lined up waiting to tear me in half.

'Not gonna lie to you, Latif. This is the worst leaving do ever.'

Latif smiled sadly at my attempt at mistimed humour. I shrugged, it was all I had, my last line of defence.

'You must learn, Javid? Action… Reaction.'

'Sounds like something a father teaches his son.' I smiled tightly at him. 'Must have missed that lesson.'

Latif leaned in, his face close to mine. His aftershave was strong and confusing, like the fragrance section in John Lewis. I had the urge to wrap my teeth around his nose and rip it clean off.

'Your father. It's become something of an obsession with you.' Latif smiled. 'You see, Javid, Abdul Bin Jabbar was more of a father to me than he ever was to you.'

His words stung.

I dropped my head so he wouldn't see the hurt, and focused on my Jordans and focused on my breathing and focused on getting my fucking hands free. Balaclava wrapped his fist around my hair and wrenched my head back up. Latif seemed pleased to see my teeth gritted, my nostrils flared in anger and my eyes red from holding back tears.

'And I,' Latif continued, 'was more of a son than you will ever be.'

A hand slipped free from the restraints and I leaped to my feet screaming and spitting, my fist coming around from behind my back and taking flight towards Latif's smug fucking face.

I connected to the side of his head and it was perfect.

His glasses flew off his face and landed close to where he did. Latif scrambled on his hands and knees searching for them. The leader of Al-Muhaymin seemed so small and insignificant in front of his men. *I fucking did that!* My action may have accelerated my death sentence, but, fuck, it was worth it.

I accepted the fist that drove into my lower back, sending me heavily to my knees. I accepted my fate as I waited for the machete to swoop down and split me in two.

It was time. I squeezed my eyes shut and saw Mum. I held onto her as long and hard as I could.

Around me, the atmosphere had changed. An eerie silence broken only by the sound of a squeaky wheel moving closer and closer and closer until it came to a stop somewhere in front of me.

Latif was back on me, recomposed after the punch I had delivered, ready to deliver one of his own. His tone a furious whisper.

'I want *him* to recognise that unlike Ghurfat-al-Mudarris, Al-Muhaymin has no place for sentiment. I want *him* to recognise that Al-Muhaymin has no place for weakness.'

I opened my eyes and they adjusted to the figure in front of me. I blinked again. Slowly. Dreamlike. The tears that I'd tried so desperately to hold back raced down my face.

In front of me was a shadow of who my father once was.

Confined to a wheelchair and broken beyond repair.

Chapter 69

Imy

I estimated that we were approximately twenty minutes behind Jay and Latif. Despite the urgency I ensured Haqani kept to the speed limits as I'd figured that Latif would have done the same, in fear of being pulled over and the police discovering a hostage.

Haqani kept tight to the border and around the four-hour mark, as night gave way to dawn, we drove on the outskirts of seemingly untouched green land within the Laghman Province. It was an area that I had never seen before but I knew we were deep in Taliban territory.

The geography made me wonder.

When Ghurfat-al-Mudarris was at its inception phase, it had received the attentions of al-Qaeda. Though their directives and methodology were at odds, they shared the same objective. Al-Qaeda lent support initially by sharing ground and facilities with Ghurfat-al-Mudarris, before they grew and were able to stand on their own.

Al-Muhaymin were currently at a similar state and stage. External funding for the splinter cell would be an issue, a risk in light of recent events surrounding Bin Jabbar. They would require the support of an existing network. There was a real possibility that support for Al-Muhaymin was being provided by the Taliban. If that was true, I dared to believe that the Taliban had provided Al-Muhaymin passage, and a safe haven for Abdul Bin Jabbar.

I dared to believe I was close.

Chapter 70

Jay

I knew he'd suffered badly. But my mind could never go there.

Now, in my eyes, the horror was complete, and I was unable to turn away. I couldn't even blink, I had to take him while I still could and search for a part of me in him.

His body slack and lifeless, his clothes hanging off his skeletal frame. The skin on his face was burnt and tightly stretched. A grey threadbare blanket was placed over his lap, below it his feet pointed inward on the metal foot rest. His head was tilted to one side and his mouth was flopped open. I remembered the last words he'd said to me, to anyone.

It was always going to end this way.

The only life that was left in him was in his eyes. And his eyes were on me.

This didn't change a fucking thing! I found the resolve to snatch my eyes away from my evil fuck of a father. Latif had moved behind the camera and was recording every fucking emotion in my face. I wouldn't give him any more.

My hands were free, but heavy hands on my shoulders held me down. The six men had moved closer towards me, and six guns were pointing at me. I nodded. *Defeated*. It was my time. But it wasn't to happen in the way I'd expected.

A noose was looped over my head and I didn't fight it.

It was tightened around my throat and I didn't fight it.

Fuck Latif if he thought I was going to let him capture my struggle. Fuck him if he thought I was going to let my dad see me suffering. I would not allow him to see me beg for my life.

I looked past them all, past the camera, past Latif, past my father, searching for something real to focus on. The green rolling hills in the distance. Pure and beautiful. I took a breath that I'd never taken before and wouldn't take again and watched as a burning car rolled down the hill.

Chapter 71

Imy

On my instruction Haqani stopped at the foot of the rolling green hills, vast with a gradual incline. I met his eyes in the rear-view mirror and noticed something close to victory in them.

'Where is he?' I asked.

'On other side. Follow track, two, two and half kilometres.'

'No,' I said, eyeing up the hill. 'We go up.'

Haqani snorted.

I was asking the Honda hatchback to go beyond its capabilities. With no knowledge of what lay on the other side of the hill, height advantage was all I had.

'Reverse,' I said. Bemused, but with my gun dictating, Haqani reversed the car. 'That's enough,' I said, eyeing up the thirty-yard run. From this vantage point I took another measure of the hill; the climb looked aggressive. 'Get the car into third gear as soon as you can and hold it there. When you hit the hill, drive in a horizontal incline and keep your speed steady.'

So there was no mistaking my intention I clicked the safety off the gun close to his ear.

Haqani shook his head as he pulled the seatbelt across. I did the same. He slipped the car into gear, but before setting off, he locked eyes with me in the mirror. 'You risk your life? For Javid?' he asked, his eyebrows knitted, as if he genuinely needed to know.

'I'm not doing it for him,' I said. 'Now drive.'

The mud kicked up underneath the tyres, as Haqani moved through the gears quickly into third. The car was already whining as we picked up speed, begging to be released from the constraints of third gear. We hit the hill with a thump. The wheels crouched and the chassis rattled as we climbed. Behind me, black smoke billowed out of the exhaust. I glanced out of the window, the car was nearly at a forty-five-degree angle. Any hidden obstruction in our path and it would topple back the way we'd come. The Honda kept on going; slowly but surely, it climbed.

'Slow down gradually and stop at the top.'

Haqani pulled up at the peak and wrenched up the handbrake. I heard him hiss quietly in discomfort, the effort of driving the car up the hill had agitated the tourniquet around his leg, the gunshot wound had reopened and coloured his shalwar dark red. Haqani massaged his thigh with his fingertips, but he was bleeding out heavily. In defiance of the pain, Haqani focused on evening his breathing, but there would be no let-up.

I placed the gun by my side and picked up the length of rope. In one quick movement I looped it around his chest and arms and pulled back hard.

Haqani thrashed wildly in his seat and grunted through his teeth. He threw his body forward hard enough that the momentum pushed my face into the back of his seat. The car rocked from side to side, threatening to upturn and send us spiralling. My eyes darted to the gun sitting beside me but using the gun would announce my arrival to those below. Haqani reached low and pulled the seat lever and slid back hard, trapping my legs between the seats. I leaned back hard, twisting the rope around my fist and I pulled with every ounce of energy I had.

I felt Haqani weaken, his breaths coming ragged and hoarse as his body finally slackened.

Before he could get a second wind I looped the rope around him a second time, before tying it into a constricting knot. Haqani dropped his head, his hair escaped from his hat and curtained his face.

I pushed down the passenger seat and pushed open the door. I practically fell out of the car. I stood bent at the waist, panting as I looked down from the peak of the hill. I was unable to make out anything except that it was around a one-kilometre drop.

I straightened up and rounded the car. From the trunk I removed the Go-Bag. At the peak of the hill, I stamped at the long grass so that I had a flat twelve-inch square area. I removed the sniper rifle, slotted it onto the bi-fold legs and steadied it on the surface that I'd prepared.

I lay flat on my stomach and put my right eye to the telescopic sight. A small robin came into the crosshair, its red chest a stark contrast to the green hill opposite the one that it sat atop. I angled the rifle on its axis thirty degrees lower and peered through the scope. Cartoon sharks circling palm trees on light blue linen came into view. I turned the dial on the scope anti-clockwise decreasing the magnification. Jay was sitting in a chair, I could see the red in his eyes, the tears streaking down his cheeks. Behind him stood a well-built man, his face covered in a balaclava. He held a machete low by his leg.

I angled the rifle thirty degrees lower so it was parallel to the decline of the hill. At the foot stood six men dressed top to toe in black, lined up six feet apart and stock still. They were all cradling assault rifles. I could take one of them out from this distance without hesitation, but I wasn't ready to give away my position yet.

In between the six men and Jay I recognised Latif's small figure. He was leaning over a mounted video camera. To the side of the camera was a frail man hunched in a wheelchair. I adjusted the sight a fraction and the side of his burnt face came into view.

I watched him carefully, everything and everyone around him melted away into nothing. I studied every scar, sear and burn on his face. I'd never met him before, but I was in no doubt, in my crosshairs was the man I had once worshipped, the man that the world knew as The Teacher.

Time slowed and then time stopped.

A feeling from within clawed at my insides, threatening to slice me open and burst through to the surface. My finger found the trigger and sat firm against it. A touch and he would be gone. I'd walk away, never to be seen again.

It wasn't enough. I needed more. I needed him to look me in the eye and recognise the hurt before I unloaded my all rage into him.

I took a breath. My finger relaxed away from the trigger and I moved the sight away. It landed back on Jay. A noose was being placed around his neck.

Time started again.

I scrambled through the Go-Bag, picking out a zippo lighter from one of the front pockets, and liquid paraffin in another. The Honda was sitting still at the peak of the hill. I rushed across to the car and flung open the door. Exhaustion and heavy bleeding had rendered Haqani unconscious. I flicked the lid off the paraffin and doused the seats of the car, before emptying the last of it over Haqani.

He stirred, opened his eyes. Unable to admit defeat, he growled from underneath his hair, 'I will send your family a video of your beheading.'

I flicked the lighter, the flame catching reflection in his eyes, and lobbed it onto his lap. I released the handbrake, as the cotton quickly caught alight. I gripped the doorframe and helped the Honda along.

Haqani's desperate cries mixed in with the crackle of the fire consuming the interior of the car as it made its descent down the hill.

I rushed back to my station and watched through the sight.

Jay was suspended six feet in the air. His leg flailing and his hands ripping at the noose around his throat. I adjusted the scope. It was near a 1km shot, thankfully, there was little to no crosswind. I willed my body to be still and held in a deep breath and counted three in my head.

It was time to put Jay out of his misery.

Chapter 72

Jay

I felt light. As though my soul had already left me. My hands scratched at my throat. Fingers clawing and prying hopelessly at the noose flush around my neck. The white stars were back and there were many of them. I could feel my eyes bulging, popping out of my eye sockets as I chased but failed to catch a breath. I fought unconsciousness with everything I had and for as long as I could, but it was coming. I could fucking feel it.

I waited. Looking down through slits. Below, my Jordans furiously trod air. Past them I could see black-masked faces looking up at me. I could see my dad, his eyes on me. I pleaded silently to him, *get the fuck up, do something, say something. Fucking help me, please!*

From somewhere in my peripheral vision, our little red Honda continued to grumble down the hill. *Too late.* Even from the distance and my fading state I heard the muffled explosion as the fire reached the fuel tank, the windows shattering, body panels being ripped away.

Through heavy eyes I watched masked faces turn away from me. Confusion and barked instructions and then bodies scattering towards the fireball on wheels. Leaving only my dad with me.

Heavy now, my head dipped. My chin rested on my collar bone. My body swayed gently. I don't know when I stopped struggling.

I felt the bullet a second after a prayer left my lips. It whizzed over my head and caught the rope above me. It wasn't a clean hit, and my body tilted as the rope tethered. I threw up in my mouth as a second shot hit the rope clean and I was in free fall. The ground rushed up at me so quickly that I didn't have time to change my position and somehow my arm took my body weight.

Biting back the pain shooting up across my shoulder, I viciously pulled at the noose, managing to get my fingers in and pry the thick rope away from my throat. I scrambled it over my head and threw it as far as I could as though it was a venomous snake.

I rolled onto my back and searched desperately for that long overdue breath. It caught somewhere in my throat as I looked up to see Balaclava standing over me.

C'mon, man! Cut me a fucking break.

Toe to toe, Balaclava was head and shoulders above me, but from my position on my back he looked like a masked fucking giant. The sun caught the machete as he raised it above his head ready to strike down upon me.

I squeezed my eyes shut as two bullets whistled past me. I felt a warm spurt on my face. I opened my eyes to see Balaclava staggering over me like a piss-head, a bloody hole in his chest and another hole torn in his mask. He dropped like a fucking tree and I rolled away before he collapsed on me, and finally I took the breath of a newborn.

With limited medical knowledge, I pushed my leg out and poked his ribs with the toe of my shoe. Satisfied that he wasn't getting up, I crawled over and patted his dead body and retrieved my phone that he had jacked. I stared at the gun in his holster and took a second to decide, *I'm fucking having that, too.*

I turned it around in my hand, trying to suss it out. I know very little about guns. But I know a little. This one was a Desert Eagle semi-automatic handgun and all I needed to know was where the safety was and if I had it in me to pull the trigger.

I held it close to my chest and moved away on my haunches, keeping myself as small a target as possible. I found refuge behind the tree I'd just been hanging from. The six Jihadis at the foot of the hill were fully distracted by the burning Honda careening down towards them, as though the Devil himself was laughing behind the wheel. They fired blindly, the sounds of their AK assault rifles relentless as they ripped holes and kicked up grass and earth. Unable to find the threat they scattered in different directions looking for cover that they would not reach.

Six shots, equally spaced out. Six composed shots, whistling down from somewhere above where my eyes couldn't reach. Six fucking shots is what it took, and I watched six of them drop one at a time.

It took a moment for my ears to stop ringing and tune in to the growl of a diesel engine. Latif wasn't sticking around, he'd used the distraction of death to make his escape. I swung the gun and pointed at the moving Q7. My finger stroked the trigger. Latif's son and daughter decided, at that very moment, to pop into my head. I recalled how they giggled behind their hands.

J. That's not a name. That's a letter.

It couldn't be me that took away their father. I couldn't have that shit hanging over me.

The gun suddenly felt heavy, forcing my arm down, answering the question I'd asked myself. Maybe I didn't have it in me to pull the trigger. To take a life.

I watched Latif disappear just as our little red Honda reached even ground. It'd lost some of its momentum but it burned brightly and roared loudly. It slowed down and came to a natural stop as if recognising its part in this was complete.

I searched for my dad. Dust and dirt swirled in front of him before dissipating and revealing him unmoved in his wheelchair.

It was just me and him. And I couldn't figure out my fucking reaction.

I felt anger, I felt love. I felt like screaming and crying. I had to work pretty fucking hard to shut down every contradictory emotion, because it wasn't over yet. And I had to be quick.

Imy would have made the call to Teddy Lawrence, and any minute coalition forces would turn up in their big helicopters with their big guns ready to take away the most wanted man in the world. Hide him away from the world. From me.

I couldn't accept that. I couldn't let it happen again. No longer was I MI5's puppet to be used as they pleased. I've come too fucking far. They can't shut me down.

The world needed the truth and I was going to deliver it to them.

I slipped out my phone and opened up the BBC news app. I glanced down the latest headlines and memorised whatever I could before switching to the camera app. I flipped to video mode.

Before starting, I looked up towards the hill. I could see the peak but I couldn't see from this distance if Imy had started to make his way down. I had time.

I pointed my phone at my dad and he came softly into focus, his eyes beckoning me to him. I pressed the red button and started recording.

'The, uh… date is December 20th 2018.' I cleared my throat. 'The EU are offering Theresa May a delay on Brexit. Uh… Facebook accused of cashing in on user data… There is drone chaos at Gatwick Airport… Trump announces he'll pull US troops out of Syria.'

It wasn't exactly a newspaper with today's date sitting on his lap, but it was close enough to validate the timing and authenticity of the video. I pinched the screen and zoomed in. My heart fucking dropped as his gormless form filled the screen. I held it for a moment, taking him in through my camera. Despite his pathetic state, I think his

373

eyes were smiling. I had to hold it the fuck together. I took a breath and exhaled loudly.

'The man that you are looking at goes by the name of The Teacher, AKA Al-Mudarris, AKA Abdul Bin Jabbar. The world presumes him dead, he's not. Abdul Bin Jabbar is alive.'

I ended the recording.

I calculated the time in England. It was about half-past six in the morning. I made a phone call to the only person that I thought that would do this. My heart accelerated with every ring and when it was answered, it raced a little more and just for a second I'd forgotten why I'd called.

'Jay,' she said.

'Sophia,' I said. 'Did I wake you?'

'No,' she lied. I could almost picture her shuffling up against the headboard. 'Tell me you're okay?'

I turned my head back over my shoulder and glanced at my dad.

'I'm okay,' I said. 'But I need a favour. You can say no if you—'

'Yes!' Sophia said.

I smiled. I think she did, too. I told her that I was going to send her a video and explained what had to be done with it, and I think I trusted her to do it.

'Go,' she said. 'I've got work to do.'

I pocketed my phone.

Now… it was over.

There was nothing left to do but turn my attention to my dad, and I wasn't sure which one of my contradictory emotions would emerge.

374

Chapter 73

The Teacher

One year ago Bin Jabbar first set eyes on his son. He knew, then, that nothing would ever be the same again. It would be the start of his downfall and the demise of his life's work.

The victories he'd celebrated when he'd driven a hole through the West, and the failures he'd suffered when he'd watched his people perish seemed insignificant, whenever he was near his son.

Bin Jabbar had long lost the ability to express emotion on his face, but he smiled anyway. Smiled as he recalled trying to convince his beloved Afeesa that their firstborn would be named Javid. It meant *eternal*. He knew now that he was wrong, that nothing lasts forever.

Besides, Javid preferred to be called Jay.

If he could find a voice, *Jay* is what he would call his son. If he could find the strength, *Jay* is what he would whisper in his ear as he held him tightly in his arms.

But he couldn't do any of that.

So he just blinked at his son and took in every word that came out of his mouth.

'They're coming for you, again.' Jay stood in front of his father, his face that of a child, small and innocent. One that didn't belong there. 'But this time won't be like the last. I made sure of that.' Jay nodded to himself. 'Me and you, we're even. I don't owe you a fucking thing!'

Bin Jabbar watched his son carefully, committing every detail to memory. Jay forced a hand through his hair and kicked up earth under his feet as he walked in small circles, as though doing so would take back what he'd just said, but it just seemed to make him angrier.

'You should see yourself. The fucking state of you. Is this what you wanted when you set out to be a hero, the big fucking man?! Can't move, can't talk. Can you even fucking hear me?'

Bin Jabbar heard every word. He let it in, cherished it.

Jay smiled to himself, there was great sense of sadness to it. 'I didn't know how I'd feel when I saw you again, but now that I have, I don't ever want to see you again.'

Jay took a step closer to his father, and another until Bin Jabbar could almost feel him, almost touch him. He crouched down and reached out, gently touching his hand.

Bin Jabbar's enemies may have riddled his body with bullets and transformed him from a crusader to a cripple who had lost any sense of feeling in his body. But he felt his son's touch.

Jay looked up at his father and said, 'I wish they'd killed you.'

Chapter 74
Jay

I chose not to say another word.

I sat back and dug my palms into the dirt either side of me and stretched my neck up to the heavens and wondered whose side God was on. The sun had now gone into hiding behind grey clouds and a drop of rain rudely slapped me on my forehead.

Beside me, my phone rang. I reached for it, expecting Imy.

'Where are you?'

'Jesus! I've called you a dozen times.'

'Teddy?' I said, as tired as I was feeling.

'Can you talk?' he asked.

I got to my feet and moved away from my dad.

'Yeah, I can talk.'

'We found Omar Bhukara.'

Omar! That was the last thing I'd expected him to say. As exhausted as my body was, my brain started shooting. Why hadn't Lawrence mentioned the fact that I was surrounded by dead terrorists? Why hadn't he mentioned that I was sitting three feet away from Bin Jabbar? I looked towards the hill, finally catching sight of Imy. He looked tiny in the distance, half walking, half sliding his way down.

Imy hadn't made the call. Lawrence didn't know.

I reached out for reason, but before it could come to me, Lawrence staggered up to me.

'He was found along with his associate, Wasim Qadir, in the back of a camper van at a disused aircraft hangar in Coventry. They'd both been shot dead from close range.'

The rain picked up, a droplet dripped down the back of my shirt adding to the chill already travelling up my fucking spine.

Wasim Qadir was a forger and a weapons dealer. I knew this because last year when I was undercover for MI5, I'd met with him to secure sawn-off AK-47s and Glock 19s.

'Tommy wasn't there,' I said. It wasn't a question.

'No.'

I swallowed hard, and started to test my theory out loud. 'The van was empty. No weapons. No documentation. He killed them and took everything.'

'It's a theory that we've considered, but… it doesn't fit. According to your intel, Omar and Tommy were going to meet with Wasim Qadir. Qadir was willingly going to supply them with guns and forged documentation. What motive would Tommy have to kill them?'

'He never converted!' I said. 'I told you already that there was something off about him as soon as I set eyes on him. There was coldness there.'

'It's a stretch, Jay.'

'No, it's a start! Tommy was a fucking loner, and in the absence of anyone likeminded, he used Omar, got close to him and spun him a fantasy about setting the world on fire. Don't you see, it was just an in! It was the only way he could get his hands on weapons and documentation.'

I heard Lawrence sigh, his brain taking time to catch up with what I was trying to tell him. The idea that Tommy was on the other side was MI5's very last fucking thought. I had once gone undercover to infiltrate Ghurfat-al-Mudarris, and now Tommy had done the same fucking thing for his own hateful gain.

'There's got to be a target,' I said.

'Where?'

'Are you serious?' I ran a hand through my wet hair, and laughed incredulously. 'You really don't know shit! This man was born and raised in Southall amongst Muslims, it's all he knew, and all he knew is all he despised. That's got to be the starting point. Look at surrounding Mosques, especially Fridays, there are four in Southall alone, and a lot more in surrounding areas. Look at Asian festivals, at Muslim weddings. Work it the fuck out, Teddy!'

He took a moment to reply.

'As soon as you step back in the country, I'd like you to come in. Your experience may be of value.'

It was a clumsy way of asking for my help. I didn't think I had a part left to play, but on the flip side I saw things that they never could. I had the ability to play devil's advocate and see the war from both sides.

I opened my mouth to answer, but somebody else had his attention. I heard hushed and rushed voices.

'Hold the line, Jay,' Lawrence muttered.

I pressed the phone tight to my ear. There was some rustling followed by silence. Followed by the sound of a tinny voice. My voice.

Sophia had executed her task by creating dummy accounts and uploading the video via every possible social media channel.

I switched the phone to speaker, and opened up Twitter. In the search bar I typed in *Bin* and it quickly picked up **#BinJabbarAlive**. It had already hit 482,973 views, and that number was climbing rapidly. I didn't expect the impact to be so quick. I should have.

Social media does not fuck around.

The world would wake up to the truth.

Lawrence was back on the line.

'Jay…' he said. 'What have you done?'

I disconnected the call.

Chapter 75

Imy

It fell still around me. Silent. Flat on my stomach and looking through the scope of the rifle I watched Jay carefully. He had a way about him, uniquely his. He was pointing a phone at Bin Jabbar. It was clear what he was doing. Jay never bought into assurances that MI5 would present Bin Jabbar a fair trial. This was his insurance. I don't think I could have stopped him even if I'd wanted to. Let it be. Let him enjoy his victory. It'd be short-lived. My actions would soon see him a broken man.

I got to my feet, and with my heartbeat hammering in my ears I started my trek down. I wouldn't rush Jay. He had earned his moment with his father and right now, he was screaming and gesturing, expressing his love through anger. The moment was too personal for me to consume. I remove the sight away from my eye and focused on my footing. It had started to rain and the terrain had become slippery.

I reached the bottom of the hill, and walked past every cold body that I had put down. Jay acknowledged me nervously with a small nod before approaching me. He stood in my path, stopping me in my tracks.

Before I could react, he was on me, arms around me, his face nestled in the crook of my neck. I could feel the sheer relief coming off him. I looked over his shoulder, the back of Bin Jabbar's fallen head in my sight.

'You didn't call it in?' he said in my ear.

I took a step back and broke the embrace. 'Go, Jay,' I said, as I removed the Browning from my waistband.

Jay blinked at the gun, and I watched him with sadness as realisation dawned on him. I looked into his eyes and hoped that he understood what was in mine.

'Call it in,' he said, softly.

I released the magazine, it slipped smoothly out of the gripped handle and fell to the ground. I replaced it with another and retracted the slide, lifting a round into the chamber.

'It's over,' Jay said, 'Make the fucking call.'

I shook my head and brushed past him, blocking out his protests in my ear. I felt his fingers dig into my arm, an attempt to pull me back. I lashed out blindly with my elbow catching his head. Jay dropped to his hands and knees.

I strode away, the gun in my possession felt natural, as natural as it had when I'd executed each member of the Kabir family. I rounded the wheelchair and finally, I came face to face with Abdul Bin Jabbar.

With a steady hand I pointed the gun at him.

Chapter 76

Jay

Imy knew better than anyone what this meant to me. It had never once occurred to me that maybe, it meant more to him. I'd been blind enough to think that this was my story.

It wasn't.

The rain picked up, warm and dirty and thick. I lifted myself off my hands and knees, wiped away the rain from my face, and blinked away the blood that had escaped into my eye from where Imy had struck me.

I moved cautiously towards him, past my dad, my eyes only on Imy. I held my hands up high, palms forward. I didn't get too close, didn't want him to react.

I remembered with such clarity the very moment when this had started, the day Imy had entered my home and pointed a gun at me. I remember the uncertainty in his eyes, the tremble in his hand. Make no mistake, this wasn't that. His eyes were like stone and in them I saw nothing but absolute determination.

I stopped a few feet from him, making up the third point of a triangle, and tried to get a measure of the magic fucking words that I needed to reason with him.

'Don't,' I said, softly. 'Please… Don't do it.'

He didn't reply, didn't acknowledge my fucking presence. I moved in a touch, an arm's length from Imy. He didn't flinch, knowing that he could pull the trigger quicker than I could make my move. I risked a glance at my dad, the rain racing down his face and drenching his clothes. I wondered if he was even aware of what was going on, if he realised that this was just another fucking consequence of his actions.

'Let Teddy know we've found him,' I said, desperately trying not to let my voice betray my emotion. 'Let him rot away for the rest of his fucking life. Just make the call, yeah?'

Imy remained unmoved, steady. He was savouring the moment.

'Do not make this personal,' I said. It sounded arrogant. I was a fucking hypocrite.

His jaw tightened as he inhaled and exhaled short sharp bursts through his nose, his thirst for revenge was palpable. I could feel it, I could fucking understand it, but I couldn't allow it.

'It's always been personal,' Imy said. 'For you. For me.'

I couldn't tell the rain from the tears that were now falling freely down his face, and I had the urge to fucking cry along with him.

'Look at him. He's already dead. He's fucking nothing, he *means* nothing to me. I get it, I fucking get it now. After everything I've done to find him, I want him to stay the fuck away from me.'

I couldn't help it and I didn't care if Bin Jabbar heard. My emotions were out, and every word that was flying out of my mouth was the truth. But it was the truth *for now*. Fuck knows my relationship with my dad was complicated. Fuck knows how I'd feel if something happened to him. I felt furious at him, at myself, for putting myself in this situation. *For fucking what!* The thread that connected us was so fucking thin, but it meant something to me, it always had.

'He took away everything,' Imy said, his free hand reaching up to steady the gun, his finger tightened upon the trigger.

'No, wait!' My feet scrambled towards him. 'Please, just fucking wait. He didn't kill your family. He didn't give the order.'

'It started with him. I'm sorry, Jay.'

If I'd stopped to consider it, if I'd had the fucking time, probably I wouldn't have done it. But my heart was calling the fucking shots and my arm came up, my fingers wrapped tightly around the Desert Eagle handgun. It felt like a fucking canon in my hands and I had to fight to keep it up. My thumb reached across, flicking the safety and I pointed it at Imy.

It was hard to tell through the rain, but I saw it. I saw him nod. Barely fucking perceptible, but I swear to God it was there. The realisation struck me like a hammer to the head.

It's what Imy wanted. It was the only way I could stop him.

'I'm not doing it,' I said and then I screamed, '*I'm not fucking doing it!*'

Imy's finger whitened and tightened against the trigger.

The gunshot exploded in my ears.

I'd pulled the trigger before he did.

Acknowledgements

Over the last eighteen months, the one thought that had constantly sat in my head was *I don't know what I'm doing*. The thought of filling page after page with words seemed like an impossible task. I needed support and I was lucky enough to have some amazing people around me to motivate me, inspire me, and just be there for me. I'd like to thank you.

My beautiful wife, you make me laugh like no other and your compliments are always delivered as an insult. But I see through them. My two boys, watching you grow is my true inspiration. My mum, dad and brother, I do this to make you proud of me.

The Soho Agency and Julian Alexander, my supercool agent, a much-needed calming influence in my life. I think you would have made an excellent crisis negotiator.

My amazing new editor, Katie Seaman. I didn't know what to expect, but you have been an absolute delight and your advice is always on-point. I've really loved working with you, and don't worry I'm working on my inner Sasha Fierce. Lisa Milton, Lily Capewell, Isabel Smith, Jon Appleton, and all those at HQ/HarperCollins who have contributed to this book. Your support is forever appreciated.

A special mention to Clio Cornish and Jamie Groves. There are signs of you all over this book.

To the reader, where would I be without you?

Finally, and most importantly, I thank God. Each day that I don't get struck by lightning is a good day.

Enjoyed *Ride or Die*?

Make sure you've read the rest of the Jay Qasim series

Don't miss a Jay Qasim short story and prequel to EAST OF HOUNSLOW written exclusively for Quick Reads 2021

Business has been slow for Hounslow's small time dope-dealer, Jay Qasim. A student house party means quick easy cash but it also means breaking his own rules. But desperate times lead him there – and Jay finds himself in the middle of a crime scene.

Idris Zaidi, a police officer and Jay's best friend, is having a quiet night when he gets a call-out following a noise complaint at a house party. Fed up with the lack of excitement in his job, he visits the scene and quickly realises that people are in danger after a stabbing.

Someone will stop at nothing to get revenge . . .

Go back to where it all began with the first book in the Jay Qasim series

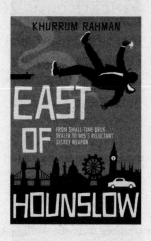

Meet Jay. Small-time dealer. Accidental jihadist.
The one man who can save us all?

Javid – call him Jay – is a dope-dealer living in
West London. He goes to mosque on Friday, and
he's just bought his pride and joy – a BMW. He
lives with his mum, and life seems sweet.
But his world is about to turn upside-down. Because
MI5 have been watching him, and they think he's
just the man they need for a delicate mission.

One thing's for sure: now he's a long way East of Hounslow, Jay's life will never be the same again . . .

Don't miss the explosive second book

KHURRUM RAHMAN

HOME GROWN HERO

Reluctant spy. Trained assassin. Whose side are you on?

Jay Qasim is back home in West London and in pursuit of
normality. He's swapped dope-dealing for admin, and spends
his free time at the local Muslim Community Centre or cruising
around Hounslow in his beloved BMW. No one would guess
he was the MI5 spy who foiled the most devasting terrorist
attack in recent history, but it hasn't gone unnoticed.

Imran Siddiqui trained to kill in Afghanistan by
the terrorist cell who saved his life after his home was
destroyed by war. The time has finally come to repay them
– throwing him headlong into the path of Jay Qasim.

Now they must each decide whose side they're really on.

ONE PLACE. MANY STORIES

Bold, innovative and
empowering publishing.

FOLLOW US ON:

@HQStories